CALE

By Sylvia Wilkinson

Moss on the North Side
A Killing Frost
Cale

CALE

a novel by
Sylvia Wilkinson

HOUGHTON MIFFLIN COMPANY *Boston 1970*

11/1970
Am. Lit.

FIRST PRINTING   C

Library of Congress Catalog Card Number: 76-120828
Printed in the United States of America

A portion of this book originally appeared
in the Hollins College *Bulletin*.

for my parents

Book One

Book One

Chapter 1

IT WAS A TIME of blossom, May in Summit, North Carolina, hardly the summit of anything, just a small hill in flatness, calling itself a grand name and never really fooling anyone. Still, the North-South driver in 1940 might have remarked, "Pretty little town" because the flowers and trees were a bit above average. Two smokestacks rose over Summit, but the air was as fresh as a farm, no smoke for ten years. The old residents feared that someday the stacks would topple over on the town when people had long since forgotten how and why they stood. But no one did anything about them because no one in Summit knew quite how to take down a smokestack and the man who put them up was long gone. In fact, the last time a Summit resident had felled a large tree, it had taken down three power poles and left the town grumbling in darkness for ten days. So the stacks would stay until the ghost of Zeb Soloman, who was responsible for them, came to push them over.

Lonza Lemirt, retired telegraph operator and farmer, rushed up one day to tell the men on the courthouse steps the stacks were falling. When it was certain that his eyesight had been the victim of a fast-moving cloud, someone remarked that he better go tell the king the sky was falling. Lonza Lemirt was a small man, just over five feet, which didn't hasten the end of the ribbing he had gotten for trying to save the world.

"Lonza Lemirt is a squirt."

*

He once had a dream where a river of boiling red water poured from the top of Summit, bubbling in the smokestacks like a percolator top but he just watched; sat on the riverbank, baited his hook and watched. He got to watch quite a while because he was keeping his mouth shut and didn't have his own screaming to wake him up or start Sarah Ann to beating on him with her little white fists.

Sarah Ann, the rose, sixty years old and still a tight little rosebud, frosted with the dew. Sarah Ann, the blossom of Yellow County, who, instead of birthing another rose had squeezed out Falissa Lemirt, tiny but in no way to rival her mother. Just a few too many bones poking out here and there and a much too matter-of-fact way of walking. That Sarah Ann had her a serving woman, couldn't afford to hire one so she had her one in childbirth, just one. Someone to tend her wishes; she wasn't going to be the cause and deliverer of a rival, no sir. Maybe when Sarah Ann was dead and buried, Falissa could give birth to her own little flower but while Sarah Ann was the queen of Summit, it was just not to be allowed. And that was that.

Falissa grew to know that in the life of a girl who is not a blossom, people are always there to remind you of it, that you're not a blossom by any means. If you are not a flower, not pink-soft petaled and light, you move quietly on quick feet to do your work, like a lady bug under a leaf, dust away the yellow fur of the beetle, without admiration, just consent. You have to work and work hard and push yourself along on your own steam and never let up. No one finds you pleasant to look at in your illness.

But maybe your work will be better than you. What is there to shame you in that? A perfect row of peach jam from two not so perfect hands, a bit short of thumb. Maybe it is good that life is not your rival, that you can look at your peach jam, just the right color, a weed-clean row, a bowl of fat marigolds and say, well done, Falissa. Well done.

*

Falissa Jenkins, wife, and mother soon, dropped the breakfast silver with a clamor. She stood a moment, dizzy in the stillness, and told herself consolingly, "No one heard. No need for explaining."

She moved slowly, tugging herself away from the sink, feeling on air inside but stumbling to anyone who might have watched. But who was there to watch, a fly sealed to the curtain back, waiting to start its flight over the dirty dishes, of too small a mind to know this wouldn't happen again, his chance for enjoyment was just this once because Falissa Jenkins was not one to allow a dish to get cold before it was washed. She moved up the steps, one at a time, sometimes both feet on one landing, always both hands on the railing. She went into their room, hers and Jerome's, settling atop the covers. As she shut her eyes, the back of her hand touched the pillow. Satin, Mama Sarah Ann had said satin would make your hair curl, so she had stitched it over the ticking. Cool and slick for her, it was better as a wet towel; as a curling iron, it was less than successful.

At least the bed is made, she thought, and I won't have it undone until I am to be in it for a while. With every ounce of life and muscle in me, I vow upon this moment that this bed will not hold me if I have the power to stand. Then she giggled, feeling a bit girlish and silly at the ferocity of her thought. She had never been allowed such grand thoughts, why she wasn't pretty enough. Mama can swear she will never lift her hand to skin a scalded tomato, that it will spoil the skin. Falissa Jenkins looked at her hands, freckled though she had to use a charcoal stick to freckle her nose in front of her mama's mirror. When was that, such a faraway thought to be having. Forget her bonnet and feel the sun warm her head and tighten the skin on her nose, hold her hands in water until the nails peeled to the quick and her fingertips crinkled up. She could shell butter beans ten times as fast as Mama who opened each green shell with a knife, sparing the white oval nail on her thumb.

Honestly Mama could remember something a lifetime I would forget in a minute.

The bell on the bedside table, like an ice cube after that hot bed. No noise, don't want it to ting-a-ling and send them all running just yet. Just want to be sure I can reach it. Two bells in the house now, Mama's bell which is china and has roses on it and rings like a tinkle of glass, ever so lightly so as not to break it. And mine, the old one I use to call Jerome out of the field for supper and one there is no mistaking as far as he is concerned. He would drop his plow and leave the mule in the field if he heard it. Well, he would do it for food so I expect as much when I ring about his first born. He'll do his own cooking tonight. One day in my life I ought to be allowed off.

Those curtains sucking in and out that window. I'd tie them back if I could get myself over there. No, it'll take more than that to move me. Like I woke up an old woman this morning. Had to hit the bed before I did the breakfast dishes, for shame. I'm hoping Jerome will think to put them in soak or I'll never clear the place of flies. And a dead fly on the windowsill is to my mind as bad as a live one in the stew. Won't take this house two days to go to wreck with both me and Mama down. Mama ain't but sixty but the way her mind is going I got a fear she is down for good.

When the baby is on his way, I'm to ring the bell and they all run to see my baby boy. Oh, don't I wish it was that way. I do wish it. I'd hear them all coming, Papa Lonza and Jerome thumping up the steps and they would run to the door and I'd hold him up and stop them dead in their tracks. A little naked boy and they'd both smile and point at his little tallywack and I would hold him to me, touch those tiny ears and tell Jerome they won't about to stick out like his. And the swelling would be gone. Oh no, no, not that way at all and I know it is getting late for me to think such foolishness. Women were not made right. Mama says that denies God but I declare it doesn't, God. You know there are some things out of kilter in this world and that people messed them up and if Eve hadn't misbehaved you might have made it easier for us. And I don't mean so much the hurting, Lord, I'd lie to say it didn't, though the vomiting up everything I looked at was hard to bear. No, I just want to do it myself. I just don't want a soul to have to help me with it. If I could just be like the old cat and go off and have them in my own privacy and clean up my own mess. I declare I hate for people to fuss over me when I can't lift a hand to protect myself. People ought to learn from that old cat. She don't want no interfering in her kitten raising and she'll pick up every last one of them by the neck and haul them off and hide them if you mess with her.

That's the main thing wrong with me today. I been dreading this part all along and putting it out of my mind, seeing me hold up my baby no bigger than a doll baby and just as pink and pretty as can be but that's not it at all. Now that it's near, Falissa Jenkins, you got to understand that's not it at all. He's got to come out between your legs which will just split you open like Mama said I split her open. Now you know that's being made up wrong and if there wasn't such a history of babies I'd never believe a word of it. I heard of one of the nigger girls who cut her own off when he come in the field with a topping knife. Mama said that was a lie and the kind of filthy talk she don't want to hear me use if I ever expect to be a lady. She still says things like that to me though I do think she's losing her head a little now and might really think I'm still a little girl. She fretted me until I flat told her I was almost thirty then she laughed and winked at me like she had caught me playing dress-up in her closet and there I was, big as a barrel. He's tied to his little navel hole and I can't feel where in this world he's hooked on to me but I know he is because I've eat enough for ten people these last weeks and that's the truth. It's terrible not to know what's inside you and how many holes there are in you and you know I asked Mama and she told me to hush up which means she don't know either because if she did she would tell me. A while ago when she was in her right mind is when I asked her, I wouldn't fret her now. She wouldn't tell me then either and I'm ashamed to death to ask anybody for a book. I like to have died when I went to that doctor last winter and love nor money won't get me back there again, no sir. But I guess them pioneer women didn't know a bit more about their workings than me, and not as much in some cases and they had them just the same or I wouldn't be here to jabber about it. I would like to know what is going on when it pertains to me like it does but when I went to school they only showed us the pictures of the insides of people with nothing in them, no baby I mean, and wouldn't have dared show us one. From the way I hear people talk them things is changing now which means my baby will know more where he came from than me who made him. Oh, I'd give every penny I've got if I didn't have to depend on them. Not a bit of sense fretting. I been over it a thousand times and even once thought of cutting him loose myself. But hers died. Oh, I can't have mine die and if I was the cause of it, I'm as good as dead in hell myself for my wickedness.

I got cramps in every inch of me, I declare my stomach don't feel any worse than the ends of my toes. And I can just feel the sweat trickling off me. If I get this bed sheet wet enough I reckon it will turn to cooling me off. That's one way I take after my mama, I hardly ever sweat a drop and when I do you can be sure there's something wrong. You know it's just like when you get a leg tired from swimming or going in after lunch before your stomach is settled. I remember that lake water, hot on top and just as cold as ice when you dropped your legs churning out of them springs and around your legs like somebody was threading a cold rope through your joints and pulling it with every bit of strength he had so you had to fan out of there quick before he pulled you under and tied you to the bottom. I pulled every pound of me up on that pier one time with nothing left worth using but my fingers though I guess I was only every bit of sixty pounds. Lying there on my stomach, praying Mama

hadn't seen me struggle because she is scared to death of the
water and would of skinned me alive if she knew I swam alone
and wouldn't let me down there again all summer long. The
mud from the pond water stuck to the hairs on me where I didn't
even know I had hairs. The white fuzz would turn me brown
from that water like a hairy man till I rubbed it away. Life came
back to my legs, my feet stung like they were thawing when
the blood started running, mud dried crusty, smelly on me and
I was right back in the water before I knew it. How long has it
been since you could go for a swim in the pond and lie on your
stomach? That is the way I'd much rather sleep. Next to that
vomiting and puffing up and running to the bathroom for nothing; sleeping like a hog flopped over in the mud left me many
a morning dragging about. And the dreams, Lord, the dreams
were hell itself.

A childhood gone too soon. I've said it many a time. Young,
old, with not a bit of in-between and never a chance to go back
and get it because as soon as I felt the first soreness in my chest
and had to start putting on two or three shirts before I found
one thick enough I wasn't shamed to be seen in, Mama said it
was time to teach me to cook and clean and keep house. And
that wasn't fair a bit, not a bit. When I found the first drop of
blood in my pants when I was sneaking down to swim in the
river and took off my clothes, I went running to her just crying
my heart out because I surely thought I was dying. She should
have told me to expect it. And then she said that was wrong,
to take away my childhood before nature said it was due. I
declare I hardly knew a boy from a girl until I was married
to one. I screamed my throat raw that day when she told me I
couldn't go swimming on those days which was the first thing
I asked and she said, "It happens to everyone, dear. All the other
little girls your age at school are going through the change
too." What did I care about the other girls at school then, not
a whit. Not a one of them could swim halfway across our pond.
That was the ache, same as now, same as everyone when I was

sure the world was mine to do with as I pleased and now it was
a dirty secret I had to hide and fib from the boys. Ugly secret
and she knew it all along and she would tan my hide today if
she knew I hadn't changed my way of thinking. I could have
sat quietly and looked every day and just waited for it to take
me, and not run and played and learned to love things
outdoors more than I'll ever love anything again.

Except maybe the child. Maybe the child. Mama knew
from the beginning and didn't tell me that I was destined for
something different, this swollen belly, and this tired sigh that
comes without my knowing it, that's what Mama would say,
is what you are destined for. She knew I was going to grow old.
But I declare nothing in this world made me even dream of that
until the blood came and she told me I could give life someday,
in the proper way of course, and now I had to watch my way of
acting, and I never felt more in my life like I was dying. To this
very moment, knowing I could give a thousand lives don't make
up for what was took from me so I'll just wait on tomorrow.

If I had known, maybe I could have been thankful for every
precious moment, right then, on the riverbank dipping up tadpoles and turning them loose in the rock pool by the house.
They hopped away when they turned. No. I don't know
how to make life more precious until something is gone away
and that's a fact. When I was a little girl, I built what I pleased.
I laid awake nights dreaming of what I would build next and I
planted everything imaginable. A whole fenceful of them
colored gourds. And I built me a swing. Now when there is
something I'm supposed to build, I do it just as they say. I just
copy down a recipe and when I get it just like Mama's then it's
right. Even Jerome throws that up to me. I am shamed by everyone that knows me if I don't, I declare I am; if I make one
little mess of something in the kitchen I never hear the last of
it. It gets so I hate to open the oven door just knowing my cake
has gone swoosh in the middle and I'm going to have to fill it
up with pineapple and raisins and make like I planned it that
way. Shamed if you do, shamed if you don't.

Well anyway, there I was married before I knew a thing in this world and here I am ten years later and don't know much more than what I could have imagined. Hardly a peep I've made these ten years if that is to be believed of any living soul. And this fretting and carrying on inside has been going on every minute when I wasn't so busy I quit thinking about it. I have gone to church and kept my house and made do with what we have. And they thought I was as barren as a rock. Or Jerome, poor Jerome that none of my family likes, not because he is less than they but because he didn't act as though he liked them or make as much over them as they would like. Keeps to hisself on those occasions, maybe a little bashful if the truth was known but not one for a lot of loud laughing and talking and they are bad to tell stories and talk about people that don't mean a hoot to him. I know just as good they blamed it on him until it was certain the baby was there all right and they laughed about it behind my back. I know my family that well. And here I've gone and let the child to get built up to mean more than it should just to be proving that I'm important and that Jerome is as good as them and there wasn't any need of it if I didn't let them throw off on me. Maybe no child could mean more than it should, that might just be foolishness because it just has to take first place from now on out.

A mother will defend her own if they are as wrong as the blackest sin, Mama said. That needs no explaining, she said, and I remember that fighting hissing wildcat I stepped into, clawing up my leg because of her babies and I didn't have no mind to harm a living thing, I just stepped into her. And I thought sure as everything I would see her hide pinned up like a chicken hawk on the fence. And not a soul blamed her. Because of her babies, that's why no one blamed her and Papa would not kill it. And my legs swelled and the red streaks filled with pus and the poison made pink paths under my skin and I seen them moving clean around my feet. When the old doctor dressed my leg, him too, it was a mother's rage, he said, and he bathed and dressed my leg while Mama, white soft hands, watched but didn't see a bit of the ugliness on my leg because I could see those blue eyes go just as hazy gray when they were duty bound to look at something but didn't have any intention of seeing it, shut but open wide. I knew Mama good. That was when I was Papa's girl, the only one, a family that was growing thin. Maybe the baby would make Mama happy. No, nothing would make Mama happy. Never could please her for a minute.

Those curtains are still floating, in and out, just as quiet, yes, like in an empty church. You see he was putting on them, Jerome. No reason he shouldn't because Mama and Papa had long since made a mess of keeping up the farm and if the truth were known they were living off Jerome but they threw off on him anyway because it was them who owned the land but it was Jerome who paid the taxes. There's a lot of people who can't do a bit better but will throw off on everybody who tries. Jerome hadn't really done much of anything but we were making it. We hadn't gone hungry and I can sure as stuff remember being hungry when I was little. It's just that I thought when I was a little girl, in a dream of mine, that I would go away from this old brown house that has never seen a coat of paint and have a white house with a mowed lawn and green shutters on the windows. That is a silly thought because if I wanted it mowed here I could do it but somebody would make some to-do over it. We're too far out to mow up around the house, it would appear wasteful. I know these people out here just as good. I wanted a mowed lawn where everybody done it and I would buy my stuff from the store in town, even vegetables if I was a mind to in little paper bags and pick out just the ones I wanted from the stack and just use my garden for raising flowers, tulips. I wished every one of them butter-and-eggs in the yard would come up tulips and every spring they come up messier butter-and-eggs, messiest flower I've ever seen and you can't kill them, look like they already been stomped on and I've often wondered if they won't a buttercup a cow stepped on a thousand years ago and they just keep coming up to spite you.

But here we live next to that chip-peeling sign, YOU ARE AP-
PROACHING SUMMIT, NORTH CAROLINA, THE CITY OF TOMOR-
ROW, that every boy I knew in high school had busted a beer
bottle on. They still do, boys I don't know but I'm too old, almost thirty, don't number boys among my acquaintances anymore. That sign had gone up after the first war and hadn't had
a coat of paint since the depression. Summit got no tomorrow
or yesterday neither since the people who opened the hosiery
mill put up the sign and didn't take it when they closed and
left. When they started laying people off back in '29, I had to
haul off the busted glass in a bucket because Papa had a automobile and popped a new rubber tire on it when rubber tires
were hard to come by. They busted out the windows at the
mill, my cousins as bad as the rest of them, and never worked a
day in the mill. They just saw it was meanness they could get
away with. There was even women throwing bricks and throwing mud with it smeared up to their elbows, heaving it at anything that happened to read Soloman's Hosiery on it and never
had on a silk stocking in their life. I wondered if he might be
any kin to the king in the Bible but I don't hardly think you can
go back that far but he was a Jew because somebody put the
Hitler mark out on the sign out front in black paint just last
week though it's been ten years. That's what Jerome said he
figured it was, the Hitler sign, I forget the name, and that he
hates Jews worst of all, Hitler does. Said he's going to get that
whole sign down one day if we run out of stove wood and that'll
be the last of that bottle-busting in the middle of the night.
It would take running out of wood to get him to do it. I don't
think I hate nobody. That's something I get from Mama. Not
that she don't just despise people inside but she says hating on
the outside makes you ugly and when I was little I was sure a
frown might freeze on my face. But I don't try to rub out those
wrinkles between my eyes anymore. They're there for good
now though I did hear letting soap dry on them might smooth
them out.
Sunshine spreading through them curtains. I hear Jerome's

old radio. I didn't even hear him come in. Somebody could steal the house out from under me today. I'll just wait and see if he thinks to do the dishes, looks like he could this once. That old brown and ugly radio, nowhere to hide the old thing and I just wish it would blow up. All about it that interests me is that orange light that swells in it and tells you the noise is coming; I'm telling you the truth, it's just something to dust and take up space. War. Always just as soon as you think you got a friend in a country it will turn on you. Can't keep me interested in that because as sure as I would say I liked the French they would start shooting at us and people would say I was letting down my country. All I ask them is that they keep them away from here and leave me be. But I declare I couldn't ever hate the Dutch, if they just shot me down, I couldn't. I came from their stock, not just Scotch-Irish. Everybody around here was Scotch-Irish but I've got Dutch blood, Papa said. I just love those wooden shoes and tulips, just thousands of them in every color in the rainbow. Don't you know it is just the prettiest thing in the world to see a field of them tulips and one of them wind-mills? And them little white hats that turn up at the corners and they wear aprons even with dress-up clothes, ruffly aprons. And they wash their steps with a scrub brush and a bucket every single day and sing and dance and show their petticoats and have the best time. And they built dikes to keep the water away; I tried making me a dike once, in the creek, not the field and I'm telling you it is a good thing I wasn't born a beaver because me and my younguns would have washed away into the ocean. I never thought before but do you reckon that is where Papa got the idea for diking the tobacco? Oh, if that water were to break away and rush down on them. If someone were to drop a bomb and it would bust through, the wind-mills and the tulips, no! All those pinwheels broken and scattered, soldiers walking them in the mud. Jerome, turn it off!

The Nazis. There too it says. Belgium, Luxembourg, where are they? Oh, it's enough to make me cry just hearing about it. I only know Holland is over the ocean and they say he is there,

Hitler. Like a cuss word, that ugly mustache. I laughed at him
like that Chaplin fellow in the picture show with the funny
duck walk when I first seen him in the paper and now he is
the most hateful man in the world. Jerome, turn it off. Turn
it off!

It will be all over when my baby is a man. Maybe he will
build me a windmill, like Holland. He might just know how
since my baby will be part a Dutch boy. It will be all over then.
That radio has made my heart thump so fast it scares me. It
is quiet now. Jerome has gone back to work. And he's left
the dishes. Kicked up the chickens. Stumbling through the
yard like an old dog; sometimes I love him more when I'm away
from him just watching him move. He didn't a bit more think
to straighten up the kitchen than the man in the moon. Just
expects a woman to always be after him picking up.

You would think them curtains had a string on them. I wish
to heaven I could get my mind on something else. I declare
this hurting can make your mind go bad. I can still hear good
though. The tin swells and pops when that sunlight slides
across it, stretching at them nails and sucking its belly up and
down with the heat. I'm hurting. The chickens, rustling
back to the shade where Jerome kicked them, lazy fat ladies in
the shade. I wish I could get myself to that window to watch
them. And to know for sure just exactly where Jerome is. Pecking in the fresh dirt he turned up, the grubs turned up and
blind in the sun and the chickens, quick as lightning now before
it dries out and the grubs work back down deep, away from
them. The sunshine. It will perk up the wild grass first and I
got to get to pulling it soon, for shame, the wild grass will take
over the garden before it is even planted. Got to get it planted.
Jerome should have waited until I was up and around before he
plowed. But he couldn't wait no longer, I reckon. He never
was one to hurry, you can't accuse him of that. Well, I know
what it is like to wait and I'm tired to death of it. The rain will
come soon and the seeds should be put away, each tucked underground to split and grow and send out little feet, little arms,

a little head to peep from the dirt. I declare that is what I like best about living. The seeds must be there before the rain, Jerome. I've told him a thousand times how he has to beat the rain. He's going to give them something to talk about if he lets a gully-washer catch up on him.

I keep things from him, I do. The things that should have come in the in-between time I'm imagining, the big-girl time before you're full grown up and people start to guessing what sort you're going to be. The time I wasn't allowed if you want the truth. I'm making up for it and I think I have every right in this world to. Even good to be by myself now though I wouldn't have thought it. Only a few more days, maybe less.

There mustn't be a single missing hill, for shame Jerome to have a missing hill. Wasteful. We must plant before the rain, so we can replant, soon, so it won't be shadowed, a dwarf, trying to make it under the big ones. Oh, it hurts to see one, best that it die and dry away. If my baby is a dwarf, best that he die. Oh no, no, no. Papa has got no size to speak of but he shouldn't be. He won't be. I just won't have my baby being no dwarf. Mama said we didn't have many but we didn't lose them, our babies. But there are baby graves on the hill, flat stones and no names. Mama said they must be another family or some of the niggers, that neither hers nor Papa's side of the family ever had babies that died, that we plant what few seeds we have well. But this has always been our family place. The Bible said so, that Papa's daddy cut it out of the wilderness, Aaron Lemirt, all the way back a hundred years ago. Somebody put those stones there and you can tell they always been plowed around. My baby won't be no dwarf. Won't a soul be able to shadow him and he'll put this whole family in its place when he gets to be a man. And he can just take his own sweet time getting there.

Growing things. The Lord would think it right my mind should be on growing things and not them graves on the hill. Put them graves out away from me, growing things now. If only to have someone to tell that to. Jerome. He'd grunt and say, "Don't see there's anything in common. I'd step on a plant and not think a thing but the dime it cost me. You are bringing me a mouth to feed, woman, and this here child will cost me till it's working age. You don't see as yet how this is going to make things harder but you wait and see. I won't trouble you now in your mother's glory but you wait and see when time turns the newness out of it."

That Jerome. Old Billy Goat Gruff. He wouldn't let me have a playful thought. Make fun of me and sometimes hurt what I say. So if I know the answer I keep the question to myself which is a way Mama taught me to live and don't lay myself bare to no man to trample on. That was the only way to live with a man like Jerome who had no respect for your woman-ness, that's what Mama said and she was right there. Didn't have a caring bone in his body. Married him before I knew any better and as much a fault of Mama's as anybody else's be-cause she'd keep pushing and worrying and talking of thin pickings for a girl who wasn't the prettiest the county turned out. She *was* the prettiest is why she could say that. She sat back like a queen and took her pick and I believe that is the truth because since I was a little girl I seen men make a fool over Mama and seen Papa beam. But I do love Jerome. Everybody can find a fault but I wouldn't have it any other way, except I would like to change what I got a little. He don't drink bad and if I push on him all the time, we do all right. But that don't mean he'll ever be fit to talk to. My boy is going to be that. When I have my boy, we will talk about them things and Jerome can just go jump. He won't care a hoot anyhow. Better for all concerned. That's what Mama would say. I don't mean it a bit when I catch myself talking like her. I know just as good I don't mean it and it gets me so mixed up I don't know what's me and what's her and I'm too old to have somebody else mixed up inside me.

It is a good time to have a child, spring. By winter he should be strong as a little mule. Make him strong. I can't even dream of it any other way, Lord. Don't give me a girl. I know a woman ought to think any baby a blessing, but Lord, being a woman ain't no blessing. You got no life of your own. No sir, you just live till you can have a boy child and watch on him.

They say I'm breaking already and it never happened to Mama. She just went from a pretty rosy-cheeked girl to the most elegant of women. Mama said what prettiness I had, I'm not the ugliest around that is to be sure, that what prettiness I had was not the kind to endure. Breaking and not yet thirty and not yet with the first baby in my arms. Yes, there were lines, some from laughing, mind you, but my skin has taken on a shine, time will make you slick as an onion, I've seen it. You got to powder down to get your softness back and I hide that powder box away in my dresser drawer, even from Jerome who couldn't give a hoot and a holler if I was slick as a peeled onion for all he notices. When I die, bury me in a closed coffin, oh yes, Lord do. I'll not have them looking on me when I can't help myself. Oh so vain, how can I be so vain when I hate it so in her. Oh no, I don't hate but it hurts me in her. Make him strong as a little bull. He is hurting so now, time to come out, he is going to start swinging his fists and feet and bust up everything inside me.

Lord, make me stop thinking on death. It is not good luck to think on dying. I ought to be on growing things again Lord, that is where I prefer to dwell. Time to come out, time to grow. Give him both of our minds, give him both of our minds together, dear God. Hardly enough for such a hard world. Both of us. The bell. I see my hand on the bell. There, I got it sure enough. Feel it cold as a well bottom. I've still got my mind about me. Ting-a-ling. Jerome, it is clanging like a fire wagon. I can hear it just as good. Jerome, get your mind on what you're supposed to do. That man will come running and just throw what he's doing sprawling, here in a minute, and think halfway to the house that it won't just his supper he was running for.

Chapter 2

JEROME JENKINS moved through the screen that morning, catching it with a thump on his heel. New door spring and it was too tight. Had to wear something out before it would work right. He heard the clatter of silver falling from Falissa's hands. Like a brass band, Falissa in the kitchen. When he would try to talk to her from the front room, of all the banging and clanging you ever heard. On Mondays he could hear that screen, whap, whap, whap, with her going in and out with the wash. One swish of the tail was all it would take to soak it up and shut quiet, one swish of the tail. That won't his remark but his brother Roe's who got Falissa's goat one night when a bunch of people came for dinner trying to give her lessons on how to do her tail just right. Roe was three sheets to the wind as usual, red-faced, but there was one thing you could say for Roe, he was an expert on tail swishing. That was Roe's remark too. But that Falissa could stir up some noise and you had to choose your distance from her, treated you like a house full of deaf people. She could scrape a pan of wet mash out for the chickens and make the pan wail its heart out. There was no cutting out her raking. He had seen her fish for the food caught in the corner of a can; she'd use up a dollar's worth of energy to peel the good out of a rotten tomato. Line up all her food for the defrosted refrigerator, open the door and put it in so fast you couldn't see her, slapping it in rows on the shelf, and shut the

door, leaning on it and measuring with her bottom how much
of the precious cold she had let get out. How had he married
such a woman? Maybe he carried it on a bit but it was sure
nobody would ever accuse Falissa of being a wasteful woman.
All those times, though. All those times and she could only
make one child. Not being wasteful must not have been natural
to her.

When he was a little boy, Jerome could remember the garbage, cans and canfuls for his mother, though he grew up dirt
poor, burning sometimes like food cooking, sweet, but sometimes
sending him running into the woods until the smell was far
enough away not to make his stomach heave. And that
Falissa hardly had a speck of garbage, which was to be expected.
You could carry out her week's garbage in a paper sack. He
had made her go to bed last night when she had already spent
an hour rubbing away on an orange rind, making it into the
sweet-smelling sawdust, putting it in jars, saving it to sweeten a
cake. Saving. Watermelon rinds were pickles in her mind before you got the knife run through it and she would pick out
the black seeds and dry them on the windowsill. Could get to
be irritating if you want to know the truth, damned irritating.
Now there was a woman that didn't mind telling everybody
that she near 'bout starved to death once. During the depression
her pa had said and she was at the growing age. He had seen
her get an overfilled plate at a neighbor's once for dinner and
force the better half of it down bit by bit. Sitting looking at
the left food, hardly able to say a word until every speck was in
her and then it took half a night of walking in the hall at home
to settle it in her, burping every five minutes. Now that was
taking a matter too far, no matter what your raising. There
were the times he felt he had married beneath him instead of
the other way around like most people figured.

She was slowing down these last few days and sighed a lot.
Wouldn't admit it was anything if you asked her but he had
lived around a pregnant woman before, his mama with Roe

and the one she lost and Roe's women with theirs, and that was a sign. Don't know why women are so intent on hiding it coming unless they just want to spill it on you at once with a bloodcurdling scream and scare you into the reminder of how hard life is on them. That they tell you enough. They want you to know with their sighing but won't have you making mention of it. No, no it's nothing and they spread their fingers across their bellies. And frown at you, superiorlike, like pain is reserved for them and they are to wear it like a crown on their heads. Even a silence wasn't silence.

When Jerome walked to the barn door, he opened it wide, sending a stream of dirt fanning across his face. It caught in the hairs on his nose and fouled one eye, sifting through the lash. He cursed himself for hurrying, rubbed the watery eye and sneezed three times. He wiped his eye and nose with his handkerchief and cracked the door slowly. It wasn't that he was superstitious but there was something about a bad start, a day that started tumbling in on you before you even got warmed up. He opened the door wide again, standing back for the thinner sift of dirt and moved in, darkening the knife of yellow light that stuck out in front of him. He heard a flutter of wings, small ones. It startled him though he had heard it a thousand times before, the early morning sparrows finding a crack in the door and coming in, fighting for the lost seeds, and the wrens, hunting in the corner shadows for spiders. That was a weakness of his, the birds. Well, he wasn't sure it was a weakness. Maybe it's a weak spot in my head but I don't like anybody messing with my birds. Farmer's best friend.

Fussy Jenny Wren. And if your Johnny Wren doesn't like your tin can you'll find a new Johnny Wren. Last year Jenny Wren nested in one of his gloves on the tool bench and cussed him out before he ever reached for it. She run Falissa in the house for taking his overalls off the line, already had a pocket half filled with sticks. Little scraper.

He read every bird book. In every corner was a magazine on

birds. Even a subscription to *Bird-Lore* that he told Falissa he got in a drawing at the feed store to keep down a row on wasting money. He'd never hear the end of her ranting on his wastefulness. He didn't know where or what this bird thing came from but it was real enough. He still had a spot of hate for Will James next door for letting his boy Stevie have a BB; he give him a Daisy for Christmas just because he asked for it. He'd seen that kid hear one singing and run off in the woods after it like he couldn't stand it another minute.

Didn't reckon he loved them just because of the singing though it was true that was something of it. Singing away any time you take the time to listen to them. Saddest sound in the world is a mourning dove. And it ain't none of that bird watcher, messing-around bunch of sissies he saw in the magazine prissing around in the woods for days on end trying to find a prairie warbler. No, it had all started with that English sparrow business when his brother Roe knowing full well he was inclined to have an interest in birds sent him that book, *Ridding a Menace*. That was just like his family. Knowing he liked birds sent him a book on how to build a trap and kill them by the hundreds. It was on birds and that was as far as they were to think. Ain't that something to give a person?

"Nigger birds. See here, it says as many as two dozen babies a year, five broods."

That was what Roe called them, nigger birds. Asked him about crows and starlings, he mumbled to hisself nigger birds too but that killed his joke because he knew as good as anyone they looked that part better. And it's a fact starlings breed twice. Ain't too often you can get one up on Roe. They do look the part. But he did have to read to Roe the chapter on their roosting habits on cornices and gables, "These they defile with excrement." Old Roe lost his balance and busted up on that "defile with excrement" and he just had to say it because he knew it would get Falissa's goat who don't like dirty talk, "I wish I knew such a fancy way to say shit all over something. I ought to get

a fancy education so I can learn myself how to talk like that."
They sent Roe home from school in the first grade for saying a
dirty poem in front of the class about little Finger putting his
Peter in the dike. That Roe was something.

Jerome walked to the side shed and stepped down through the
stall toward his tractor. A bird flew over his head and he ducked,
heart taking up a faster beat, and then he saw it head on into
the one glass window in the whole barn.

"Bird. Oh my God, bird."

He climbed out of the stall and walked to the window seeing
spider webs hanging in the air in the light film and the dust
flakes that made his eye water again.

Bird. Poor stupid bird. And there was a hole big as day you
could have gone through. One pane. Out from the broom handle I let slip through it. Sparrow, you probably came in through
the same hole and just got mistaken.

He reached down and touched the bird, feeling first the
warmth that always startles you with a just dead thing. He sat
it upright in his hand, folded its wings, turned his own head as
the bird head cocked sideways, English sparrow, striped like a
chipmunk. Broken neck.

He walked back to the stall and stepped down into it. Dry
packed manure, empty for some time now, cow'd been out since
March. He took the pitchfork, lifted a clump with one hand
and dropped the bird in the opening and let it fall shut. One
step and it shut up like it never moved, a trapdoor grave. Keep
the dogs from rooting him up, heavy.

Jerome let the fork go with a thump and stepped onto the hub
of the tractor tire and lifted himself into the seat. It took all of
the tobacco money, two years, but it was well worth it, well
worth it. He threw it out of gear, turned on the switch and
pulled the gas lever. The engine turned over slowly, popping,
bucking, then with a crack fired the first shot. Smoke poured
from the stack and when the first yellow flame licked out from
under the cap Jerome shut the engine.

"Oh goddammit." He ran for a bucket and to the rain barrel. He threw the water from the barrel, a long silver streak that landed with a fizz. Already out before he hit it, washed a shiny red spot on the tractor's nose.

Jesus God, Jerome Jenkins, you have finished your day's business and there are those whose alarm ain't gone off yet. You would think I started out with the full intent of wiping out the whole bird population on the farm in one day's work. Might have been her second brood.

Jerome reached for the remains of the nest in the stack, catching hold of a sprig wound together with the caterpillar webs from last year's persimmon tree. It came out in pieces but the cupped center was whole, four black scorched eggs on a bed of singed feathers. They didn't smell cooked, not like his garbage fire, like a brush fire. No, just four little black marbles. He tossed the eggs and nest in the stable and had a vague quick thought about just as well, without the mother, but the whole thing didn't go together for him. That one might not have been the mother, might not have been the right kind of bird even. The female sparrow has a browner back according to the book. Could dig her out, brown all over now, oh shit. It was just the world was out to get him today.

Jerome took his tractor on out and started cutting circles in the field. The bird was soon gone. Things didn't stick on him anymore like they used to. It was too weak to hang on to him long but Falissa would have fretted all day if she had known. This was the best part of plowing, the first turn. The popping of the roots and not a thing short of a boulder would stop those big discs from rolling. The soil turned up the first round, a rainbow of colors around the edge. Yellow, blue, red. Not many would think all those colors was there but this was Yellow County living up to its name where dirt was yellow and as red as blood in veins so when you cut in, it was like hacking into an animal skin. The second round scattered the rainbow clay and sifted through the winter rot, the stalks he had chopped in. No, that was Falissa come to think of it. He was down with a crick and she had gone and borrowed back her papa's stalk cutter from Will James and run them in for him. That Falissa could run a tractor like a man. But that was his favorite work; he got peeved when she took it on.

Jerome drove around for a long time until the clods were almost gone and the dirt was fine. The smell of crushed ants filled the air and severed earthworms twisted in the dirt. The chickens were at the edges of the field, running into the road each time he came by on the tractor, the rooster daring him until the last minute. Then he lifted his wings and ran like a woman with her skirts hiked up, dirty-assed thing.

Plowing was like fishing. He could watch the dirt turn just like he could watch ripples on the water, for hours and not have a thought go through his head. He could lose track of time if he could just find him a job to do that didn't require thinking. He looked for those jobs, and put off the others where he had to watch himself, stretching wire, driving nails, where he had to make measurements, damn he hated to take measurements and do figuring. Just give him something he could decide on in the morning, go at it all day, and just stop when his stomach told him or the top of his head started frying in the sun. Burned the part in his hair yesterday and it itched up a storm. Jerome stopped the tractor, left it running and stepped off beside it. He stood up close to the tire, looked down the road, over next door where James was busting up land too. As he listened to the siss of his pee under the tractor and watched it run toward his feet, he saw Mrs. James run out across the field. The tractor, no matter with her looking, she wasn't concerned about him. He buttoned his overalls and just as he started back to his tractor seat, he saw James shut off the engine and start back toward the house with his wife. Something must be the matter. Then they both stopped like they read his mind and he saw James cup his hands around his mouth. He shut his engine too and as it sputtered heard, "War! Get on your radio!"

Jerome went in and listened for the first sound in the brown box, watched the orange light take its time swelling up:

Chamberlain resigns as Prime Minister of Great Britain
Churchill takes over
Nazis invade Netherlands, Belgium, Luxembourg . . .

Then it repeated. Was to be expected. James had a boy though, almost grown. Give him something to shoot at other than birds. That boy was nothing to be proud of. Pretty soon that Hitler will have him one big country.

Jerome heard it through then cut it off and went back to the yard. The chickens had flocked to his field while he was gone and they ran in all directions when he came up like they were guilty of something. He got back on his tractor and worked, his mind blank, free of war except once when he wondered why a man would want land he never saw and so much it would be a burden to him to keep check on it all. He noticed James hadn't returned so he would get his garden planted first this time. He heard the bell, took the tractor to the barn and it wasn't until he went into the kitchen and saw his and Falissa's break-fast dishes still there that he remembered.

"Oh my God. It wasn't supposed to call him to eat today. We should have got a different bell." He went quickly up the stairs to her room.

"It ain't even lunchtime. Now what was I thinking about."

He opened the door to their room. She was shiny with sweat which made him frown.

"You better get somebody to help me, Jerome, and I'd prefer it to be that lady you spoke with. And you and Papa Lonza make do for dinner on what I cooked up for you and see if Mama wants a bite." That was the last Falissa said to him until the next morning.

*   *   *

The child came that night, just before midnight, May 10, 1940. Her labor was long as she might have expected because from her first sickness, that left her cheeks with seven round holes in them and three between her eyes, life had never given Falissa Jenkins an easy go of it. Winston became a name she heard frequently through the brown box that ran almost constantly now. Winston became in her mind a little elf she could hold in her hand, found one day under a bean plant. A haughty little elf but one she liked. And she saw a church on a hill of green grass, like fresh rye you could lie down in. Churchill. Church hill. The newsman liked him and she did too, his fancy voice, but she didn't listen to the words much anymore. She could have named her baby that, Winston, but people would have thought her too fancy. No that wasn't it. He was part of the brown box and that might all go away or it might keep coming and remind her of something bad. Even when her baby was grown. In the middle of a song, *Bell Bottom Trousers, coat of navy blue, I love my sailor boy* . . . Brussels, brussel sprouts, a little cabbage for my elf, blistered leaves. The song would snap away, baby fruit carelessly knocked off, it wasn't proper to play "London Bridge" anymore, not proper to play at all unless you were a boy soon to go off. The music would wind down slowly in the background. A big red hand wringing it to silence, choking it. News of Europe, war, meaningless now as a word said over and over, war, war, war, an unlatched door beating in the wind, forgotten, an old man she once knew that she hated to hear laugh, haw, haw, haw, all on the same note.

Her little boy was at her breast and she had meant to order her some bulbs but it was all over now, boats had no room for such fancies, soldiers trampling her tulips, breaking down her windmills with their cannons, flooding the land until Holland was no more, just a faraway ocean, brown water. Best the water would cover it over if it had to be scarred.

If that brown box had never been here I wouldn't know it and could look at the fields and never see in my mind soldiers tramping toward the house. Oh, that's not true for a minute with every boy in this town signing up. All this waiting and saying goodbye and their mamas sniffing by my mama's bedside. Visiting her more now like they want just this little taste of death so when it comes they can stand strong and feel a familiar taste in their systems. I know them just as good. And I've been guilty, Lord, as guilty as the day is long gloating over my baby's youngness. They was telling me I was waiting too long and here theirs is marching off to war and mine not out of the crib. Oh Lord, forgive me for my gloating. But I'd do it again. And I wouldn't let them send my boy off to war. I'm asking forgiveness too soon, dear God, because as sure as you are in your heaven, I'd do it again.

"You'll never raise him."

The old woman squinted at the child, the mite in his mother's arms, and shook her head. "You'll never raise him," she repeated, surer this time, she had spoken, so much for the child. "What a shame for the family that has never lost a child."

The old woman coughed, bouncing in her bed, even in her death, graceful, featherlike. Her gown was pressed, each ruffle separately. She wouldn't have it any other way. She was the color of the sheets but for the blue veins on her hands and neck, and the blue eyes. Blue now, so sure she would never raise him, looking at him hard, never lifting those blue-veined hands to touch his warm skin. You could make me hateful, Mama. You make me burn inside and sting in my head like I'm going crazy I'm so hateful. You could make me wish he would live past you so I could say I told you so. It ain't in me to be so mean but I could bring up the graves; they are up there in the corn field and no amount of denying is going to carry them away or taking Papa into your lying silence, six babies dead up there and a grave rock will outlive this house and all that are in it. He'll live past you, and me too for that matter. Your mouth is pinched. You are no cameo anymore, you hear. There is many a man who would rather look on a living, blooming girl not so perfect of feature but filled with the life about her and not herself.

He is a cute little mite, all his little energies gone into the black hair that curled on his head, leaving the spindly little arms for later. He *is* cute, she could have said that, his round blue eyes looking in any direction you pointed him. He was cute, little Cale Jenkins. Not much special about a baby it was sure but the fact such a thing could come out of you. But that black hair in the most perfect rings was special to more than a mother's eye. And he hadn't cried a peep since his first spanking. He just looked at things, trying to touch everything that got close enough for him to see and not getting his arms to work properly. And he was a hungry little fellow, kicking those legs like he won't content if he couldn't just pump the milk out in bucketfuls. He'll grow up slow and easy and take in all there is to see and there won't be a June bug on the place he don't catch and tie to a string and he'll be the terror of everything around that tries to sleep its days away. Give him time. I'll raise him, Miss Sarah Ann, if it's the last thing I do.

Chapter 3

June, 1940

PAPA LONZA LEMIRT had been a telegraph operator but even Summit didn't need him anymore since they got telephones down at the railroad station. The passenger service cut down to one car a day from Raleigh when the mill closed and the freight traffic thinned until the hobo camp by the trestle was empty of campfires and their tin cans rusted in the ground. The bus to Raleigh was cheaper. Papa was far from useless when the news came of his retirement time coming. But they tricked him, got him out of there before the pension come into being. Could have been fixed for life, sixty dollars a month. He was always good with his hands and he figured the war would set them back to telegrams anyway. He had seen one war and how it made the world just turn itself around and start going backwards. Had to have wars to keep people from getting ahead of themselves. But that didn't mean Papa liked wars. He had fears in his dreams about his sisters' boys getting killed. He had been distressed bad about them since he saw that movie one of his sisters took of the boys home on leave and before it got back from developing, one of the cousins was dead and there he was just as alive in that movie, popping the girls on the tail.

Falissa watched Papa holding the baby, but there was a sadness still. Papa is distressed about Mama too, which he has a right to be. She is going out. I am convinced of it. And Papa does love her. He admires her too. She is a lady to Papa. He has never stopped thinking for a minute how lucky he was to get her and you can be sure she has never stopped reminding him. It has done Papa good for me to have my baby. Why he can just sit there and hold it and talk to it for hours at the time until it messes in his lap. He is just the best babysitter you could have and I had never dreamed he would take to it so. But you know I think maybe it is because it is a boy. Papa just got left completely out of having a boy. Mama never had no sense of making a family and didn't think twice Papa wanted a namesake.

It's just as well because Jerome doesn't make a thing over it but he thinks it's woman's work for now. He better just watch me or I won't ever let him have a thing to do with my baby, thinking he can just have it at his choosing, probably waiting till it's big enough to work the fields to pay any attention to him. Then just come in one day and try to snatch him out from under me. I wrapped my baby up this morning and took him out to walk the garden with me and I bet there isn't a month-old youngun in this county had a cutworm explained to him already. Bad this year and why in the world they want to chop a plant down. I can see their eating on the leaves if they're hungry. But just leaving it to die, that's just meanness.

"Papa, the swallows are low this afternoon. They aren't halfway up the locust tree."

"Gonna rain."

"We need it. Things are wilted."

"Sarah Ann don't like the rain, makes her fidgety. Told me somebody was shooting at us until I figured she was talking about the rain on the tin."

"She has less of a mind every day. She has heard the rain a thousand times and went off to sleep with it."

"Well, I can see how she might think that about the tin loud as it was. It ain't so hard to imagine she could be mistaken. We can all let our ears mistake us. I tend to have a bit of a ringing myself . . ."

*

He won't let a soul say a thing against Sarah Ann. He will think her perfect until her dying day. And that day is coming on us soon. I'm sure of that. Under all that prettiness there wasn't much spunk. The life in her faded fast and it do make you think about that prettiness on top, how little it is worth to you if the life is slipping out. But so long as she can be grand, if it is in a box with her hands crossed, just so long as she can be grand. I don't mean to sound ugly like I don't love my own mama but I suppose I was kind of hoping being sick might humble her a bit. Just keep hoping and see what it gets you. When I quit listening to Papa, he just starts talking to Cale. Just took the little fellow away from me. I do all the having just so he can get all the pleasure out of him. I declare I don't know what he is going to do when the little fellow gets old enough to stick his finger in his ears. Lord help me in my old age to have my heart fail me before my head. But I am glad he had a grandpa. It is well that a boy have a grandpapa and I hope he'll be old enough to remember him. Anybody who loves a baby like Papa ought to have had a wife who give him a dozen.

"Hey little button, hey, hey, hey. Lordy, when are you going to look at me like you know something I'm talking about. Now you needn't expect me to go on telling you stories if you don't pay no attention, you hear? Got to the funny part and you didn't crack a smile for me. You supposed to laugh at an old man if it's just for politeness' sake. Gotta little horsie and he's going to town. Ride him up, ride him up, ride him up to town."

"Papa, slow down a bit. He's awful little for all that jousting. You're going to make him lose his breath."

"Yes'um. Yes'um. You hear that, don't you. She is going to make a no-count sissy of you. Dress him up in his little suit, girl. I want to take him out walking. Shouldn't oughta keep him shut up all the time. Needs the sunshine. He's as pale as a girl."

"How far you going?"

"Just down the road a piece."

"He's going to be starved to death in an hour."

"Won't be gone thirty minutes."

"You can take him." Falissa took Cale and went up to the bedroom. She felt him and he was wet. She undid the wet diaper, showered him with powder and watched him twist on the bed while she folded two together. "Think there is enough juice in you to soak up two, do you?" He opened his mouth and his eyes brightened with her voice but he wouldn't laugh. Just couldn't make him laugh if you tried. Not out loud yet anyway but he didn't cry either which was something. She zipped him up in his playsuit and he frowned at her when he tried to move inside the stiff cloth. "Now don't you take all of this so seriously. Looking at me like a little old man already. Like a turtle on his backside." She bent down close to him and saw her shadow darken his eyes. He waved his hand but no smile, just that frown like a little old man. Never like a baby for a minute.

She started down the steps and saw Papa by the door, his hat already on. "Aren't you going to take your cane?" Then she saw it, the same frown. "Just don't let me interfere with you menfolks. You just do as you please."

Papa Lonza took the child in his arms lifting its head up over his shoulder. "Now you at least want to see where you've been."

"You just make sure where he's been isn't the Rebel Bar."

Papa laughed and jousted the little boy up and down when he went out the door. He thought he heard her laugh too, probably did. Falissa was a good sport. He hadn't drank like he used to in years, ever since Sarah Ann started getting weak. She wouldn't have a thing to do with him when he touched a drop, not even a beer on a hot day which was what would keep some fellers drinking but was the best thing in the world to make him stop. Made him hurt bad those times when he couldn't help himself. She stuck up her nose and locked herself in her room; could carry her punishment a long way, Sarah Ann.

"You know why them birds is down so low, boy, huh?"

The baby grunted.

"Well, because that's where the bugs are. They don't just come down on their own. The bugs come down and they come after them but what you got to know is why either one of them come down in the first place, right boy?"

The baby was silent.

"Right. And that's because it is going to rain and it is already halfway down the sky and the bugs get lower to keep the water from squshing them and there ain't much space left for the birds to go bug hunting in. And I hope they ain't much space for the bugs to go hiding."

Papa walked on out of the driveway and started down the road. "Boy, you see all them cedar trees?"

He turned the baby around in a slow circle and tossed him back up to his shoulders again. The baby squinted and sneezed. Papa took out his handkerchief and wiped under his nose.

The old man sniffed loudly and the baby sneezed again. He looked at its nose but it was clean. "You must be 'lergic to bitterweed. It's in the family because it's always given me and your mama a fit. When she was a little girl I saw her sneeze many a time until her supper would come up. I was hoping you'd be spared that. I declare, my mind do wander now. It can take off from something and get switched off on a side rail and never find its way back home again. And if I'm telling you any of this too soon you let me know and I'll tell you again."

The fences were furry with cedar trees but the dark evergreen softness had long broken away, honeysuckle already taking off up the post and scenting the air. A mule tearing the green strings off the posts stood at the fence, pressing down the wire to pop off the new leaves, the pasture behind him picked barren but for the bitterweed, yellow and dusty.

Papa took the baby over to the mule. The mule lifted its head, slinging a circle of green slime on Papa's leg. The big thick ears flopped forward when it saw the baby.

"Well now, you know a fine boy when you see one."

Cale reached toward the mule with both hands and it jumped back, blowing its nose over both of them.

"Now don't you go and dirty him up, you old fool."

Papa wiped the green specks from the baby's face then tried to rub them out of the cloth of the playsuit. "Your mama's going to skin us alive. And you were brand clean."

Papa went back into the road and headed toward town. "Mules can't have no babies. Now, that there came from a jackass daddy and a mare woman horse which is the way it's done around here but now I've heard tell of a hinny which is the other way around but that will near about kill that poor mama coming out, I mean the mama was a jackass and the daddy a horse, but around here you won't catch nobody calling one a hinny if you know what I mean."

The old man started to laugh. "Naw, you don't yet. You're too young for that kind of talk yet. This little thing here Falissa's got all that padding on is your hiney. Reason we use mules is because they got little feet and all you got to do is see them sawmill horses to imagine what a mess they'd make of a row. Got feet on them as big as a dinner plate. You just missed seeing them. Left here two weeks before you come. We let them use our pasture while they were cutting off the backside. Shame there's no use for them because they were fine critters. They were as fine as them I saw on show when I was a little boy, pulling a beer wagon.

"Look a yonder at them stacks. You can see them from here a little bit now, but when it is full summer you'll have to be around the next curve before you can get them in your sight. Ugly things. I remember the fellow who had to lay the bricks for it and that son of a bitch Soloman made him spell his name in white bricks and you can't read it now to save your life. Son of a bitch Soloman. Heard it so many times I almost forget that's not his name like when I said it at church and Falissa almost clobbered me, hacked me in the leg with her pocketbook like a sickle. And they called me Chicken Little because of that thing

but I'm not telling you that story until you're old enough to understand my side of it because I know it's going to be everybody's
in this town's word against mine and they're all just waiting to
be the first to tell it to you. Even my own kin turned on me. I
hope you are tall as a tree, boy. People'll watch their mouths
around you. I am sixty-one and one-half inches high, at least
I was before I started leaning a bit, sixty-one and one-half inches
high. Kept me a mark on the door and I won't sixteen before I
had to quit moving it up. Boys are bigger now, no doubt about
that to my mind, but that don't fool me into thinking I won't
little before boys started being made bigger. But I swear to
God in heaven above that them things were falling and still
are and if the clouds were as still as death, you could still see
them falling. They going to go a little at a time, especially that
biggest one, the mortar has give away and the first thing you
know all that leaning will pop the bricks out, won't take but
one for the whole shooting match to go, and it is going to be
the biggest catastrophe since the floods in '16 took every bridge
clean to the ocean."

"Mr. Lonza Lemirt, yuh bring that boy over here. Talking
up a storm. He gon' think you crazy as a bedbug."

Papa stopped to see who called. It was the big tenant woman
from their place coming in from the sawmill with an armful of
scrap wood.

"Aunt Bynum. Yes'um, Aunt Bynum."

"Woo, now look at that. I would say he is going to be a lucky
one. He don't look a bit like yuh. How old?"

"Four weeks, two days."

"He's growing like a weed. He ain't going to be no squirt."

"Well, you won't find me crying over that, no sirree. I'd just
soon him have to learn to duck his head going through doors
myself if you want the truth."

"Uh-huh. Miss Falissa getting on O.K.?"

"Was up the next day."

"Naw."

"Yes'um, she was. No dust going to settle on Falissa."

"With the first born. She's a strong woman. My first one like to have killed me. That one says how-de-do when it pleases. No more nine months than a frog gon' hop backwards. I got me one coming on next month or so myself. What did yuh name him?"

"Cale Leroy Jenkins."

"Starting off on a new name. I'm agreeable to that. I won't never much for all that junioring and the thirding myself."

"I got to be going, Aunt Bynum. Falissa don't give us much time together."

"Well now, don't yuh let me hold yuh up. But yuh bring him to see me again yuh hear? I want to be keeping an eye on the new man around the place."

"Yes'um."

"Oh, one more thing, Mr. Lonza, before yuh get off from here. How's that woman of yuh's? I hear she sick and I ain't seen her in well over a year."

"She's not doing so well, Aunt Bynum. We don't 'spect her up again. She is lying in that bed just as pretty as a picture but it don't seem likely she'll be out again."

"I'm mighty sorry to hear that. I didn't think I'd seen that parasol around the yard. Now yuh call on me if yuh need me, Mr. Lonza. I be glad to set up with her for yuh. She was a fine lady."

"Thank you, Aunt Bynum. I'll tell her. She thought a lot of you."

Papa walked on back down the road. He turned over his shoulder and could see the back of Aunt Bynum's head, tied up with a rag, the hem of her dress jiggling as she hurried along.

"Now that there, little Cale, is a nigger. But that is a fine one, one of the finest I've ever known. She is as strong as a mule, standing there holding that wood like it was a bundle of matchsticks. You got to get used to her ways but if it was the end of the world, she would be the last one there helping you out, just yelling at you like she was the only grown-up on earth and working herself to death for you. She's smarter than most white people. And your daddy Jerome don't appreciate her properly because what he don't know is most people have to keep up three niggers to do what Aunt Bynum does. She is the workingest woman that ever lived and so was her mama and her mama's mama, my Pa said, who he found up in Virginia after they been turned loose with no man to look to them. Runs in the family 'cause the only thing I ever seen get the best of Aunt Bynum is keeping that husband of hers at home. You should have seen what your mama made her for Christmas. She come up whispering to Falissa what she wanted more than anything and me just dying to hear and Falissa told me as soon as she was gone. She wanted her a pair of big old-timey drawers that you couldn't buy no more in the stores made right with pockets in them to keep her money in. You ought to have seen how big they were. We made Falissa hold them up, couldn't get her to try them on for love nor money, and we all got to wondering how in this world any man could find any room in bed with that. And her man's skinny as a fence post. But she loved them drawers. That was a sight, the way she carried on about them drawers and brought Falissa a pack of Old Maid cards as a present for making them. Old Maid cards. That would have just killed your Mama to get such a present a few years ago. Why I can remember when she was scared to death of being an old maid, that the family would come to an end and she'd be the cause of it.

"That was as much my doing as anything. Not Sarah Ann's like Falissa is prone to think. No sir, it was mine because of that pa of mine. You see, little Cale, I know just as good I'll have to tell you this all over again, I ain't that much an old fool but it don't hurt practicing up. You see my papa, your grandpa, no, great-grandpa come over on a boat. It was long before they got the good ones. You see he come over on a boat all the way across the ocean that won't hardly big enough to go down the river in. And he had done made him a family before he started, a woman and two boys I never seen even in a picture because he didn't own any, and they didn't have land big enough for a pea patch he said, so he decided to pack up and come over where he'd heard people could put his whole farm in their parlor. Now he didn't know what he was getting into but he was sure of one thing, that was he couldn't get into no worse because he was going to starve where he was. So he set out looking for a boat. I ain't going to bore you with the details now. I just wanted to tell you about Falissa and the Old Maid cards. I declare I'm as rambly as a briar."

The old man walked into the town, by the feed store at the edge. People started to nod but most of them shook their heads when they heard him talking.

"Look at them, boy," he whispered. "Jealous as they can be of me. Well now, he told of the cities, my papa in his funny way of talking. Like people had dumped all of their houses together with not a bit of self-respect and privacy and not a patch of dirt big enough to grow a tomato in and people was living off nothing but bought stuff and if the money were to stop coming in the factories, they would all go hungry as dogs and it had been so long since they'd planted a garden, they had forgot how. I declare he would have been right in style if he could have lived in twenty-nine, if he could have seen the messes they called gardens around here. All sleeping in one bed and him starting to think his pea patch was the biggest place in the world when he got himself on a boat and decided that city was just a little taste of hell. And his two baby boys took the smallpox and died. Fifteen days and he was a man without children and people was rushing them to get them out of the boat because it was spreading and he and his woman had to take them up top and drop them off in the water like they was no better than garbage. The sea birds come dropping down at them and his wife let out a shriek. Lia. She shrieked at them birds to stop and that was the last he heard her talk because it was like she broke everything

inside her. He said she watched them, pecking down at the
water and lighting in a circle, squawking at each other, until
they were white specks and lost in the blue water. And in seven
days he had to take her to the top and drop her, at night when
the birds were quiet. She was wasted as a little stick, my Mama
used to shiver when he'd tell that. Him who had decided there
was nothing worse found hisself with nothing but hisself. He
stood on the top that night thinking it was his last night to
breathe that air and he might go over hisself and that not a soul
would grieve. A man would just spread over more in the straw
and be thankful for the room but he started into thinking something he told me never to forget and I won't at that. He told me
it is a sin for a man to die and leave no one grieving because it
takes those that care about him to measure his life. That was
all there was to it, no man is going to give up.

"Then come the sickness. He turned up his stomach until
there was nothing more inside him. He didn't even get the
sight of the land that others were to tell him about, that light
green that come when the water turned shallow and the air that
got thick with birds, but he woke up in the port being doctored
by people he didn't even know. And he was lonesome and tired.
He started to walking soon as he was able to put one foot in
front of the other, weary before the start and said to hisself he
was thirty-four years old and had to make his way alone. I'm
'bout to get back around to them Old Maid cards, now you just
hold on. Quit being such a wiggle worm. He looked out there
in front of him and seen mountains and white rocks just rolled
about since the beginning of time and looking at him like come
and pick me up and put me together right and you can live here
but I ain't letting you have me for nothing. So he went out
after them rocks and what you know the first thing he started
thinking was how a woman would want her house put together.
Then he started in to thinking just like he was a young man,
wanting him another woman, because it won't right for no man
to come that far and live his life and rot back into the ground
and all he had to offer to a women was him and the work of his

two hands. He could have rotted into the ground over there in the Dutch ground, he didn't need to come clean over here where he didn't know nobody to watch his woman and babies shrink away. And my Papa won't going to be wrong. He come to raise a family in a new land and build him a big farm and he won't going to come all that way to wait out his days by hisself. So he spruced hisself up and went out and found my mama in no time flat. He was a fine figure of a man for what good it done me. So that is why I won't having your mama to be an old maid, no sirree. I didn't get me no boy firsthand like I planned on, and Falissa didn't get no prize husband, but she give me a boy and I can go to sleep in my grave just as peaceful as you please knowing you are going on in this world and going to find you a woman and grow you some fine crops and fix this back up into the farm it was. But my name is going to the grave. There is some things you just got to give up no matter what you are thinking to do. That was done when Sarah Ann said Falissa was the last. When things start looking too good something comes along to remind you you are on earthly land. And when Sarah Ann said it was the last, then it was the last. And Papa didn't want us to spend the money writing on his stone. My name's gon' get plowed in the ground with nobody to carry it."

Papa could hear his name, Mr. Lonza, coming behind him and further back, a thin "Papa." He could see the big Negro woman running, almost falling forward in the road but propelling ahead of Falissa who was still in her apron. Falissa wouldn't leave the house in her apron.

"Mr. Lonza! Mr. Lonza, yuh woman . . ."

The big woman stopped and caught her balance and her chest began to heave.

"O Lord, we done come running when there is nothing ahead but eternity."

She turned to Falissa who was just arriving. Falissa reached for the baby and he handed it to her. She wrapped her other arm around his shoulder and they headed toward home.

There was no use anybody saying anything. Sarah Ann was

dead and he won't there with her at the last. Took out with that baby without so much as a goodbye to her. Tending to his own wishes and left her to go alone. Worrying about leaving his mark on the earth while all he had worth living for went away. The Lord would punish him for his wickedness or he would do it hisself. Sarah Ann was dead.

Chapter 4

CALE was on his stomach on a quilt, pounding his fists into a
velvet square. Aunt Bynum had put him there purposely in
the velvet area so she could leave his shirt off and the cover
wouldn't scratch him. His body was powdered but the white
flakes began to roll into tubes in the folds of his skin and he became shiny and wet. The day was swelling outside, wilting and
twisting the leaves, lingering on the edge of a storm, whipping
up the dust and spraying it through the front screen. The day
was teasing and toying with the idea of tearing up the funeral,
cracking through the leaves and into the stones, leaving the
preacher saying his final words with his hair running into his
face, the good book clutched against his chest while he recited
from memory, the red clay cutting into furrows and filling
the grave with orange water, bubbling white foam like it was
filled with poison. Something won't right about buying a plot
of dirt when you had a hundred acres. And you oughtn't be
buried away from your own kinfolks.

Aunt Bynum had kept the baby in the back room until all
the people were gone, humming and rocking with him on top
of her big belly, eight months gone. She took him back out
when she thought the parlor was empty but she had forgotten
about the old woman, still there with the lid open. She wasn't
going over close, no sirree; over here on the other side of the
hall was close enough and from here Miss Sarah Ann didn't look

like a person, just so much more lace and flowers and Aunt
Bynum didn't have to think there was once something living
and running under that blue-white skin. Just filled the front
room up with starched doilies and frills, just nothingness, and
little glass dolls in full skirts. Didn't like to walk through there
for fear of tipping one and busting it, even with her dead as a
doornail. And she picked and chose them dolls what she thought
looked like her, the spitting image with their pinched mouths,
skin slick as a frog's belly. White like dead.

"Yuh don't do much laughing, do yuh, booger?"

Cale continued to beat the velvet, the red of it lighting up
his sweat-slick face.

"Yuh done lost you a grandma 'fore yuh even got to know her.
Lord, that is something to say because I don't think there are
many souls on this earth that are prided with knowing Miss
Sarah Ann. She could put the fear of the Lord in yuh just walking down the road, make yuh stand so still you didn't stir up a
speck of dust 'cause if yuh was to spot up her dress, she would
strike you dead. Did yuh know that, youngun? Every little
nigger on this place learnt that before he learnt to walk. Learnt
it soon as he learnt to stir up dust. Every white man in this town
would make a jackass of hisself if he thought Miss Sarah Ann
might look up. She kept folks away from her like she'd freeze
the hand that touch her. Naw sir, that was a fine lady and it
won't a few times we spent imagining how your granpa got
his seed in her 'cause she sho won't gon' let him touch her."

Aunt Bynum laughed, deep inside her throat so the dead
across the way couldn't hear her.

"Ain't yuh got no sense of humor? Huh, ain't yuh got no tick-
lish spot? How 'bout yuh coming from a seed on a lavender
powder puff? Strike me dead didn't no angel of the Lord put
no seed in that woman. She was the devil hisself."

Aunt Bynum stooped and struck Cale lightly in the side, rolling him over. He wound his fists and feet like a hard-shelled
animal, reaching for the ground. "Why yuh just a little ma-

chine, wiggling yuh feet. Don't yuh know little boys supposed
to laugh, not just run like little motors? Let me set yuh back up
and quit messing with yuh before yuh start hollering and yuh
mama give us both down the country."

She turned Cale back to his feet and he stared at the velvet
a moment then reached for one of the white knots on it.

Aunt Bynum bent over to whisper to the baby. "Yuh know
something, little booger? If the little niggers on this farm
knowed there won't nobody here in this house but me and yuh
and knowed she was dead in yonder, they'd give me a quarter
apiece to come spit in that box."

Aunt Bynum's mouth flapped shut and she looked around
her. "And I'd shut my eyes and get rich." The house was still
and no one was coming up the walk. "I gon' be struck dead
someday for such as that. Yuh wait and see, youngun. Lawsy,
what makes me so mean?"

Her chair started to rock. "But it's the truth."

Four pallbearers came up the walk. They moved in the
open door and nodded at her. "It's the truth, Lord, it's the truth,"
she repeated.

"Amen, Auntie," one of the men answered.

"It's the truth."

They closed the lid and one man pinched a finger in the latch.
Half a cuss word came out, before there was quiet again. They
carried the creaking box to the door, white with gold handles
and white gladiolas on top.

"That little woman got enough box here to sink her to China."

"Shut up," and they moved out the door.

"It's the truth, Lord, it's the truth," Aunt Bynum said again
and watched them shove the box into the black hearse.

*　　*　　*

"Sam Fariss forgot to turn his headlights on."

"It don't matter, Jerome. There's no traffic to speak of and folks can see he's in line if they needed to," Falissa said without turning around.

"He could have an accident just the same. Just like him to forget."

Papa Lonza sat by the window and Falissa was between him and Jerome. He didn't look up, almost as if he couldn't stand to see what they were passing by outside. He was crouched down, even smaller than usual, his head bare and hair combed smooth, still thick gray-black. He wore the white shirt he wore on Sunday with the collar tips pointing up.

"I never been in one of these fancy cars before, not this fancy. I know you ain't, Falissa. This is finer than the Packard my old man bought," Jerome said.

"Well, these are not the circumstances for enjoying a fancy car if you want my opinion."

"They sure spruce them up. Family live like dirt all its lives and ride out to the graveyard in one of these like that's what it's supposed to. Don't seem right to me."

"We never lived like dirt, Jerome."

"Well, you didn't never go for rides in nothing like this."

"That is not what it's for."

"I bet old Soloman's got him one now just for riding around in. Got him a fancy nigger driving it with stripes down his pants and is picking him another town clean."

Papa groaned and turned his face toward the window but squeezed his eyes shut. Falissa put her hand on his arm and he relaxed again, his face back toward his lap. Jerome was quiet now.

"Do you think it's going to rain, Papa?"

The old man looked up and batted his eyes but did not look at Falissa. "Naw, don't reckon."

Then he looked slowly out the window again. "It could rain, I reckon, if it was a mind to. Wind's up. Looked like it yesterday." His voice trailed off, tired. They passed a boy with his hair blown up flat on the back of his head and a bald spot showing. He looked at the procession, staring, craning his head to see in the hearse. Falissa hoped Papa didn't see it but he did. He balled his fists and said, "Got no respect for the dead. Low living scum."

"He don't know no better, Papa. He didn't mean any harm."

"He won't see her. She's shut up tight."

Lonza heard her name, way back in his head. Sarah Ann. Sarah Ann. You don't even mind being dead. I seen you lying there in your prettiness just like life was a botherance to you and you had just as soon it leave and take with it the ugly hacking. Your Lonza saw you lying there in that parlor and the old men had a special way of looking at you. And I was proud of you for not letting the world beat you up, as soft and pretty as the day you were born. Don't no young man know what us old men see; we see Lonza's woman. When they shut that lid she turned to stone, to marble with smooth blue veins and she is like the body on top the casket in the town church, too sacred for a person to reach out and touch. I saw that pretty body there in the church when I was a little boy and my mama told me never to touch it but I did when she turned and it was smooth and cool as anything I've ever touched. But you, Sarah Ann. You turned to stone when you were touched and not a living soul will touch you again.

You could have had anyone you wanted. But I don't think you wanted nobody at all. That's why it was me. I was the one you poked your finger at. It's 'cause this town didn't have nobody special enough to offer such as you. We didn't have no princes or kings and you knowed I would treat you proper. You knowed I was little and would never lift a finger to hurt you. There was times I had to work hard at it, Sarah Ann, and you never knowed it. But don't think I minded. Never for a minute. I was bound and determined never to put a spot on your whiteness with no rough handling if you wound me in a knot inside. Not a spot on you, nowheres, Sarah Ann.

*   *   *

Sarah Ann's was a dry-eyed funeral. Papa trembled when he saw the box go in the ground because it looked so much like her and he didn't like not having anything between it and the dirt. But she had picked it out herself. Falissa had felt her eyes cloud up, she had tried to get her crying done before she came in order to take care of Papa. There was always something terrible about finality and she would always search her mind at these times, wondering if there might have been something that would have made her going mean more. Yet Mama herself had been determined to die, just as determined as she was to have a plot in the graveyard under a tree where the land was tended and not out in a corn field in the hot sun with the rest of the family. Mama dead or Mama alive would always be part of her mind; Mama was gone and left herself sunk into Falissa's skin like a dye. She came back every Sunday to pay her respects, bringing flowers when she had them, letting Papa place them by the stone while she straightened up, pulled grass, clipped around the edge of the stone where the mower missed. Papa never talked much when they were there which wasn't like him, but she could see he was pleased when it was sure her grave was the best kept. He took his handkerchief and wiped off the stone. How long will this go on? It is all for Papa until he is gone.

*　　*　　*

When Papa was tired he hurt himself by thinking of when Sarah Ann died; he whined and cursed himself until Falissa had to put him to bed. He would mumble awhile in his sleep but would soon be snoring, old man sounds in a dreamless sleep and he never wanted to take to drinking again even to clear his mind. And come morning, he was in to see his Cale. It had been so long since there was something around that could change for the better. Most things just rusted, got old and broke, and people wrinkled and slowed down. But every day that came made Cale more of a person. And he had started to laugh. Papa

could make him laugh just by peeping over the edge of the crib
now since that wonderful day when Papa sneezed twice and
Cale broke out laughing. And soon only when Papa was very
tired or sick with a fever did Sarah Ann dying come up, just her
living and he framed her in his mind like the women with bus-
tles and long dresses that hung in the circular frames over her
bed. It was best that she be there, both of them would be pleased.
And Papa stayed in the bed under the stairs, where he stayed
while she was sick. The white crocheted coverlet on her bed
was never turned back even for company.

Falissa watched them through the windows, Cale walking now
and squealing when he was happy. And the babble, the talk
that Papa had called her out to hear when the child had a bug
in front of him, picking it up and putting it on its back, blowing
it until it turned over and laughing as it tried to run and couldn't
escape the little fingers. But gentle, he never crushed it and his
talking stopped when it tired and curled up, worn out. He came
running to them. Knees pointing outward, got your father's
crooked legs.

March was coming again. Her last March she was swollen
with Cale but now she was feeling the tightness coming back
across her stomach from bending and lifting. Her clothes didn't
need a let-out after Cale, not even the finer ones with the tight
fit at the waist, she saw to that. The bones in her pelvis even
flattened down a bit she thought. It was only the baby she let
herself gain. But what a lot of work that child had brought her.
If not for Papa to tend to him and let her forget that he was there
now and then, her house and cooking would go to ruin. She
made his little clothes, resisting the fancy stitch since Jerome
had made some comment when she trimmed a little jacket for
him about saving that stuff for her girlchild.

Winter wouldn't let go and the wind that blew in was cold
and hurting. She could see the back of Papa's red and black
checked coat, out by the wood house, his shoulders rolling forward and hiking it up in the center back. He stood smaller

than ever before, permanent now. And at his feet, little Cale,
stacking up the kindling blocks. Sitting right flat on the cold
ground; Papa should know better than that. And she watched
the old man stoop and tie up the blue hood around his head.
Knocked it right back off. Couldn't stand to have a thing on
his head.

There were still snow patches, glowing out of the darkest
shadows, freckled black with soot. But the snow had fallen clean
since the coal-burning trains were gone and Soloman's was no
more. The smoke from their own chimney had dirtied the snow
on the ground. Mama never let them make up snow cream because of its dirtiness but now it was fresh-falling after the first
snow swept the air, the only thing about Summit that seemed
to get better not worse. The cream was so flat without vanilla
but she couldn't waste it for playing, not with the war still on.
The sky kept the snow color, cloudless except for white strings
and with a pink glow even in the early day. Snowbirds pecked
around in the thawed places after some old seeds she'd thrown
out. It was going to snow again before spring broke; nothing
acted like winter was over with. Jerome had gone out to patch
up the stalls but she hadn't heard a sound out of him. Likely
as not he was sleeping, she had caught him at it more than once,
if he could find a place big enough to spread out. Even had
two of her old bed quilts out there to wrap up in. She had found
them in the hay. And likely as not when his hammering would
start he would just be doing it for her benefit. She had tried to
get him to go in town and work the winter months after the
tobacco was sold, but he would stay all day and not come back
with any money. Just stand around and talk, that's what he
would do. He had a funny way of making like he was working
hard. And he believed himself with all his talk about the baby
and how much it was costing like it was all her doing and none
of his. But that won't the way you should look at a child, like
the only changes it was making was hardships. And she didn't
see how it made a single hardship on Jerome anyway, she had

to work a little harder to keep doing her regular work that filled up her day before he came and so she could have a little time each day just to talk to him and play a bit. No more time than Jerome took with him, he was likely to think that Papa was his daddy anyway. As slow and dull as Jerome's life was, wouldn't you think he would want to find a little time for Cale? Like he was bound and determined not to give him any attention and keep everyone else from doing so if he could. Had been just as cross as could be with Papa about it. What in the world was wrong with an old man enjoying himself? If Jerome had worked half as hard as Papa had to, we wouldn't be where we are and have the place look like it's falling down. How can any man really think he works so hard and do nothing? Maybe she was being harder on Jerome because he was so trifling about the child but he hadn't helped out a bit. Makes you wonder if he really does think about it.

Papa had made a tall tower of the kindling and it went toppling over and scattered in the yard. Cale started to laugh and hit his hands together; she could hear his laugh even through the shut window, that laugh was twice his size to make up for so long in coming. But maybe there wasn't enough laughing and good times around here for him to learn it when he came along. Papa tossed the scattered blocks back toward the shed, landing them around Cale's feet. It made her heart jump a little, thinking one might hit the child and wondering if Papa knew he was slipping. Then she saw it, worse than she could have imagined. Cale started throwing the blocks into the air. The old man's back was turned, stacking the blocks up against his chest. He couldn't hear her beating on the window, trying to push it open but it was stuck. Two of the blocks had gone over Cale's head and hit beside him. By the time she was out the door and down the steps, it had happened. In the soft brown-curled hair on the child's head, there was a gash, bleeding already and running toward his face. She didn't even see it happen but was sure it would be there.

"Oh Papa, you've hurt my baby. Oh, it's bad."

Papa was frozen and could not move when she picked up the baby.

"Go start up your truck."

"Falissa!"

"Go start up your truck and don't stand there like an old fool. Isn't this enough? He's got to go to the doctor."

The baby was screaming now, and she held it against her almost smothering it to get the crying to stop.

"Falissa, the truck don't run."

Falissa felt a terrible silence come into her head. She could see the open, screaming mouth of the child and his blood on his face and on her chest.

"Jerome. Where is Jerome, Papa?" she said weakly.

"I'll get him honey. The truck ain't run in years. Now don't you worry and you try to wash out that cut and stop off the bleeding. I'll get him." The old man began to find his feet and voice as he moved off toward the barn.

Falissa started down the path toward the tenant house, smelling the woodsmoke of the only house nearby. The baby had stopped screaming and was only whimpering in her arms as she went through the barren woods, the limbs cutting across her face. "I'll get you to the doctor, now don't you fret no more, little Cale. Mama'll take care of you."

She could see Aunt Bynum, with a hoe handle, breaking the ice on the mule's trough. The dark woman's breath came in puffs and the mule's breath went about her feet like smoke as it pawed the ground.

"Aunt Bynum!"

"Lawsy child, what's the matter with yuh?" The mule pushed her aside, dropped his nose in the hole in the ice and began to suck at the water. "Land, child, yuh got a sick baby."

"Aunt Bynum, he's busted his head wide open."

Aunt Bynum took the child from her almost roughly, fingers pulled up the flap of skin and the groove was clean a moment then it filled again with blood. "It'll require a couple or three stitches I'm figuring. Jason!"

Falissa felt the wind cold against her chest where the baby was taken away. "Yuh ought not be running around without a coat. Yuh'll catch yuh death of it. Jason!" Falissa watched Aunt Bynum stuff her handkerchief in the cut and hide the bleeding.

"Next time he do that yuh get yuh a handful of spider webs or some soot if there ain't none at hand. That will stop up that bleeding. Jason, get yuh black behind out here while yuh still got one to get on."

Jason appeared on the porch, stuffing in his shirttail and pulling on his jacket. He started to button his shirt over his chest and Falissa could see the ribs, each separate like steps on a ladder.

"Yuh hear me calling yuh. Get that mule up and take this youngun on down to Dr. Paulson's and get his head looked after." Jason moved to the mule, his eyes widening when he saw Falissa. Aunt Bynum took off her sweater and wrapped the baby up in a bundle. Jason stepped on the edge of the trough, swinging up and over, and headed the mule toward them with his knee. "Now yuh hurry up there, Jason. And yuh remember one more thing. Can yuh remember one more thing?'"

"Yes'um."

"Yuh ask Dr. Paulson to call Mrs. Falissa as soon as it's taken care of."

Jason nodded and took the baby in both arms and headed the mule off down the path.

"Aunt Bynum, I could run that fast."

"Chile, you couldn't run that far. It's most three miles to Dr. Paulson's. Jason take care of yuh baby for yuh. Jason love a baby better than anything. He'll get me full of one and he ain't here a day but let it come and there he is just fooling with it up a storm. You come on up in the house and warm up and we'll wait on him to come back. I got a good fire going and I want yuh to see my little Floyd. He ain't but two months younger 'n yourn."

"No."

"What yuh mean, no? Yuh come on and do as I say before yuh get a chill."

"I said no. I'm going home to the telephone."

"Well, yuh do as yuh please but that man will have that baby taken care of in no time and the best yuh can do is get yuh wits about yuh and wait. Ain't no sense fretting around the phone till he's had time to get there. Ain't no sense fretting no way. The chile ain't alive who don't bust his head open before he's grown."

Falissa turned to go back up the path, her face burned like cloth warmed in front of the fireplace sinking against her flesh. Like a child. Aunt Bynum talked to her like she was a child and it was her baby they were concerned with. Her mama never bossed her around like that. Never since she'd been grown had anybody talked to her like that and that black woman had just snatched her baby away like it was her right to.

She saw the house through the clearing. No one was around so Papa was still to find Jerome. Now where had he gotten to? They would have been in some mess if they had to wait on him to do everything. Probably asleep or ashamed to answer, leaving her at a time like this. They must be to the main road by now, Jason and the baby. Do you reckon Jason would have enough sense to flag down a car and get there quicker? What would he do with the mule? The baby was warm; if just that bleeding had stopped. Aunt Bynum said it wasn't deep, but all that blood; niggers just don't worry about things. They're just tougher. Falissa dropped to the top step and pulled her knees up against her. The yard was quiet, not even a chicken but there was a hateful blue jay. Somewhere she could see him, it would be good to even see him move. It was starting to snow, the sky had been right. And her baby was out on the road with a cut-open head. He was cold and in the snow and bleeding and crying and nothing but a stupid nigger with him that probably wouldn't think to cover his face. The blood was on the front of her apron, shrinking and puckering the cloth as it dried and turning dark. She pressed her face against her knees and there was pain inside, like having a baby. She was cramping double and nothing she could do could straighten her.

"Mrs. Falissa, don't you reckon you ought to go in and listen on the telephone. I declare I want you to know you're going to freeze."

It was Aunt Bynum again. She had no sweater on either. It was on the baby.

"Mrs. Falissa, yuh taking it all too hard. That youngun will be all right in a day or two. Little tuff will grow over it and yuh won't even see it."

Falissa was crying, hard now.

"If you're worrying about depending on Jason, I can tell yuh just as soon put it from your mind. He could be as no count as the day is long but he won't let no harm come to your youngun. He would die hisself before he'll let a scratch come on that baby. I would never have give him to him if I believed he won't going to take care of it right. That's what I come up here to tell you, that you don't need to go worrying on Jason."

"You don't need to talk on, Aunt Bynum."

"Yes'um. I was just worrying that you thought . . . Yes'um."

"He should have called by now."

Aunt Bynum started to speak but turned instead and went back down the path, mumbling to herself.

"Where you going?"

"I left my baby by hisself."

Falissa felt her face burn again. There was an edge on Aunt Bynum's voice and Falissa felt hate inside herself burning to get out, just like the preacher said at church, Devil's living inside you. She didn't know there could be such hate in her when she saw the snow-dotted head of the Negro disappear in the trees. You got to fight off the devil in you.

The phone was ringing. Falissa ran into the house and lifted the receiver off the wall before the second ring.

"Hello."

"Mrs. Jenkins?"

"Yes, this is Mrs. Jenkins."

"Dr. Paulson here. Stitched your boy up. Took four little ones so it wouldn't scar. You want him sent on back home with the boy who brought him, don't you?"

"He's all right, the baby's all right?"

"He'll be a little sore and fussy for a day or so but he's as good as new. Soon as the hair covers it back over, you won't even notice it."

"Yes, send him with the boy. And wrap him up good. It's snowing."

"And where you want it billed? The boy didn't have any money."

"Here, to me. Falissa Jenkins, Route 3, Summit. I'll pay you soon."

She put the phone up and went back to the porch. Everybody telling her the same thing, hair will grow over it just like nothing happened.

The snow was in small flakes and blew along the ground, sticking like fine salt. Still no Jerome and Papa. If Papa had been rushing all this time, he might surely bring on a stroke and wouldn't they be in a fix then. She rang the dinner bell over the porch then let it swing silent. Everyone had left her. She was sorry she rang the bell. If it were to bring Jerome, then he would be there when the baby came. Then she would have to explain to him. He would call her foolish. She was truly sorry she rang the bell. But Jerome was not to be moved. Her fears were wasted because she waited until she heard the steps and saw the jostling head of the bareheaded mule coming into the yard and she was still alone. She ran to the side of the mule and Jason handed her the child. Jason moaned softly when she took it from him but he was smiling, relaxed, and the fear he left with had gone.

"Was just having him a fine ride down the road and he fell sound asleep."

Falissa lifted back the sweater and saw his face, sleeping quietly, it was past his nap. The heat from his body warmed her face. And on his head was a clean circle, his pretty curls shaved away for the dark line of the cut. The cut was tiny, not even an inch.

She looked up at Jason who was watching the child. "Ain't he something. Just had him a fine time. Didn't holler a bit till the doctor started cleaning him up. Didn't like them cold clippers. Said to keep it washed off but go easy on it, that's all he said."

Falissa walked to the bottom of the steps. "Thank you, Jason. You tell Aunt Bynum I'll send her sweater down soon as I get the blood washed out of it."

"Yes'um." Jason turned the mule slowly and started down the path to the house.

Falissa bent to kiss the child and smelled Aunt Bynum, fatback and woodsmoke soaked into the sweater. The blood had made dark brown spots in it, deeper than on her apron. Cold water before it sets. She would take them into soak. No need to replace the sweater, just her everyday one.

She put the sweater in the sink and turned on the cold water while she watched a thin brown ring form on the sink at the water's edge. She should send Jason some money. She would ask Jerome how much.

Chapter 5

IT SEEMED that winter had finally broken. The trees blossomed and grass clumps spotted the fields. The peaches had budded first, soft white in their youngness, popping out on the twisted limbs like moths that had lighted, opening and closing with the breeze. Yesterday Falissa had taken the child into the yard. Though Cale had grown hair over the cut, she made him tip his head up constantly for her to examine it. She watched Papa and the child play, closely now, seeing them now as two children, one to be watched as much as the other. And she had learned to do her work with her hands only, saving her eyes for them. The jonquils were fading, hanging paperlike on their stems, and the yard filled with dandelions and buttercups with a dusting of johnny-jump-up, white as the last snow that spotted the yard.

But then the frost settled again, taking the first buds with it. The petals vanished in the cold night, never hitting the ground, just drawing up on the black limbs. Jerome always saw the first warm week in April with a certain uneasiness and this time his fears had been grounded. Usually with the first pale light of the morning, the birds started singing, so loudly that when he opened his eyes, he was awake for good. He didn't mind that; he slept during the day in the barn so it was good to hear the morning come in with the birds. And that was a good time because Falissa always slept soundly until the alarm went off and he felt comfortably alone with her asleep.

Lying in the bed the morning after the week of the spring-time, he knew what had happened. He hadn't gone to bed too early to know there was a chill in the air last night and this morning's sunlight danced in colors through the frost on the windows. And the birds were quiet, huddled together from the strange winter that they dreamed they were free of. And the insects weren't humming in the hedge bushes. They all must have known before him; while he was sleeping warm inside they felt the cold close around them. He wanted to get out before Falissa woke up. He didn't want to see her rush to the window, complain, cry about the loss of the peaches, maybe even the apples, say there would be no jam, and walk around gloomy all day, sighing when she looked out the window. He hated that sigh. She had jam enough for three years in the basement. They were still eating on '37.

Jerome slid from the bed without disturbing the covers on her side. He took his overalls and shirt from the chair and his shoes from under the bed then slipped through the crack in the door without her moving. He was into the overalls quickly but the shoes laced slowly, stiff from the wet. He should have hung the socks out or slept in them, one. Damn, he hated to start out with wet feet.

The frost sparkled more in the living room, through the white dotted swiss curtains, off all the knickknacks she set around, her mother's junk still in the glass cases. It was starting to melt and drain in streaks on the front window, squirming down the glass like white worms. It was enough though. As Jerome went out the back door, shutting the screen behind him, he saw the yard, wet like a spring rain but the unmistakable chill was in the air. Maybe the birds know it's coming; they know a lot we don't give them credit for, I'm betting, and don't make the mis-takes we do. As he walked toward the orchard, he saw the one sure sign, the color was gone. The pink that was alive like sun-burnt flesh drooped with sickness, pale, bruised. The peaches were gone unless a miracle gave them another spring. And they had budded thick, wouldn't be enough fresh spots left for a bloom to color the orchard. False spring. Only a man is smart enough to know. And he can't tell anything short of another man. He'd seen them down east once where their life depended on those fool peaches, burning salamanders at night, staying up to keep them going when they expected a drop. That's when he and Roe were working the peaches, pulling them, but they were so picayunish they fired them when they caught Roe throwing them in the baskets from the tree. He was a good shot. Jerome had been glad, he remembered, because he was near about lame from stepping in a rotten peach full of yellow jackets and wanted to go to the ocean and heal up.

He felt no remorse about the crop. Didn't like peaches, maybe that was it. If they fall off they ain't worth a damn and you got to work yourself to death to get them down. Ate himself sick on them when they were picking, go the rest of his life and never miss them. Nope. Just couldn't get upset over that kind of crop. Those trees were there when he came and except for a few sprayings to keep Lonza quiet, grew on their own. Lonza said his papa planted them after the war, Civil War he reckoned. The only thing that bothered him was that Falissa would make a to-do out of it, nothing could go against the plan or hit a bump that she didn't make a to-do out of it. This was a pleasant silence and he could have it when he pleased by just walking on his land. Almost his land, and all his when the old man went. He didn't wish the old man dead; it just didn't matter one way or the other, it was as good as his. Having it legal would be a blessing though, making it his for certain in case something should happen to Falissa. The old woman Sarah Ann he was damn glad to see go. Useless and weak, he paid her no mind when she started in to giving him orders. Comes from her background, treated like a queen. He'd have put her in her place if it'd been up to him but it was two to one when she got high and mighty and wouldn't do her share of the work. High-toned old bitch. Take her out of the city limits of Summit and see how far her fineness would get her. Her fine family won't a hill of beans in Raleigh. His family won't one to search out its tree. That would be some tree. Roe used to talk about his limbs and splinters in every sweet ass in North Carolina when he saw that tree on the wall. Got drunk and told Sarah Ann if she didn't watch it, he'd cock up his leg and pee on her trunk. She shut up in her room over that, stopped that harping on her tree. He would have done it too, cocked up and peed on her tree.

And old Lonza, even he knew where he come from, from a Dutch immigrant who ran out of land over there and got his land on a homestead back when it was plentiful. Jerome's family didn't even know where each of them came from. He had so many half sisters and brothers he couldn't keep up with them, most of them bastards if mention was to be made of it. But he had him a father all right. Willie Jenkins. Crazy as a loon, mean as a snake, and likely as not to be sleeping in some whore's bed right now with her picking his pocket on the bedpost. But he would get it back. That was the damndest thing how he could squander money and get drunk and lose every cent and not remember a minute of it and before you knew it his pockets were full again, gambling, bootlegging, no telling what, just had a way of getting his hands on money. Bought him a Packard back in '39, brand new right out of the showroom window in Raleigh, when people were lucky to buy a piece of tin, and had to have them deliver it because he didn't know a bit more how to drive than the man in the moon. Whether he paid for it or not and they just couldn't run it down, it was still sitting there, seventeen miles on the speedometer and all the old fool even learned to do was start up the engine and race it up and then the battery went so he left it there to rust away and get grown over with honeysuckle and have a snake curl up in the seat like it's been run in the ground already. Spit fire at me if I were to touch it. He can have his goddamn car. Hotheaded old fool.

Jerome went into the barn. It was already warming up outside but inside the barn was as cool as underground. He went to his quilt in the hay; Falissa hadn't found it this time so it won't folded up and hid. He stretched out and shut his eyes, quiet and dark here.

*　　*　　*

Twenty-five years ago in 1916, when Jerome Jenkins was eight years old, he spent what was probably his first and last sleepless night. It was winter and cold; there was no heat in the house because the fire had died untended hours ago and what little heat there had been had gone through the cracks in the wall or up into the rafters. His mama had stuffed the wall cracks with newspaper and the bare wood ran with silverfish, the shiny many-legged bug worms that shredded the paper and sifted it around the edge of the walls. They left pictures of the trees outside through the cracks and blew cold air across his eyeballs. He and Roe were in bed, and the ticking rose over and around them as they worked into holes; better to wrap in the straw and lay against the hard slats than feel it soft under you and freeze. His mama had told him not to do that, that he might smother and to stop burrowing like a mole. Jerome lay on his stomach and reached around his legs, pressing the straw sticks back through the cloth so they wouldn't scratch his skin. He had started with his face under the cover where it was warmer but Roe who was next to him had said, "Duck under the cover, quick," and he farted and made it unbearable. Cabbage fart. He breathed the cold air outside the covers that went deep inside of him all the way to his stomach and made him shiver. He could hear a rat moving inside the wall, pulling the paper through the cracks to the inside and shredding it with a crackling sound. The rat ran down into its nest, swooping up and down and making him keep his eyes open so he would not see flames in his mind, coming through the wall and burning the house down. Won't no good trying to sleep. The green log in the fireplace still popped out pieces on the floor and made him jump. Roe, who was four years old, was breathing loud and he thought he was probably asleep, he was little enough to sleep easy. He heard Papa Willie come through the door and go to the fireplace and dump in a bunch of logs. He shivered again and thought of the fire, hoping Papa Willie would open the door and let the heat come in to them if it was to catch up again. He didn't hear him scratch up the coals. He was afraid to call out to him because he might be mad. He had been drunk early in the afternoon and even when he could control his temper when he was sober he lost it if he had been drinking. It was only good when he had been drinking so much he got staggery and clumsy and Jerome could get away from him before he could grab hold of his shirttail. Mama was sick and in bed, her stomach swollen full of baby.

He was almost asleep when he began to hear the fire sounds cracking and snapping again and the smoke sucking up the chimney. Through his window glass he could see the hot sparks falling. Papa Willie was always impatient and used too much paper and one summer night when Mama smelled smoke Willie had to climb up with a bucket and put out the fire in the pine straw on the roof while they handed him up buckets full of water from the rain barrel. But the dancing sparks looked nice tonight and the roof was frozen slick from melted snow, sending them down a slide into the air, almost like lightning bugs in the cold winter, a dream.

He could hear Roe start to snort in his sleep because he had rolled over and pressed his nose in a fold in the ticking. The sparks came across the porch, he watched them through the windows, they bounced, swirled, and fell over the edge into the snow. The wind caught them in the air and Jerome watched their light turn out and go away with them. He followed them through the darkness, down an icy tunnel where he could not stand up to walk and sat down, sliding away with the wind cutting his face, his fingertips numb, until he lay back and his backside warmed up as he slid faster. The ice was black for a long time but soon it began to flash, with colors, blue, green, and soon it was reflections of sparks, red. At the end of the tunnel he found himself walking across wet ground that made his feet cold. He should have remembered to bring his shoes. And he never should have come in his bobtail nightshirt; he was glad he had kept on his long johns anyway but he couldn't reach to get the flap up. Mama left it down so he wouldn't have an accident at night.

Here at the end of the tunnel the tiny sparks were larger than he was; they were in their own home and much the boss of everything. At least it looked that way at first glance. They had faces and arms and legs when they wanted them. And they made cracking and popping sounds when they walked, like they were getting the kinks out of their joints. And they could roll and tumble like you've never seen. He should have brought Roe along. He would have if he'd known he was coming because Roe would have gotten a kick out of this. At the end of the path he saw something that surprised him. It was Roe and he had gotten there ahead of him. Now how in the world did that happen?

"Roe, how did you get here?"

"It isn't something you get overnight, you remember that. It takes many a year," Roe said quickly.

Jerome didn't think Roe a liar because sure enough, he was old with gray hair and wrinkles. He was more than a grown-up.

All of the sparks were lined up and marching in pairs toward Roe who stood by the river. Jerome got in the line but a spark pushed him out.

"You fool, don't you know what is happening? Get out while the getting's good, Run, run, run, as fast as you can."

He ran out of the line and he saw what Roe was up to. He was making the sparks jump into the water and die, each one sending up a puff of smoke as he hit and Roe saying, "Hurry up there. One, two, three, jump! One, two, three, jump!"

Jerome went to the edge, he wanted to scream, to ask Roe why he was doing such a terrible thing. It was cold by the water and the sparks traveled in faster, sending splashes of water on him, the water warm at first and cold as it spread in his clothes.

"Faster, faster," Roe screamed. The sparks were crying out before they hit the water, terrible dying cries.

Jerome started to speak to Roe of the terrible thing he was doing, when Roe said, "It don't matter. They're cold-blooded. It don't hurt them none."

Why did they scream so? Soon Jerome was wet and cold and he sat on the ground and drew into a ball. Something is wrong. He had told Roe that about frogs and lizards and fishing worms, even crickets. He had learned it at school when he asked about putting them on fishing hooks and if the hook hurt the fish's mouth. He should never had told Roe that about things being cold-blooded. He wouldn't have if he had known it was going to be leading to such meanness.

Roe turned to him and the noise was almost deafening.

"You're not Roe." And he wasn't. Of course not. Roe wasn't even there, Roe was a little boy, and Papa Willie had lied and said he was Roe gotten older. It was Papa Willie killing the sparks. Papa Willie. And he was wet and cold and now Papa Willie beat on him.

"Shut up, you little bastard. You hear me. Shut up!"

Papa Willie beat on the covers with his fist and Roe cried and rolled under him. Then Papa Willie turned and left, slamming the door to the room. Roe was screaming but someone else was too. The noise went fainter when the door shut but it most surely was Mama, screaming in the other room. He was wide awake now and Roe whimpered stuffing his face in the pillow to keep from crying out loud.

"Mama, Mama."

"Shhhh, Roe. Papa'll beat us again."

"Mama hurting."

"Roe, you peed in the bed." The bed was wet and cold and Jerome felt the whole side of his nightshirt, soaked.

"Roe, you peed all over me."

"Gotta go pee pee."

"No you don't neither. You done peed enough for a week right in the bed."

Roe went back to sleep leaning against Jerome's side. His little head was rubbery, soft, and Jerome didn't like to have him touching him. It was like if he moved he would hurt him or break him. Roe pressed the cold wet nightshirt against Jerome and he smelled pee and baby burp, milk. The pee dried slowly and it was morning before it was stiff in his clothes. The smell of it was fading now and he could only smell the sour milk where Roe had burped up the rest of his supper on his front. All night long through the door Mama screamed until he could not be sure he heard her anymore. And the front door opened and shut, banging all night. When the morning light filled the whole room he could see the snow, still on the edge of the porch. He was sleepy but his eyes burned and it hurt to shut his lids over them. Now he had to pee, bad. Soon Papa Willie opened the door; he was red-eyed and ugly.

"You stay put in this room until I tell you you can come out. And don't you try going out that window because it's nailed from the outside, you hear!" They didn't speak and he shut the door; Jerome heard him slide the furniture against it. All morning long, people came and went, talking but not loud enough for him to hear. Roe still slept, squirming tighter against Jerome until he wanted to push him away but couldn't make his tired arms do it. Roe's head buried against his chest, his mouth sucking the front of his nightshirt.

Jerome's memory quit him from here on, beyond that morning in bed with Roe, but the day went on and they weren't fed. They cried a lot and peed off the edge of the bed, because it was too cold to get out. Jerome found the pot, reached under the bed and set it out but Roe couldn't hit it. Night came again and a colored woman was the first to open the door, a tenant woman pushing away the furniture, bringing them cornbread and milk and finding their sweaters for them. They went to sleep when she left, Jerome too tired to try to listen to the voices in the front room, and they slept well into the next day. The woman woke them to scrub them and dress them in their Sunday clothes on Wednesday and they went to bury Mama, only no one told Jerome and Roe that Mama was dead. It was Jerome who figured it out at the church service. He saw the box up front on the altar and they put it in the ground. Papa Willie had his hair slicked down and had on his necktie, and Mama wasn't there with him. He wouldn't never forget Mama screaming. Jerome told Roe when they got back home.

"Mama's gone away for good, Roe."

"How you know?"

"Because she ain't here, dummy."

"Where is she?"

"She's dead," and Roe had turned around and walked off. He went out to play in the yard. He didn't know what dead was and he wasn't interested. Jerome knew, he knew two things: That what was bad already was going to be worse because Mama wasn't there to take up for them, and that that baby inside Mama had tore her up and killed her. That baby had tore up Mama worse than Papa ever had beating on her.

Jesus God, you can't get no idea of a family out of that or a name tree or nothing. All this family talk and tale telling, it makes me sick. I'd spit on the old man if I saw him in a ditch drunk like he was anybody's trash and I'd kiss his ass if he was in the position to go lording over me. Every man for hisself. I didn't do nothing to make him and he didn't do nothing to make me with any intention behind it. My old man might well be the sorriest person who ever lived. And Roe ain't much better in some respects but it's been just me and Roe up against the world too many times. I know who my friend would be if the chips were down. Roe would be there pitching for me.

Listen at them birds fussing in the loft. And that fancy woman thinks it's her it's over. That's what you think, Miss Sarah Ann bird. No sirree, it's that little patch of property he's picked to put his nest on. There is something to that, I can tell you. You just let the government or the Yankees or anybody you mind come try to take my land and you'll see you some fighting like never was. I'd kick their asses off. You give me my dirt and I'd get along. Come spring if I got a hoe and a package of seeds I'd make out mighty fine. I seen it when a five-dollar bill wouldn't buy you a how-de-do. And of all of the sorry gardens that you ever seen when those town people tried to spade up and plant in their backyards. They'll do well when this war is over to go back to planting grass. Ain't it something to see those people planting grass and mulching it and watering it like it was something. Goddamn grass, I'd plow it under.

Willie Jenkins had him some land, yes sirree, my old man Willie Jenkins had him some land, and he was going to have every last grain of dirt until they put him in it and if he knew how, he would blow it all to kingdom come right before he departed this earth. I remember him saying it the first time when I was seven years old, how he was thinking of getting him some dynamite. Willie gave me an acre a year by the time I was nine. I could break my neck and not get pocket change off that acre. He made us eat cabbage and corn bread till it ran out our ears and made Mama can and put up until the pack-house was four years deep with food and still it was corn bread and cabbage and collards until we laid in bed at night and listened to each other fart and blow up the sheets. The old man ate meat with his cabbage and picked every bone until it was slick and sucked it so dry the dog didn't even want it. Never even left us fat and skin. Made me want meat for so long that when I got it, pigs' feet and hot dogs in town, it made my stomach sick.

You didn't say nothing to Willie. And he lost his temper and went through us all slinging us against the wall like we was troops marching on him, breaking things. Kicking me between the legs, the dirty old bastard, and I saw my big brother Tom try to fight back when the old man had shoved him in the crotch with an ax handle and Willie beat him bloody. Tom was nearly a foot bigger but the old man come at him with that ax handle and messed his face up so that the next day when he left and never come back I wondered if he was ever going to look like Tom again. Mama doctored on him all night pinching his face together. I seen her stitch those flaps of skin down with a sewing needle. But that was the end of Tom, no letters, nothing, he never come back, not even when they buried Mama. Don't know if he even heard of it. Don't know the whereabouts of none of them but Roe and don't nobody know his until he shows up but Roe knows I'm put so he'll be back. He signed up to fight but he'll be back with a mouthful of stories. He'll be back when he needs money and he knows there is one of us that knows the value of land under his feet. Roe wouldn't never leave me for good.

Roe was four years younger than me but he took out before I did. I used to have to hunt him down for Mama when he just started into walking and I'd find him half a mile from home. Reason he had to take out was before they come after him, he knocked up the girl on the next farm and she won't but twelve.

Well Roe won't but twelve either but they would have sure made him marry her. She said he was the one, that he had took her down in the woods on the way home from school against her will. That I can believe, that it was against her will, because she looked like the prissiest girl you ever seen and it must have been dark in them woods for Roe to even get going with her. And her with a belly already showing before her papa came over and screaming and saying she didn't know that was what it would do to her and he made her do it and told her it'd make her pretty if he stuck her with his magic wand. That Roe was something — twelve years old and out in the world taking care of hisself and me sixteen and still at home. He had been bad to take to women since he was ten, I mean it, but he usually went into town with the money he got from the crops and spent it on whores. That Roe really is something.

Next time I seen him I hardly knew him. I was in town killing time after we had sold the tobacco when I seen this dude in a zoot suit come up to me and say, "Buddy, you got a dime?"

Well, I'd know the way he talked anywhere but not the way he looked. He really took me back. He was skinny as a rail but decked out to beat the band which made me think he was just recently prosperous and had been hanging on in some hobo camp until he found him a woman to buy him some clothes. And him just thirteen. That Roe was a mess. Said he'd been to St. Louis and New Orleans and had come back to see if the nigger girls here was half as good. He did look like a man though, already.

It was Roe who put me on to Falissa. That's the truth. It was near about six years after that when me and him had just got out of Fort Bragg and come back to town and he told me he had gone to one of them church socials and met a girl with a nice ass that he wanted me to see. He said he was getting him a free meal, just fell in line at one of them reunion things where everyone brings a covered dish and he seen one whose ass twitched real nice when she moved up and down serving the plates that he had picked out just for me. He said she didn't have much meat on her all around but he could tell that was going to be a nice ass when it finished filling out. Roe was a funny one. He took after Papa Willie about women and me about the land. Papa Willie didn't need him anything permanent 'cause he had him his land. I'll hand him that, he knowed how fast everything else could take out from under you. Roe and Tom were gone before he could turn around. That's what your sons can mean to you. But I'll tell you he can take his land with him to hell. I don't want it. He acted like he might let me have it and I stuck around when ever last one of them had left him and he got drunk one night and said he had gone down to the courthouse five years before and made it

legal that all three hundred acres was set aside as his cemetery
and he had no heirs and I asked him about me and he said
bastards didn't have no rights and laughed at me. And I was
the only one of the three who won't bastards and I told him to
cram his goddamn farm up his ass and went out and got drunker
than he ever dreamed of and left at twenty-one years old telling
myself I was the stupidest bastard on God's green earth for
trusting that S.O.B. And I got my own. I wouldn't have his on
a platter. When he's six feet under it and can't do a damn
thing about it, I'll just let stink weeds grow on his grave.

Jerome got up and walked behind the barn where he stuck a
shovel in the plant bed, the earth cracked with ice for an inch
before the blade slid in the ground and the compost smelled
hot in his face.

Chapter 6

July, 1942

FALISSA walked in long skirts, her sleeves down and her head covered with a wide-brimmed hat in the hot sun. The cloth on the back of her blue dress was already bleached light from the sun. Her feet were bare and dusty, the skin drawn across the tops but Mama or no Mama, she couldn't stand grit in a pair of shoes. She and Papa Lonza were going down the rows yanking the bunch beans from the ground, their vines spent and yellowed, and their taproots breaking loose with a thin pop. Cale ran in circles under the locust trees, rolling in the grass that grew up to the trunks, talking with the chickens that cooed and talked back to him but stayed at a safe distance. The flowers were dropping from the persimmon tree, tinkling across the tin at night when the wind blew. Cale stayed out from under them because he had already picked up a bee sting on the bottom of his foot, his second, the first one from a yellow jacket on a rotten apple in the orchard. Bees and black spiders, those were the bugs he was not to touch.

And in the lower field Jerome worked his way toward them with the tractor, turning the dirt over and listening to the snap of roots under the blade. A flock of blackbirds had swarmed behind him and walked longlegged and flat-footed through the dirt. He watched them as they searched the clods, filling their beaks full of grubs, racing each other for every split, broken worm. They didn't swallow them, just scooped them up, chewed them down to size, and kept walking, looking for more until they had enough to start the flight, low through the trees, with the weight to their nests. The nests were hidden somewhere in the pine woods and the babies cried out, not a pretty noise and one that started with the sunrise. Jerome watched one blackbird break his flight, a tiny Jenny Wren attacking him until he dropped his grubs and she swooped under him, catching them and zooming away before he could chase her. The blackbird stopped in the trees and fussed until the birds behind Jerome flew up to join him. Jenny Wren got her a nigger to do the work for her. Probably been stealing from her.

He looked into the bean patch and Falissa and Papa had cleaned it down to the wild grass. Falissa and Papa sat at the head of the row, going through the plants picking away the few beans left. Jerome could see the green beans cupped in her apron, her hands stuffed as she snatched away. She could probably find a mess there in what he would have just plowed into the ground. And if they were tough as whitleather she would cook them to death and make them eat them. Strings in your teeth.

Cale ran up to Papa and the old man covered the front of the child's T-shirt with the yellow leaves. They were laced and furry and stuck to him like the decals Falissa put on her kitchen cabinets. He made a snake, a big S. Cale ran to the back of Papa and hung around his neck, turning the little man over backwards, sending his feet into the air. Falissa laughed and Papa hurried after the child, caught him by the shirttail and swung him over his head, wrapping the short legs around his shoulders. With the two of them, one head over the other, Papa was the height of an average man. Jerome watched them over the roar of the tractor, like a silent movie, slapstick.

He saw Cale begin to jump up and down and point at the tractor. The child pulled at his mother's skirts until she went down to the edge of the field and opened her mouth, her hand waving.

"Jerome, take a minute and give him a little ride. He's just dying to go."

Jerome pulled over beside them and shut off the engine. Cale jumped up and down and laughed.

"What'd you say?"

"Take Cale for a little ride on the tractor with you. You've got plenty of time and he's having a fit to get up there."

"Wanted to get this rowed up and seeded before supper."

"We got an hour after supper before dark. Take him up, just for one turn around. That's what he asked for, last night when he said his prayers."

She lifted up the little boy who reached out to Jerome. He slid back in the seat and sat the child between his legs. Cale took hold of the steering wheel and tried to turn it but it wouldn't move.

"Tractor," Jerome said.

"Tract," Cale repeated.

"Now get ready for a lot of noise."

"Weady."

Jerome started the engine and Cale bounced in his lap.

"Sit still mind you or I'll lose you."

Cale sat still and held on to the bottom of the wheel. Jerome pressed the clutch and put the tractor in gear and when they turned around, the plow blade turned around, dragging through the tight dirt. Jerome looked at the top of the little blond head as they went down the field and noticed for the first time a little tuft of white hair on the side of Cale's head. The cut, must have come back that way over the cut he got from the block of wood. An onion in a petunia patch. They reached the end of the field on the far side and Jerome stopped the tractor.

"O.K., now we got to lift the blade to turn around. You see this lever?"

"Uh-huh."

"Pull it to you."

Cale took hold of the lever but it didn't move. Jerome cupped his hand over Cale's and slid the lever, the blade lifted up, hissed, and dropped away grass-clogged chunks of dirt. Cale turned and looked under his arm as the blade went up. Jerome pressed one brake and spun the tractor around on one turned wheel.

"O.K., now put it back down. Push the lever the other way."

Cale pushed it forward and the blade dropped and rattled into place. The tractor moved again down the row. Jerome went back to the other side and stopped in front of Falissa.

"O.K., boy, end of the line."

Cale's face tightened and he let out a wail. The tears were instant and before she had him in her arms to lift him away from the tractor, he was coughing and choking.

"Now see what you went and started," Jerome said. "Can't leave well enough alone." He backed the tractor from them and started back in the row. Falissa patted Cale on the back but he kept screaming and kicking so she set him down and let him run back into the trees, like a wild animal set free.

"If you'd give him more attention every now and then, it wouldn't hurt him so."

"What? I can't hear you."

"Never mind," she said and shook her head.

She turned and went back to the snap beans, watching the little boy pout from behind the locust tree, the chickens cooing at his feet. He kicked at them and yelled, sending them in all directions and under the house. Then he threw a cob but it fell short and landed in one of Falissa's geranium pots.

"Showing his temper," Papa said.

"And a temper he has. I'd make him pick it up but if I won't a grown woman I think I'd be throwing too. Jerome's showing himself too, acting like he's Mister Big and got so much to do he hasn't time for playing. He don't do half a man's work. And he hasn't an ounce of patience."

"I don't think he cares a thing about that child," Papa said. Falissa looked at Papa. He hadn't said anything like that about

Jerome before. He was noticing. People were noticing. Cale was still in her sight but he didn't know she was watching and soon his whimpering stopped. His eyes followed the man on the tractor. He walked down closer to the field and watched until the dirt formed a pattern, dark behind the tractor and white-crusted where the sun had dried it out. Soon he grew tired of watching and threw clods in the edge of the field.

Chapter 7

JEROME was in his workshop in the barn, light on in the daytime because it was cloudy outside. He sat on the dirt floor of the tractor shed, a burlap bag spread out in front of him and with a pile of paper sacks and seeds scattered about. The rats had gotten into the barrel and chewed into the bags, running the seeds out and eating part of them. Now the weevils were at them, the insides sifting through little holes in the side of the seed like sawdust. He had dropped them down in there to save for replanting and hadn't thought to put on the lid. When he had gone to tip the barrel up, two of the brown rats ran up his arm and leaped into the hay, burrowed away and were lost before he could think.

Used to sell you seed in cloth bags but with all this cheapness nowadays this is what you get. Paper this and paper that. This planting had brought on many a missing hill. Land acting like it's wore out. Makes you think maybe they let the seed go bad, give you last year's seed but there ain't no reason for hard times there. No reason I can think of except somebody trying to get an extra nickel out of you without working for it. Falissa done the squash and cucumbers herself and the watermelons and pumpkins, dried them on the window sill, all the vine stuff, and they came up fine but the bunch beans acted like they never got in the ground.

Papa Willie like to have broke me and Roe's necks one time.
He told us to plant out the bunch beans and we got hold of the
poles by mistake and they come up pretty as you please until
one day Willie noticed they were slow in blooming and had
started sending out runners. He come in and slammed us good,
one then the other up against the wall and asked us which seeds
we used and we hadn't thought a bit more about it than flying
when we did it so we couldn't tell him. He started whaling me
and Roe run out and Willie got holt of him and tore his shirt
clean off him, shot them buttons off the front like bullets and
he went sprawling and Papa kicked him in the balls and Roe
told me while we was putting up the posts to string the beans
that he was going to cut the old bastard's balls off while he was
asleep or passed out drunk and feed them to the hogs and let him
priss around with his knees knocking together. Or he might
just paint him black and tell the Ku Klux Klan to do it for him.
He heard of them fixing up many a nigger if he started looking
too hard at a white woman so he'd get Papa fixed up like that
for messing with him. That Roe acted like he meant business
but he won't like brother Tom who come at him swinging and
got his ass whipped. Roe won't going after no balls when the
old man passed out drunk; Roe was just turning his pockets inside out to see if he had any change left. That Roe was a snake.
Didn't a bit more care about anybody but his own hide. He
said he would have sold his mama for a nickel if you offered
it to him. Cut her throat for a dime, I betcha. But he didn't
know Mama like I did. He didn't know enough to cry when
she was gone. He didn't know her being there. He just got
mad at her and hated her for not being there no more and she'd
been dead as a doornail for years before Roe had enough sense
to know what a mama was like. I knowed that Mama done her
best considering what she had to make do with. She had marks
under her eyes that were near about blue whether he beat on her
or not. And her legs were knotted up in the back, I hated to
see them. I hated to see her bend over the washpot and her

skirts come up and show them knots. And she got sores that wouldn't get well. She won't strong stock to start with but I did like her corn bread. Falissa ain't never done it right. I liked Mama's corn bread when it was cold as ice. Get me a big slab of fresh butter and nothing would beat it except maybe a little damson jam with it. She put a bit of spring onion in it to give it a little bite. Make me hungry to think about it. But Falissa don't believe in such. She don't go for sprucing things up. She just has a set way of doing things and you don't make a comment on nothing around her or she takes it as criticism and gets fighting mad. She ain't never even thought her hair might comb in another direction, not since I known her. She does take criticism bad and that ain't no way to be because she ain't never going to learn nothing. She's got so prissy and snotty since she had that youngun. I don't even like to be around her. Going to wear him out washing him. Mama just hung up Roe's diapers and let them dry out. Made the kitchen pissy smelling but she never made no production out of raising a youngun. Falissa thinks that child has made her God Almighty. Damn, I hate that sighing. I stay out much as I can.

I hear something in the front room. Them rats out loose I bet and me without a thing to shoot them with.

Jerome walked through the door to the inside of the barn. In the thin light he saw Cale playing in the straw, rolling over in it.

"Hey boy, how did you get in here?"

Cale looked up and ran to the door but stopped. Then he looked at Jerome and laughed. "Me play." He fell sideways in the straw and began to roll over again, from top to bottom of the stack.

"You going to get the itch doing that."

Cale jumped to his feet but didn't brush the straw from his clothes.

"Brush off."

He tried but it still stuck all over him.

"Where's your mama?"

"Dun' know."

"Where's Papa Lonza?"

Cale shook his head.

"Well, which one you supposed to be with?"

"Me help you work."

"You'll get to do that soon enough. If I was you, I'd spend now getting in my playing."

Jerome walked back through the door. "Stay in here and play but let me know when you get ready to take off and tell me which way you go so I ain't responsible for you."

The child followed him through the door. "Papa work?"

"Not much. Just trying to sort out some seeds. Rats mixed them all together. Ate holes in the bags."

Cale sat down beside the seed cloth. He began to stack the beans in piles, the brown ones, the white ones, the red-striped ones.

"Hey, you're pretty good."

Jerome sat down and began to work with him. When Cale put a bean on a stack he looked at it a moment and when he got a wrong one, he moved it.

"Who taught you that?"

The child looked up and said, "Dun' know."

"How did you know one from the other?"

"Red. Blue. Green." He pointed at the three stacks.

"That's not right. Red. White. And striped."

"Striped not a color."

"Well, striped a bean. Or speckled. Whatever you want to call it."

"Green, blue, yellow."

"You just got you a bunch of colors in your head and don't know where they go. Who taught you that?"

"Dun' know."

"Dun' know, dun' know. Is that all you can say?"

"Dun' know."

"Why don't you go out and play and quit bothering me?"

"Me work."

"You not work. You get on my nerves. What you got against playing outdoors?"

"Big bear out there."

"Who told you that foolishness and don't you dun' know me or I'll pop you where it hurts."

"Papa Lonza."

"That's a fine thing to be teaching you. Are the gypsies going to take you and sell you? Did he tell you that?"

"Uh-uh."

"There is no big bear out there. There are none anywhere around here, do you understand?"

"Uh-huh," Cale said without looking up from the beans.

"You just watch out for snakes and spiders."

"No. Bees and black spiders."

"And snakes. You add that to your list."

Birds began to come in through the stalls, whistling low over the straw and resting on the high rafters. The light from outside was gone and darkness slid in around them.

"Nighttime."

"Nope. Storm time. Going to be bad. The birds are in."

"Papa Lonza says birds don't like to get wet."

"I don't know that that's true, about getting wet. They hurry up their business before a storm. Little ones have a bad time flying in the wind. Not the wetness that bothers them. Washes out the lice."

"I don't like to get wet."

"As many baths as you get? I thought you liked it."

"Nope."

"Then why you let her give them to you?"

Cale looked blank and said, "I saw a redbird."

"Don't go changing the subject on me. Why you let her wear out your hide scrubbing it if you don't like it? I wouldn't let my mama do such. Why don't you say two baths a week is enough? You're your mama's boy. You are, aren't you? You belong to your mama."

"I belong to Mr. and Mrs. Jerome Jenkins and I live on Sherman Highway."

"What would you rather do? Ride on the tractor or go walking in the woods with Grandpapa Lonza?"

"Me ride tractor."

Cale dropped the seeds and started to climb onto the tractor on one of the big wheels. He fell backwards in the dirt but was to his feet quickly. "Me ride tractor."

"No, not now. I was just checking."

"Me ride tractor." The child began to jump up and down.

"I was just asking you. I wasn't offering you a ride. A tractor's not for playing. I don't have time to take you for a ride. And didn't we just say a storm was coming. You want to get struck by lightning?"

Cale walked to the edge of the burlap bag that held the seeds. He stooped to his knees, watching Jerome. He grabbed the bag and stirred the beans up and ran before Jerome could get to him. Jerome ran after him and caught him by the arm at the door. The child began to scream and try to pull away.

"Shut up. Shut up! Nobody's hurting you. Not yet but you are not getting away with that ugliness. You got to have a spanking for that."

The door to the barn opened and Papa Lonza stood there.

"Cale, what's the matter with you? I have been looking on every inch of this farm and you scared me to death. Don't you run off like that on me again, you hear."

The child ran past him, screaming, and hit him with his fist. Papa Lonza looked blankly at Jerome.

"You straighten him out," Jerome said. "You make him like he is and you find the time to straighten him out. Shit if I'm going to do it."

"What is the matter with him?"

"He thinks he can just tear up what he pleases because he's got a mama that can't see the devil in him. You straighten him out."

He walked back to the seeds and the old man turned to follow the child. Cale had stopped screaming and was walking slowly in the road deciding not to run to the house. The rain was starting to fall and Papa hurried after the child, the drops already making dark spots on his shirt. Falissa was on the porch ringing for them to come in.

The lightning filled the barn as Jerome counted the seconds until the thunder rumbled. Six miles away and moving over us and the seeds still in the barn. He kicked them up against the wall and left them for the rats.

Chapter 8

I SAT IN THE TUB last night and watched the patterns on my stomach. I get the water just steaming hot and all I do is puff up red and they get whiter, like white lightning bolts. It drew back tight quick enough after Cale though everyone told me it'd be different. They just don't know how much stooping and squatting I do in a day. But they told me a lot of things would be different. It hurt when he came along but hurt is so hard to remember. The best and the worst always are I'm coming to realize. I can remember the in-betweens and see them and even tell about them, lying there balling up the sheets in my fists and sticking my fingernails into my hands. And yet the hurt is not something I can imagine. I can just see in my mind what kind of woman all that hurting would turn me into if I let it. But I'll have it again. Those patterns, they're spreading already and getting thinner colored and there is another one growing in me and Mama should be here to see it. All her talking about we don't have many but we have them well. Pshaw! I am near about sure I could have as many as I pleased if I didn't take precaution. It ain't like Mama and I come out of the same mold; the older I get the more I think she was the strange one, not me. But maybe that's because she's not here telling me how to be a lady. And maybe it's because I've quit believing every little word she said and thinking being a lady ever amounted to a hoot anyway and won't just a way to keep from working.

Jerome didn't seem a bit more excited about this one than the
last. It's a good thing I got Papa to show caring or I might start
thinking I was being the fool. Ain't it something. I fretted
about that before Cale but people made me just as sure as everything that any man alive once he really was a father would be
excited to death and he would just break down and give up his
coldness and just be itching to get his hands on him other than
to pop him. I've watched Jerome, watching to see if it was just
his crazy stubbornness and that he really wanted to reach out
and grab the little bugger and just talk to him up a storm. I
think I know him well and talk on it a lot but I'm not settled
to believe he won't show a little something come time. Like
Papa, poor old Papa that everybody makes fun of. But he has
enough love in him for ten big men. Papa just don't hate a
living thing and he loves the stuffings out of that little boy
and sees no shame in showing it. I was brought up believing
there won't no shame in showing you were pleased. That was
Papa's doing. I declare I think it has made him live ten years
longer because he just couldn't stand not to see him grow up.
And I give my husband a manchild which every man is supposed to want and as sure as I'm sitting here he loves his
dirt better and all I'm asking in return is just enough loving for
the child so he don't grow up thinking something was wrong
about his folks. You can live with someone and think you know
them, even know their funny ways but not a bit more be able to
understand what was the cause of them. I've heard that what
you had as a little child makes you what you come to be as a
grown-up but how can that be true? When I was a child I
wasn't a bit more like I am now than the man in the moon.
We had some happy times though. But it won't good for Jerome
as a child. It won't so much going hungry like it was with some
who come up during the bad time. To this day I got to yell my
head off to get him to set down to the table. Jerome just don't
have no people to care about. Jerome just never had no one
to teach him you was even supposed to care about your people.

That sorry Roe. I would be hard put to care about him even if he was my brother. I don't see why Jerome couldn't just change today. He could if he wanted to and set his heart to it. Just put a little bit of that caring he has about his garden and his birds and cows and give it to his little boy. Just like the Bible says, love God and Jesus and your fellow man. I'm old enough to get on by myself and Lord knows I'm used to it but I do think the little boy needs it. If we end up raising him wrong and he turns bad I'll blame myself even if I don't have nothing to do with it but the birthing. He's got caring in him I think, Jerome does. Everybody got to have caring in him. God made man in his love, you don't have to be taught it. Jerome just puts it to the wrong things. Well it's not wrong to care about your farm, that's right, but you ought to care about your people first. I'd say it to him in a minute, he's just got things turned around sideways, I would but I know just as good and well that he'll get mad and snap and make me hurt, he'll say all the things that people do to each other, how the boy next door ruined his daddy, how his daddy did his mama, how he hates to see a man let himself go moon-eyed over some girl, and then he'll ask me how I can put truck in that and I'll have to listen to all that over again about his land and his dirt and how he goes out by hisself and feels just right and I'll almost hate him for loving being by himself so. I know what he's going to say before he opens his mouth. So we'll just go on hating what the other one has, I reckon.

I keep believing I can change things but it takes youngness to change and neither me or Jerome got it no more. You can see a bad child turn good or a weak one get strong as a little mule but then comes a day when they're set, froze up, like a jello, and you just go making a mess if you try changing them. I'm not the smartest person in the world but I know that's the truth. I ought to feel sorry for him. I do sometimes I suppose, but he can get so trifling that I have to take to meanness just to take care of myself. Maybe there's nobody who likes people who acts different from them and that is what is wrong all over and we don't like them unless they do just like us. And we know we're right and they're wrong. But there has to be some right and wrong. When I get up against this I keep remembering what Mama said about turning to religion. I know I let my mind wander all those years sitting in church and I probably got the barest nothing to go along with my believing, I mean I did use that time for daydreaming about who I was going to be and who I was going to marry and pretty clothes I wanted to have and I didn't hear half of what I was supposed to, but I come out with the essentials. Good old Papa always said that. He wasn't much for all those trifles and remembering this and that Bible verse if you just come out with the essentials. Come out believing that Christ was good and trust His way of doing things to be the best way for you to live and love God and each other. Them was Papa's essentials. And with all his faults, he does seem a better man than Jerome though many would say that was a sin against your husband. I'm not sure but maybe if you're not allowed to do all your growing up before you're married, you do a bit afterwards though there are many who would say you should be grown the day you get married. But I wasn't, not a bit of it. I had the biggest dreams in the world and didn't know no better what I was bound to come to than the day I was born. I'm getting to more of looking after myself. I was always one to look after myself but I was scared of people, I was scared to death of Jerome and going against him but if I'm believing I'm right and he's wrong, I'm going against him when it comes to that little boy. It don't matter about me; I might just as well of lived my life for all it's going to change for the better. But I am standing here and making a judgment against my husband that he's wrong, that he is doing wrong against his little boy and that he will have to answer for it if there is a hell. And I believe that there is.

Things has changed so. So many handsome young boys have gone off and died, just so people around here could go around

feeling bigger and better than everybody else. I don't know
nothing about people in them other countries but I've seen many
a pretty picture that tells me they are finer than us if you were
to look at some things. They got fine houses, one on a calendar
in Germany, and it has got a grass roof and Jerome was poking
fun at it and how a big old cow was going to start grazing up
there and fall right in on the living room. He just makes fun
of everything he don't know nothing about. It makes you wish
somebody real smart would come up and just tell him off good.
I don't know if they let the cows or goats or what eat up there
but it makes a pretty house and I bet they got a good reason for
doing it that we don't even know about. I wish I did know.

Sometimes I wish I had me more education. I went through
high school and I can speak the King's English proper if there's
need to. I went all the way and even skipped two grades but
sometimes I think the teachers didn't know much more than
we did. I used to read books a lot — murder mysteries — but
Jerome made so much to-do over it that I got so I hid them and
he made me cut out the light at night and I did so like to read
myself to sleep. And before long I stopped altogether. Well,
I suppose Cale had something to do with that, don't go blam-
ing Jerome for everything, but I do read to him and he is real
quick. I can tell already that he is quick the way he memo-
rizes things. He near about reads the books to me. That little
Billie Bantam getting after Reddy Fox:

> I'll scratch his face
> I'll peck his nose
> I'll bite his ears
> Till away he goes!

And the one about out west, I declare he got me so tickled when
we come to that part about the buffalo turds. I'm ashamed to
think it and me trying to read over it quicklike because I
couldn't think of no way to change it and that little rascal caught

me and asked me. They were using turds to start a fire though
I never heard of any such thing and think the fellow who wrote
that ought to ashamed of himself putting something like that
in a child's book but that cowboy built himself a fire with turds
and that little boy of mine probably will before it's all over with.
And then I got tickled over it right in front of him which is the
last thing I should have done. And I wonder if that isn't the
reason he makes me read him that same story over and over
again. I'll just die if he has an ounce of that sorry Roe in him.
He gets so tickled when I get to that part he just gets tears in
his eyes. What makes them such little snakes? You can be just
as careful as you please and leave them alone five minutes with
a bunch of little rascals like those at Vacation Bible School and
they learn more meanness than you could have taught them
in a year if you tried.

Maybe I was the same way. Honestly I just can't remember
anymore. When Mama was still here I could use her to remind
me of things and she did know me before I was able to remember.
No, with me things didn't seem to come in little bits and
snatches. I was young and old. I've said it before. Cale would
have liked me as a little girl. We would have had us some fun
together and I would have been able to keep up with him. It's
funny how life is. It just does things the way it pleases but if
the design had been put together with the best in mind for all,
Papa would have been the daddy of that little boy of mine and
Papa could have spent his young years with more than a bunch
of women. He has got a mighty few years left. But I reckon
he has had a better life than most. I give him a boy though he
can't ever have his papa's name. I would have done that for
him had the law allowed it. And I didn't cause him no trouble.
Maybe that made up for some of Mama's foolishness. But I'm
just patting myself on the head. He loved her better for all her
foolishness than he ever did me for causing no trouble. There's
more to making people love you than not being a bother. But
there was a time when things were different. It is getting so

far back now I almost think I dreamed it but I was a spindly-legged little girl and I remember running up and down out yonder in that thin white dirt and just loving how hot and tight it made my feet, pouring it over my legs. And I was always finding things. To this day I can't go by a shiny paper on the ground and not think I found me some money and have to look and see if anybody is watching me pick it up. Woman ran right into my behind downtown one day when I was picking up a shiny that won't a bit more than a chewing gum paper. I ought to be ashamed of that. I noticed the little things outdoors more when I was little. My little boy's head is just full of dreams and things I can't see a bit more than nothing, just like my own head was once upon a time. Now for me it's just fretting around about spots here and there in my house and in here I got my hand in everything and it runs to suit me. But out there it's just any way it chooses and if you don't put up a fight it'll grow right over you like a kudzu vine. Papa used to kid me about the kudzu because I got upset when it ran away down from the railroad track and went over that old car up there somebody left and over the tobacco barn and Papa said it would sneak up behind the cows one night and grow right over them and they'd just be bumps in the field the next morning. That Papa. He didn't mean to scare me with his tales but that one scared the daylights out of me until I was old enough to know that vine couldn't move as fast as me and won't going to sneak up my backside and smother me.

I used to have these dreams when I was a little girl. I wanted all the trees in the woods in rows and the ground under clean with no brambles and the weeds cut down and the bushes trimmed and the same kind of flowers in the same place until it seemed like everything inside my head was in little blocks and in straight lines and it got good to go out and set by the pond and see the mess everything was in, cattails growing this way and that and bits and pieces of everything under the sun in the ground and everything all zigzagged. That's why I like my boy to go outdoors with Papa and have him learn all about loving things the way they are. I think Mama did this to me. I can't help myself and people call me a fine housekeeper so it ain't meant to be wrong. I just don't want my boy to put things in his head in little squares until he starts thinking that's the way everything is supposed to be. I don't want him spending all his time fixing and straightening and thinking that's what matters. Mama seen I was getting wild and she put the clamps on me, I declare that's what must have happened. That must have been what happened because I cut out my digging and hunting and finding and keeping things in my room and started not being about to stand it if things won't straightened. I got so I quit catching moths and things to let them out and started pinching them dead in a handkerchief like Mama.

I remember once I saw a broken spider web down by the pond. I remember it special because a bird must have flown through and didn't even feel it and he cut a hole, clean like he'd used a biscuit cutter, and didn't even leave loose threads. I watched the old lady spider winding her eggs, her legs all bunched up and working as fast as she could go and with that hole big as day over her head and not paying it a bit of mind. I told Papa and his eyes just sparkled and he said it was the kind of thing he wanted me to see. He wanted me to see the animals caring for their babies and just letting the house go. He whispered that to me so Mama couldn't hear. I was Papa's girl then. That's the kind of thing I could tell Papa and I saw them and saved them just for him. He always listened to me. And when my Cale is old enough I will save them for him and maybe he will bring them to me the same without my having to ask.

I took something else to Papa. I will always remember this one just as good because it bothered me and bothered me but Papa was there then for me to take things to, when he was young and I was young. I saw a flower, one I didn't know, blue-fringed with some needles in its flower that had stuck some water drops it was holding. It was just covered with little black-

shelled bugs but it was an awful pretty color. I bent to look at it
and I heard a buzzing, loud and ugly buzzing of big flies, the
green ones that won't shoo off and I stooped beside the flower
and saw what it was. It was a dead mouse and the flies were eating on it and then I smelled its dead smell and the flower lost
its smell before I could take my mind off the mouse. I told Papa.
It made me cry for a while before I told him because I didn't like
to find dead things. I won't ever scared of mice and Papa used
to catch them and put them in my pocket when we were getting
the hay. And Papa told me the flower was a trick, it brought
me up to it with its prettiness so I would see the mouse because
the flower was alone with the mouse and couldn't move away
like I could. It wanted to bother me too, only bother me inside. It did bother me until me and Papa went out with a
hoe and I got him to chop a hole and bury the mouse and that
flower didn't move. He was careful not to cut the roots and I
thought of why people do things, how something like that
could make people do things. Jerome is like that. He'll sit on
the porch and see a big weed and he'll look at it until it bothers
him and he'll get up and go get a hoe and chop it down. It's
being inside yourself that makes you do things. That weed just
comes inside him and bothers him until he has to go get it and
if he had just glanced at it and not let it inside, it would still
be there. And that pretty flower, bringing me to it and making me hurt for something I'd never known about. If Jerome and
me both are like that then all people are because there is not
another alikeness in us. And we'd both go out of our way not
to hurt a pretty flower no matter where it picked to come up.
Weeds and flowers. Lawsy, don't I know something about that.

I suppose I'm saying to myself that I got nothing else. All
this remembering being a little girl is just idleness. Everything in my life is gone or decided on but that boy and whatever
is to come now and I'm not going to see anything else to surprise
me. Not up close anyway, I might happen to read abut it. I'm
not even going to see what the ocean looks like or the moun-

tains unless something changes my life because we are never leaving this spot until the good Lord is ready for us. And everything is set up inside me now, even in my dreams and I can't make them move. I let it get away from me. I'd do it over different. I would have waited longer on a man and not got scared. I would have knowed him better if I knew what I do now. I would have looked harder for loving in a man. I wouldn't have thought loving come so easy to people. By the work of my hands I know that I don't ever have to starve to death. And I'm better than most at things and I didn't need to be scared of that like I was. But I'm still afraid of things. I am afraid my children are going to break away from me and not be right. I'm afraid God is going to think I am wicked and take my children away from me. I can slip and chop off a bean plant and I'll set it back up in the row and hope Jerome don't notice it and think it died naturally. I got fears that come up in me as soon as my hands get busy and my mind starts wandering. I'm not to get far away from my fears. It was not meant that I be without them.

Chapter 9

CALE AND PAPA LONZA walked down toward the creek. It had just showered and Cale had on his bright yellow slicker and boots. Papa had pulled on his galoshes but hadn't hooked them so they flapped around on his feet. He guided little Cale in front of him because the wet branches were bent down from the rain and were dropping water on them as they walked. All through the trees they could hear thumping sounds when the animals broke the water loose. The trunks of the trees were black-wet and speckled with light green moss. In the rotten stumps from the sawmill cutting in 1940, the mushrooms glowed orange and grew in bunches like oysters around a pier post. The gnats were rising now and flew around their faces, catching in Papa's lashes. When they reached the hollow, Cale began to notice the puffs of steam that rose from the rotten leaves.

"Look at the smoke, Papa."

"Nope. Almost smoke but not quite. Steam."

"Steam."

"Yep. Remember that smoke comes from fire. There won't no fire here. It just got hot and then it rained and cooled off and got hot again and that stuff is the water drying up and going back where it came from so it can rain all over us again. Look here."

Papa stamped his foot and a puff of steam rose.

Cale started to laugh and jump around in the hollow like a

frog, stopping each time on all fours to watch the steam go up around him. The sun was breaking through the leaves and the fog slid around and through the trees. Two starlings lit over their heads and the water came tinkling down on Cale.

"It's raining again, Papa."

"Naw, honey. Just them old heavy-footed birds up there shaking it loose."

Cale looked up as the starlings took off, dumping water in his face. "Wet me, old bird!"

"Come on. Let's go on down closer to the water. This is my special flower place."

They walked toward the edge of the creek and soon there were colors all around them. Tiny blue iris at the foot of the trees and yellow flowers on vines in the trees, sticking out long red tongues. Papa showed Cale a jack-in-the-pulpit, its green topknot sheltering the flower and its leaves filled with water like a funnel. By the edge of the creek stood the prize, Papa's favorite, three lady's slippers, their pale pink bulbs trimmed with pink petals.

Papa pointed to them and said, "Now that one there is as pretty as a woman. Ain't many I can find to speak so of but them lady slippers. Got a right name. Lady slippers of the orchid family for a fine-bred lady not just any common farm woman."

Cale walked to the flower pinching the bulb shut.

"Now quit that," Papa said quickly and Cale jumped back, his eyes clouding up. "You went and bruised it. Now, don't go harming things. You got to learn what to respect. What in the world makes you do something like that?" Cale pinched the flower again and Papa popped him on the behind and took his hand and pulled him away. He whimpered a little but Papa ignored him, holding in his temper. Why? Nobody ever taught him to be mean.

They sat on the big rock over the river; they always came to this particular rock on their walks but this was the first time when the summer flowers were out. Vines hung over it, inviting someone to swing across on them. The pools quivered with water bugs and Papa could see their shadows on the bottom. Foam gathered around the bottom of the rock, white now not yellow like it was when Soloman's mill was going.

"See them bubbles. I can remember as good as yesterday when them bubbles was yellow and the water won't fit to look at. I seen them blue and green and every color in the rainbow and first I thought it was kinda pretty. Almost looked richlike until I saw you couldn't see the bottom no more and I could have kicked myself for not hollering sooner. I took to seeing fish turned up and bloated, with their scales coming off like feathers. And they were eating at each other when they started swimming sideways and you didn't see bug one swimming on the water. Then Soloman went back to just dumping the water full of yellow. And it had a stink too. Some people said they didn't notice it and you could get used to it but I thought it had an awful smell, especially if the morning was wet. I don't like the idea of getting used to a stink anyway whether it's hurting me or not. But it's fine water now. Took it five years to run out fresh and God only knows where it went. And full of fish. See them."

Cale bent over the edge and when his reflection fell over the water the fish darted into the shadows. "Fish. I see it, Papa. One, two, five, seven."

"Hold on, one, two, three, four."

"One, two, three, four, two zillion."

"Zillion? Where in the world did you get that? I declare you could raise a youngun in a closet and he'd pick up something you never heard."

Steam lifted over the water and it moved slowly, sliding with the water around the bend. Near the bank spiders walked on top of the water, wobbling when the water bugs ran through their legs. Cale dropped leaves in the current and watched them spin, shoot between the rock and bump their way downstream.

"My papa looked out over this very same water. Did you know that's the reason he picked this place for his? Back then a man had to put water and shelter from the weather first. The rest he could take care of hisself. And he wanted to put his house right down here by the water but that woman of his said she didn't want no mosquitoes and snakes and what not infesting her house so he give in and put it where it is. That's the difference between a man and a woman; a woman got inside to worry about and a man got outside. Did you know my papa built your house?"

"Papa built my house."

"No, my papa built your house. He built it back when it was enough to claim your homestead and farm it and taxes didn't eat you alive and every man who was ready and willing to work got his fair share. The country has come to shame when it had to take so much from a man to run its wars that he has to give up his land. Used to be a man worked to feed his family and now he has to feed the city folks just to pay his taxes. Man got five mouths of his own to feed and he got to raise to feed twenty-five. If I was a man, I'd be ashamed to live knowing I won't feeding myself. But times has changed. Papa wouldn't believe how times has changed. But it is still mine and it will be until they put me in it, this land. But I'm too tired to fight, child. Too old and too tired. Jerome knows that." Papa stared quietly across the water while Cale drew in the moss with an arrowhead. "I even thought once that we might someday have to pack up and leave just like my papa did in the old country, just go looking for us another country but pretty soon they ain't going to be none left. Nothing fit to live on. My papa left where people were fighting and dying and walked right into somebody else's war. He didn't have no way in this world of knowing that a war was brewing but he did tell of the road coming south, how he seen black men chained together and walking and it won't until he got to Richmond, Virginia, that he knowed what people was up to. Selling people. Lord, I'm glad it's not in my time but it do look like they would have thought a little when they set them loose. Now you can set loose a wild rabbit and he knows just what to do. But you set loose a tame one and see what happens. He'll get et up by the dogs before sundown. You don't set loose nothing what don't know how to take care of itself.

"Papa didn't even own him no slaves and he had to fight him the Yankees when they come marching through. He told me they come through here hungry and mean and took every chicken and pig he had and he locked Mama and the children under the floor of the packhouse when he'd seen fire lighting up the sky over toward Raleigh and heard them laughing and camping out in the woods. Yankees left them with nothing but a stack of sweet potatoes they had racked up and covered with straw so it looked like a haystack. You'll see soon enough what happens when people mean well but don't know much." Papa looked at Cale who had moved down the riverbank and was throwing rocks in the water. The boy looked up and grinned and kept throwing.

"They was seven years catching up and Mama didn't have a child what lived until me back in 1869 and I was her last. And there is two dead baby boys on the hill named Lonza. But that's what war is good for, Cale, and I'm hoping you won't see none of it. But I declare you will unless people do an awful lot of changing. Aunt Bynum told me once that sometimes she wished her mammy had been nice to the white folks so she'd have something.

"I'm talking this way about wars, Cale, and I'd fight them like a banty rooster if they come trying to let on like what was mine was theirs to plunder. It's just what a man has to do and what he wants to do is usually two different things. I'd be 'shamed of you if you wouldn't fight if they called you but I don't ever want to see you going out looking for it. If I'd had my wants things would have been different. I'd a had me a boy of my own and not had Jerome in between. Come take what's mine and put his name on it. I got to depend on you to do right by my farm. If I'd had my way no sawmill would ever have come in here."

"What you want to be, Papa?"

"Huh." Papa laughed and looked at Cale. "It's what I want to been."

"I want to be an airplane flyer."

"Well, that's not a bad wish. You'd probably get quite a view of the world from up there. I reckon by the time you're grown the sky'll be full of them."

"I want to be Superman."

"How about Captain Marvel?"

"Nope, Superman because bullets don't hurt him."

"I thought Captain Marvel could take care of that too."

"I don't know. I don't got no books on him. Mama read me Superman."

"Captain Marvel was one of my favorites. I don't want to be none of those fancy things, though there was a time when I thought I wanted to ride the fire wagon but that was only because of the horses and those polka-dot dogs. Then I saw me a bad fire in the general store and I didn't want no part of that. All that fine merchandise just ruint and scorched . . ."

"I want to be Superman."

"Hush interrupting me. I thought one time I might run off with the circus when I watched them big fellows pull up the tents and seen the trains come in with the animals. And you know, Cale, I seen them animals years later when I was working down at the railroad station and it was pitiful. I had thought it was really something seeing all those big cats snapping their jaws at the man with the chair and him going in there with them. I mean it hurt me inside to see them all shut up in those boxes in the cars, each one of them by hisself and walking back and forth and no room to stretch his legs. You can tell they hate it the worst of all, them cats. I went out with a light one night and saw those big eyes, glowing back at me."

"I never seen a cat in a cage. Aunt Bynum got a cat. Floyd says it's his."

"That ain't the kind of cat I'm talking about. I'll take you to the circus sometime and let you see. We'll have to go clean to Raleigh but you ought to see yourself a circus. I've heard many a time that they will be gone before long. Naw, those cats were lion cats and tiger cats. Fifty times as big as Aunt Bynum's cat."

"I seen a tiger in a picture. There's one in the Tarzan book and he rides a lion."

"Superman and Tarzan. Ain't it something the stuff they put in your head."

"I can read A's."

"Now that's real good. What was we talking about? Circus, fireman. What I wanted to be. If I had me a big pile of money, I tell you what I'd do. I'd build me a big glass house and I'd grow me flowers, every kind in the world and there could be snow on the ground and on the roof and I'd have me flowers in that glass house. I seen a fellow had one. Growed flowers and oranges and bananas. Had stuff growing that didn't live nowhere else but the jungle."

"I want me a gun."

"You're talking awful big. What you want such a thing for?"

"So I can shoot me things."

Papa was quiet a moment. He looked at the little boy who threw pebbles in the water. "Bang, bang, bang."

"Where'd you hear that?"

"I seen a gun in the store."

"I mean where did you get the idea for shooting things?"

"Dun' know. I bet I could hit that old fish from clean up here."

Cale threw a big rock and all the fish ran into the shadows. The ripples moved outward and the fish moved slowly back into the outside rings.

"You got it at the picture show I bet, or one of these little boys you been playing with. That's nothing for someone to be teaching you."

"Can we go to the picture show this week?"

"I reckon we can if your mama will give us the money. We'll just get in the way and bother her until she does. What would you rather have, a gun or a fire truck?"

"A gun."

"A gun or a puppy dog?"

"Puppy dog."

"That's better. Who you love best, your mama or your papa?"

"My mama."

"Why?"

"Dun' know."

Papa patted the boy on his knee. Four years and knowing so much. It won't like it was when he was four years old. He wasn't so serious already. His mama would be out picking cotton and dragging along a burlap bag. He would play in the pile of cotton until they ran him off. Then he'd play in the hot sand, with an anthill or inside the shed with a doodlebug. He'd catch a black ant and put it into the doodlebug's dirt funnel, watch the ant claw up the sides and slip and fall until he got to the bottom and the doodlebug reached out and pulled him under. He won't thinking of such things as guns. People didn't want to think guns then. They had seen enough of them and all the boys with legs and arms off. Neighbor boy had an eye gone from a gun and it was stitched shut. He saw guns for sure, people kept them. He heard one boy's father brag about how many Yankees his gun killed and they looked at it hung over the mantel, kept polished blue and the wood shiny but it was battered from the war. Hearing how many people it killed didn't make him want to shoot it or kill anyone. He saw his papa take down the gun once, it was for a chicken hawk, and he crawled under the bed with the dog when it went off. Same old dog that didn't like thunder and that knew the Yankees had killed the old cow he slept with in the winter. His papa hit the hawk and it fell from the sky with its wings open, but its glide was gone and it fell hard and fast. Wasn't any good seeing that chicken hawk dead either. Fence strung with seven foxes and the chicken hawk and the buzzards came in for them. All the birds pecking away till nothing but an old skin dried up. There was nothing in this world good about killing anything and he'd have to get that sorry gun notion out of the boy's head.

"Jerome talk about guns to you?"

"Huh?" The boy had crawled away and was stacking up flint rock.

"Your papa. Did he talk about shooting?"

Cale looked blank and wrinkled his nose.

"Never mind, never mind. I can't blame him for everything I can't figure out." But I could kick him in the seat of the pants for not paying you any mind. It's a shame before God to have such a fine little boy and pay no more attention to him than if he was a chicken. And you're already getting away from us. Falissa's going to make you a mama's boy and Jerome's just waiting till he can work you in the fields. That ain't no way to grow up, though I don't blame Falissa. That's the best a woman can do. And my time is getting short. I wake up wore out and Lord, I can't run you down. Talk yourself blue and got no idea of what goes in that little head to stay.

"Cale, you hear about the Indians?"

"What Indians?" He was interested.

"Used to live right here. See that scooped-out place in the rock? That's where they cooked. And they used those rocks there to make arrowheads and hatchets."

"What for?"

"To get them something to eat." I ought to just shut my mouth. Ain't no use lying and pretending to the boy that people ain't full of meanness. Don't take me two minutes to find my way back to what I was trying to get away from.

"Buffaloes."

"Don't talk foolishness. You know there ain't no buffaloes here. That's just for those Indians in the west. Possums and squirrels and sometimes bears."

"There are bears here?"

"You just go play and don't pay any attention to me. I'm an old fool."

"Black bears or white bears, Daddy said there won't no bears."

"Black bears. Go play."

"Apaches?"

"Lumbees."

"Geronimo?"

"How do you know so much? I'm going to crawl under the bed. How old are you?"

Cale held up his hand and looked at it, four fingers.

"Old enough."

Cale shook his head. "When I'm this many I can go to school." One hand, one finger.

"Six. You got two whole years to go. Don't rush yourself. I didn't even go to school. I was ten years old before they taught me my numbers and letters in Sunday school and they didn't teach me much good at that. I write as good a hand as that Jerome though he'd not admit it but that Falissa can go circles around me. She's quick to catch on. Got your mama's features and your papa's fixtures." Papa laughed and Cale ran to him.

"What's funny?"

"You are."

"Uh-uh."

"Yes, you are."

"Let's go to the picture show tomorrow."

"Have to ask your mama."

"You know what's on?"

"Nope."

"Uh-huh. We seen it last week."

"Oh, coming next week . . . I forgot what it was."

"Red Ryder and Hopalong Cassidy."

"Oh."

"And three Bugs Bunny cartoons. What's up, Doc?"

Both of them looked up as the supper bell tinkled through the trees.

"You know what that is."

"I'm not through."

"Yes you are or your mama'll take care of both of us."

"I'll take care of her." He made a pistol with his finger and hissed twice. "Got her." He holstered his gun and ran up the path.

Chapter 10

SHE THOUGHT of the morning, the start of the day, when she had almost felt herself go back to that time when she had Cale, the fear and being alone, when it mattered so much what happened to her daydreams. This morning she had felt the war come over her, bother her not because of the people of Europe and Holland, but in her life and in her way. Maybe it was because the baby was so near. She was weak maybe, but she had hated the war all the way to the mothers who had sons in it.

She had gone to the store to stock up before the baby came and to get her sugar with the stamps while they still had some. She was there when they opened and the line was already clean around the block. She had brought it home, like five pounds of gold, and poured it into a mayonnaise jar; it only filled it half full. And when she started to the pantry with it, the jar slid through her hands like water. Just dropped it kerspat and broke it in a million pieces. The glass went in her shoes and she saw the white mound, neat, hardly spread about at all, but with the glass shining in it like jewels. She had spent the morning straining and sifting it, trying to get it all in another jar before Jerome and Papa came back, with the sweat popping out on her face, picking out the last shiny bits that went through her flour sifter until her fingertips were as sore as could be. Her floor was clean enough to eat from, it shouldn't hurt them. It was sure just as pure white as it was in the beginning, it looked to be anyway. She ran it through the sifter three extra times to be sure. She didn't use it in her coffee but the men always did and Cale liked it on his oatmeal. But she had heard many a time that a person couldn't eat enough glass to kill him and she had never heard of a soul who had died of it, that your throat just wouldn't let you swallow enough to kill you. Choking on seeds and gum balls and even a bit of gristle but never on glass so she wasn't going to fret. You can't fret yourself over ever little thing.

Yes, indeed. Things were different now. Four years ago she would have blurted it out, apologized, confessed because she was so afraid of him and of him finding out, and ducked her head and stood there and taken it with him ranting and raving as if he never made a slip in his life when she had even seen him plant the wrong seeds in the garden. Just last summer they had to pole and string up a whole acre of beans when he got hold of running bean seeds instead of bunch beans, worse than a child sometimes. Certainly he was not perfect though he claimed to be. But now in this day she kept her secrets, even ones he might find out about. She won't scared of him like she used to be.

And last week she had washed Jerome's liquor stamps right in the pocket of his shirt and ironed and starched them to boot. So she just let him find them hisself.

That afternoon news had come that Hitler was wounded and Falissa nodded her head and smiled at Papa. That was what made it certain the second baby was to come tonight, the war was almost done with, so she had told the doctor when to arrive, after she was done with the supper dishes. This one was going to be right on time, not like Cale. The feelings inside that she hadn't thought of for four years were coming back, just as clear as if it had been yesterday. But just the hurt in her body, the rest seemed far away now. That Hitler who had been so big was starting to lose, even Roe had said that and he was over there. This baby would probably be a girl, but somehow it seemed almost better this way. That Cale be the man of the house and not have any competition. And two would be enough. It had all frightened her so back then, the baby coming and the war all running together in her mind. She had thought so much dying was to come and all the houses would fall and burn and they did but not here. And a dream of something you've never seen can die so quickly, is so easy to kill, so much that you shouldn't let them be real enough to die. Now she saw how little the war had been to her, how her life went on almost untouched but for the lack of a few things at the store, no sugar for seasoning the vegetables, the walking and pulling her purchases back in Cale's little wagon when the bus stopped running. She heard the sound of human feet every morning, an occasional mule in front of the house as everyone walked and left their gasless car in the drive or saved it for a Sunday afternoon drive to Raleigh, coasting down the hills out of gear. And when and if it came time for the war to affect Cale, he would know how to take care of it and he would tell her how.

She had sat downstairs with the three of them, Papa Lonza, Jerome, and Cale, until the smoke from the men's pipes began to hurt her eyes and the child had sneezed twice. She took Cale up to bed, telling him it was bedtime a half hour early but wanting to get him down while she could. As soon as she saw the brown bag with its top twisted, she knew she couldn't depend on them, either one of them. Papa would be drunk in five minutes like it was the first drop he'd ever touched. She watched Cale brush his teeth and say his prayers, and she told him to ask God to bless in addition to Papa and Mama and Grandpapa and Uncle Roe, who had been added to the list since he sent him a German helmet for a present, to bless his new little brother or sister that might come to stay with them that very night. He did and got in bed and she pulled up the covers; his eyes were wide open because he wouldn't be sleepy for thirty minutes but she pulled his door to and went on to her room.

Downstairs as she looked over the banister, Jerome was pull-

ing out the fifth of whiskey. She waited to see if he was going
to share it with Papa and he did. That was a gesture that always
surprised her coming from Jerome, except maybe he wanted
someone else to be as much to blame as him for his foolishness.

"Jerome, just send the doctor on up when he gets here. I'll
stay ready for him and no need for you and Papa to come."

He nodded and watched her disappear from the top of the
stairs.

They sat silent a moment, Jerome stuffing his pipe again; tobacco was still plentiful and if not he could have grown his
own. Enough wasted in the floor of the packhouse to last him
a year. The liquor was working on him fast. He had eaten a
big supper but it had been a long time since he had had any.
He was relaxing now, didn't want to make any fast moves with
his head, didn't want anyone to talk loud. The old man was
quiet, thinking.

Jerome thought of his old man, always drunk but never the
same. Sometimes mean drunk. Falissa said he was that way.
Must have took after him there. Did get drunk and give Will
James the stalk cutter but if James had been a decent sort he
wouldn't have taken it.

"What's that?" Lonza said.

"I didn't say anything."

"Thought you did."

"Nope, was just thinking. Thinking about my old man and
his boozing."

"Your old man make his own liquor?"

"He made it, he stole it, he made the niggers make it, he did
anything to get it. He didn't have enough sense to make it right.
He'd pick the bugs out of the mash like they mattered a damn
bit and turn right around and get metal poisoning. Like to have
choked his insides out."

Jerome stopped to laugh and Papa frowned and turned away.

"Aw, I won't laughing over his choking. Don't wrinkle your
nose at me. I was just thinking of how me and Roe used to

want to go off to town without him because he'd go get drunk and make a fool out of us and keep the girls away and pass out in some whore's room and lose all his money and we'd have to tote him home in the back of the wagon. And once we got near-bout to town and thought we had shook him and I got to getting that followed feeling and I'd turn around quick and almost catch something move until finally I was sure I saw a shadow, so me and Roe started running and jerked around quick-like and caught the old bastard trying to duck behind a tree, had followed us all the way to town like that, running in and out of the woods so we wouldn't know he was back there. But me and Roe fixed him good the next time. He was about half passed-out drunk in the bed when we decided to leave and I was to talk to him and get his interest, telling him how we wanted him to go to town with us while Roe went about and tied his feet to the foot of the bed. He had got all but one of his hands down and the old fool caught on so we had to jump him to finish tying him down and he bit the blood out of my knee. You should have seen him pulling and yanking, working the hardest he ever did in his life and cussing like you have never heard until the woman who was living there come in and threw a glass of water in his face before she knew he was tied up. That was Jessie. She was one of the meanest women he had, I'll say that for her."

Jerome looked at Papa's chair and he was gone. Then he heard the doctor come across the room and tell him to keep his seat, which he planned to do, and start up the stairs leaving Papa at the foot. Papa came and sat back in his chair.

"Doctor's here."

"Well I'm not blind. Drunk maybe, but I'm not blind."

Papa began to rock slowly in his chair.

"Going to have me two grandchildren before I go."

"Go where?" Jerome grunted again and said "Oh," answering his own question. His eyes brighted up. "I was telling you about my old man and his drinking. I'll tell you what I think the best one we pulled on him was. That Roe. He really could think of them. The old man was passed out cold just inside the front door and me and Roe took his arms which was as limp as dishrags and pulled them out straight and Roe took the broom and run the handle up inside his sleeve, cross his back and out the other sleeve. Then we buttoned up his cuffs around them." Jerome laughed and his eyes watered on his face. "That Roe took the old man's liquor bottle which was about half full and set it up on the mantlepiece where he could see it and when he come to, he busted up everything in the living room, knocked the clock over and all the pictures off the walls trying to get that liquor bottle and it won't till he passed out again and sobered up that he thought to go shut the broom part in the door and pull that handle out."

Papa Lonza was laughing now.

"He beat the hell out of us. Not Jessie, just me and Roe because he didn't hear her laughing. That's what he always did. But damn if it won't worth it that time. Damn if it won't. We got the best of him."

"That must have been something."

"Don't know why somebody didn't kill him. He killed a man once."

"What? In a fight?"

"Naw, no fight. I know it won't no fight but he told the sheriff it was. He was drunk. He won't never much of any other way and me and Mama, that was way back before Roe, when she was living, me and Mama spent the night hiding from him up under the house. Then we heard this car drive up and this man start talking to Papa and they got to arguing and Papa went in the house and shut the door saying he was going to get some money and next thing me and Mama heard was Papa's gun go off, that man stop walking on the porch and fall clean off on the bushes and me and Mama could see his legs hanging down in the porch light and he went stiff and was just as dead as a doornail."

"They send him to prison?"

"He never even went to jail. They got a petition on him. Everybody signed a paper on him about what a hardship it would be on the family. He was kin to every one of those bastards who signed it nearabout but they got enough names, hundred it took for them to set him free."

"Who was the man?"

"He was a bootlegger. They said he was part nigger which is part of the reason for all the names. But Papa was so mean mad at me and Mama he probably didn't even have to have anything against him. I'd be dead as a doornail today if he'd thought to look under the house. Mama is anyway and there wouldn't have been no Roe. Mad as the devil at us and killed somebody to show it." Jerome moved to get up from the chair but fell back.

"Where you going? Falissa was wanting us to stay down here."

"I reckon I ain't going nowhere. I ain't going up there."

Jerome looked in the fireplace, the firedogs sitting by themselves, the fireplace swept clean of the ashes.

"I shouldn't ought to drink. I shouldn't ought to drink after what I seen it do."

Papa turned toward Jerome. When Jerome saw the old man's face, he threw the empty bottle, breaking it inside the fireplace, the last thing he saw or heard before he fell asleep.

*　　*　　*

Cale woke up about six-thirty the next morning. The house was quiet and his mother hadn't opened the door so he could smell the breakfast bacon cooking. He went into the hall and saw their door was closed but he could hear voices. From the top of the stairs he could see two heads in the living-room chairs, Papa Lonza and Papa. They were asleep so he went in the bathroom and peed without flushing the commode and walked by them quietly down the steps and out the back door. He went down behind the barn to his hole. It was just like he had left it, the straw still covering the lid. When he lifted it, he saw his candle, the box of matches he had taken from beside the fireplace, the paper sack with three biscuits in it and his Red Ryder book. He sat down in his hole and lit the candle. It blew out once but the next time it kept going. He pulled the lid over him. He could see through the cracks he had left for air but the straw would hide them. He turned the pages in his Red Ryder book. He didn't know the words in this one yet so he looked at the pictures. It was hard to see in the flickering light and wax dripped on the book and one drop made a hot place on his hand. When he was through the book, he flipped up the lid and got out, walking back to the house peeling the wax off his hand. In the kitchen, Papa Lonza was fixing breakfast. He didn't speak to him when he came in but he didn't fuss at him either for going out of the house before breakfast without permission. There was a strange man in the corner, drinking coffee.

"Who are you?" Cale asked.

"I'm Dr. Paulson. And I've come to tell you that you have a new little sister."

"What's she called?"

"Pearlie Sue Jenkins."

"That's ugly."

"Well, my boy. That's between you and your parents and her." He finished his coffee and dumped out the grounds in the sink and went out the back door to the strange car that was in the drive.

Chapter 11

AN AIRPLANE flew over, rattling the windows in their sockets. The chickens in the shrubbery kept right on kicking out sprays of dirt but Falissa, Papa Lonza, and Cale all looked up, missing sight of the plane as it disappeared behind the locust tree. The sound was soon gone and there were only the bees on the white locust flowers, a steady summer hum.

"I saw a bummer plane go by. Yesterday. Right over there." Cale pointed to the sky over the barn.

"That was just a regular plane, Cale. A people plane. That was just like a car or a bus or a train only it was up in the air."

"Falissa means it ain't got no guns and no bombs, Cale."

"How do you know? It had bums on the wings."

"Well, because it's got no reason to have. No reason at all flying over this country."

"Makes Mama jump every time it goes by."

Falissa frowned and her long, bony fingers moved through the beans in her lap. "I just don't like loud noises, Cale. And where you got the word 'bums' I'll never know. It's bombs. If you want an example of a bum, just think of your Uncle Roe."

"Papa Lonza, where them airplanes?"

"They're up in the air, dumbo. You can see that as well as I can."

Cale turned and drove his fist into Papa's arm. "Not them planes. In the movies."

"They're over the ocean and no concern of yours."

"Where are they dropping them bums?"

"It's bombs. Over the ocean. Nowhere near here so you don't have to worry. They won't drop nary a one on Raleigh I'm figuring, nothing to attract them but cigarettes around here."

"Papa, don't tease him so."

"It's the truth, Falissa. I heard down at the steps that cigarettes made us figure higher on the target list because they could drive half the people in this country crazy if they didn't have them."

"When did you start believing anything you heard from that bunch on the courthouse steps? Do nothing but run their mouths."

"We don't have to worry yet about them coming over, Cale, as long as we can keep whipping them over there, but that is about all of it we don't feel, because so far as I can see we're using up our people and our money to beat the band."

"Who we shooting?"

Papa looked at Cale and said, "We're shooting the Japs and Germans mainly, Cale. That's who we're shooting for now. They just got too greedy and wanted too much. But there is no need in the world for you to concern yourself. They let that Hitler put them up to it and that will all be taken care of soon enough."

Papa looked over at Falissa. She was frowning but her hands kept snapping beans.

"Your Uncle Jack said it was just little boys they were shooting, pretty little blond boys and when he first saw them he didn't think he could shoot, but they had guns and was going to shoot him so he had to do it. He had to stand right there and kill little boys who didn't know no better but they would shoot him like a rat in a hollow if he give them the chance."

"Papa, hush. You never know when to quit. Just give him an explanation of war and leave it at that. When he gets old enough he'll get all that at school."

Cale put on his helmet and they couldn't see his face, only the shiny dome of metal. It was too big and his ears kept it from covering his face. Roe had sent it for him with a letter that said he took it off a dead German. It came from the ten-cent store but Lonza had read him Roe's letter before she had a mind to take it away from him and now it was too late.

"Uncle Roe shot a German. He shot a bunch of them."

"Falissa, there ain't a thing in this world I can do to stop such talk and you ain't helping me."

"Well, don't talk so much and learn how to change the subject. You know he'll keep asking as long as you keep answering."

"Papa Lonza is crying."

"I am not. It's my eyes getting bad. They're burning me like they going to sting out."

"Papa Lonza crybaby, Papa Lonza crybaby."

"We didn't want to shoot the Germans, Cale, or nobody else. It's just they made us have to do it and I don't want you ever wanting to shoot nobody. This killing has been bad before but I declare I don't remember all them flags in Summit. I don't remember having to count the flags and trying to remember who they were. There won't but two the first time it happened, two here in Summit."

"Papa, don't you think it's time you just quit talking?" Falissa bent from her chair and poured her snap beans off into a pan with a clatter, lifting up another handful of beans into her lap. "You have got to wait awhile to explain some things and that is most certainly one of them."

"I ain't got time to wait. No, I most certainly don't as he is already talking guns."

"Well, Papa, you'll just have to let me take care of it then. And stop feeling sorry for yourself. You've got plenty of time."

Falissa's fingers moved through the beans, looking down occasionally as she pulled off the ends, both hands working, never still. Cale ran to the end of the porch, hanging his feet over the edge so he could kick the bushes and make the flowers fall, and then watch the chickens cluck and run to catch them and sling them from their beaks.

"I'm thinking, Papa, that when he is grown this fighting will all be done with."

"What makes you think such foolishness? I've lived seventy-six years and I've never seen them quit."

"Well, it doesn't affect us and I don't think we ought to dwell on it until it does, and I just don't want to be around all those crying women and if that's a sin before God, I'm sorry."

Papa Lonza smiled. He heard an old voice in Falissa's, Sarah Ann's, almost hateful but it was her voice to his ear.

"I sounded like Mama, didn't I?"

"Yes'um, you did."

"She put her meanness in deep." She saw the hurt in his face, still, after all this time. She was her mother, that gave her the right, blood kin could criticize. She deserves it. No one should have let that woman get away with such . . . but everyone did.

"Look at that Cale pout at me, Papa. He's still mad at me because I had to tan his little hide this morning."

"What did he do?"

"He glued every last one of Jerome's ration stamps for the gasoline and mine for the food on the leg of the living-room sofa."

Papa and Falissa laughed and Cale ran and punched Papa in the arm.

"Why you laugh 'cause I got a whipping?"

"It's what you got it for, Smarty Pants, too big for your britches."

"I tied them up with damp rags and think I can get the most of them off without ruining them. It was just flour paste. You should hear the town people fighting at the store, Papa. All of them trying to grow a garden and having it dry up and die on them and Lord knows, water is one thing we got plenty of."

Cale went down the steps, into the yard, bored. He liked

to be away from them when they did something else and talked
and wouldn't answer him. He would run to the edge of the
yard where he saw their lips moving and the bees were louder
than their words. His helmet rocked on his head, the leather
band tightening with the heat and pressing his forehead. He
ran into the yard, staying in their view so they wouldn't holler at him and ran in a circle, nodding his helmet back and
forth on his forehead. His pants rode below his tummy and
his shirt lifted over his navel in the hot sun. He tried to feel
where Falissa had spanked him but it wasn't there, not like
Papa Jerome and his switch and the red whelps that he could
go to sleep thinking about and feel smooth-swollen with his
fingers. He fell in the yard, over something. His knee was
green but there was no blood. Didn't hurt anyway. A trapdoor
covered in the grass and a pit, under his bare feet snakes that
wiggled, and he climbed up the side on roots and pulled over the
top on his belly. He lay back in the grass and his helmet rolled
off, wobbled. He made dying sounds. He would play like he was
dead. Then the German wouldn't know. Hold in breath. The
grass itched. Ants crawled up his shirt, over the top, under
the bottom, up his pants legs. He smelled dead ants. He had
to get to the bush before the German could hit him. The German had seen him rolling in the grass and knew he was alive.
He was unarmed, his rifle smashed. He made it to the bushes
and hid in the shadows. His helmet. He had lost his helmet.
He saw it. It glinted in the sun. The German would want it.
The German knew it came off a dead German and wanted to
get it back. He threw himself on the helmet and rolled through
the grass, dodging bullets, a flesh wound in his leg. No, in his
arm. The blood trickled through his clothes. He had lost too
much blood to go on. He slept. In the morning the sun came
through the leaves, woke him up. The wound had closed over
in his stomach. He felt it with his fingers. It had healed and the
skin stuck up in the center and he would carry the scar in his
belly where the German shot him.

Chapter 12

PAPA LONZA walks like he got wet pants. 'Cause he got on his scratchy wool pants but they're the only Sunday pants he's got so he is wearing them in the summertime anyway. When we get where there is a lot of people, he pulls on my hand tight and I can feel the round spots on his fingers that are cold. We got an hour before the movie starts but we got to keep an eye on the line. That's why me and Papa Lonza are in the feed store, so we can see out through the window when the line starts. When there's as much as ten we go over because we want the front and I got to get me a Lash LaRue star. Superman and the Molemen, Lash LaRue, and ten cartoons.

They got biddies here because me and Papa heard them thump-thump from out of the door. They got them in boxes in the back with holes in them and you can see their yellow sticking out the holes, and hear them scratching and peeping up and down. We got biddies at home and ours look better.

"Papa, they is sickly."

"Shhhh. You want them to put us out to wait on the street? You talk louder than you mean to. They are a bit poor-looking after you seen Falissa's. Haven't got much color. They was unnatural raised you know."

· "Huh?"

"They was incubated . . . raised with a light bulb in a hot box without no mama. They take the eggs and heat them up and fool them little biddies into thinking they're hatching under a mama. Then they take out all the puny little roosters and dye them blue and pink and sell them before Easter for twice as much as they're worth."

"There's one dead."

"Maybe he's just asleep."

"How come he don't wake up and go back in? I'll tickle his foot."

The leg begins to pull itself back inside the hole.

"See, smarty. It won't dead." Papa said.

"They just got together and pulled it back in. They took it and throwed it in the quicksand."

Like in the show last week. The badman had killed an Indian and took all his arrows and shot them in the settlers so that Lash LaRue would think it was Indians who done it and they didn't have no fingerprinting back then and the settlers were all teaming up to go kill the Indians when Lash LaRue started thinking it won't the Indians and I forgot the part about putting the Indian in quicksand, they done that first after they took off his arrows and feathers and his tommyhawk and he went slurp under the mud and never was to be seen again, but Lash LaRue found his feathers and bow in the woods and knowed no real Indian would go off and leave his feathers and bow which took him to suspecting the badman. Trying to make it look like an Indian and not wanting to get caught with the stuff. If he had had fingerprinting like in *Superman* he would have known already.

"Papa, how come Lash LaRue ain't got no fingerprinting?"

"Hasn't got no fingerprinting."

"Hasn't got no fingerprinting, how come?"

"Lash LaRue has got fingerprints. Everybody got them. Even you. You leave them all over enough things to know you got them."

"That ain't what I asked."

"Well I'm glad somebody knows what you asked."

"You remember. When he found the bow in the woods. He could have put a fingerprint on it and done like in *Superman* and knowed right off it was the badman."

"Now how would he know? Do you think the Dodge City Sheriff's Department has a fingerprint on every badman and Indian in the West?"

"You said everybody got fingerprints."

"Go see how many people in the movie line."

"Four. I already looked. How come?"

"We better get over."

"How come. How come. How come!"

"You want to go home without the movie?"

"No."

"Well you keep that business up and see if you don't."

The badman had killed an Indian and took all his arrows and was in the bushes beside the farm. He saw through the trees his first victim, an old man with wool pants on walking across the yard like he had wet pants and zap, he got him. Then he shot mother and daddy and the little boy ran and hided in the wash pot and the badman thought everyone was dead so he left and the real Indian came and a strong brave found the little boy who was pretending to be asleep in the wash pot and he took him up on his white horse and galloped across the prairies with him and raised him to be his own son and called him White Cloud. Silver Arrow. No. Creeping Bear. Big Black Creeping Bear. That's Floyd. Fox. Wolf. Silver Wolf, the bravest Apache in the West. Blue eyes.

We go out the door and across the street. There are only six in the line ahead so it's for sure that we'll get the front row and the Lash LaRue badge.

"What does that say?"

Papa Lonza looks at the poster and sees the girls. One bunch of pictures has people getting pies splashed on their faces.

"It says you don't come."

"Naw, it don't."

That was the boy in front of them in the line, eleven or

twelve. "It says 'Fiery Faye and her Fabulous Follies — girls, girls, girls.' " He starts to giggle and turns around.

Silver Wolf went into a saloon and all the white men looked up. He saw Fiery Faye and decided he would take her away to be his squaw. A cowboy drew a gun but Silver Wolf was unarmed except for his knife. He pushed a table over on the boy who shot down the chandelier with his gun and everything got dark and Silver Wolf ran away with Fiery Faye . . .

She looks too heavy. His horse couldn't carry her and Silver Wolf don't want her. She's a painted woman. He don't want no Indian squaw either. He don't want no woman. Just his horse. And when the lights came back on in the saloon, Silver Wolf was gone but Fiery Faye was still there. And she remembered the rest of her life Silver Wolf who left her. Naw, no Fiery Faye. Silver Wolf comes in the saloon and fights the cowboy who draws a gun but Silver Wolf grabs his arm and he shoots down the chandelier.

"What you and me going to come see next week, Papa, if Fiery Faye is on? What happens to Part Two of *Superman?*"

"That's just the night show. Me and you will come to see Part Two."

The Indians came and took an old man and a little boy and let the old white man sit on their tribal council until his dying day and then Silver Wolf let him be burned like a hero when he was dead.

The lady started selling tickets. It cost twenty-five cents for Papa and nine cents for Cale and five cents for a box of popcorn with extra salt. They handed Cale a silver star and one to the kid behind Papa. He had hoped Papa would get one so he would have two. They went to the front row and all four of the people in front of them were already there. The first seat Papa sat in smelled like pee so they moved on down the row. Cale stuck his silver star on the right-hand side of his T-shirt. "It don't weigh nothing."

"What?"

"My star. It said solid silver."

"Solid tin."

"Two boxes of popcorn, one for me and one for the rats," Cale said.

"Where'd you hear that?"

"Last week behind me. Are there rats here? Where does that door go to?"

The door glowed with a red light EXIT.

"Outside, I reckon. That's where you go if it catches on fire. But you wait for me and don't go running toward it. That's how people get hurt."

"On fire!"

"Back long before you were born the opera house over at Salemville caught on fire and burned up ten dancing girls and a piano player. More people than they could count got trampled down when everybody started running out like a herd of cows. That was during the war, the first one."

The piano player comes in and sits down and opens his music. Looks like he wouldn't still need music. "The Sweetheart of Sigma Chi" . . . he don't know but one song. The newsreel comes on. Same news as last week and the week before. Soldiers running over hills, ducking from the bullets, loading their guns, moving fast, scared, their backs slammed against the dirt.

Then the first cartoon, *Bugs Bunny*, then *Looney Tunes* and *Superman*. The Molemen are very short but they have tall heads and each one of them looks a little different. They march in little rows down under the ground. When they come up they can't see and bump and stumble. I like the Molemen better than the people. Superman floods their hole under the ground by picking up a tree to change the river. Everyone is hissing. Papa is hit in the head with a popcorn box. The screen is shaking from being hit with popcorn boxes and a big wad of bubblegum sticks in the middle. It is continued next week but just before it went off we saw a bunch of Molemen crawl out and mumble to each other in Molemen language. They'll be back next week.

We walk out into the sunlight after cartoon number ten. I had already seen the Lash LaRue movie and three of the cartoons.

Mild-mannered Clark Kent stepped into the alley, looked both ways and saw that no one was watching. He pulled off his necktie and undid his shirt.

"Papa, what do you reckon happens to those clothes he takes off?"

"Who?"

"Clark Kent, dummy."

"Oh, I don't know." Then Papa laughed.

"I mean what if some bum comes in the alley and put them on and walks off and when Superman comes back he doesn't have any clothes."

"I guess he has to go in a store in that funny-looking little blue suit and buy him some."

"What happens when he takes a bath? Will the blue suit come off?"

Superman undid his shirt and beneath it he found a large letter M and his legs shrunk up and the top of his head grew up and he squinted and took off across the sky and said, "This looks like a job for Moleman." And his cape flapped off and he crashed and his head cracked open and inside was an egg yellow.

"Let's get an ice cream cone, Papa."

"We don't got enough money. We can get a bag of peanuts."

> The boy stood on the burning deck,
> Eating peanuts by the peck.
> The flames amounted to his chin
> But still he poked the peanuts in.

"You want some, Longfellow?"

"I'm not Longfellow. I'm Super Moleman."

"O.K., Super Moleman. You want to spend our last nickel
on a bag of peanuts and split them?"

"Yep."

Papa Lonza and Cale went to the railway station to eat their
peanuts, cracking the hulls and putting them back in the
bag. Papa liked the station; it never changed. They hadn't
even taken down the sign that said telegrams but he knew somewhere behind that window was a telephone and a sweet-voiced
woman who had replaced him. For Papa, time put on the
brakes when he saw the black porter pulling the baggage cart,
at the same speed, in the same uniform with the porter cap
hiding his age in the gray fur on his head and his blackness hiding his wrinkles.

He nodded, and spoke his name, " 'Noon, Mr. Lonza. You
looking well."

"Thank you, Jalob, and you too."

"How you, Mr. Cale?"

"I'm fine, thank you very much."

Cale looked at Papa as Jalob pulled the cart to the siding.
"Am I supposed to say 'sir'?"

Papa shook his head. "Jalob would think you were being a
smart aleck if you did. Just be polite. But you remember to
say it to white men."

"Yes sir," Cale said and giggled. He liked the dark cool station. His mama would call it 'old-timey' he thought, and she
would try to guess where the people with their cardboard suit-
cases and lunch boxes were going. They were all exciting people from the gray rooming houses in the city whose names they
didn't know. Some rented rooms for a dollar a night and Papa
said some others tried to time it so they could sleep in the station
and say they had a train coming before six so they wouldn't
get arrested for loitering, a word for hanging around. The train
came and Cale and Papa went to the edge of the platform.
Cale's heart always beat fast when he saw the engine the first

time because it was so much bigger than it seemed from watching the train on the track. The white steam came in around their feet and black and white clouds spread and caught under the edge of the roof. When the steam went across his face, it felt cool then wet and it formed in little water beads on the side of the engine until it moved again and jarred them off. There were always sparks from under the big silver wheels when the long arms moved over and around and rocked to a stop beyond them with the passenger cars by the platform. When the engine was stopped, Cale and Papa went back to the bench to get out of the people's way.

"You want the last peanut?"

"I flip you for it," Cale said.

"Got nothing to flip."

"If it's got two inside we both get one."

Papa opened the peanut. "Two."

"I get the big one," Cale said and popped it in his mouth.

A woman got off the train with a bird cage. In it was a little yellow bird that jumped back and forth and kicked out seeds as she walked. Its feathers were ruffled up and it was squealing. The woman looked very tired.

When the people were out, the train jostled as they undid and unloaded the freight cars, the couplings lifting like they would come unlatched.

They started to vent the engine and steam rolled out the top in great white clouds. Cale's heart began to beat faster and while the men worked, he noticed his feet wouldn't touch the ground. He curled up against Papa who patted him on the head. The train got quiet and Cale saw the mail bag fly out and swing on the hook. They could hear the yellow bird in the cage whistling shrilly as the woman went through the front of the station.

"Papa Lonza, where can you get a little yellow bird like that?"

"I don't know, Cale. I reckon that woman brought him from a long way off."

"You ever had a little yellow bird?"

"No. I knew a woman who had one though. They're mighty delicate little birds. She had one in this tall cage and it used to sit in this little swing and sing and chirp. And she used to sing and it would sing with her and one day this organ salesman came and was demonstrating to her what a fine song you could play on this little organ and that bird took into whistling with it and was just carrying on a piercing song until the organ got up near the end where the notes were so high they hurt your ears and that little bird went quiet and fell right off that swing with his heart burst open and never sang another note, just dead as a doornail. Just broke his little heart that something had come into his house that could outdo him."

"Is that the truth?"

"Cross my heart. In fact she started hollering to me out in the garden where I was weeding her flowers to save it and I told her I heard you could dunk them in cold water sometimes to bring them back to, and she did, and it didn't do no good and she got mad and threw me out like I done it in the first place. Told me she didn't want me touching her flowers again and started ranting about the poor little wet thing like I'd drowned it when it was dead before it ever hit the water and it was her that killed it. She killed it when she broke its spirit."

"What's its spirit?"

"Uh. That's a hard one. A spirit is different to break than anything. Not like an arm or a stick. If I were to break your spirit I would say you can never go to Lash LaRue movies anymore and you have to stay home and practice piano lessons."

"I would break your head."

"You're too big for your britches."

"So are you."

How can he just go in and out of being good and bad before I get him through something? Can't keep up with him anymore. I been through one war and come through standing up but there ain't going to be no place for me after this one. I can tell just as good that I have lived out my time. I hate to admit it but I liked that little boy better when he couldn't talk back to me and we just laughed. At least I could make like he understood me. Here I am acting like an old fool after I said what an old fool my papa got to be before he went and how it never was going to be me that way. But you can't help the truth, I declare you can't. And I don't know if I could make him any different if he was mine. He's near 'bout mine as it is. But I reckon that's all I got anyway. Something near 'bout mine. Got no job. Just an old railroad station going to pot and a talent no good anymore and too old to learn a new one. I wonder if my equipment is still sitting in there just collecting dust or if they took it out to get it out of their way. Probably threw it in the garbage or in a back room somewhere. Something to be replaced by some little old twirp of a girl just because she happens to have a fancy voice.

"Papa, when we going to go on a ride on the train? You said you'd go to Raleigh this summer."

"Well, it isn't summer yet." Papa looked down at the child and saw his bottom lip begin to roll out. "We'll go soon as we can. When your mama says its O.K. and will give us the money."

"You're bigger than she is."

"Well, that's a fib."

"You're older anyhow."

"You're talking right now. I'm the oldest man in the world and sometimes I think I'm the tiredest."

"I want to ride the train in one of them cars."

"Hobos used to ride them cars, that was men with no money that just went from place to place and hung around under the trestle. A whole bunch of them got killed when I was a little boy, track buckled up when the temperature got up over a hundred degrees and the whole train came off the rails and went every which away. You don't want to ride in them cars."

"What happened to the people cars?"

"Won't none of them on the train. Just animal cars and box-cars and a couple loads of coal that the niggers hauled off and stole before they could get the train going again."

"I want to be a hobo."

"Naw you don't either. Didn't you just hear me tell about them all getting killed?"

"I wouldn't be a hobo here. I would ride way off and be one in Raleigh and go where I wanted."

"And just what do you think you would eat?"

"I'd shoot me a rabbit. I'd eat me one of them old cows in the car."

"And where would you sleep?"

"I'd sleep out under the stars."

"What would you do for people? How about your family and your mama and daddy."

"I don't need none of them to go with me. I can go by myself."

"And who'd protect you while you was asleep?"

"I'd get me a great big dog named Fang."

"He has to sleep sometime too you know."

"He keeps one eye open."

"Oh." The train whistled and began to puff and slide out of the station. The passenger car went out with an occasional cameo in the windows, a man, a woman, a man asleep with his chin against his chest.

Cale reached for Papa's hand and pulled him to go home. Papa got up slowly, hating to leave the damp cool of the station but knowing this was the four thirty-three when it went by the house and it would be there long before they were. Papa squinted in the light, not orange yet because the days were already longer. They walked in the grass beside the highway, beside the ditch that was filled with what people threw from cars, papers, cans, and bottles, and he thought how it didn't used to be there, how he used to run down the side to pick up a scrap and find it was a white morning glory all twisted up in the heat. Too much to pick up now. Cale ran ahead, stopping each time the old man hollered and waiting with his hands on his hips for Papa Lonza to catch up. Soon Cale saw the house and started running toward the yard. When Papa got there the child was sitting on the front porch swinging his legs.

"What took you so long? I been home an hour."

Papa walked up the steps to his chair and soon as his weight settled in the chair he heard Falissa ring for dinner. His legs were very heavy and he felt a flash of anger that she had let him get his weight settled down before she did that.

Chapter 13

THE TIME IS SOON when my papa is going away. He has had a good long life and he has seen two grandchildren so the Lord would call him fulfilled I am certain. But it doesn't make it any easier seeing him go. And seeing Papa not come out of his bed like he used to, holing up under those steps like a sick animal in a burrow and walking out once or twice a week, reaching out to catch against a tree to get his balance. His body is breaking, I can see it now in every move he makes. There's no lightness there anymore, just a jerk here and there and wobbling to the spring like an old wound-up toy. And his eyes cloud up over the least little thing. But I can rest easy over Papa because if he were to turn into the devil hisself before he passes, the Lord would take him to the good place just on what he's done so far. My papa never had a hateful streak in his body. I can't be so sure he'll see Miss Sarah Ann up there, unless the Lord has a weakness for her too and believed all that fasting and Bible reading was done for Him like she made like. I'll leave the Lord to His own judgment and if my papa wants to join her in the hereafter then he has my grace to do so and we can hope that an angel body is given the same to everyone and she won't be holding a place of beauty with the angels. It should do her soul more good to have that happen than to rot in hell, to be one of all the women who have passed and not be a bit the prettiest. But she is gone from me already and Papa soon too.

It is right that I put my life out for my children. And I have
all I want, two will satisfy me. It is best there be no more so I
can give to them all that they need of my time and my love.
And I am not letting that boy of mine turn to pure meanness.
I would die before I'd take the boy out of him but all this talk
about guns and shooting people I am going to put straight in
his head. If it means he doesn't go to another picture show
I am setting him straight. I want him to grow up knowing
what it takes to be a man in this world . . . as soon as I get it
straight in my mind.

It would be good to find him a mortal man he could see and
follow by, and though my papa set a good example in some
ways, I can't see I want him to be like that. Papa had a few
too many weaknesses for my choosing. And my husband and
his brother just aren't anybody's measuring sticks if they want
to amount to anything as people. I don't know what keeps that
Roe out of trouble with the law if what he says is true. So it
will be outside my house. But I will give that boy a picture of
a man to build hisself on and he will jump up right over any
picture on this earth.

You can't go changing his mind to suit you, that is for sure,
little button that he is with a will of his own already outgrown
him. From the time he wouldn't give you a laugh except to
please hisself, that little fellow has been his own boss.

You would think I didn't care a whit for my little girl if a
body could hear me thinking which isn't so. It's just I know
which one I'd let sink first and I'd tell a fib before God if I
didn't admit that I'd let that little girl go down with me because she is just part of me. Just as pale and sad with nothing
out in front of her but to bear children and find her glory in
that way. I would never slight her, not for a minute. I just
know she is in for the same as me and I will try not to be the
mother to her that mine was to me and let her know in due
time what is out ahead and maybe tell her some of the good-
nesses that will come when she has a boychild.

I see him from the window where I can always find him,
thinking he is alone and talking to a bug. But he is by hisself
if the truth were said, in that place where he won't let grown-
ups go, talking to hisself. You can almost let yourself get as
jealous as can be knowing he might as well be telling you that
you got no business interfering. But that's a little fear. I guess
my wants and fears just aren't as big as most but I just want to
stay right here where I can see my little children grow up and
raise families and do smart things . . . And then I say to myself what a silly I am thinking that. Why, what in the world is
anybody going to find to do in Summit, North Carolina, that
hasn't been done a thousand times before? But honestly I do
want them to have more than me. I would miss him if he were
to grow up and go away but I could live in the proudness. Not
that I begrudge my station, not a bit. I got a good life and plenty
to eat and a place to be a bit proud of but it do get samey. Samey
it is. I want my little boy to say soon as his life gets samey, well,
I'm just going to take off and do something different in a different place if I please. Not that I want him to have a fine car and
a fine house, he can have that if he pleases. I just want him to
be able to do as he pleases and say not a soul on this earth can
do a thing to stop him. Not have somebody hanging over him
squshing the life out of everything new he thinks up.

But I *do* want him to be older when he starts thinking such.
I want him to stay out of these wars we got coming ahead
and invent him something or build fancy buildings or even go
to college if he pleases. That's for rich people, I know, but he
might get somewhere on his smartness.

But I don't want him thinking like one of these soldiers that
just wants to go killing. The war is done with for now. Let it be.
I declare I don't mean to go against my country but I don't want
him telling hisself that there is something fine and great in
being a soldier and killing like that foolish Roe. They make
so much to-do over it, everybody does. I ran into a lady I knew
when I was a little girl and she was bragging on how many men

her son wrote her he killed. Now who in the world brought her to think such was great? There is going to be none of that in my house, none of it, and the first time he catches his eye on something away from that helmet, that helmet is going to find its way away from here.

Chapter 14

FALL HAD COME and Cale was in his first year of school. Falissa walked him to the bus stop, gave him all his instructions and let him go on from there by himself.

The labor shortage was over and Jerome's winter job at the warehouse had ended when the young men started coming back from overseas. He stayed around the house in the morning, much too long to suit her because his being there interfered with her work. And too, she had never had to explain things before. She watched Cale from the window to see him get on the bus safely each morning while she dried the breakfast dishes, strolling back and forth into the front room and hadn't had Jerome's "What you walking back and forth for? Can't you let him out of your sight a minute?" which wasn't fair at all because she had worked hard to teach Cale to take care of himself. He always had his money for milk at lunch, he brought home his lunch box and the one time he laid it down, he remembered where he'd left it. He never missed the bus, his teacher gave him good reports, said he was attentive, he was not a mama's boy. Jerome wasn't being fair at all. It was just a nice sort of feeling to see him go up the steps on the bus, the stop sign folded out the side of the bus and watch his head bob to a seat as he went on his way. No harm knowing for sure he was on his way. Especially if he didn't know she was watching him.

Jerome had taken to reading the paper. He would check the want ads first which hardly ever changed in Summit, and the ones over in Raleigh did him no good. Then he would read her news of prisoners, war trials, executions. He would talk about maps of places he had never heard of and point them out to her. The war was done for the soldiers but people wouldn't let you put it out of your mind. The paper was bound to talk about things you were sick of, just to keep filling the pages up. People seemed happy for a short while until they started in the business of cleaning up, and coming home and finding jobs. Stevie James down the road was killed and she just hated to run into Mary James and hear her talk how we ought to go to Japan and kill every last one of them and burn it to the ground, that it wouldn't be over to her mind until there wasn't a slant-eyed person on the earth. She would get right wild-eyed and it was two years since her boy died. It seemed a lot more bad was going on now than it used to be but it might just have been the paper. They used to just read the weekly in town and already knew pretty much of what it reported. Just as soon not have the paper. It made you worry about things you could leave alone and that weren't close enough to worry you unless you let them.

Pearlie was in her playpen, a quiet baby, easy to amuse and required just the necessities, which made her wonder if it wasn't people who made their children into a bother instead of the children themselves. Hard to say if Pearlie was pretty yet since all babies were somehow beautiful. She had Cale's hair, only hers might have a mite more curl in it, just enough to poke it up above her ears. Also when a baby didn't cry and wet up its face you couldn't help but think it was more beautiful. Just humming away in the crib with just a wooden spool to suck on.

But life was somehow duller for her; the fall of the year did that because you had to know winter was coming. The maples by the drive were taking on a fine glow, it had been a wet

August, and the trunks were black, almost elegant in their darkness. And her mums were good this year, bright yellow and rusty. It smelled nice out now, tobacco, things drying up and the wind whipping the smells around in all directions. She had always been partial to dry colors, orange and gold, and with Mama gone she had taken down some of the white. Cale tore up the starched doilies and she was glad because they made things look too old-timey. People were starting up to Durham to sell their tobacco, saw more trucks than wagons these days, and Papa was itching to go. He loved an auction. But he wasn't up to it. She worried more about seeing him go off than Cale. He was getting shakier fast and he would be a burden on somebody if she let him go off with them. He did love the auctions though, got him so tickled. But if he were to take a fall he'd be too old to mend. Maybe he could go to the bazaar at the school tonight and take his mind off hisself. She hadn't been to the bazaar in years, not since she was at the school, but now with Cale going, there was an excuse.

Cale had gone through a series of fights tonight, trying to decide on his costume. She had hoped the soldier was out of his mind, especially since she had long ago given away his helmet when they were collecting for the white elephant sale at the church. He had been a cowboy since Christmas, forgetting the helmet and wearing the guns and hat he got. She had put the tin helmet away as soon as she noticed he had quit wearing it. But he didn't want to be a cowboy tonight since that wasn't special and he was that all the time. She started with ghost since that would be easiest, no, that wouldn't do, then fireman, policeman, engineer, until finally Cale told her the answer. Pirate. That came from Papa's stories of Blackbeard off the North Carolina coast, so he was pleased and she went to work fashioning his disguise.

They went into the fish-the-apple-out-of-a-tub room and at the end of the room was a big sign that they were directed to that

read, "Please hold your breath or your nose when fishing for
apples." It was handwritten and Falissa asked and found that
the mayor's son had gotten strangled and his mother had taken
him home furious and threatened to put an end to the bazaar.

Cale and Papa went into the Hall of Horrors and Falissa
waited outside. It was a row of flashing lights and dangling
paper skeletons, one large rubber spider that caught in Cale's
face, all leading to the final horror, a human heart that you had
to touch before the door would let you out. Papa touched it
first and then Cale, sticking his hand into the cold slippery mass
that wiggled like jelly under his touch. He got outside and
said to Papa, "Do you really think that was a heart?"

"What?" Falissa asked.

"A heart. You had to touch a human heart they had before
you could leave."

"Goodness. They have added a few things since I remember."

"Just an old pile of hog innards," Papa answered.

"Ugh!"

"Ugh yourself. You two boys just go find a rest room and
wash your hands."

Papa and Cale walked toward the rest room and Falissa
called out through the crowd, "Wait up. Just a minute."
She caught up to them and said, "I think I'll go to the auditorium and watch the picture show and just let you two meet
me at nine to go home."

"What's the picture show? I want to go to the picture show."

"It's about a foreign country, England or somewhere," Falissa said.

"Oh, I thought it might be good. Me and Papa will just stay
out and look around, won't we, Papa?"

"That we will."

At nine Falissa came out of the dark auditorium and squinted
in the light. The wall clock said five after nine and the boys
weren't back. The movie had seemed slow but the charm of
the accents was still in her ears. Even the farm people talked

fancy. And England looked like around here except they kept
up hedges for fences. And here and there they had these stone
castles. At the end of the hall she could see Papa and Cale, her
eyes still blurred and making spots. There was something silver
on Cale's head. As they got closer, she recognized it . . . the
helmet. Oh for goodness' sake, and she had given it to the
church bazaar so he would never see it again and forget about it.
She could see his lips, pouting, and his pirate's eye was around
his neck. Papa looked at her and shook his head; he knew she
had given it away.

"Cale, where did you get that hat?"

"It's my helmet."

"Where did you get it?"

"The lady made me buy it and I told her it was my helmet
because I could tell by the dents."

"Cale, you should have let some other little boy have that
since you don't play with it anymore. You're too grown-up to
play soldier. How much did it cost?"

"Twenty-five cents."

"Oh for goodness' sake. Roe didn't pay that much for it."

"Uncle Roe didn't buy it. He took it off a dead German."

"Why don't you take it back and see if the lady will give you
back your money. You can buy a lot of things with twenty-
five cents, fifty more comic books which will last you till next
year."

"I got to have it."

They went out the door and Falissa and Papa were silent
as they walked home. When they got to the yard of the house,
Cale ran to the edge of the porch, climbed up, jumped off and
hit the ground. The helmet rolled off and he put it back on and
marched up the steps.

"Now don't you get all sweaty and grass down your shirt. I
don't want to bathe you again tonight. You just march yourself
through the door and go brush your teeth."

"Mama, why did you give my helmet away?"

"Cale, you didn't play with it anymore. You hadn't touched it for weeks. I'm sorry I did it, I really am, but I didn't think it meant a thing in the world to you. You know I wouldn't have given it away if I'd known you wanted it."

"I got to have it, Mama."

"Well, I can see that now."

"I got to have it. I got to have it to fight the Germans when they come."

Chapter 15

PAPA LONZA hasn't come out of his bed under the steps for three whole days now and Mama holds his head with her hand when she goes to feed him. He don't eat nothing but two spoonfuls and starts shaking his head how he don't want no more. She was leading him to the bathroom yesterday and he didn't make it and messed all over himself and she made me go in my room but I already seen it come down his legs under his nightshirt. He has got a stroke Mama calls it and says he is not going back to being right. He makes her leave his shoes by the bed but he don't wear them none. Mama spanked me Saturday 'cause I put an egg in one of them and Papa put it on and she said I should save my cuteness when she wasn't worked to death with an invalid and a baby. Mama don't spank hard enough to hurt but I cry and make like it so she'll quit and give me a spoon to lick or something.

We went right by Saturday and when I asked him about the movies he just looked at me and he said something was going to fall right on the theater and we better not go and Mama heard him and said pay him no mind but that I couldn't go by myself. And we went right on by Sunday and Mama didn't go to Sunday school and me and her stayed home and Daddy went and when he come home he sat out on the porch till it was time to eat. I got to talk to Papa because my turtle ain't et a thing and won't come out of his shell and I got to know if he's

dead. Mama don't care if I talk to him but she is at the kitchen
door listening.

"Papa, I got to talk to you about my turtle."

The old man turned his head and looked at the child. He
opened his mouth but didn't say anything.

"Papa, I have give my turtle a snail, a caterpillar, three red
ants, and he just lets them walk right across his shell and
won't come out to eat them."

"He's dead."

"How you know?"

"If he don't come out, he's dead."

"Papa." Falissa walked in from the kitchen. "He might not
be dead. He don't eat much and maybe he is just like most wild
animals and don't like to eat when he's penned up."

Papa grunted and turned away from her.

"You hear about Blackbeard?" he asked Cale.

"That's fine. You tell him some Blackbeard stories but don't
go getting him scared his turtle is dead."

"Blackbeard and his band of men decided they were going
to pirate them some ships and decided they didn't want to work
hard for it. I tell you this one?"

"Nope." Cale sat on the floor and leaned against the bed.
He didn't like to look in the old man's red eyes and see the
cracked skin around his mouth.

"Blackbeard and his men got down on Hatteras Island right
on the edge of the ocean on the coast of our own state. They
looked out one day and figured them out a place where the
water was mean rough, where there was some places the water
won't deep enough to take a bath in or float a toy and made sure
it looked just fine to take a big boat through at night when you
couldn't look over and see the bottom and watch the blue-
shelled crab walk by. They were going to get the big boat
stuck on this shallow place that was called to them a sandbar
which is like a mountain only is under the water, I'm told.

So one night when it was stormy they all got together and when they sighted a ship they lit them a lantern and they started swinging it, making like they were a fancy harbor to tell this big ship loaded with jewels and gold that this was the place to come home in the storm and that ship just turned right in like a dog to bacon and got itself stuck on that bar and those pirates plucked it like a chicken. How you like that?"

"I like that, Papa."

"Well, you ain't heard the best. I got men today who go fishing to tell me 'bout it down there at Hatteras Island and they say that it is called the Graveyard of the Atlantic and there is pieces of ships scattered as far as you can see like they was seashells. Big ships with fancy working in the boards."

"Papa, are you telling that child the truth? He's believing every word of it, you know."

"Every bit of it. We'll take us a ride down one Sunday and see."

"Well, I don't know what we'll ride in but we'll see."

"Let me get to the best part. And to this day there are men who say they would be in their ships off the dark water just out in a fishing boat and they would see a light swinging and they would check their compasses and find out they were off the coast of Cape Hatteras and there won't supposed to be no one there and certainly no fool would land a ship there and they would get people to check and they couldn't find a soul and it is said that the ghost of old Blackbeard who's buried on Ocracoke Island just comes up out of the sand when there's a storm brewing and walks that beach with a lantern and is just cackling away and wrecking ships to this day."

"Papa, you send him out if you need me. And Cale, you stay here with Papa till I get back. I got to get some picking done or things are going to rot in the field. You're sounding a whole heap better to me."

"Don't you mind me. I'll get along."

"But you call me if you need me, you hear. And don't wait a minute too long. We don't want a mess like last time. Soon as you feel the least little bit of an urge, you call me."

"Yes, ma'am."

Papa grunted and began to squirm.

"Papa, tell me another Blackbeard."

"Don't know no more," he snapped.

The child began to bang his head against the bed.

"Be still, you're jostling me."

Cale got up and ran to the window, then started to the door.

"You stay here, with me. Your mama said for you to. I might be needing you to help me."

"I want to go outdoors and play."

"You do that some other time."

Cale sat in the chair in front of the fireplace. His feet still didn't reach the floor when he leaned back.

"I got shot last night, Papa," he said after a while.

"You what?"

"I got shot. The Germans shot me. You wanna see?"

"I suppose I do."

Cale lifted his shirt and pointed at his navel and began to giggle. Then he was quiet for a while until, "Hey Papa, you ever seen the tattoo of the chicken I got on my stomach?"

"No, I guess I better bite that one too."

Cale lifted his shirt again, "Uh-oh. It's all wore off but his ass hole."

"You are so funny you ought to be on the stage." Papa rolled over and faced the wall.

"Papa, you know why the ocean roars?"

"Nope."

"You'd roar too if you had crabs on your bottom."

"Now you watch where you tell that one."

"Why?"

"You don't know all of what it means, that's why."

"I want to go outdoors."

"Well, I said you stay in here. Looks like you could do that much for me. I ain't got long."

"When are you getting well so I can go outdoors?"

"You wouldn't be such a smarty if you had to lie here and feel like me. Ain't no pleasure thinking you got to let go of all those years. No pleasure a'tall. I worked hard to stay living and I don't like nothing sneaking up on me. I should have knowed it though, soon as that war was over and I hadn't found me no job. Soon as people were getting back on their feet and I seen the railroad station half shut down. If you can't find no job after a war then you outlived your usefulness."

"I don't know what you mean, Papa." Falissa was at the door. "There's not the man in Summit that is as useful as you. What in the world would I have done without you to take Cale out when Pearlie came along. What would Cale have done but just sat around bored as a stump. Do you have to go to the bathroom?"

"No, and I'll tell you when I do. You don't have to ask me like I'm one of your brood. I got a mind about me to know when I have to go."

"It's hot as a firecracker out there. Near 'bout cooked the tomatoes on the vine."

Falissa went in the kitchen and set down her bucket of tomatoes. Cale walked to the door and watched as she poured the steaming water from the kettle into a tub on the floor. Then she slid the tomatoes in the water and they bobbled like the apples on Halloween only they smoked.

"Whatcha doing?"

"I'm getting ready to skin some tomatoes."

"Can I go outdoors?"

"I suppose so but don't go out of the yard."

Cale walked back by Papa's bed and the old man called his name.

"Cale, I won't be holding you but just a minute. Just let me have one more minute of your time to tell you something I been meaning to before I forget it. And get over here close so I can whisper it because it's a secret and we don't want your mama in on it."

"O.K. Tell me."

"You know them smokestacks downtown?"

"Sure."

"Well, ever since 1930 after old Soloman who put them up has been gone from here they been slipping a little, you know what I mean? They been slipping ever so little at a time 'cause he made them shoddy, got a local to lay them who never laid nothing bigger than a fireplace in his life, just like them silk stockings that run if you looked at them and nobody around town would wear to a dogfight, and he left here with no more mind what happened to them than the man in the moon. Left his troubles for somebody else to bear. I'm passing this on to you because when I pass away, people are just as likely to forget about it because if you go around talking about them stacks, they act like they going to take you to the loony bin. They'll tell you your grandpa was crazy as a tick and to put them stacks out of your mind and then Summit won't have a soul left to save it. Don't you pay no attention to those old fools on the courthouse steps, you hear? And I tell you which way they going to fall. They are headed this way, due north. Now they might not be tall enough to make it, I ain't never been much for sighting a measurement but I can tell you by golly they're coming this way because they ain't never swung in no other direction, due north. And I ain't able to tell you when they are going over, might make it slowlike, and pop out a few warning bricks before they go, and they might just come undone and go all at once, but I'm able to tell you they are going and that's for sure and I'm depending on you to figure when and if they are going to hit here. But they are going to make one mess when they go and the Rebel Bar and the store are going to be right there under the thick part and then the movie house and mind you it will take half the citizens of Summit. So it is up to you, boy, to convince them that it is going. And I'm lying here on my back not able to do a thing in this world, telling you I'd just as soon be able to fly to the moon as make them citizens know

what they're in for. They going to sit there chewing and spitting and gossiping about who ain't there wasting time, and
what things was forty years ago and before you know it they'll
be nothing but a greasy spot under a pile of busted bricks and
mortar. But you take care of that, boy. I'm depending on you."

Cale sat down by the bed. "I'm going to take them down."

"Well, I think an older man than you had tried to think of
how and he ain't come up with nothing. But you're a smart
little youngun. You get to work on an idea and don't you ever
forget about them."

"I'll remember, Papa."

I'll walk out to the edge of the yard when Mama ain't
looking and undo my shirt and put my clothes in the woodshed
and fly up over Summit and look down like it is little boxes
and toy cows and people and spy the smokestack. I'll just wrap
my arms around that old stack and pull it from the ground like
it was a weed and take it out and throw it in the desert and do
the other the same way. By that time a crowd has gathered.
And I'll come back and ride in an open automobile with stream-
ers and people will come throw money in my car. Money
enough to buy me a bicycle.

Before the end of June, Papa was dead, in his sleep. Cale
stayed by his bed a great deal before he went, listening to the
endless barrage of stories. Papa's mind seemed straight then,
when he was telling stories, as long as things were behind him;
but he couldn't deal with now, eating, going to the bathroom,
sleeping. In the last week people came from all over, his neph-
ews, his cousins. There were Lemirts everywhere to carry on
his name. Papa Lemirt had been fulfilled.

In the last day, Papa began to whisper. No one was dead,
his father, his mother, all there. He talked to Sarah Ann. He
sent her to the kitchen to bake more bread. There just wasn't
going to be enough with this many people here. She hadn't

planned for this many people. The doctor gave him a shot to ease the pain saying, "This is going to hurt," and Papa answered, "You shouldn't ought to do that to anybody." They all laughed at him so he laughed too. Late in the afternoon the preacher came. The family all gathered in close to hear Papa's last words. The preacher sat down beside the bed, took Papa's hand and bowed his head.

"Lonza, you want to say some words to your Lord now? He is waiting ready to hear from you now. You want to speak to Him?"

Lonza's eyes opened in surprise at the preacher and he pulled his hand away. The family began to move back when he said, "Don't see no need of it."

The preacher got up and went to the door. Falissa shook her head, ashamed when the preacher patted her on the arm. "It's all right, Miss Falissa. Don't you worry about him. The Lord takes care of His children even when they deny Him." That night after the people had gone, Papa asked her who was that young preacher he had never seen before. What in the world was Pastor Sarles trying to do, get a youngun to run his affairs. Falissa hadn't the heart to remind him that Pastor Sarles was dead too, soon after he preached Sarah Ann's funeral.

Falissa kept the room clear after all of them had spoken to him because they made him uneasy. He wasn't used to a lot of company. He finally fell asleep and she didn't know when he died, his face just stopped twitching when she said his name. She called the doctor to come take him and went in the kitchen while the men carried out the body. Then she took the sheets from his bed and went to sleep the four hours until dawn. She would have to tell Cale in the morning. He was old enough and he would have to know now what dead was. And there was no backwards to her life anymore and she would be the next in line to die.

Book Two

Chapter 16

JEROME had told Cale not to leave her, to stay with her until she started birthing the calf then to come get him out in the lower field. He was trying to get the hay up before the rains hit and there was no way he could wait around until the spirit moved her. The calf was going to come early; she should have gone several weeks more but Cale had learned that that was the way things happened around here, his father waited for things and they happened while he was still waiting.

He had found himself a place, propped between two bales out of the reach of the light from the open door, spread over with an old quilt he found in the hay. He watched his father's tractor bounce down the road, it seemed more alive than the colorless form in the seat, shiny red with the old yellow mule wagon hitched up to haul the hay. The dark sky made it glow brighter and the fields were an unreal green like in a picture book.

Cale knew the rains were coming. It had gotten black as night early in the afternoon and the birds were squealing. No false promise this time because the wind just stirred and twisted the clouds and made them look meaner. They blew down from the north, an endless strip with more behind them as they moved across the whole farm. The clouds settled down lower over the trees now, bringing darkness inside the barn and making him feel small like he was in his bed.

He watched the cow eat, her tongue sliding into the corners of the box and he imagined another creature, living inside the stupid square head and allowed to run out every morning and night for food, looking for light between the teeth. An oozy creature that moved like a slug and left a slime trail. It didn't work though, he couldn't laugh even at himself because her eyes looked right at him, they wouldn't let him be by himself. He wanted to go play in the yard and if it started raining, he'd get out his train.

He knew about the birds. He knew that from Papa Lonza who was so proud of knowing all the answers about the animals that he would fib before he would say he didn't know. They had watched the birds before the snow last winter when Cale was in first grade, rushing to get food before the ground was covered. Today they were flying for food before the rain beat them in the bushes. Papa Lonza had said they would do that. The sparrows were diving in the stable, stripping seeds off the straw under the cow's feet with her stepping at them like they were flies. Through the door Cale could see the starlings, pecking at the seeds in the manure.

Heat lightning had started, filling the sky and outlining all the cows huddled together in the pasture. The thunder rumbled like things were falling down slow somewhere, taking a long time to settle into place.

Heat lightning didn't frighten him because it felt like the headlights that had drifted by him and Papa when they walked on the roadside at night to the filling station. Like switching on and off the light in his room, making ghosts of the furniture and trees that would fade away. He knew where the heat lightning was, and he could watch it from his room at night when it let you see everything for a second, clear as day. But he hated the storm lightning, the kind that streaked down hard with no noise until it was over with. Flash, bang. You didn't know where or when it was coming until it was there.

He watched the double pine the cows always stood under,

the one that lightning had already hit twice. It rattled in the wind, the dead half trying to split away, making noises like it was hurting. Cale looked at the cow, hoping the first rain would crack in the dust and scare her back against the wall. He didn't like her anyway; she would stand until you got right up on her then throw her head and run. There was something wrong with her. She had not gotten bred the first time his daddy brought in the bull and had torn down the fence and gotten herself bred by the neighbors' old scrub bull they were saving to slaughter. His daddy got mad and cussed Will James and the bull, said he was going to kill it. They called her calf the goat, the one they switched from cow to cow to keep down the milk fever when they lost their calves. It won't really a goat, it just didn't look good enough to be one of the calves and it had white whiskers on its chin. And this cow kept getting fat and blowing up like people do when they have a baby in them only it's harder to tell on a cow since they're all fat anyway. And she never had any calves, that is until last year when she finally had one that was all right so his daddy decided to keep her. But even then, she dropped it and walked off and left it. Just let it fall out of her in the field and left it like a pile of manure. Here her water had already broken, that was what his daddy said, and she was just eating and slopping her lips around at the grain like it was any day of the year.

Cale didn't hear the birds anymore, except a few noises squeaking way up in the loft where they were getting to shelter. Jerome had cut the hay at the wrong time as usual and it was either let it get wet and rot in the field or get it in the barn before it was dried and have it rot and go to heat there and smell up the whole place. Cale saw dust fly up in the cow pen like someone had thrown a rock there, then another and another and the rain was starting to hit the tin on the roof. The cow's head came up and hit him on the knee when the first drops started to hit. He felt a sharp pain, knowing her thick skull didn't feel anything.

He rubbed his knee where the soreness of a swelling was

starting. The trees in the gray square through the door looked
still and afraid. A white ball, marble size, slid over the edge
of the roof and bounced down into the drain, then another
until the tin started rippling over his head. It was going to be
hail; he had only seen hail two times before in his whole life.
It had come at a bad time before and they had stood on the
porch, watching it rip the tobacco off the stalks, then melt away
in the sun like it had never been there. The worms and heat
spotted the tobacco until it yellowed in the field, the leaves so
thin they flapped in the wind. Cale had seen the white stones
land on the tin, dancing around like they were alive, like jumping beans, and he wondered if he cracked one if there wasn't
a worm inside it too.

The cow was not eating anymore; she held her chin up and
the skin down her side moved in ripples. The white in her
eyes was clear as a light in the stall. She had quit chewing and
the grain slid through her lips, hanging in slime strings in her
whiskers.

Cale took her by the ear and tried to pull her up further into
the stall because her rear was almost out in the rain. "Come on.
Move up before you get rained on." She threw her head up
when he touched her and hurt him again, his arm this time until
tears came in his eyes and he knew this animal was too big and
strong for him to stop her from doing anything she wanted to.
He wanted his daddy to come back, to take her by the ear and
hack her in the haunches until she was up in the stall, to yell
with a man's voice and make her do as he pleased. There was
no gate so he couldn't shut her in, just watch her jump in and
out of the door as the rain started to hit her, her thick sides
beginning to swing away from her spine.

It was real lightning now and the thunder was close. The
whole barn was beginning to shake as the water and hail was
thrown against its sides. He heard the glass break in one of
the packroom windows and the wind blow in and scatter it on
the floor. Better not go barefoot in there. The cow started to

walk in circles, like a circus animal in the ring, spinning by in front of him and making crying sounds. When she turned in front of him, he saw blood under her tail and her circle game stopped when she rubbed the blood off down the side of the stall and started to whine. It was time to call his daddy.

Cale went to the front of the barn and pulled open the door. The rain blew in and wet him all the way down the front. The fields in front of him were a green blur because the water fell in a solid sheet over the edge of the barn. He called his father's name and heard it echo behind him, up through the barn where the birds started chirping and he knew that was as far as the sound had gone. He looked where the road was, trying to see if there was a red blur of his father's tractor coming, but there was nothing. Every time he screamed "Pa" the cow would roar from the stall and he could hear the wood sides of the stall straining under her weight. He looked down the road again and heard the animals behind him making more noise than he could. He ran through the barn back to the stall and saw the cow with her hind quarters out in the rain. Her sides were quivering and the skin moved in waves, a stick rolling under her skin.

She had dropped her calf. It was there, already dropped and lying in the drain ditch outside of the barn. The water rushed over it, tearing away its white cellophane skin and tufting up its fur. Cale dropped into the straw in the stall and felt a sharp pain in his leg and then another. She was kicking at him and wobbling on her thin legs.

"Stop it! You better quit that!" She ran against the front wall and he watched her bunch up her muscles. She was the dumbest thing he had ever talked to and he knew what could happen now; he knew if there was one thing his daddy told him never to do, it was never to stand in the door of a stall. In an instant the cow could come through it and trample you in the ground; they waited for the day they could catch you in a hole and stomp you, Jerome told him that. They acted like they didn't mind you but don't let them get you cornered. And it would not only be him but the little calf in the drain ditch.

He crawled to it and lifted its head up above the water. The membrane was all broken away and rolled into threads but the calf didn't move to push it away, not even from its eyes that were sealed shut. As Cale tried to pull it to its feet, it fell against his legs. The water was falling so hard from the gutter, it was choking him and stinging the top of his head, inside behind his eyes. When he tried to pull the body away from the water, it felt as though it was coming apart in his hands. Its legs pointed toward the stall so he couldn't get it out of the rain unless he could roll it over. Each time he lifted it, the mud sucked it back so he cupped his body over it, feeling the water cut on his back like a whipping. He had to think. He had to think of what was right to do. There was no breath coming from the cold nostril and its lashes didn't move but there was some warmth deep beneath the fur. What were all the things you were to know to do? He could hear the mother dragging her feet through the straw, pawing like a bull and banging against the walls, crying out. He didn't care if she hurt, if she just fell dead in the stall so he could rest from the fear that she would come through the door.

He felt her hot breath and looked up into her face, snorting, and watching him.

"Why do you do that? Why do you? Just leave me alone, leave me alone, you old ugly. You are uglier than anything in the world. Why don't you sit down and be still and leave me alone."

He pulled on the body again and heard the mud suck away from it. He had moved it a little. He stuck his hands in the wet fur, clasping them around the narrow body and tugging until it gave under him. He had moved it a little more, not much but it had sucked loose and the head had flopped forward inside the door. He was far enough inside for the weight of the rain to be off his back.

Suddenly Cale jumped backwards. The mother cow had knocked against him with her head, butted him. She shoved him back again then dropped her nose, touching her calf for the first time. He heard a moan inside her stupid body and he pressed tight against the wall as she walked out the door, across the calf's body, pressing one of its legs into the mud under her feet. He was crying now, out loud, he could hear himself, but he was too afraid to move to try to help the calf. She started to roll it inside, easily tossing its legs up and over until it was inside and twisted in the straw. Then she started to lick it and Cale stood there so still she would forget him. He wouldn't move a muscle until she had forgotten him. He saw it start to squirm. Its tail flipped once and it stretched but could not lift its head. But it had squirmed, he saw that; it was living.

"What have you done, boy? What have you done?"

Cale looked up behind the feed trough and he saw Jerome, his clothes black with water and his black hair stringing across his cheeks. His fists were drawn and his eyes followed the boy as he edged to the door. "I told you to call me. Didn't I tell you to call me? Are you going to stand there blubbering, huh, like a crybaby girl?"

That was when he had run from him the first time and gone to her. He heard his daddy yell "Wait," but he wouldn't stop running, if he got soaked clear through, not for anything in the world. He ran into the kitchen and wrapped around his mama's legs. He wasn't mad at himself for going to his mother because he knew how it would be. She would make it easy; she would dry him off and change his clothes. Then she would fuss at his daddy when he came in and make him slam doors because she said Cale was still a little boy.

Chapter 17

CALE JENKINS had begun to get people straight in his mind, to put people around him in their places. He knew what Papa Lonza had been. He could tell when he got sick and all those people came he had never seen, that Papa Lonza was more important than he acted like. And now Mama wouldn't let him go downtown by himself. And it wasn't near as easy to get a question answered as before. Nobody knew as much as Papa Lonza. He knew to stay out of Daddy's way. Don't ask him nothing he don't know the answer to which is just about everything, because it will sure as stuff make him mad. He knew what to tell Mama and what not to tell her because in that way he could please her and there was something nice about pleasing Mama. The way she smiled maybe but mostly the way she went about things after she was happy. She sang some, always the wrong words with the wrong tune and she laughed at herself and said she couldn't carry a tune. She put a special shine on things when she was in a good mood, rubbed all the specks off the glasses, always let him lick the spoons. He didn't know if it was because he liked to see Mama happy or if he hated to see her sad, to see her look away from Daddy and not talk much, to get quiet when she was snapped at, just tell him what she had to. Now, it was just that Mama was always too busy and she didn't have any fun.

He was gone most of the time now with school and it was best

because Mama made him stay around the house too much now
and come home from playing when it got the least little bit
dark. Even on weekends she wouldn't let him go downtown by
himself so he had to play with Floyd a lot when Aunt Bynum
wasn't making him help her. Mama had got so she didn't always
watch him walk to the bus stop but some days when he looked
back as the bus was leaving, he could see her shadow behind
the lace curtains. For a while she just tended that basket that
had Pearlie in it and let him do pretty much as he pleased. He
didn't see much of Pearlie then, just heard her noises and saw
the bundle his Mama lifted up but he did watch her sometimes
getting a diaper and see the dirty one get pulled away and see
her little behind that was split all the way around. She was all
bent and twisted like she had a string drawn up on her and
she made a lot of noise. She made noise almost all of the time
and reached at him and he liked to get away from it and just
stay close enough so he was hollering distance, then could
answer his mama so she would leave him alone where he was
and not think he was too far away. Now Pearlie was around and
talking and following him. Everything he'd say, she'd say it
too. And she wouldn't stay away from his things and Mama
made him let her hold them when she took them up.

Pearlie don't mess with my monkey though because I hide him
and if she did, I'd break her head. My monkey has got kinky
hair on him like Floyd. He has, and he wears a red corduroy
suit with suspenders and he says Zip across the front. I can feel
his stuffing coming out through where Mama sewed him up in
the spot I chewed on him when I was little. I still like him
sometimes when I'm not sleepy and I don't want no baby spitting
up on him. I swallowed one of his eyes and Mama had to reach
down my throat after it. I don't remember. But she said she
did and that the prongs were up or it would have been the end
of me and none of my animals don't have no eyes anymore.
Mama took them all out. I sucked in a sourball once and hung

it in my windpipe, I think. I got a tick in my ear and had to
go to the doctor. Mama said I'm accident prone. Floyd had
an accident in his pants the other day. That ain't like Floyd since
he is eight like me but he got the runs from eating strawberries
and that will do it and he went to run to the woods and didn't
make it and squirted in his pants so he went running to the
pond and we like to have laughed ourselves sick. Me and Floyd
found a snap bug today. He gets to keep it today but I get it
tomorrow. You seen one. You can put it on its back and it will
kick till it sees it ain't going over and then it'll snap clean up
in the air and come down on its feet everytime. It'll try everything else first before it uses its snapper. We like to have wore
it out making it snap till it would play dead to make us leave it
alone. I got my radio down so low . . . if they just wouldn't
play that music, it makes more noise than the talking and I
have to keep my finger on the sound button at the start but
you bet if my daddy come through that door I'd have it off 'fore
he'd see me. Next is Yours Truly, Johnny Dollar. Mama lets
me listen to Gene Autry and puts me to bed and she don't know
I keep listening.

> I'm back in the saddle again
> Out where a friend is a friend,
> Where the longhorn cattle feed,
> On the lowly jimson weed;
> I'm back in the saddle again.

That's Gene Autry's song. I know it by heart and can play it
on my harmonica.

I can hear my crickets singing. They all do it at once like it's
one long note and you can't even hear them breathing in between. I'm going to make a hundred dollars with them. I get a
penny apiece for them. And if I can get them to hatch then I
won't have to catch and can just set back and raise. I let Floyd
have a quarter for every hundred I told him. We got bed quilts

with biscuits under them set out and before morning there'll be a thousand I bet.

You should have seen it today when the Pepsi-Cola man came over the school and wrote in the sky. That was really something. He went out of smoke when he had Pepsi C and had to go get some more and when he come back his writing had blowed out so you could hardly read it but he done it out anyway, O L A.

Floyd said he seen a man electrocute his compost pile to make the worms come out. He did. That he took a battery and stuck on these wire things and put them in the ground and shocked them old worms one good time and they come crawling up top and all he had to do was pick them up. I bet I could get more than a penny for them since people thinks they is so much trouble. I could if I could get me them electric things. Floyd said his daddy won't home or he'd make them. Uncle Roe promised to come see me by next Christmas. He'll get them for me. Only don't nobody fish in the winter.

Floyd says he has to ride twenty-five miles to school and I told him he lied like a dog. He did and he said he won't going the day they told him he didn't have to because he didn't like his teacher and he has had the same one every year since he come there, which has been going on three and he don't get to change till the year after next. I got a pretty teacher this year who just come out of school and ain't got married yet. She's got the smoothest legs you ever seen and wears shiny silk stockings. Tommy Grinnin said he might just marry her if she was still around when he got ready. But she's real pretty. She'll get married. She don't have hair on her legs like Mama. One I had last year used to show her pants. We'd go out on the playground and she'd sit on the wall and show her pants and Tommy Grinnin went up one day and said "You just took my picture" to her and we liked to have died laughing and she made him stay in and didn't even know what he meant because she was out there taking pictures the next day just as big. He'd get us all to line up in front of her and pose and he'd say, "Now click that old Brownie." She got so she didn't even bother to make him stay in. Tommy was out to get in bad with her because one day he was playing softball and she was turning rope over at the tree for the girls and he hit her square up beside the head with a softball and she went the rest of the year pretending she was having these fainting spells and have to go sit down in the lounge. Tommy said she was just going for a smoke. That Tommy could be a big ball player if he wanted. He can hit the ball over the fence just any time he feels like it and he don't even have to wait for a good ball. He's bigger than most of us because he's been in the third grade two years already. They don't give him the best athlete medal because he's failed. He ain't going to be there long anyway because if they find out what he done, they'll put him up in the training school. Two of his brothers is there. They closed up school one morning last week to have the wall outside scrubbed off. It was white and Tommy went out on the outside of the window and walked along the edge when we had that art teacher who don't come but once a week and don't watch you much and none of us knowed it but he took his red paint and painted "Fuck you" down the side of the wall in red letters big as him and the principal wouldn't let us go home when the bell rung until he got the janitor to go out and tape up newspapers over it but Tommy had done told us what it said. You can learn some things from that Tommy, I'm telling you. But Mama don't want me around him because he's got bugs, you can see them crawling in his hair. They look like maggots and are enough to make me sick. I asked him how he could stand them and he said he didn't feel them none and if he was to say anything his mama would wash his head with kerosene which he did feel and he'd rather have the bugs. I don't know how his mama don't notice them. My mama would skin my head if I got them.

I asked Mama what was wrong with her stomach before she had Pearlie back before I was in the first grade and she wouldn't tell me. I didn't know what in the world made her swell out like that until I seen another lady who was worse and it won't a week before I seen another one so I just asked Tommy and sure as anything he knowed. I asked him if it won't a baby in her since Pearlie come about that time and he said yeah. I asked him what put it in there and was there other ways to get babies. He said no and that my papa had screwed his peter in her so she could have a baby. I asked him when and he said after I went to bed. Well that don't make no sense. But you don't think I told my mama I knowed that, no sirree. She would cry her heart out if she knowed. She's like that. I told her I saw the cat eat up the mess after the kittens was born and she went in her room and cried like I said something bad. I'm not going to tell her nothing. Tommy wanted to come over here and show me how to smoke and I thought at first I might ask him and we'd go down in my hole out back but I got to thinking about all that smoke in there and I don't know if I want to get all that close to Tommy. Nobody ever been in my hole anyway, not even Floyd and he don't even know where it is because I built a top and covered it with pine straw and I took all the dirt away with a bucket when I made it. I might go over to Tommy's and have a smoke with him. I been wanting to see his house but he has got some awful-looking brothers and sisters. They all smell like peepee. He's got five of them in the school I go to. Tommy said his big sister used to go out and get naked with men in the old cars they got out in the backyard and he and his little brother would try to sneak up but they were afraid the men would kill them. And if his daddy were to catch her he would cut her heart out and hang it in a tree. Tommy come home with me one time and wouldn't go home when suppertime come and he eat nine biscuits and he grabbed at things like somebody was going to take it away from him, Mama said. I was kinda glad he didn't talk much because he talks ugly but he just ate the whole time, and I seen him put the left-over biscuits in his shirt when we was clearing the table. I seen Mama get up and look down in his hair and frown at me and she washed behind my ears till they hurt that night. She said I should pity him but not associate with him.

Tommy's always making me feel up under the edges of his desk at school 'cause he's got it crusted up with boogers. I put my chewing gum under mine one day and got him tickled but then I got it stuck on my pants leg and Mama made me scrub on it with gas till it was gone. Got in the corduroy grooves. Tommy plays in his spit on the desk. He spits out a wad and draws pictures in it and if the teacher's coming he wipes it up on his shirt-sleeve. They're poor and all, but Mama says "Soap's cheap." Mama'll scrub you raw if you let her. I don't want to be like him in most ways but I sure do wish I could hit a ball like him.

I asked Daddy one time if he ever wanted to be the best person in the whole world at something. I was thinking about Tommy who is the best ball player for his age I ever seen.

"Where the hell is that sort of thing going to get you?"

"I just would like to see my picture in the paper like that man Papa Lonza knowed who was the world's champion flagpole sitter. When he went up he was just like me and when he come down he was the champion."

"What the hell good did that do? Make like a fool sitting up on a pole. You got some kind of funny ambition if you ask me."

"Jerome, I do wish you would watch your language. It does seem like you get worse on his account. I hear you twice as much if he is in the vicinity . . ."

"You having a talking contest, Falissa?"

Cale had turned his porch chair around and had his legs through the back. "I bet Papa Lonza was the world's champion flower namer. He knew every single flower on the whole farm."

"That he did, Cale. And he knew two for some of them."

"And most of them were wrong," Jerome said.

"Jerome, do you have to run down everything? Papa did

know the flowers and the trees and the birds. He had a way about him outdoors with all his trifling."

"He ran his mouth like the world was going to come to an end before he could say all he knew. I got no fuss to pick with you, Falissa. Let's just drop it."

"I didn't pick a fuss with you, Jerome. You were the one who started the snapping when the child asked a sensible question."

"Drop it," he said. "I can't stand that whining." Jerome moved in his chair and made a grumbling noise, either in his throat or his stomach did it by accident.

"Tommy Grinnin can hit a baseball further than anybody in the whole school and he isn't in but the third grade."

"Who's Tommy Grinnin?"

"He's the boy who came for dinner, Jerome."

"Oh, the filthy one. He's just white trash. Why is it my boy can't find anything for friends but white trash and niggers? Is that what we have to send him to school for?"

"You just have to make a point to something, don't you?"

"What?"

"You know you are talking too much and you are just doing it to fret me. Don't you think the boy gets tired of hearing fussing all the time? It's going to have an effect on him, you wait and see. And it seems we don't get along a bit bad except where he's concerned and children notice that. He asked you if you wanted to be the best at something, which is something a father ought to be proud to tell his son."

Jerome was silent. He wasn't listening. He could cut her off when he wanted to and she never knew it until he was silent.

"I wanted to be the best at something, Cale. I wanted no woman in this whole town to say she could keep a house better than me. Your daddy is just tired but he knows what you mean. It is the same when I want to make the best peach jam and the best potato salad, and pumpkin pie and watermelon rind pickles. He wants to grow the best garden."

"I don't give a damn if it's the best garden. I just want to get by and not have anyone bitching at me that I didn't furnish them with enough food."

Falissa turned her chair around so her back was to Jerome. Cale was trying to pull his legs through the chair slats.

"Are you caught?" Falissa asked.

"Nope," and he sat still.

"What do you want to be best at, Cale?" she asked quietly.

"I hadn't made up my mind yet. They call me Wildcat at school 'cause I'm the best fighter. I mean *scuffler*, Mama, it ain't the same as fighting."

Falissa rocked in her chair a moment. "You want to be a farmer?"

"Not much."

"Well, why not?"

"Not unless I could have me a quarter horse and a thousand head of cattle and a forty-hundred-mile ranch and a bunkhouse full of cowboys."

"Well now. That's out west. There isn't that much land here and it's too rich just to use for grazing."

"I'd just as soon be one of the cowboys and go to different places and not have to be on one ranch all the time."

Jerome got up and stood in front of his chair. "So you've been to enough movies now you know all the answers. They've told you it was some good to go around all over the place and not have no land of your own. What you think those movie men do between movies? They got no place to go home to, that's what."

"Oh Jerome. Now don't go making him think those movie people are really cowboys."

"Lash LaRue is. When he come to do tricks with his whip he said he learned them on his ranch in California."

"Probably a ranch with a concrete swimming pool and a Cadillac instead of a horse."

"That's not true. That's not true, is it, Mama?"

"Now don't put me in the middle. Honey, I don't know a thing about Lash LaRue."

"You better start thinking real hard about being a farmer, you hear. You've got sixty-five acres to start thinking about and when I get old and your mama gets old, you are going to look after this place."

"Jerome, what you want him to do — pack up and live with the hobos? Cale is eight years old."

"Eight-and-a-half, Mama."

"And he doesn't have to be a farmer if he doesn't want to. He doesn't even have to live in Summit if he wants to go somewhere else."

I know one thing. I don't want to be no farmer like my daddy. He thinks he's going to make me. He don't know nothing. He don't never go to the movies. He don't read nothing, just his bird book and he reads with his finger. He has never read my comic books like Papa Lonza used to. He don't know a thing unless it happened right here in Summit and he don't believe nothing new that people tell him. I can't wait till my Uncle Roe comes to see us. My daddy said that Uncle Roe was really something. He has been to every country in the world. He has been in the war and got him a Purple Heart two times and just went right on back to fight some more. He went out in the battlefield with people shooting at him just so he could get me a helmet and he sent it to me. He is going to bring me a sword he got off a dead Jap when he comes. I been telling Tommy about my Uncle Roe and even Tommy don't know nobody like him. Mama don't like him though, Mama don't like Roe one little bit and I don't know why. Me and Mama agree on most things and what I know she won't, well, I don't tell her. We just don't agree on Uncle Roe, though I never seen him in person. Maybe Mama don't remember him good and got him mixed up with somebody else. I'm gonna get him to tell me that verse that he said and got kicked out of school in the third grade. Old Tommy said that must have been a dilly because he hadn't said one yet they'd throw him out for good for and he's said some fine ones. Give us beans again for lunch three times last week, and Tommy said just as loud so Miss Spenser could hear.

> Beans, beans, the musical fruit
> The more you eat, the more you poot.
>
> Beans, beans, are good for your heart
> The more you eat, the more you fart.

That ain't what she made him stay in for. It was funnier than that what she got him on. We was having the art teacher again and when she went out of the room, Tommy took off his shirt and pulled his pants down under his belly button and when Miss Spenser walked in, he jumped behind the art table and he sure as stuff looked like he was naked as a jaybird and he hollered out, "Look at me, Miss Spenser," when he jumped out and she hid her face and squealed and when she saw he still had his britches on, she got mad as fire and made him stay in, every afternoon she said, until he could learn to act like a gentleman. And that's just what he wanted her to do. She's going to find out what kind of gentleman he is. She should have known not to get by herself with Tommy. He is going to pull up her dress, he told me, easylike with a yardstick so she won't know it and is to report to us tomorrow if she wears ruffly drawers or colored ones or the kind like his sister has with the days of the week written on them. Or Tommy said they might just be holey ones since teachers don't make much money. Tommy has holey drawers. We went in down at the creek and his hadn't ever been mended but he don't care a bit. Mama would have a fit if she saw Tommy's drawers. Mama can't stand nothing ragged.

She oughta see Floyd. He don't wear none at all. Shoot, Floyd don't care neither. That Floyd sure can throw. He can hit a bird on the telephone wire. I seen him do it. Got that old starling before she batted her eyes. He and Tommy ought to get together but Tommy can't stand niggers. Floyd is fun to play with sometimes. He'll do anything. I can get him to go along with anything I think of. Floyd ain't got much to play with though. We mostly have to use my stuff.

Last summer when everybody else had gone to Vacation Bible School, I had a ringworm and Mama wouldn't let me go because she said I'd show it to everybody there and they'd think I went dirty. Graham crackers, that's all they feed you with some kind of sour juice or hot milk. But they'd been drawing this big scene around the wall and I was getting to paste up cardboard to make the camel and I was trying to decide on one hump or two humps, one like on the cigarette pack maybe. Anyway, I was afraid somebody else would work on my camel and that was still worrying me when I got to Floyd's house to show him my ringworm and to get up somebody for baseball but nobody was there but Floyd. Floyd was pissing when I came up, by the tree that shaded the house, but I couldn't see his gun because Floyd turned just as I came up and drew a wet line on the tree. Floyd tucked it inside and came running up and stopped still like a dog getting to the end of his chain. Then he fell down and rolled over and jumped up laughing.

"Whatcha doing?"

Floyd grinned, "I'uz pissing."

"You ain't been pissing all morning or you'd dried up and blowed away."

Floyd grinned again but didn't say what he had been doing.

"Where's everybody?"

"Momma took Judy and Junior. Rest's picking."

"Oh. Why you here then?"

"Momma forget me. Shooed me off down to the barns and Momma done gone when I get up."

"Whatcha been doing?"

Floyd didn't answer but started picking up things and throwing them at the privy.

"Throwing?"

"Yep."

A rock rattled across the tin roof and a guinea hen came running out with a bunch of keets. Floyd took off toward the porch and then I saw why he was so scared. She was mad as the devil. A guinea'll fight you. She's a watchdog. I ran to the porch and jumped up and she stopped at the bottom of the steps then strolled on under the house.

"Woo'ee!"

"What you keep such a bitch for?"

"Ain't mine."

There were a bunch of dead flowers in some cans, too dead to know what they were. No paint on nothing but they hadn't painted it. It was just yellow when it was new and now it had turned black. That was when I got this funny feeling that I wanted bad to see inside Floyd's house. I hadn't ever seen inside a nigger house.

"You got a room by yourself?"

Floyd laughed and didn't answer.

"Well, do you?"

"Shit, man, I got two rooms." Floyd sounded funny, like one of his big brothers that worked the tobacco barns but he turned away quick and went running down his steps and was Floyd again.

"Woo'ee guinea bitch. I cut yuh craw out. I take me a knife and cut yuh gizzard loose." Floyd was jabbering to the guinea but she didn't come out. If she had, you bet Floyd would have been right back up on the porch. That was when I walked to the door and peeped in. You know all I saw, I saw some beds, four of them, but they didn't have no legs and were all over the floor. Through the door I saw the other room and it had a table and a wood stove like the one Daddy throwed in the pack-house. I hadn't thought that would have been the way it was. I had forgot they had to have a kitchen.

Floyd went running off down the path to my house and kept coming back a few steps, trying to get me to go with him, trying to get me away from his house I betcha.

"Let's go to yuh place."

"How come?"

"Get yuh bat 'n' ball."

"Aw, we can't have no fun with just us."

"Roll the bat."

"Naw, I don't wanna."

There was nothing in the house. I stood at the door and couldn't see nothing but the beds and a stack of clothes in the corner, and there was a big old radio.

"Let's play your radio."

"Won't play."

"How come?"

"Dun' know."

"Are there any plugs in there?"

"Huh?"

"Plugs, electric plugs."

"Dun' know."

A wagon came up to the front of the house and we went running off around it and the guinea hen chased us halfway across the yard then Floyd was called and went off with his momma and left me by myself. I went home then, 'cause I wouldn't go in nobody's house when they won't there. I went home and played with my electric train until Pearlie got home from Bible school. I put a new thing on my transformer, an electric cross-roads signal bar that I could work with one hand and make two color of lights work and my trains with the other and get it up so they could go faster and faster and I crashed one into it and it turned over like a real wreck. Floyd didn't know what a plug was.

Chapter 18

CALE had enough money now to get a secondhand bicycle. He knew where he could get one for $5.00 and he already had $6.73 from selling worms and crickets and weeding gardens. It was rusty and needed a new seat but he figured he could get the chain to go again by oiling it. But he decided not to spend his own money yet, to wait and see if he might not get one for Christmas. He remembered all the times he and Papa Lonza went over his list to Santa Claus and Papa always seemed to know what he was going to get and what he won't. Then he found out from Tommy Grinnin that was just kid stuff, believing in things like that, the good fairy when you pull a tooth, the Easter bunny, and Santa Claus. He never did believe in that Easter bunny stuff in the first place because he and Mama always dyed his own eggs, they poked holes in the ends and blew out the inside so they wouldn't have to waste them. Some of them little kids at Sunday school said the Bunny brought them and they had the same decals as his did that he and Mama got at Kress'. He never was much for animals that talked. And he was pretty sure about the dime under the pillow coming from Mama because she tried to get him to pull his own teeth to save money. But the Santa Claus stuff was hard to believe, that it really wasn't true anymore because he got two sets of presents, one from Mama and Daddy and one from Santa Claus. And he was sure he saw him one night, walking in the chicken lot with this red shine around him like the stoplight downtown when it was raining, but his daddy said it was the devil. And he was almost sure last Christmas he saw a sled go by his window before he went to sleep and he heard something in the living room.

He told Tommy who said, "Shit man, who you think is going to fly around in a sled and get to every house in the country in one night, huh? You could fly all night and not get to all of them in Summit. What about New York City?"

Tommy had been to New York City. He got sent there one summer to stay with his aunt while his daddy was in prison and his mama had to work. He lived in a building with hundreds of people in it, forty levels high he said.

Cale had asked Papa Lonza who had said that the elves helped him so it certainly was possible. That he covered all over the ocean and brought the Dutch children new wooden shoes, and the Eskimos snowshoes and him a new pair of saddle oxfords.

When he told Tommy, "Oh sure, man. Elves and fairies, shit. And when was the last time you went down a chimney, huh? Little tight in there for a guy with a stomach like that. That old red sonovabitch try to come down my chimney, he'd get himself right in the middle of the circulator and cook alive."

Mama told him that "Santa Claus is the spirit of Christmas. He is the spirit of giving for all the little children in the world."

"Can you see a spirit?"

"Well, you can if the spirit wants to be seen but not unless he does."

"Is that why Santa Claus comes at night?"

"Yes, of course. So he can go about his work undisturbed while all the little children of the world are asleep."

"Who's that guy in the Christmas parade? I saw him."

"That is one of Santa's helpers."

"He said he was Santa Claus."

"Santa Claus is everywhere. Everywhere little boys and girls are good and giving and kind and love the little Jesus baby who God gave to the world so we could have Christmas and celebrate a joyous time."

"Tommy Grinnin says there is no such thing as Santa Claus, that it is just somebody inside your own house that does it."

"Well, Tommy Grinnin just doesn't have the spirit of Christmas. And don't you go and spoil Pearlie's Christmas, you hear? She is looking forward to it so."

So Santa Claus, the flesh and blood man, was no more. The North Pole didn't exist, the sled, the reindeer, the elves, the toy shops.

On the day before Christmas Eve he was in the living room with his daddy. He had been painting faces on cookies all afternoon for his mother and was a little sick on the stomach from eating raw dough and licking spoons. He had newspapers down and was painting some pine cones and gum balls gold for her. Pearlie had a briar bush and was sticking gumdrops on the thorns and eating all the black ones. There was a knock at the back door and his mother answered it from the kitchen. She walked into the living room and whispered to Jerome.

"Jerome, it's Jason again. What do you want me to tell him? I can't tell if he's been drinking or not."

"You can tell him to go to hell for all I care. I'm not giving him any more money."

"Jerome, I wish you would talk to him. I think it's your place to do it."

"Look, do me one favor. Just tell him I said if my own kid has to do without, no little black bastard is going to get one. What's the matter with him? Has he lickered out his sense?"

"I have told him two times now that you are not going to loan him the money and that you don't have it to loan if you could. I just think it ought to come from you directly or he'll be right back up here again. That woman is nagging him and sending him back and he is going to keep coming until you put it hard and straight. You know how she is when she gets her mind made up."

Jerome slammed his paper down and got up from the chair. He walked into the kitchen and Cale could hear him talking. His mother listened from the door but he couldn't hear what he was saying because his father wasn't talking loud like he expected. Soon he came back and sat back down.

"He won't be back, Falissa. You have got to learn to be firmer with the niggers."

"He just always looks so pitiful. I just know he don't eat right. Not an ounce of meat on his bones."

"They don't go hungry, Falissa. Aunt Bynum is a good provider and he knows damn good and well he wouldn't have his ass here if she didn't put out so much work. Take ten of him to make one of her."

"She just got her mind set on that present, Jerome. You just wait and see. They'll be back just as sure as anything."

Cale thought about what they had said during supper and by that night he was pretty sure of two things. He was almost certain he wasn't going to get a new bicycle. The reason he knew was that was what Floyd wanted. They had both decided that was what they wanted, and Jason was coming up trying to get the money to go buy him one.

The other thing came just after they had finished supper and were clearing off the table. They heard a horn blowing real loud as someone drove by. Falissa pulled open the front curtain but no one was there. In a few minutes they heard it again. She went back and opened the curtain and got a glimpse of a truck going by. They all waited by the windows. Jerome looked over Falissa's head and Cale and Pearlie stood beside each other at the long window behind the Christmas tree. The truck came back and this time it stopped at the foot of the driveway. There were two Negroes in it, one they didn't know driving and in the other side, Jason. Then they saw it, in the back of the truck, a shiny new red bicycle. The men blew on the horn again and the truck backed up in front of the house, the bicycle in full view, then they pulled off and didn't come back. Floyd was going to get a red bicycle.

"That black bastard is going to go find hisself another place to live."

"Oh Jerome, wasn't that the most childish thing you've ever

seen? I don't believe for a minute that Aunt Bynum would have approved of such as that."

"So he's found out that Sears, Roebuck ain't got no more sense than to give a nigger something on time. That kid won't be on that thing two weeks before they come after it."

Cale was right. He didn't get the bicycle for Christmas. He got mostly clothes and a dump truck and a little town to go with his train set. It had "made in Japan" on the town set and Pearlie got doll clothes and he knew good and well his mama had made them though they came in her Santa Claus stack. He was sure now that Tommy was right and Mama and Papa fibbed to him all along. He went down and bought the used bicycle but it wouldn't roll home. He had to go back for a can of oil to get the chain to turn and stop by the filling station for air. One of the tires wouldn't hold air so he had to push it all the way home with the chain grinding away. He made him a working place under the shed and took the whole bike apart, piece by piece and started to work sanding. He had seen Floyd on his bike but not out of his front yard because he couldn't balance it yet and it had trainer wheels on the back so it wouldn't fall over. Floyd took them off once and turned it over first thing and skint the paint off one fender. But Floyd hadn't offered to let him try it and he wasn't going to ask. He had ridden over at his cousin's and got pretty good at it and could teach Floyd a thing or two.

Early one morning, a week after Christmas and the day before school started back, he saw Floyd go by the house on the bike. He was standing up on the pedals so he could reach them and the trainer wheels were gone. In a few minutes he came back the other way and turned up the drive. He rode through their yard and down the path to his house. Cale heard him drop the bike with a crash and he guessed that was the only way he had learned to stop it since he couldn't reach the ground. When the bike hit, a lot of kids started laughing and Cale could hear them fussing over who was to get to ride it next. Floyd had the only bicycle on this end of the highway that he'd seen. He walked down the path and turned up in the trees, where he could see Floyd's house and they couldn't see him. The red bike was on its side on the ground and he saw five niggers, Floyd and four others, all sizes. One of them picked the bike up and tried to jump on the seat. It fell back down and on top of him. They all laughed as he wiggled out from under it.

" 'Ey man, wen yuh gon' jine the circus?"

"Yuh is going to the Big Top."

"Yuh see that sign man, down't the siding?"

"Junior gon' ride in the circus."

"Dey comin' in."

"Wen they comin'?"

"Shut up, nigger. Yuh ain't goin'."

"Dey put yuh in de cage."

"Dey put yuh in wit de monkeys, nigger."

"Dey feed yuh to de snakes."

"Dey let the lions pick yuh bones."

"Dey let an elephant shit on yuh."

They all started to laugh and the boy picked up the bike and came crashing down again.

"Woo'ee! I wish I was good enough for de circus."

"How come we ain't all fancy riders like Junior?"

"Hey Floyd, let's git yuh bike and go up to de tracks in de mornin'."

"Why man?"

"Why man, 'cause the circus coming in."

"Man, we got to go to school tomorrow."

"Who sez?"

"Dey sez."

"Who dey?"

"Shit, I ain't going to no school. I could learn that old woman something."

"She gon' learn yuh something yuh don't know."

"She don't know what her pussy's for."

They all started laughing again. Floyd was trying to stand his bike back up on the kickstand.

"Yuh going man or ain't yuh?"

"Yeah, I'm going."

"We gon' set them animals loose."

"Naw."

"Gon' have lions and tigers loose in Summit."

"Naw."

"Yuh gon' open your shit house and find yuh a bow constrictor curled up on de seat."

"What's a bow constrictor?"

"A snake, man. Yuh stupid. Dat's the biggest snake in the world and dey got to feed it live pigs to keep it satisfied."

"Naw."

"Yeah man, and it eat 'em in one bite and yuh see this ol' lump go sliding down 'em. Dey twenty feet long."

"And what happens to it?"

"Yuh stupid. It's shit man. Dey is making it into shit."

They all laughed again.

"Yuh lying."

"What yuh ever eat yuh didn't make into shit?"

"I seen a snake with a lump."

"What kind?"

"A big old chicken snake and we kilt him and cut him open and he eat dis white doorknob."

"What'd he do dat for?"

"He thought it was an egg, yuh stupid."

"Yuh lie like a lizard."

"Naw, man it's de truth. But he was going to die anyways. Man, dat was going to bust his ass wide open."

"Woo, I don' wanna shit no doorknob."

Floyd rolled the bike up by the house.

"Let's play Hell, Over."

"Shoot, yuh always win."

"Naw, I stand back further. Yuh get to pick my rock."

"Cliney bust a window glass in my house last week. He got me tanned alive."

"Cliney can't throw none. 'Sides he ain't here."

"He beat yuh ass he hear dat."

Floyd picked up a rock and walked to the front of his house. He stopped and yelled, "Hell, over!" He dropped his arm and threw the rock. It went over the peak of the house and rattled across the tin on the back porch. They heard the plop as it hit the front yard.

"I get yuh, man."

One of the other boys picked up a rock and yelled, "Hell, over!" It went sideways and hit the chimney, bounced across the roof and landed with a funny sound, a splash.

"Yuh hit the rain barrel, nigger. That don't count."

"Why don't it? It's same as the ground."

"Ain't nothing but the ground same as the ground."

"Well, it's on the ground. Shit, yuh can go play with yourself."

They all giggled until a big woman appeared on the porch, Aunt Bynum.

"Who throwing rocks at my house? Floyd, you throw that rock?"

All four of the boys ran to the woods. They didn't stop but kept on running.

"Naw. I didn't throw 'em. Cliney done it."

"That won't Cliney I saw."

"He run home. Soon's he done it because I tol' him yuh gon' tan his hide."

She stopped talking and looked at the little boy who looked at the ground.

"Yuh learnt to ride that bike?"

"A little. I ain't learnt to stop."

"Well, yuh get to learning because yuh don't never know when it is going to take off and leave."

"I kill anyone steal my bike!"

"Yuh talk big, youngun."

She turned and went back in the house. Floyd picked up a rock and dropped his hand, aiming at her. Cale thought he was going to throw it but he spun around and threw it through the woods, whizzing it by him. Cale ran out before he thought. Floyd saw him and stared for a minute. Then he turned and ran around to the other side of the house. That wasn't like Floyd. He usually wanted to play.

"Hey, Floyd. We can 'Hell, over' at our barn," Cale called.

Floyd appeared around the house. He hadn't gone far.

"Dun' wanna."

"What you want to do?"

"I wanna fight and beat yuh ass."

"I beat your ass."

Aunt Bynum was out on the porch, swinging the door back against the wall.

"I will not have sech talking in my yard. Mr. Cale, if yuh and Floyd can't play nice yuh just go on up home. And Floyd, if there is going to be any ass beating, it is going to be between me and yuh, yuh hea'?"

Cale turned around and walked back up the path. He could hear Aunt Bynum soon as she thought he was away, "Yuh don't ever fight the white boys, I beat the livin' blood out of yuh yuh ever touch him. Yuh fight them little niggers till it thunders but yuh ever touch Miss Falissa's boy yuh good as dead. Yuh want us put off? 'Tween yuh and yuh sorry daddy . . ."

Cale went back to the woodshed to work on his bike. He wanted to sneak down and get a good look at Floyd's so he could get the stripes on the fenders right but he won't never going to ask to ride it. No sirree. It could rot behind the bushes before he would touch it.

Chapter 19

CALE was suckering the corn, popping the short green off-spring from the base of the corn stalks. The corn was already over his head and he moved through the field in privacy. His mama had said the harm had already been done and if his daddy had planned to sucker he should have thought of it a week ago. But he made him do it anyway. The sucker shoots were filled with water from yesterday's rain and they flicked out water that dried stiff on his arms. The long thin leaves from the mother stalk brushed his shoulders, tickling him and leaving itch across his back. But he liked it in the field, in the semi-shade and with the good sound of a light wind moving through the hum of the stalks. At the end of each row he wound up and tied the suckers with a leaf and left them stuck on top on the fence posts to dry for fodder. The grass had come up thick after the rain and covered over the exposed corn roots but he was still going to have to plow because his mama wanted to plant pole beans and use the corn to run it on. It was too shady for beans to come up but she'd make him plow it anyway. He didn't mind plowing when it was just over tractor height but now the old mule would give him a fit snatching at the stalks, trying to get a meal off the thin green leaves. Papa Lonza had him a wire basket he put on the mule's nose but he had a way with the animals too. Cale had never been able to use it without having to put up with getting kicked at every other step.

He wanted to get done early in the day if he could because

he wanted some time left for his own work. The morning glories had already twisted up; it was middle afternoon. After his tenth birthday, his daddy had started giving him a list every day that left little time for anything else. Yesterday when he finished up early he asked him if he could take off and work on his pond and Jerome made up a job for him to do. He should have just quit and not asked or just piddled around making like he was working, that was his mistake, because the afternoon was hot and sticky and almost unbearable. His daddy had been cleaning up in the barn trying to make room for the new crop of hay to load in and his forehead was stuck up with hay dust. That was a bad time to ask off, when his daddy was working. He had made Cale go down into the lower field that they hadn't even sown and carry out rocks. Cale wasn't even sure if he planned to sow it this year because it was too late for much of anything but corn and it would take a lot of breaking up to get that land ready, even had a three-foot stand of young pine coming up on most of it. But there he was, all afternoon picking up rocks and carrying them out. And with most of them you couldn't move but one at a time so he went up to the house and got his wagon that he got for Christmas seven years ago and filled it up and hauled them out. He had a big stack at the edge of the field beginning to look big enough to build something with when he started to notice how dark it was getting. So he started on back to the house, trying to time it so he could be just at the edge of the yard when the storm broke, so he'd be close enough not to get real wet and far enough away to make his daddy think he just quit working. The woods were filled with blackberries and he almost ate himself sick before he got home and then the drops started dashing through the trees and he started running, pulling his wagon so fast the wheels flew up in the air most of the time instead of on the ground.

The rain yesterday really messed up his pond good, you couldn't see a thing in it now, just as red muddy as the ditch beside the road. Didn't see how the fish could see where they were going in it. He was raising shiners and he wanted to get down and seine up a couple of dozen in buckets to sell for bait this weekend. He could put a sign up in the front yard and catch people on the way to the lake. Just wasn't any way he could make himself get interested in the jobs his daddy thought up for him to do, no way. Never gave him any money for helping, not even an allowance and he could make fifty cents just for weeding a flower garden somewhere else. It was just get it done quick as you can so there is some time left for your own doings. It was just planting, growing, picking and spending the winter watching things get eaten up so you could start all over again. His mama fixed and canned stuff all day long. And never having any money to show for anything, not having much of anything you couldn't make except with what little money came from the tobacco or selling a cow. And they never used any of that to go anywhere except to the State Fair once a year. They hadn't yet been to the ocean and even most of the kids from in town had been there. He had learned to swim in the pond pretty good but now it had gotten so shallow from all the mud washing in that he could touch bottom almost all the way across. He rode his bike a lot after supper when his parents set on the porch. He had it so everything moved perfectly, smoother than a new bike. Usually they would leave him alone then and he'd ride off for an hour or so, go down to the farm at the end of the highway where the pony was. The man that owned it let him ride it around in the pasture some and said he would let him keep it for him when they went on vacation if his daddy would let him. Said he rode pretty good not having anybody to teach him. He hadn't asked about that yet. The man said he would bring over his own corn so he didn't see why his daddy wouldn't let him, he wouldn't eat much grass and they had plenty. It wouldn't cost anything. But he was scared to ask just the same. Had to pick the right time.

He walked up toward the barn to put the tools up, the knife

and the hoe. Right by the entrance to the tractor shed was the rain barrel where he dunked his arms and splashed his face. The water was hot on top but when he stood on his tiptoes and bent over he could feel the cold down deep. His skin felt good where he rubbed the water and the corn itch began to go away, so good he didn't want to get out of it. He could make the corn itch roll up in balls on his stomach. Suddenly he heard the front door of the barn slam back against the wall and the bunch of pitchforks fall over. Then he could hear his father cussing.

"Cale! Cale, come on up here."

"I'm already here. Right out by the rain barrel," he called back and then climbed through the stall into the barn.

"Cale, I want you to back me up on something."

"O.K., what is it?"

"You know how I told Will James two times that I didn't want his niggers cutting through our property anymore."

"Yes sir."

"Well, Falissa just told me they came through again, this time on the goddamn tractor pulling a harrow and it was getting so she was scared to let Pearlie play out for fear she would get run over."

"Why don't they take the highway?"

"Because they're niggers, I guess. They figure it is two feet shorter coming through my property and they ain't never done nothing else."

"Why don't we put up a gate?"

"I'm not spending any money because of him. The law is on my side. I checked it at the courthouse. It says if there is another access to a man's property then you got a right to make your road private and there is another access to his property right down the U.S. highway to be exact."

"What are you going to do?"

"You come help me put on the big disks and I'll show you right quick what I'm going to do."

Cale and Jerome went into the tractor room. Cale took

the bolts off the harrow and the tow bar and Jerome pulled the
tractor away from it and backed up to the disks. They moved
the arms down and bolted the disks' handle in place. Jerome
dropped the blades halfway down so Cale could ride up on the
back of the tractor. He held on hunched over as Jerome pulled
out into the road. Cale knew what he was going to do now but
he hadn't really believed he would do it, he was going to plow
the road under. He had told his mama he didn't need the part
that went to Will James' because he wasn't going to see that
bastard again. Jerome stopped by the house where Falissa
stood in the yard with Pearlie.

"Falissa, you keep Pearlie up in the house. Cale and I got
work to do and we don't want her getting in the way."

"What are you going to do, Jerome?"

His mother looked frightened as she walked up and touched
his father's arm.

"I'm going to put a stop to that cutting through."

"You've just hollered at him from the field. Why don't you
go over tonight and set down and talk it over with him? Why
don't you try to talk sense with him?"

"Talk sense with who? With Will James? What do you
think I've done the last two times?"

"I know." She bowed her head and stepped back away from
the tractor. "You be real careful. You too, Cale, you understand? I don't want you to make anything big out of a little
squabble. I just wish you'd try to settle it without hard feelings."

Jerome put the tractor in gear and they moved out toward the
road. "Going down."

The big disks began to move down and Cale felt his back
straighten automatically. He stepped back onto the bar over the
blades and his weight pushed them in deeper into the hard-
packed road dust. They went the length of the road and on the
first trip just scratched the surface. When they turned around
the road hardly looked touched except they had chopped down
most of the bitterweed. But on the trip back to the house the

big disks began to sink in the road that had been packed for a hundred years and the white sun-faded top dirt sifted over the ridges of the disks as they broke through like flour in a sifter. They turned up the lower dirt until it looked like breaking a new field, the red-orange clay that squirted out in long shiny strips. As they started back down again Jerome edged the tractor over.

"Hang on good. I'm going to take care of the ditch too while I'm at it. Don't need no drainage now."

The big tractor wheel dropped in the ditch and clawed to the other side while Cale swung his weight back so he wouldn't fall off. Jerome lowered the disks another notch and they broke into the ditch, this time easily flipping up the honeysuckle and crusted mud that had been there ever since Cale could remember, cracked up in squares. As they neared the end of the road Jerome turned his head around. "Don't look now but James has come out in the yard."

When they got to the end of the road and started to turn around, James walked down toward the tractor. Cale could see his face good now and there was no doubt how mad he was, ready for a fight as far as he could tell. Cale saw his lips move as Jerome shut off the tractor.

"You got something to say to me, Will?"

"You goddamn right I got something to say to you. Is that your boy up behind you?"

"It is, and anything you got to say, you say in front of him."

"You get down off the tractor so we can talk."

"I can talk fine from up here and I'd advise you to do the same." Cale saw Jerome's hand drop down just over the wrench he kept by the seat but he didn't pick it up.

"I'm going to get the law onto you. I hadn't planned to say nothing about it but you leave me no choice but to get the law on you. I'm going to get the sheriff out here before suppertime."

"Law on me for what? For plowing up my own goddamn land? Think I just might plant me some late tomatoes in this strip. So far as I know my land goes to your fence and your land goes to your fence. And right at the moment you are standing on my land."

"Don't get wise with me. You know goddamn good and well I'm talking about that road you just plowed up. My granddaddy got a right of way on that road with Lonza Lemirt and it still stands."

"That's where you're whistling through your teeth. It stood till the day they built U.S. 18 out there and now it don't stand no more."

Jerome smiled and leaned back in the tractor seat.

"I'll get you, you sonovabitch."

"Now don't go threatening me, Mr. James. You just done it in front of a witness. And if you want to find out about the right of way, why don't you just take a visit to the courthouse and they'll show it to you in black and white."

"You just wait. I'll get you."

Jerome's hand closed around the wrench. He lifted it up and Will saw it. "The only getting you'll be doing is off my property."

Will turned and went back to the house. They watched him walk in the door then Jerome started the tractor and started back up and down the road until it was level and the clay had grown fine. By the time they had finished, and pulled the tractor back to the front of the house, the road looked like part of the field and it was though it had never been there, except for the hole in Will James' fence.

"Tomorrow we are going to seed it and in a week or two we won't even have to look at that bastard's house. I might change my mind and plant something tall and thick."

They headed back to the barn and Cale felt the disks lift up and bend him over again. Out of the corner of his eye he saw Pearlie on her tricycle on the part that went in front of their house, riding up and down like nothing had happened. They put the tractor up and started toward the house. Falissa had already rung for dinner.

"What you think Will James will do, Daddy?"

"He'll go in the house and steam and spew and cuss at his wife and after supper we can go out on the porch and listen to him beat his mule. There ain't a goddamn thing he can do. But if he wants to try it we'll be waiting for him."

"You mean he'll get so mad he'll beat his mule for nothing?"

"Won't be the first time I seen him do it."

"That sure is mean."

"And I want you to promise me something."

"What's that?"

"When I tell your mama what happened I want you to back me up on what I say. And if I tell anything wrong you correct me but you back me up on what that sonovabitch said, you hear."

"Yes, sir."

They walked in the kitchen and sat down at the table.

"Well, are you two done with your plowing?" Falissa said and frowned at them.

"Yes ma'am, we are," Jerome said and reached for a biscuit, winking at Cale.

*   *   *

That night Will James beat his mule. They couldn't see him because he tied it up somewhere on the far side of the house but they could hear the mule squeal after each whop.

"What's he using?"

"The harness strap probably.'

"He sure is a mean sonovabitch."

"Cale, don't you ever let me hear you say that again. Jerome, I told you that would happen."

Jerome smiled and put his feet on the railing.

"He's quit, Daddy."

"All that exercise wore him out. Will James ain't worked that hard in years."

"He ought to be ashamed. I hope the Lord punishes him for that," Falissa said.

"Can they put you in jail for killing an animal? Is it like murder?"

"It's not like murder, Cale, but the Lord takes care of that kind of sin," Falissa answered.

"What do you think, Daddy?"

"Oh, I don't know. I heard they used to hang people for stealing horses."

"Well, Jerome, that's because they belong to a man."

"You ever see a hanging, Daddy?"

"Saw one. Me and Roe seen one in Louisiana. Hanged a nigger for rape."

"What's rape?"

"It's for jumping on a woman."

"Did you ever have a horse?"

"Never did."

"Man down at the end of the road says I could keep his for two months while he's on vacation and he'd furnish the food if I'd just look after him and I could ride him all I wanted."

"Wondered why you were being so nice."

"What you think?"

"I guess so if it's all right with Falissa, but you got to do all the looking after."

"It's fine with me . . . if you'll just be careful."

Cale ran down the steps.

"Where you going?"

"I got to go tell him it's O.K."

"You tell him tomorrow."

"Aw, why not?"

"Because it's getting dark. I don't want you out tonight because there is going to be some mean, mad niggers out tonight."

"Oh." Cale ran back up the steps and sat in his chair. It started to look darker and he could see the headlights bounce off the barn from U.S. 18.

*   *   *

The pony arrived in the back of a truck. It was red with a
bull nose, one of the little ponies from the Ocracoke Island.
At first it wouldn't get off the truck then it got frightened at the
metallic sounds under its own feet and bolted, knocking down
the Negro who brought it and dragging him until he scrambled
to his feet and yanked the pony to a stop. Falissa had her first
misgivings when she saw him, Johnny-Step-Up. Yet all went
well for the first few weeks. She had never seen Cale so happy
and she had gotten Jerome to boost up Pearlie and the pony took
both of them for a ride, Pearlie laughing and pinching Cale
she held him so tight.

It was a stomping pony, stomping flies, the straw, the water
in the pond. They were told that was because it was a beach
pony and it was true he wouldn't drink from a bucket. He pawed
out a hole at the edge of the pond and watched it fill before he
would drink.

One evening in early July she was in the garden and she saw
Cale riding on the far side of the pasture. The pony seemed to
be bucking more than usual, tossing the boy forward on its
neck. Suddenly both of them went mad. She stood there and
watched the boy fly off his back and roll over. Then the pony
started to roll. Both of them were on the ground, rolling down
low from her sight then flinging back up into the air again, their
legs kicking wildly. It was like a strange pantomime at first, the
two figures moving in the air trying to tell her something she
could not understand. Then the squeal of the pony cut through
the air. Falissa was running through the rows and stalks, lifting her skirt out of her way, feeling the pain in her ankles as
they sank in the uneven ground. She went through the barbed
wire, snagging her dress and tearing it loose.

She could hear their sounds now, first the pony, screaming
from its nostrils, the tiny animal like a large mad stallion, rearing
and falling and rolling on its spine. And she heard her boy,
"Quit, stop," he was saying but he didn't cry. He just waved his
hands and slapped at his body. She took the boy and pulled him
to her, sliding her hands down his thin limbs and ripping away

the insects, their insides hanging to him, still pumping the poison through the thorn in his flesh.

He was crying for his pony and as she took her handkerchief and started pulling the wild bees away from him, one by one, she saw it running away, half sideways down toward the creek. He was crying hard then but he was calling the pony and pounding on her head. "Got to get my pony, Mama. Got to catch my pony."

"You just let him go. Your daddy will find him. We got to take care of you."

Then he started to walk toward the house away from her, his legs straddled like he had wet himself and his arms stiff and away from his body. She followed and saw the wiggling bugs still on his flesh, even burrowing into his hair until it was alive with their movement. But the boy didn't cry out, just walked ahead of her every time she caught up with him. She fell behind, her breath coming in gasps and her calves tight with cramps.

When they got to the yard, he changed. His body started to tremble, at first letting him keep moving but then his shoulders shook violently until he started to fall.

She rushed and grabbed him to hold him up and he said, "I'm freezing, Mama. I'm freezing to death from the cold."

She carried him into the house, took a knife and slid each of the stingers from his body. She should have done that in the first place and they wouldn't have hurt him so bad. Why did she snatch them off so, just filled him with poison. Thirty-seven she counted plus what she couldn't find in his hair, thirty-seven. And he lay there and trembled, his heart beating too fast to count when she put her ear to his chest. She dressed him in his pajamas and his skin twitched each time she touched him. She felt foolish warming covers to wrap him in the summer-time, but he kept freezing, whimpering it was the ice she put around his throat to keep his breathing open. His head was hot as fire.

Where was Jerome? Would he know better? She couldn't

call the doctor without his permission. If he was just here he would see she wasn't getting upset over nothing. Nobody had ever gotten stung more than three at a time, even when they had the hives. She had seen them together today, Cale and Jerome, him showing the boy how to girth the saddle, how to let the air out of the pony's stomach and catch him right. He had laughed and showed her his accomplishment and ridden the pony for them up and over logs and around bushes, the pony as much like him with his tossing head and kick-up-at-the-heels run as an animal could be like any human being. That pony had thrown his head up once when she went to lead him in the barn and cracked her so hard under the chin she saw stars, until she felt her tongue to see it wasn't bit in two.

"Got to catch my pony, Mama. You let him run off. He is going to be dead on the highway like a dog." The boy cried out, almost in his sleep.

"Hush now. He is not. Your daddy will find him and pen him up for you."

She sat all afternoon watching the boy and wiping the sweat off his head. He was asleep now but she didn't know if that was good or bad. She had rung the dinner bell for Jerome but he hadn't come. Then about six o'clock she turned and saw him at the door. "Jerome, you frightened me."

"Falissa, I have found his animal and it is tore up," Jerome said.

The boy cried out when he heard.

"Oh God Jerome, please don't say that. It isn't true. He is hurt enough. Just look at him."

"Why didn't he hunt him up if he got throwed?"

"He won't throwed, Jerome. He got into a nest of bees and they stung him out of his head. He is burning with fever."

Jerome walked to the side of the boy's bed where she sat with a cloth on his head. The boy's eyes were open now. Falissa looked up at Jerome and said, "He got thirty-seven stings, Jerome. He got enough poison in him to kill him."

"How you feel, boy? You hurting bad?"

"No sir. I just feel funny, all puffy. And I'm dizzy. Did my pony get run over?" A tear rolled from the boy's eye and Falissa wiped it away with the cover.

"Naw, he ain't dead but that little horse has tore his skin off in chunks rubbing up against things. He's got patches bigger than my hand where there ain't a speck of hair and he's as blood red as a skint pig."

"Hush, Jerome, don't let him know."

Then the little boy had opened his eyes and said, "He throwed me off and kicked me in the ground. I didn't fall off of him ever. He throwed me off and hit me with his shoes."

"He's out of his head talking, Jerome. Had we ought to get the doctor before night comes?"

"Well, you just might have ruint your little horse because you didn't watch where you was going."

And the boy's eyes opened wide and didn't blink as he looked up at his father.

She said, "You had it on your mind to get after him and he'd of just as well been lying here dead and you would have lit into him. You just came in here burning mad and wound yourself up all the way from the field. He's a child, Jerome. You can't blame him like a man. You just show me the man who could have took what he got into any better." And she put her head into her lap and cried.

The little boy got up from the bed and walked to the bathroom. They both watched him as he peed then disappeared behind the door to pull the lever. The child walked back into the room, his eyes still spread into the unblinking blue circles. He folded his pajamas shut as he walked.

"He has torn his skin off?" Cale asked.

"He's tore up bad. There ain't no way I see it healing without scarring and the more they itches the more he's going to scratch. We going to have to do some work on him before we take him back. Did you let him get loose when you fell?"

"No, Mama did. She made me come in and wouldn't let me catch him."

"You were in no shape to go running off after anybody's little pony. We'll doctor him back up, Cale. Don't you worry."

"Is that true, Falissa?"

"Yes, it is true. I don't have to explain myself to you."

"You ought to let him fight his own battles."

The child had gotten back in his bed and pulled the covers over his knees before he hugged them. He stared at his mother who watched him, her eyes red from crying and flecked with the light beside his bed. She started to speak but before she could the child screamed "I hate you," and lay down on his pillow, pulling the covers over his head. A muffled voice asked that the light be turned out and the two of them left the room.

Falissa walked in the kitchen, her mind swollen, stunned, as she went to the cabinets. Her eyes were stinging with tears but Jerome wasn't going to see her cry again. There it was, the pine tar. She threw on a pan and melted a hunk of lard, pouring the tar in slowly, stirring with a butter brush. The smell cleared her nose and her lashes dried stiff and prickly. Then she went into the yard where Jerome had staked the pony. It was ugly, white and bloody-splotched and gnats covered its sores.

"Easy baby, easy. This will feel good."

She took his halter and clutched it tight while she painted the spots, the pony kicking and stamping at her as she moved around him, up close, away from the sharp hoofs.

Chapter 20

THEY HAD ALL WALKED down to the revival tent, Jerome and
Falissa and Cale and Pearlie, dressed in their Sunday clothes.
It was set up behind the church in the place they used to play
baseball on. Cale had gone down that afternoon to see if there
was anyone out to throw with and had seen the huge tent spread
flat across the ground covering the baseball diamond. He had
watched them pull the tent up and the shadow of it darken the
church. The wind was blowing, giving them a time putting it
up and snapping the canvas flaps like somebody getting a beating. It made him think of the circus that Papa said might someday come to Summit.

He had forgotten about the revival until he saw the strange
woman in the long blue suit come out and watch the tent go up.
It was the lady preacher, he suspected, who was coming in tonight to preach from a long way off. He had never seen her before. She was tall and straight, thin he thought because her
clothes blew and flapped like the tent. She had a white face,
drawn up tight and she didn't crack a smile when the men cut
up with the tent. She walked away finally, shaking her head like
everything she saw was wrong. He decided he didn't want to
go hear her preach but he might as well forget that. They won't
going to let him stay home alone and he knew his mama and
daddy had to go.

That night in the tent they took their seats about halfway

back where they could find them four together. Pearlie had on her Easter dress that she had worn yesterday to Sunday school and she made a crunchy sound when she sat down that made her giggle. Cale sat beside her in the folding chair and it pinched his leg under his short pants. He hated short pants even if it was hot unless they were jeans he tore off himself. And then Mama hemmed them up and ruined them. He wouldn't see Tommy here anyway and the rest of the boys that went to the church had to wear them too.

He decided to try to find the pitcher's mound but soon realized it was under the platform they set up for her to preach on. Home plate must be outside. He bent over and looked under the chairs for the paths to the bases and when he looked between his legs, Pearlie giggled and tickled the back of his neck with a blade of grass.

Falissa grabbed Pearlie's hand and said, "Cale, Pearlie. Now you two sit up straight and just get settled down for good, you hear. I'm not going to have any of that out of you tonight."

Pearlie leaned back and her eyes dropped like on a baby doll. It was almost her bedtime and she was getting sleepy. Cale didn't see Jimmy Sims so he must be behind them. When he looked over his shoulder, his daddy slapped him on the knee so he sat up and looked straight ahead. There had been a hymnal in every other seat and he was sitting on his so he slipped it out from under him and handed it to his father. His father turned it over in his hand and stuck it under the seat without speaking. He couldn't carry a tune.

Everyone got quiet and only the flap-flap of the tent could be heard as the regular preacher walked to the stand and called them to prayer. It was too long as always and he had to wait for coughing to stop when he was done. He was frowning when he started talking. "Tonight we are most fortunate to have with us, all the way from out west in Idaho, Mrs. Rebecca Ruth Samuels, noted teacher of the word of our Lord Jesus Christ. Mrs. Samuels has requested that there will be no singing tonight and I would like to ask you at this time to quietly put the hymnbooks under your seats that were so kindly distributed this afternoon by the Big Brothers Bible Class."

The chairs creaked as everyone but Jerome put the hymnbook on the ground under the seats. Cale looked down the row and saw the red-edged pages glowing in the grass.

"And now it is my pleasure to give to you, our sister in Christ, Mrs. Rebecca Ruth Samuels."

The preacher walked quickly to his chair and sat down while the tall woman rose, her Bible in her hand, her long white robe showing only the toes of her black shoes, ironed so stiff it looked like stone. She did not go to the stand but walked beside it, tucked her Bible to her chest, and lifted her hand. Cale and Pearlie turned to Falissa who bowed her head so they did too.

"Dearest Father in heaven above, we come to you tonight, sinners all. We have stained the world you made for us with your divine hands and we come to repent of our transgressions. We have broken the Sabbath. We have sinned against your holy word. Oh, how we have sinned, Lord! We have sinned in our churches and now come to you, outside the walls that held us in our evil, that pacified our weak confessions. We have deceived ourselves. We come to you on new grounds and put the walls of the church behind us, in this transient tent standing as our transient bodies, we prepare to live and die for the Lord Jesus Christ. Except ye repent, ye shall all likewise perish. Amen."

Her shrill voice still echoed when everyone lifted their heads and they were quiet now, not like after the preacher's prayer. The preacher looked straight ahead and not at the woman who spoke ill of his church. Falissa watched him for a moment then turned her attention back to the woman.

The woman still stood beside the preaching stand. She lowered her eyes and looked up and down the rows of people like she was looking for someone to point a finger at.

"You have called our Lord Jesus Christ a liar!"

*

Falissa couldn't sleep. This hadn't happened to her in an age but it was that woman's doing, that slick-faced woman with her hair pinched up in a knot behind her head, getting herself up in that white robe like she thought she really was something. Where do they get somebody like that? Been looking forward to the week of tent teaching since last winter but this just might be the last one I drag out my children to. This one comes storming into Summit like she was divine sent and tells them that every last thing they have ever believed in since they read their first Sunday school lesson is no good in the sight of the Lord. Who tells her that? She says, the Lord. Now can you believe that kind of talking, people who hear things from the Lord and see the devil? I just think they make it up.

Falissa had heard of an old colored woman when she was little, Aunt Bynum's mother, as a matter of fact, who used to have visions. She walked in the streets of Summit, in a long white dress with a sheet hanging down off the back of her head, chanting every so often when she had a vision and said the Lord had told her he was coming and the people better get ready. But this woman said the Lord wasn't coming. That he was going to destroy all the people unless they changed. She would have you spend every minute of every day thinking on religion to get right half of what she was harping on. Now they can't go changing into what she asked them to. Well, they could but who in the world as hard as times are is going to let a perfectly good crop go to waste. They would put you in the looney bin for that. Why that goes against every last thing in the world I've ever believed in. And not eat pork. Who reads that old-timey part of the Bible? Goodness, that is not the way I was taught to live by people who were every bit as good in the eyes of God as Rebecca Ruth Samuels thinks she is. If you start going by all the cloven hoof and flying things there won't be a thing in this world you can eat. Why I've heard tell people who first come to this country thought a 'mater was poison and just set them on the mantelpiece to look at. Now who in the world with good sense would do that anymore? I declare I thought this world had gotten a million miles away from that old-timey teaching. Believe like her you would look in my smokehouse and the grocery store and call half of what you see poison. Saying war and sickness is caused by us. A lot more to causing wars than eating pigs and wearing wool, I say. And the killing of the young boys. How can that be so? Saying that and half the people there just brokenhearted still over the last one and afraid to death all this war talk will start another one. I wish the Lord would come to me and tell me that Rebecca Ruth Samuels is crazy in the head and he didn't tell her any such thing. Why doesn't he come to me, same as her? She gets a little sunstroke and calls it an act of God. People have always had wars whether they tried to be good or bad and the Lord didn't have anything to do with it, that was just a mess that man made all by hisself, ever since he showed his greediness in the Garden of Eden.

All this unclean woman business. And Elsa sitting there beside me looking up the scripture like she'd come on something worth reading about. You wait, some of them women will get all up in the air about that woman and do their best to do what she says. I know some of them don't have no more sense than that just because they think some preacher said it. Self-appointed, I say. She had no business herself talking like that in public and embarrassing people and bringing this unclean woman up right there in front of the children. Things were different in Bible times and they didn't have things to keep themselves from being unclean. Rebecca Ruth Samuels ought to know that as well as anyone. Talking like we ain't got soap and water. Why we just take for granted filling up a hot bathtub. She probably grew up on rags and cotton like the rest of us until somebody decided that was old-timey and made something special to take care of it. I am every bit in the world for somebody making that and putting it out where you can buy it if you please but imagine talking about something like that in front of children who don't know a bit more about it yet. There'll be some hard questions asked tomorrow. You wait and see.

And how about bringing it up in church to boot? Well, not

really in church. She didn't have one thing nice to say about the church for sure and they do a lot of good in my opinion. I hope somebody higher up in the deacons had the decency to say something to Preacher Richards about all that business. He must have been embarrassed to death since it was his doing getting her here and that board down at the church. Not right her talking against the people who asked her here. If you want to know what I think, I think they asked her because she was a woman and they wanted to show themselves, just trying to be different. They probably heard she caused an uproar somewhere. There's some of them down there who want all this hellfire and damnation kind of hollering in the church which in my opinion is not the place for it. Why I'll just wear all the wool I want to, and make Jello any time I please. Cale and Pearlie just love it with bananas cut up in it. I declare I think I heard her say it won't right to lick stamps, I think I heard her right.

Her and her twelve things, I thought she never would get to the end of that ranting and raving. And I don't think I like one little bit having a woman up there preaching. Just don't seem the proper place for a woman to be to me. I'd like to know what went on inside of them men's heads on that. I wonder what her Lord thinks of that, too, one who is supposed to find her place in the home and cook and raise children taking up a man's place in the pulpit. Oh goodness, that might be thought wrong of. I shouldn't have such thoughts, the Lord will do as he sees fit. I just don't like somebody acting so sure fire of themselves and I don't see any reason in the world why my God isn't just as good as hers. He sent me two fine children and I couldn't have wished them any better. She thinks I'm going to drop on my knees and thank God when the frost kills my peach blooms and the bugs eat things up, well, she's just crazy in the head. I think the Lord above would think I didn't have a bit of sense left if he looked down and saw me thanking him in my prayers for killing everything. He'd hit me with a lightning bolt I'd be so

crazy. And I don't believe he did it to me anyway, let the frost
come and mess up my peaches two years in a row.

Oh goodness, I know good and well he did. I must be denying the Lord above if I don't think he controls all the things of
nature with his hand. Wasn't I taught that he saw every little
sparrow that fell? I have let that woman make me so mad I
can't think straight. Did he take revenge on me for some evil?
I try so hard not to be evil, I do, but nobody can be perfect no
matter how hard you try. And I am ashamed of myself sometimes. I'm ashamed when I lose my temper with the children
and with Jerome and show myself and say something hateful.
I do get ashamed when I make a mess of something in the
kitchen or slip and hurt someone's feelings. But I know there
are a whole lot of people a whole lot worse than me and don't
think a thing of it. And that woman preacher got up there and
tried to make every last one of us feel like the commonest criminal. She did, and for doing the nearest nothing to my mind.
Like a criminal for using the hybrid seed and that was the best
thing in the world ever happened to Jerome's crop, no more
missing hills and all of it just as firm and the same size. Now
who would have thought she would have found fault in that.
She ought to come see our crib if she thinks there's meanness
in that and those fat happy cows keeping warm on it in the
winter. Why that should be to the glory of God to see such.
Back in the Bible they didn't know about that, how to mingle
seeds and goodness, not a soul I know could do it either. You
have to buy them in the stores made up by someone a whole
lot smarter than any of us claims to be. Is the Lord going to send
that man to hell for making a stalk yield three ears instead of
two and a nubbin and feeding a lot more hungry cows and little
children? My papa never could get more than two to the stalk
no matter how hard he tried.

No wait, that's not right. I didn't pay attention. She says the
man who plants the mingled ones is wrong, not the one who
makes them. That makes us wrong. According to the Bible.

According to her Bible, if you ask me. Oh no, goodness no, it is all the same one. What am I thinking about? She is just paying more mind to the Old Testament than anybody around here thought ought to be paid. Well, to parts of it anyway. I declare I didn't even know some of those funny names were even in there until I looked up front in it tonight. I suppose it's all in what your teacher chooses and we come from two different kinds of teachers. But I have seen some of these people argue till they were blue in the face over something I wouldn't have given a second thought to. Maybe the Lord knows which one of us is right, or maybe he don't see no need to choose sides neither. But that woman is going to follow every single thing word for word. She figures there is no way on this earth she can come out wrong and if God believes that other part the most, then all of us who been believing the way we been taught all our lives are the blackest of sinners and my mama and papa are in hell sure as shooting. My good papa who wouldn't hurt a flea and was about the best person I ever knew in my life and she would call him a sinner every day of his life. I just don't think she's right. I have never known a person in all my days who let his fields go unplanted on the seventh year and grow up in weeds and thought that the fruit on the fourth year was any different than it was any other year. He wouldn't think to carry on about such as that.

I can hear that Mrs. Samuels now, saying the Lord took my peaches hisself because I wouldn't give them up to him. That's the way her crazy thinking would go. And that cooking up on Saturday. I remember some old-timey ladies doing that and dishing out cold dumplings on Sunday but my mama just took that as pure laziness. I guess I do remember once putting on a button on Sunday and having my mama say to me, "Putting stitches in your soul." More than once if the truth were known. I don't know as how anyone could stitch a soul or it would hurt them if they did it, sewing on Sunday, I mean, and I don't think Mama ever thought of it having any meaning at all except it just wasn't supposed to be done. I said to her that my book said, "A stitch in time, saves nine," and she could go by her book and I'd go by mine. And Mama called me heathen. Goodness, that is the truth, isn't it? I've been called a heathen by my own mother long before this preacher woman came along. And I bet my mama's mama called her a heathen too. And just because the world outside is changing so fast we can't begin to keep up with it, that's what Preacher Richards talked on yesterday, don't mean we ought to throw out all we been taught. Maybe we just let things get to be too much trouble and we toss them out and be done with it. And maybe the Lord is watching us and saying we are sinning, not giving the proper amount of time to his will.

Oh Lord, I wish you would talk to me sometime. Why did you pick this preacher woman? I wish you'd tell me for sure you said all that to her. I don't expect all you said to her myself, just a little reassurance, just a word maybe one time, telling me you think I was doing all right by my husband and children and my house and what changes you would want me to make to make myself better in your eyes. And I would do it for you and not doubt a minute. There is not a soul on this earth can tell me so I'm sure of it. Does that make me a Doubting Thomas, Lord? I declare you just can't go around believing everybody. You just got to have some mind of your own. That is why I'm asking you to go to the trouble, Lord. So I can sleep right at nights, like tonight, and not toss about till the sun's up with nobody to ask and answer my questions but myself and not having a bit of confidence in me. Why I don't know what I'd do if I was sure that all my churching ought to go, my baptizing, just my sitting there on Sunday morning in the quiet and listening to the preacher and putting all my worries away from me with the pretty colors from the glass wiggling on the wall, using my mind to think on things my work don't let me think on.

And I just love the pretty music. That is the prettiest thing in the world hearing that children's choir at Easter time. It just makes tears come to my eyes to think about it, the sweetest voices in the world. But she don't want no music, no singing tonight for Mrs. Samuels. Nothing to take away from her. She has gotten me so scared. I don't like this scared religion. Preacher Richards don't harp on it. I don't think any good Lord would want to make people afraid. It is ugly to see people afraid, all crying and huddling together, like when them bombs came over I seen people in those news movies who were afraid and it just gave me nightmares. And is there one soul in this town come next Christmas who won't put up a tree? As happy as it makes the little children? Has she denied her children that pleasure of going out a hunting a tree and decorating it? I think maybe she is a mean woman. She is so stern I bet her children don't love her. I bet they are afraid of her too, but they don't love her good. Putting up a tree and giving to the little children don't make me think less of the little Christ child. Why it makes me think more of what we have to be thankful for, him being born to save the world from wickedness. It is part of feeling the spirit of Christmas. I feel the spirit every year and just double since I had my little children.

And does she just throw her sugar coupons in the trash pile because she didn't pay straight out for them? Why I think that is the most wasteful thing I ever heard of. If I am given a coupon for free, I most certainly am not ashamed to use it. I'm not so high and mighty I toss it in the trash. I don't care what she says. And I am not letting a soul touch my children with a rod. I'll give them a good little spanking to teach them a lesson but you just let somebody try to take a rod to my children and they'll have me to deal with. I've seen what all this rod and strap beating does to a little child. It makes him not right in the head. She is a mean hateful woman to talk of such. And to talk so ugly about people who can't help what is wrong with them. Cripple people and blind people. The Lord above must have meant you to help them. He said to love your neighbor and is she going to stop loving him because the poor thing has something wrong with him? They are so pitiful I just hate to see them but I thank the Lord because it could have been me or one of my little children. I think of that and how thankful I am that they are healthy and as sharp as little tacks, both of them, and it makes me feel sorry for the people who have something wrong with them that much more. I admit people don't like to see open sores and things that make you sick at your stomach, especially if they come from going dirty and not taking care of yourself. I'd be the first to say that it just kills me inside to see that little Judson boy that got scalded when he was a baby turning a pan off the stove and you just about can't help but stare at a man with just a nubbin for an arm. But you try not to and you teach your children not ever to and the last thing in the world I'm going to do is teach my child to be mean to someone like that. Sakes alive, where is her Christian charity? It says somewhere about the lamb and the meek, it says somewhere else in the Good Book that they get to go to heaven first. I'm going to find out where if I have to read the whole book through and I have a good mind to write that woman a letter and just tell her that she can go believe what she wants to believe and I'll believe what I want to, and teach my children properly, and I don't appreciate one bit her getting up there and talking such meanness with my children right there unawares in hearing distance and me not a having a bit more idea ahead of time what I was getting into than the man in the moon. I'll tell her and she can carry on her preaching somewhere else and never come back here again. She is not welcome here.

*   *   *

"Me and Roe used to go to tent meetings. Go slipping in the back and act like we was there because somebody told us we oughta get religion and we just wanted to see all the hopping and carrying on. I went to a few with my mama when I was little, she went for that kind of religion, all that hollering and feeling the spirit and running up front. She'd get saved every time there was a new preacher. She'd sit there by me and start in to quivering like this."

Cale watched his father stand up and put his fishing pole on the pier rail. He shook his fingers then he trembled up his arms and started to shake his face until the loose skin on his neck started to flap. Cale didn't know he had that much loose skin on his chin.

"Aw, I can't do it right. You got to make it go up and down you. Roe can though. You ask old Roe to do the quiver when he comes here."

Jerome sat back down and took up his pole again. He whipped his line around behind him and sent it over the water, the worm coming down lightly in the dark place by the cattails. "Gonna get me a wide-mouth bass. You just wait and see."

Cale threw his line again. He didn't throw much around his father because he was always criticizing him for throwing dangerous. He was with Tommy one day when the wind blowed and he got a hook in the back of his head, his own hook, but he won't about to tell his daddy that. Tommy had to cut it out of him with his pocket knife.

"Anyway, Mama would start in to that quivering and if someone else had gotten started to quivering more before her, they would get up front first and she and the rest of them would stand up by their seats. Now you would have thought I would have gotten tickled to death but I didn't let out a peep. No sirree. That preacher up there yelling with the sweat sticking his shirt to him, he had me so scared I wouldn't crack a smile for fear he'd tear my head off. He would have too. That was a mean preacher. He used to be on the road gang until he got the spirit. He won't ashamed to tell it. He got the spirit one day out on the gang when he was shoveling hot tar on Highway 18 up near Raleigh and he thought it was just so hot he had to be in hell itself. But if he throwed it down and started running, he knowed the guard would put a bullet in him, so he poured the tar off the shovel and watched it move around and the Lord come to him and told him he was going to roll him up in a blanket of tar and toss him in hell to burn forever if he didn't go straight and the Lord told him to spread the word. So that's how he took to preaching. You don't go laughing at no man who got the spirit that way. And you don't laugh at no man who ain't ashamed to tell you the way he got in the prison in the first place was from cutting a man from ear to ear in a fight."

"Did he die?"

"Of course, he died. You stupid or something? How you going to cut somebody from ear to ear and not have him die? He died deader than hell." Cale's hook had floated up close so he pulled it up. "Got your worm, see."

The hook held only one little frayed segment of the worm so he reached in the can and started to thread the hook through another one.

"Don't leave so much of the worm hanging off. Don't give him nothing to bite at what he don't get caught up on it."

Jerome threw his again, back into the quiet water around the cattails. "See him. See him," Jerome called.

"What?"

"The red-winged blackbird. Went in the cattails."

Cale watched the blades move back and forth but the bird was hidden.

"Naw sir, I don't take to preaching when some prissy woman gets up there and tells you everything is wrong except pissing standing up. And since she can't do that, she'd probably find fault with that. Boy, I wish old Roe could have been here to hear that one. He'd have took her down a peg. She wouldn't have set old Roe down on that nigger business like she did that fellow down front, old big-mouth Gudger who ought to keep it shut unless he knows what he's talking about. Old Roe would have got up and told her she was a woman so therefore she didn't know what a pretty little piece a nigger gal could be, he'd of said that right there in front of everybody. I can hear him now . . . Don't you worry, Mrs. Samuels, if one goes messing around with a white woman, we cut his mingling off. You just let me know if one bothers you and we'll cut off his mingling and throw it to the hogs. That's what old Roe would have told her, something like that. She wouldn't have gotten the best of old Roe."

"Is it true all them niggers got white blood like she says?"

"I heard it before. I won't deny it. I heard it before. You know about the slaves?"

"I know all the niggers were slaves once a long time ago."

"They tell you that at school? It won't so goddamn long ago if you ask me, won't a hundred years ago if you had a black bastard you was tired of you didn't put him off, you sold him off and got back what he'd cost you. And he got the big mouth, you whipped him down to size. But what I was getting at about the slaves, they don't tell you this in that school and don't you tell your mama I told you. I bet because those old prissy school teachers don't know it to tell and if they did they wouldn't have the guts to say it, they just tell about them picking cotton. They used to, the men who owned up a bunch of slaves, they used to keep them a hot little nigger wench, one with some meat on her bones that jiggled just right when she walked, you know what I mean?"

"I know what you mean."

"I figured you did. I figured you was on to that. Nobody have to tell you any birds and bees stuff. You on to all that. They'd keep them this little wench I'm telling you about and when the old lady started getting prissy and telling him no when he was needing some, he'd just trot on down and visit his nigger gal who was always ready to go. Those old ladies get them a bunch of kids and they ain't no good no more. You see that's all the good they thinks it's for, having them little younguns and when they get what they want, they just start getting cold as a witch's tit. And then a man's got to go looking somewhere else. And if his nigger gal starts getting too many younguns he just gets him another one. That's why there is so many little light-skinned jiggaboos running around. How's that for a story?"

"That's a good one."

"I was going to tell you about them tent meetings the kind me and Roe used to slip in on. We was there one night and this preacher had them rolling in the floor and blowing at the mouth like mad dogs and Roe grabbed my arm and like to have sent me through the ceiling. He pointed me toward this woman who was over to the other side of the tent, I probably oughtn't to tell you this, but I bet you heard stuff worse, huh, at school? She was over on the tent post right there in full view with her skirts hiked up and rubbing on this post just getting herself good. I oughtn't to told you that. That's the way women are though, boy, I'm telling you. They put on all these shines how they don't want it like they're supposed to and you get them at these tent meetings and they're the first to go out sprawling and rolling around on the floor. Proves they got it all up inside them and all their properness is just put on. Women are excitable, I tell you. Tell you what me and Roe used to do. We'd slip in back like I telled you and we'd be picking us out the two prettiest ones what looked to be the most shook up and starting to tear at their clothes. If they were by theirselves and didn't act like they were married, we'd get in behind them soon as the tent would let out and start some fast talking and get them off to the woods. Like taking candy from a baby. That old preacher knew how to get them going and we'd go pick them off and old Roe said the preacher picked him off one too, he just left enough to go around for all us boys and he was going to get her off and fill her with the spirits sure nuff. Shit, I bet that old Rebecca Ruth Samuels is tight as a Coke bottle, don't you, boy?"

"I bet she is."

"And you just watch your mama take every word that old bitch said as the Gospel Truth."

"You think Mama would do that?"

"Naw, not really. But she stayed awake half the night fretting about it, covering and uncovering, worried me to death. Your mama's like that, you know."

"Like what?"

"She's a worrier. She is a little simpleminded about some things. I don't mean she'll go let the crops rot every seven years because some crackpot lady preacher said to, she's too damn stingy for that, but you just watch her go worrying about every little thing she thinks she does wrong. She'll be sure as stuff the Lord's getting at her for her meanness. She'll worry herself sick before she puts that old bitch out of her mind."

"Don't worry me none."

"Naw, and don't you let it. You make your own mind there. But you know women, boy."

"Yeah, I guess so. They always worrying about something that don't matter."

"Now you catching on. Now you got it."

Chapter 21

AFTER SCHOOL Cale had been the first on the bus. He was wanting to get home early because his daddy had said Roe might be coming through this way. But no one else at school was in any more of a hurry than usual. He watched them poke up the steps and then the driver was late. Roe might not be in until the train but he could have come on the bus. Roe had promised to come see him before, two years ago, and at the last minute called collect to say he couldn't come. Cale had never gotten to meet him in person but he always got letters and presents. The last one was a coconut with a face made out of shells that Roe said he got in Hawaii. Last time Roe was going to bring his new wife to meet them, a tiny Oriental girl he had gotten on an island, but someone found out he had another wife in Cape May, New Jersey. Roe said he didn't remember it but she had a bunch of papers made up to prove it so he guessed he better stick around to straighten it out. He wanted to keep this Oriental one because you couldn't get them like that around here. Jerome was upset to hear Roe was married and for the first time didn't seem interested in having him visit. Roe who said he never would. But when Jerome found out there were two, he slapped his knee and laughed, "That goddamn Roe. Hadn't changed a bit!" So far as they knew neither wife was around now; Roe said that the U.S. Government had sent the Oriental back and that the one in Cape May decided she didn't want

him. So Roe was coming home alone. He had sent Jerome a telegram from Atlantic City, New Jersey, that said, "Lock up the
women and children," that was all, so they expected him any
day. It was almost four days now since they heard from him.

Cale hadn't gotten a letter of his own from Roe this time
but somehow he had a feeling it might be today. The weekend
was coming up and maybe they would get to go someplace,
maybe even on Saturday night. There was a dirt track race at
the oval at Janks Corners and a baseball game in Raleigh.
Tommy Grinnin told him there were rooster fights down at the
river every Saturday night.

The school bus pulled up at the new filling station near their
house on Highway 18, actually it was the old store with a new
front the gas people had built, and he saw Pearlie, already there
and waiting on the front bench for him. She had her red plaid
book sack in her lap and she dangled her feet down but they
wouldn't reach the ground. Her socks were slid down in her
shoes. She needed to learn to sit so her pants wouldn't show.
Tommy had already made fun of her to him. Mama had
given her a home permanent that frizzled all over but she didn't
care about that either. She had to stay the full day now she was
in the third grade and she waited on Cale so Mama wouldn't
have to walk down to meet her. Mama didn't like her walking along beside the highway still though he didn't know why
she wasn't old enough. She knew better than to walk out in
front of cars; she was more careful than she needed to be to his
mind. She wouldn't go until there wasn't a car in either direction, even if you could just barely see it down the road. She said
she might fall down and not be able to get up before it got there.
She did fall down a lot; every day it looked like she got another
circle on her knees that Mama painted with that purple stuff.

Mama didn't ever make him wait on a grown-up to be walked
home, even from the first grade. He asked her, "Mama, there's
no need of making Pearlie sit down there at the store waiting
on me. I'm twenty minutes later than her."

"Cale, Mr. Sinson knows me and he keeps a peep on her until you get there. That is the best place in the world for her till you get there. And you don't understand how important that is. Mr. Sinson doesn't mind a bit. He understands what I mean." Every day Pearlie would go tap on the window and wave before she left and Cale would see him come to the window in his white apron with the blood on the front.

"I wasn't meaning that. I mean why can't she walk on?"

"Does it trouble you that much to do that little bit for me?"

"That's not what I mean either." He had almost just gotten mad and said to drop it but he wanted to explain what he meant. "I just think you're going to make a big baby out of her. She ever gets stuck there if I miss the bus or something or have to stay for ball practice, she won't know what to do with herself."

"You let me make that decision, young man. And there are a few things in the world you don't know though I'm certain you think you know it all. There are people who go around and bother little girls that don't pay any attention to little boys. There are people right here in Summit who'd watch that bus pull up and see a little girl get off by herself and go off down the road and lie there waiting in the ditch for her. I don't intend to explain it any further to you but there are people going around in the woods and riding in cars with meanness on their minds. So just leave it at that and do as I say."

Mama has just sat and listened to what Daddy reads her out of the paper too long. You ought to hear him. He finds anything that might have been us. He found where a man's silo split and buried him alive, where a plane crashed on a farmhouse and killed all the people while they were asleep. Last week he saw one where a car ran in a house and killed a man in his living room. He has told her about every little kid who drank rat poisoning or bug spray or something. Now he's got her all scary about Pearlie. He read her about this little girl who got in the car with a stranger who said her mama was sick and her parents got notes and had to pay money to get her back. But she was a rich little girl, everybody knows my parents don't have any money. What would they want with Pearlie? Besides Pearlie is a smart little kid. She isn't going to have anything to do with a stranger. She would turn up her nose at him and run. He never would catch her if she didn't fall down. So everywhere I go, there is Pearlie pulling on my hand like she is going to squeeze it off and every time I stop she swings around my leg. And I don't think it's because she is scared of anything but just because Mama told her to hold on to me. She is a pretty strong little kid. Every time I ask to go somewhere by myself, Mama brings up me and Papa Lonza again, how Pearlie didn't have a Papa Lonza to take her places and I'm going to have to make up for it. I guess that was true, about how Papa Lonza was already around, because I can remember good every time I stepped out of the yard by myself, Mama started hollering at me. She's not going to let anybody go off by theirself if she can help it. Mama is scared of everything. You have to watch her or she would make you scared of things when there won't no need to. She can hear noises at night when there isn't a thing there. I don't know what would happen to Mama if something scared her real good sometime, like somebody broke in the house or something. She'd go crazy. She wouldn't let Pearlie spend the night or anything and it is time she did because when I was in the third grade, I used to go off with my friends. We went downtown or to the show and me and Tommy messed around the railroad yards. Of course, if Mama had known that, she would have had a fit. Pearlie has lots of friends at school because she rattles on about them all the time when we are walking, tells everything they did or said at play period, and Mama is going to have to let her play with them or their mamas are going to think something is funny about her and she is snooty or something.

Pearlie was always asking him questions about Papa Lonza because she didn't have any grandparents to talk about and the

other girls at school did. What he couldn't remember, he made
up, but usually when he got to talking he could remember more
than he thought he could. Just never had no reason to before
because nobody was asking. And she asked dumb things like
did Papa Lonza have a farm with ducks when she should have
known she was living on his farm. She couldn't get that straight
because all her other friends went out to the farm to see their
grandparents.

They had these pictures of Papa Lonza that were sort
of brown-colored but pretty clear, one of Papa in a dress when
he was a little boy. Then Mama had one of himself taken with
the Kodak in that same dress and she pasted it in beside Papa
Lonza. Someday he was going to tear that one up in a million
pieces when Mama wasn't around. It was hard to remember
Papa Lonza good though even with the pictures that Mama
took of them together.

There's this one in the front porch by the post and Papa
didn't even come as far up on it as I do now and Mama told me
it was true, that I have already outgrown Papa who would be
pleased if he was here to see it. There was the one I liked best
in front of a circus train down at the railroad station. It said
Barnum & Bailey on it in big letters and you can see behind us
there is an animal in the cage but you can't see what it is. I
figure it was a gorilla because it looks like there is a hand around
one of the bars and I don't think we would turn our backs so
close on one of the cats. Papa was fearful of those cats when
they were closed up and bolted shut because they wanted to get
out so bad.

But in that picture, with the ape, I'm not near as tall as Papa
Lonza. I wouldn't have known it was me though I knew it
was him because I didn't think I looked like that. Mama said
it was me but I told her I didn't remember those big baggy
Boy Scout pants with the pockets and zippers all over them and
in every picture I had them stuffed with something, peanuts,
Mama said. I just don't remember. Papa was so poor looking

you couldn't tell how big he really was because he didn't touch his clothes anywhere. Mama said he ate good but it all went to his hair and his mustache that he used to trim all the time because he got his food in it. He had to cut the whole thing down to a stub once when he fell asleep on the porch chair and got his chewing gum caught in it.

I'm getting much bigger now, over five feet already, almost. Since I left the fifth grade I don't need a small desk anymore and I don't think I'll ever have to have one again. Pearlie still does so it must run in the family. Tommy's not but three and a half inches taller than me and he's older. And my face is skinnier because in the pictures it's all round and puffy looking, like a pie face with my eyes and mouth all pinched up in the middle like a fly or a raisin or something. It's like that person is dead too, you know, like Papa, because it's just as gone away. I won't ever be a little kid like Pearlie again. If I was I can tell you sure I would try harder to put things straight in my mind so I wouldn't have so much trouble trying to remember them and have to believe what Mama says. Every time we remember the same thing Mama tells it so different I don't believe her anymore.

When they got to the yard, Falissa came to the porch and Pearlie ran to show her her hundred on a spelling test.

"Uncle Roe here yet?" Cale asked.

"No. But if he shows up you can be sure it'll be at mealtime."

Cale put his books on the edge of the porch and went to the backyard. He could hear Pearlie in her room already playing her paper records on her record player. They were so worn out it sounded like they were singing under the water.

Pearlie is really a little kid. She don't know nothing and when I was her age I could have told Mama a thing or two. Mama thinks she's so smart and Tommy Grinnin could have told her things when he was five years old that would have curled up her ears. Tommy said that, that he'd make my old lady's teeth fall out. You really have to watch what you say around Pearlie because she will ask fifty million questions and a bunch of them Mama would get me good if I answered. And the first thing she would do would be tell Mama. She asked me about this little boy who played with his business in her class and he was tall so he could set in the back where the teacher couldn't see him. I just told her I didn't know anything about it because she tells Mama every time I answer her and tell her not to. She gets Mama all worried over things I knew to keep to myself even when I was eight years old too. Mama is just making a baby out of her. I got to feel a little sorry for her because she don't ever have any fun the way Mama keeps her so shut up. She just plays in her room with that box of dumb paper dolls and talks to herself. She's the only person I've ever known who will color every single page in her coloring books.

Cale climbed up into his tree house. Pearlie wouldn't bother him with her jabbering up there. She was scared to climb up there because it looked so high up from the ground. That's what Papa wanted. A little house all his own and away from everybody. A place that would keep the cold out and he could have things the way he wanted them and people wouldn't go messing into his things.

If he had the glass, big sheets of it like they had in the store windows downtown, he could make his tree house so there was light, maybe even color it like sunglasses for the summertime and come up inside it through the bottom. But that wouldn't be any good, having it glass this close to the house. That would only be good if he could go down in the woods and be where he could look out and there was nobody to look in. He would have to stay in the dark and maybe even board up one more side so he could keep a close watch on who was looking in. He had made his table so it would fold up to the wall on hinges; that was in case he ever decided to spend the night up there and needed the room for his pallet. Cale had his comic books up here and the magazine Tommy let him

have with the naked women with their titties showing. If Roe
would hurry up and get here so he could show him, he could
give it back to Tommy. Papa would have had as big a fit
over that book as Mama. He didn't ever like the stuff that
went on at the movie house at night.

I kinda miss not having Papa around but he would be so old
now he'd be a lot of trouble. He got awful slow close to the end.
My daddy was sort of glad Papa died, I think because he had to
keep him up. But Mama said it was Papa's farm in the first
place and Daddy wouldn't have a knob to hang his hat if it
wasn't for Papa. Don't know whose word to take. I'll wait
to see myself because I'm not sure I ought to believe either one
of them. Mama sure don't like Uncle Roe. She gets mad as
a hornet if you mention he's coming. Mama said he is so full
of tricks he will make her nerves come apart before he is gone.
I can see the smokestacks through the trees. I hadn't yet
figured out a way to get them down right. They're getting to
looking pretty bad too, all crumbly. I asked Tommy about it
and Tommy said we could pull out the bottom bricks like
you do on stacks in the grocery store when they're not looking.
That's Tommy for you. He would just as soon knock them
down and sqush everybody in town as stand there. Tommy
got a gun now, a twenty-two, and the policeman done told him
he was going to take it away and break it over a post if he caught
him shooting too near town again. Tommy said he was going
to shoot that cop in the ass. Tommy already told me he shot
three cats last weekend. I wouldn't do that, they might belong
to somebody. We been out shooting rats at the dump, those big
ones that run over the top of the garbage and when you get one
he squirms and squeals and dies with his mouth all snarled
up so you can see his teeth. Tommy says you'll probably
die if he bites you so we poke him with a stick before we
sling him off in the fire and watch him cook. He's going to
have to go back to the training school though if he don't

watch out. They're checking on him every week. I don't see him much anymore since he failed out the fifth grade. He don't go half the time. One day last week I saw him out the window in the bushes making faces at me in class and trying to get me in trouble. He wouldn't have failed out but he didn't do no work at all and the worst thing, he hit that teacher back who whipped him in front of the class. I think they'd of let him go on if it won't for that. When she got him in the balls, he pulled loose and hit her right in the face so hard he had to have his hand put in a sling and she stayed out two weeks and still had a blue mark when she come back. He run out of the school and Tommy said she had the police come after him and they come in his house with six bloodhounds on chains and put him in handcuffs and two of them held a gun on him or he would have run off. He had to stay in the training school for six weeks but I didn't tell my mama. She don't like him anyway. But there isn't anybody way out here for me to play with. I got to stay in town and miss the bus to play with anyone and then I got to walk back. Papa Lonza and Daddy can have their old land. I'd buy me a house there in town right by the basketball court and where I could just walk across the street to the movies. Me and Tommy can find more to do just walking around than out here. He has been trying to get me to sneak out at night and come to town. I had to tell him I can't. They caught me, they would kill me. Tommy don't understand. His mama and daddy aren't there, you don't ever see them. He just goes as he pleases.

I see Mama coming up out of the basement. She's got a basket of something brown. Those bulbs. She'll make me help her, just wait and see. Maybe Pearlie will do it. There she comes down the steps, got a spoon and a spade.

"Cale . . . Cale, where are you?"

He put his magazines back in a mayonnaise jar and screwed on the lid before he dropped over the edge and caught his foot

on the plank nailed to the trees. He walked to the front of the
house and she handed him the spade. Didn't ask him where he'd
been for a change.

They started planting the bulbs up under the bushes in front
of the house. They had been down in the basement in a bin
of sawdust since the last time Papa Lonza took them up. He always took up the bulbs after they bloomed and took them apart,
breaking off the new little bulbs and planting them until his
bulbs numbered in the hundreds, mostly daffodils and hyacinths
and one little batch of blue crocus. Cale with his spade and
Pearlie with a mixing spoon were making a row around the steps.

"Now don't make them too regular looking. You don't plant
flowers like you plant a row of corn. Mix them up a bit or they'll
come up and tell on you," his mama said.

"How you know they aren't dead? They been in the basement for twenty years."

"Not that long, young man. Unless you're thirty years old
and I just hadn't noticed it. And bulbs don't die. They aren't
like seeds. They can grow over and over again. It's just your
grandpapa went to a lot more trouble about his flowers than I'm
a mind to. At least as long as we got nothing but the most ordinary."

"Papa was a sissy."

Pearlie giggled at him.

"He most certainly was not a sissy."

"Flowers are for girls."

"You have said that around your grandpapa and he would have
whipped you good, little showoff. If flowers are for girls then
they are for men to give to girls. And your grandpapa didn't
have any small weakness about girls either. Flowers and girls.
It's a shame he didn't get to see you, Pearlie. He would have
made a fool of hisself over you if he saw you in your Sunday
dress. That brother of yours just didn't show him the proper
appreciation and he told me a many a time how it was a bad
sign the way he didn't have no respect for the flowers. He told

me he would be a devil to women someday and he was glad he wasn't going to be here to see it."

"I didn't do anything to his flowers. I just couldn't remember all the names he wanted me to. He had too many names for things."

"Pretty women and flowers. Those were your grandpapa's weaknesses and your brother treats them both like rocks."

"I do not either. Why should . . ."

"I was just kidding you, Mr. Touchy. For goodness' sake. That was your grandpapa's weakness, not mine. How long those bulbs been in the basement should tell you that."

"I'm going to take Pearlie downtown one day to see the periwinkles. Can I go downtown if I take Pearlie? Maybe we can go while Uncle Roe is here. Papa had a special place down at the courthouse where he went to see the periwinkles."

"What's a periwinkle? I want to go see the periwinkles, Mama."

"Well, you'll just have to wait for spring. Your brother evidently didn't learn much from all of Papa's talking. They bloomed out last spring. They're a spring flower, blue. They were one of Papa's favorites because they were so dainty. They were dainty like your grandmama. I'm surprised to death to hear him remember it."

"You should have heard Papa, Pearlie. He made them out to be something. He said they were a sky of blue stars like at night and they were just a bunch of green plants with blue flowers, that's all. They were right pretty I guess if you like that kinda thing. The first time he said it he made me believe they were animals that hide in the grass and winked their eyes."

Pearlie laughed at Cale and said, "Are they an animal?"

"They're a flower," Falissa said. "I just told you they were a flower and Papa never told you such a big fib. You made that up yourself."

"Then I thought they were like lights that cut on and off and broke loose like a falling star."

"Cale, now stop that. You're telling her a fib and you know she believes everything you say."

"I'm not fibbing, Mama. I did so really think that. And when I really saw them, Pearlie, I told Papa they looked like a pinwheel you make out of a square of paper and fold back the corners and pin it on a broomstick and he got mad as fire at me. They didn't look like nothing special to me."

"Seems to me your memory is a little too good to be true, young man."

"He did, and then he told me they were made by God's women, they were like Santa Claus' helpers and that God used his women to make flowers and kept all the ones with little hands in a flower-making place because there won't no way a man could make such as that even if a woman made up the design for it because he'd sqush it and he was sure a woman had to make the first one for God."

"I didn't know Papa was telling you such foolishness. How come you remember all of that?"

"I do, Mama. It's true, honest, because he made me sit there till he was through telling it and I thought I was going to bust open on the ground before I got out of the woods and he got through. He did, he said women went to heaven and made flowers for God. I didn't like his flower stuff near as good as his Blackbeard stories."

"Bust open."

"Hush Pearlie. Well, why don't you tell Pearlie about Blackbeard then . . ."

"Because I can't remember them good!"

"Don't raise your voice at me, you hear?"

"Yes, ma'am."

"And leave the religion to the Sunday school teacher. I didn't know he carried on about such as that with you. I wouldn't have allowed that for a minute. Your grandpapa had an imagination . . ."

"Tell me about Blackbeard," Pearlie said.

"I don't remember."

"I want to hear about Blackbeard, Mama."

"He says he doesn't remember so I guess until he decides he does, you're not going to hear about Blackbeard. Honestly, I didn't know Papa was filling your head with such. That will worry me to death. No telling what he was filling your head with and I thought he was the best babysitter in the world. It must be the truth though. Just like him."

"It is the truth. I said it was."

"That's enough out of you. It just looks like you would do better to remember something useful. Can't you remember those Blackbeard stories?"

"No."

"Neither can I. Goodness, I ought to be ashamed as many times as I heard them. There were such good stories. Weren't they, Cale? Weren't they good stories? I wish you would remember them for us. They were about a pirate, Pearlie, one who robbed the ships off our very own seashore and took their gold away from them."

"I remember that much."

"And there was one about a harbor light that wasn't really there . . . Oh, my memory isn't worth a hoot. Couldn't tell it good if I could remember it."

Falissa poured out the rest of the bulbs and they sat around the stack and began to take apart the buds.

"Don't you wish we could tell what color they were going to be?" Falissa asked. "We'll probably get three white ones right beside each other."

"Like Christmas tree lights."

"That's a good comparison, Pearlie. After next year when they bloom we can make a note of it. Your grandpapa will sit up there in heaven and watch them bloom."

"Why did you fuss at me for saying women make God's flowers?"

"What, Cale?"

"Nothing."

"Don't you nothing me. What did you say?"

"It didn't make any sense. I said he was helping the women make God's flowers."

"Oh. I thought we had decided to drop that. You would have surely loved your grandpapa, Pearlie, and he would have loved the stuffings out of you. He just thought women were the finest things on the face of the earth and if he had thought he was going to have a little blond granddaughter, I think he would have lived forever. He would have had you made Princess of the World."

Cale yawned out loud. Pearlie looked at him and he thought he noticed her turn up her nose to him before she looked back to Falissa, listening now.

"He would speak of the gardens about Summit, the vainness of flowers. He made many a penny weeding and planting for ladies who would claim his work for their own and he didn't care a bit. I would get after him for letting them take credit. One of them won on his dahlias at the garden show even. And he said no, he didn't want it, because when you saw a patch about a house you were inclined to think there was a woman inside and it was the work of her hands. He didn't want credit for a woman's work."

"I know one, Mama. I just remembered one."

"Well, go ahead. Tell it and I'll get back to mine."

"Papa told about a man who used to set stones in rings in the store downtown, how he couldn't believe a man could get those little stones in the holes. And one day when he was in the shop, an old man come in with a rock he had found split right in two and in the middle there was what looked blue so he come to see what it was and it was a sapphire which was worth a lot of money because it was filled with some kind of stars . . ."

"A star sapphire. That is a special part of the stone."

"Anyway, anyway." Cale was breathless like it was coming to him too fast and if he didn't keep spilling it out, it would go right by him. "Anyway, the man went to work cutting out the stars in the blue stone and he hit wrong with his cutter and broke it in a million pieces and just put his head down and cried. He did, he told me that."

"That's just exactly like one of Papa's stories. He could break your heart with his stories. I suppose he told you a woman should have done that and it wouldn't have happened?"

Cale looked blank a minute. "I don't remember but Daddy told me that man was a queer."

"Cale!"

"He did! Daddy said that he was about half woman which is what a queer is and he said the man with the squeaky voice who sells magazines down at the station is the same way."

"Don't you say that word again. Do you realize what you said?"

"Well, Daddy said it."

"I don't care who said it. If I hear you say it again, you are going on a trip to the barn."

"But he told me . . ."

"Hush, just hush this minute. You hear me, hush!"

Falissa's hands were shaking. She had quit working. Cale was quiet now and looked down. Pearlie still sorted the bulbs, not listening, Falissa thought. Who knows? Who in the world knows what they hear and what they don't and how they go sifting it out in their heads?

"Pearlie?"

Pearlie looked up. "I was thinking I'd like to spend the night at Betty's. She has a double-decker bed . . ."

"Some other time, Pearlie. I was telling you about the gardens, the ones your grandpapa made all over this town. They stand to this day even after he has long been in heaven, they bloom to beat the band. And in the lightest of color. You might not remember this but I want to tell you one of the most special things about women that your grandpapa said. He used to see a garden all tangled up with zinnias and red dahlias and big

bright-colored flowers with these loud-colored blooms and just
let somebody say it was pretty. 'Pretty!' he would say. 'Humph!
You call that pretty? That is like a painted sweaty woman in
church. That is the work of a red-handed farm woman. Now
take a periwinkle. Took a fine-handed woman to shape a periwinkle.' He would say that, that red-handed farm women
were good for no better than ripping open a sack of guano, for
slinging off handfuls of feathers and pulling apart a picked
chicken, or snatching out a ragweed and beating the dirt off
its roots. Not a one of those hands could have shaped a periwinkle, took a lady to make a periwinkle, maybe a plastic tulip
but not a periwinkle or a columbine, which was another of
his favorites . . ."

"You fussed at me for telling the same thing . . . about the
periwinkles. That's not —"

"It's not the same!"

"It is too. He wasn't talking about planting a patch. He was
talking about making the flower in the first place. Don't you
know? He meant dreaming up the flower in the first place."

"You just need to get a little smarter and a little older, young
man, before you decide that you know more than your elders.
I'll let you know in plenty of time when that moment has
arrived. And your grandpapa was a humble man, Pearlie.
He knew as much as ten men but he never made like it and he
never was a braggart. He never was pushy and loud-mouthed
like some people I know. He was a humble man."

"He used to brag about the telegraft."

"That wasn't bragging."

"He said nobody at the other stations could keep with him
and they had to tell him to slow down so they could read it because he was so quick with his fingers. He said he was waiting
for everything to get broken in a storm or war or something so
everybody would come running to him and beg him to run
the telegraft."

"He just saw too many of those cowboy movies with you.

Papa never thought of himself saving the day. Papa wasn't that kind of man. He was proud but he wasn't a braggart. He was proud as stuff about this house and how it was put together with pegs and it was a hundred years old but he wasn't boastful."

"He showed me a brick, at the bottom of the chimney, and it has a dog's foot in it big as a bear, and he said they must have cut that brick right out of a mud patch. I told my teacher about it and she said it might be a custom. She said they might have done it on purpose for some reason. I wish I could tell Papa. I told her Papa saw the Civil War . . ."

"He most certainly did not. He wasn't even born. How old do you think we are?"

"Well, he almost saw it. He could have. His brothers and sisters did."

"But they were dead long before Papa."

"My teacher showed us pictures today of the women in long dresses and they looked like he said Grandmama did."

"She wasn't that old either."

"Well, they looked like those pictures in her room of her."

"Those aren't your grandmother. They came from the store."

"Papa said they were her, all those in the case that Daddy pushed in her room were of her."

"They looked like her but they weren't her. She just picked them out because she thought that was the way she looked. She was a prissy woman, your grandmama. You will never see one so prissy. She thought she looked like those white dolls and I declare she did."

"Did I see her?"

"What?"

"Did I ever see her? Before I could remember?"

"She saw you but you were too little, one month old when she died. She hardly had been outside in her life, just as white as a lily. She was a most special-looking woman. Your grandpapa and I were walking home from church one day, and we came by the colored church and your grandpapa saw those colored women in their white organdy dresses, black angel dresses going to sing in the choir just fanning back and forth those pasteboard fans with Lydon's Funeral Parlor on them and that picture like on the front of the colored funeral house, Booker T. Washington. And they were slick with sweat and had drops on their upper lips that just made me tickle because they wouldn't wipe them away, and he popped up and said, 'Look at them trying to dress out white. She never would sweat like a horse, not on the hottest of days.' Tickled me good. Papa thinking those colored women were trying to pretend they were like Mama Sarah Ann. Just because they wore white choir dresses and got decked out in organdy ruffles. Made him mad as fire and he was as light-tempered a person as I ever seen."

"Aunt Bynum told me she was mean to them, that she won't nice like you and that she hit her once in the back with her umbrella stick because she didn't get out of her way fast enough."

"Aunt Bynum told you that?"

"She did, didn't she Pearlie?"

"She did. When we were swinging on the tire. And it made a whelp on her big as a cucumber."

"You don't believe a nigra's tales, do you?"

Cale shrugged his shoulders and didn't answer.

"What else did she tell you?"

"I don't remember."

"You, Pearlie?"

"I don't remember."

"Well, when you decide to remember, you tell me and we'll see about that. Your grandmama was a fine Southern lady. Only the old, old women at the church are as fine-mannered as she was because hard times have made us rougher. She had two kitchen hands when I was a little girl, Aunt Bynum and Sister Sue, and it won't till the depression when they had to be put in the field to make ends meet. But you don't want to hear such as that. It would be the hottest day of the year and you just didn't like to be around people and you'd get near Mama, I declare it is the truth, and she would smell like powder and soap, sitting in the shade of the porch up there with her fan folded shut in her hand. She just opened it for the prettiness of it, so you could see the lilacs trimmed in gold and the pearls strung 'long the edge. And when Papa was lying there in that bed he looked up at me and said, 'My woman has skin that never was touched by the heat of day and she is whiter than the bed sheets. I would have thought that her face was the whitest thing on God's earth but those legs are whiter. White as a cloud!' Cale, you were there when he was remembering her dying, that's what it was and talking about her like she was alive with him. White as a gardenia, he said, and if she was handled roughly she would bruise . . . Cale! Did you throw that rock?"

"Yes, ma'am."

"You're not too big for a whipping. Why did you throw that rock? You almost hit me. You could have put out Pearlie's eye."

"Because I don't like hearing you talk all the time about her."

"About who? About Mama? You don't like something, you say so and explain yourself. You don't throw rocks."

"You hit me with a rock and I bean you."

"Get quiet, Pearlie. This is between Cale and I. About Mama, I said? You don't want anyone talking about your own grandmother?"

"Yes, ma'am."

"Well, why not, for goodness' sake? There's quite a lot that grown-ups can tell you that you weren't around to notice and someday your own little children are going to want to know about their kin. You won't have kin like Mama again. There aren't women like her anymore . . ."

"I'm glad there aren't . . ."

"You don't have to listen. You just act like a decent human being when somebody is talking to you. You never even knew her and don't you go getting your ideas from some nigra who'd just as soon spit on you as talk to you."

"If I'd know Grandmama, I would have pinched her until she turned brown like a nigger."

Falissa stood up, dropping and scattering the bulbs that were in her apron. "That's the last word from you, young man! You are going to get a whipping from your daddy this time. You are a hateful, ugly little boy."

"I don't care. I would. I'd have pushed her in the pond with the frogs. Ain't nobody that good as her. She thought she was too fancy. And she had a nigger slave name. She wouldn't have been so snooty if she'd known she had a nigger slave name." Cale was laughing now and Pearlie started to laugh with him.

"Didn't she, Pearlie? Didn't I show you?"

Pearlie didn't answer but kept laughing when Falissa looked down at her.

"Cale, what has gotten into you?"

She broke off a switch and he ran to the edge of the porch out of her reach.

"You look up over his bed, under the steps. You do it! Papa knew it. He read it to me." Cale ran yelling through the house.

*   *   *

After supper, Jerome took Cale to the barn. Falissa couldn't hear him whipping but she knew he was; she couldn't bear to hear it even though it was her doing. And it would be a bad one because she'd been holding Jerome off from him for a long time. As many times as she had switched him herself and hidden his doings from Jerome, now here she made him do it. But she didn't have any choice. A switching would have been a waste of energy on a boy his size. Jerome would use his belt. He would be careful of his mouth next time.

She went into the front room and opened the door to the bed closet. What in the world was over Papa's bed? The light was burned out but she could see paper on the ceiling up over the bed, just like the one someone had pasted on the pantry shelves before she was born and Mama had made her pick off. Lying on the bed was a flashlight, Cale's light. She took it and lit up the ceiling. Then she saw what Cale had told her about, a newspaper from Raleigh, 1863. Somebody had covered over the cracks in the ceiling to keep the dirt from the steps from sifting. Some little child probably way back in the Civil War. Cale ought to get that down and take it to school. And in the center, still clear, a small notice:

$100 Reward — Ranaway from the subscriber on the 29th May, a negro woman named Sarah Ann. She weighs about 160 lbs., is 5 ft., 5 or 6 inches high, dark copper color, kitchen hand, full faced, quick spoken, about 20 years old and took all her clothing with her when she left. I will give the above reward for her delivery to me, or for her confinement in any jail so that I can get her . . . my address is Samuel L. Delong, Thomasville, N. C.

Sarah Ann. For goodness' sake. It does say Sarah Ann. And with the same spelling. Why that's from back in slave times, before Papa was even born. That was put up here by somebody in his daddy's family, that didn't even know he'd marry a Sarah Ann. Imagine somebody buying and owning a person and putting in an ad like she was no better than a lost cow. Wouldn't that have gotten Mama good, a slave with her name? What a sin to even think it. The last day Papa had been in there, all his raving about the cooking and getting that nigger out of his kitchen, why I knew that wasn't like Papa. I knew it just as good. He had never talked like that about the colored people, in fact Papa was better than most not to mistreat them needlessly. Then he ran Aunt Bynum out of the house, ran her out of Sarah Ann's kitchen the day he died. Made me wash every dish on the shelf swearing Aunt Bynum had touched them when I did every one of them myself. Said he won't going to eat a nigger's cooking when he'd done it a

thousand times. I let him lie there in his dying misery with
that looking down on him and didn't know a thing about it.
I thought it was all up inside his head and there's what was
bothering him big as day. Every name on the face of the Lord's
earth and that has to be the one in front of his eyes. But it
was a common enough name to have. No matter. His poor
mixed-up brain. Poor old confused head. I live my life with that
in my house, as much as I scrub and dust and clean and not
even know it is there. I don't care a hoot about the world out
there anymore but I will not have goings-on in my own house
I don't know of. I just won't have it. That is coming down
out of there if I have to scratch it off with my nails. If I'd seen
that, I wouldn't have let Papa see it for the world and not Cale
in a million years. A man buying and selling a woman. I don't
care what color she is, she is still made up like a woman. I
don't care if she is green, that is just the worst thing I ever heard
of. I hope she got off and he never found her, no more respect
for a woman than that, asking them to hold her in a jail until
he got his sorry hands on her. That lady preacher said what
they were up to, she knew it. Acting like it was just for the work
around the house and that's the difference between hiring and
owning. Thinks if he owns something it's to do with as he
pleases. And my children were there. Cale knows just as good.
They pick up things at school. Who is to tell him right? He
can see. Doesn't have to go outdoors to see. He can see that
Jerome don't treat a woman right. And Papa did. But he
hates her, he never knew her and he hates that kind of lady.
And I declare I must have made it as bad as anybody, talking too much. And the first thing you know that Roe will come
in here and mess up his mind with filth. He won't listen to a
word I say. He won't listen to some fancy talk on respecting and
treating with kindness. No sirree, he will hear all that big-
mouth talk from those men with about half of it made up and
the first thing you know, he'll be grown-up and just like the
lot of them. Not worth a hoot and a holler. Won't take much

for him to grow up sideways. Papa, you ought to be here to tell him about women, you went away too soon. You went away with the most important thing still to be done. He won't listen to me because I don't have no filthy dressing to put on what I say like Jerome and Roe. You were as ashamed to death of them as I am, Papa. He gets to be a man like them I want no part of him. He can just call himself some other woman's son. That's not the son I raised up and I'll just show him a little picture and tell him that is my son but he has gone away. That's my sweet boy that is no more. Then he'll cry and he'll want to be his mama's son again but it will be too late for him to change his ways. Stop it! Stop it, Falissa. Stop it!

Cale and Jerome came through the back door as she jerked up off the closet bed and closed the door quietly. She moved to the window and heard Cale walk behind her, not crying out loud but whimpering and sniffing. She watched her breath form, disappear, while he climbed slowly up the steps to his room. He shut the door, hit the bed and the springs squeaked then went quiet. And she felt for a moment everything leave her, like in a fainting spell, her head went light. It was some kind of madness.

"Why don't you settle down? He's just like everybody else's kid and needs burning up now and then. You're just peeved because you can't make them go your way to save your life. Ain't that it?"

Jerome stood at the door and looked at her for an answer.

"Leave them alone, Falissa. They'll make out as good as anybody's." He went out on the porch and she watched his pipe flare up in the darkness. She straightened her hand and stroked the curtain but the veins in her skin stayed pinched, swollen. Her face burned until it felt wet.

Nothing you would look on, nothing anybody would look on and remark it was special. And it is all going to go that way. There on a little plot of land no one would ever turn their head to look at.

Book Three

Chapter 22

ROE JENKINS sat on the third seat back of a Trailways bus. He had stared at the window that was stuck shut through patterns of brown mud sealed on from the last rain and watched the headlights move through the bus. He couldn't sleep because every time he shut his eyes the combination of the diesel smell blowing through the window from the seat in front of him and the large quantity of bad alcohol he had consumed brought his stomach up level with the top of his neck. Last night he wondered where there was mud since it was paved from Jersey to Virginia but now he knew, this S.O.B. picked up every bum on every dirt road in Virginia. The bus smelled bad, real bad. The field hands who got in and out left their stink behind them. Give their fifteen cents to the driver just to ride half a mile to the station to take a frigging shit. He got right tickled at the driver when a nigger asked him where was a colored restroom and he pointed to the woods and said, You oughta be able to find somewhere out there to cock up your leg. Takes a bus to bring out the worst in people. Let them live off in their holes in the woods and you can get away from them but try traveling in a thirty-foot box with a stuck window with enough of them to fill up a state. Didn't no nigger try to hole up in the free john in the men's room, just them wops who come picking think they can act like a white man. Think that because the only thing rotten they ain't is a nigger. And not one honey worth having in two hundred miles of this box.

Gone me one onct, right on the bus. Set her on my lap and took her on the bus at night when the lights were out and no one knew a thing about it. Little bit hefty, though, wore me out in the legs. Getting too old for experimenting. That'll be the day I push up a lily. Got to watch them bastard drivers with the lights if they're on to you. Flick them on and look up in that mirror. You can usually figure on the time to the next town. You can figure it takes twice as long as it oughta and if he's going to stop somebody pulls the cord, bing! This one that come on at the last station is the kind of bastard I don't trust with the lights. Got him a fat ass wife at home he's wore out. Naw, it ain't her wore out, it's him. That's the type. Fuck a flying doughnut, man. There's one behind me tonight that would have to pay me she's so bad off and she has been going at that poor fellow running her mouth for two hours without breathing and that guy hadn't even grunted for an hour. Stick a sock in her mouth to take that one.

"Sure is a noisy place to sleep, ain't it, buddy?"

"You bet," the fellow replied.

She shut up. That ought to get me a beer out of a fellow come Summit. I'd a told her to shut her goddamn mouth. Ain't nobody on the face of the earth gives a damn if her sister's husband left her, probably not even her sister's husband. Least of all her sister's husband if it runs in the family.

Stinks. Stinks rotten in here. You watch me go thumbing next time. Damn rather go thumbing and light up on the back of a load of hogs than this. Least you can breathe while you're waiting. Here a man's got to smoke to breathe. I was late getting a move on it, too, had an unexpected delay in Petersville of the legal variety. Tied one on last night and got myself caught up in a raid with me already upstairs with one of them, a nice one too, blond and just a little plump and plenty damn young when the door gets kicked in and it won't even locked and there was a gun on me before I got my hands on my pants. But I had me one good roll and was about asleep on her. Makes you wonder when they bust in like that if Petersville ain't got them a little cooperative going. You let them get a honey, which means they ain't flat broke, then the cops get them and take care of the rest of it. They'll put me to sleep in a privy before they'll make me pay out no twenty dollars for some crummy sheriff to line his pockets. Sheriff is a Baptist and don't know no better than to act like one. But that little sweetheart last night put her up a fight. Scratched him up like an alley cat, trying to get his hands on her for free. Might have just popped in before schedule to catch her with her pants off. But she tore him up good. She won't no fool. 'Cept when it come to me. Believe on these lying lips.

Took us in and I told that little baby I was a visiting evangelist and this was a terrible embarrassment and I would work on getting us out of there. Just watch my style. I held me a meeting or two in my day talking up them dollars and cents, them fellows ain't no fools, them evangelists. It's the one who thinks he got it right to be set up in one place who's got his balls on backwards. You try to move out on the little lady and they'll string you up. But you come in and out, slam, bam, thank-you-ma'am. That's my style of gospel. Healing is my favorite, putting my hands on them shriveled up heads. Heal, baby, heal. Jump in and beg for it. This one will get old Jerome. Wait'll I tell it about the Petersville jail. Asked for me a Bible first. Now they won't going to refuse no man a Bible. In his time of trial, how could they refuse a man the good book. Not a smile. Not a smile in that long row of whores and hot pants. I turned me to Acts and when I tried to find the pages, I didn't have no doubt how drunk I was.

"And a certain woman named Lydia, a seller of purple, of the city of Thyatira, which worshipped God, heard us; whose heart the Lord opened, that she attended unto the things which were spoken of Paul. And when she was baptized, and her household, she besought us, saying, If ye have judged me to be faithful to the Lord, come into my house, and abide there.

"If the city treats you with unkindness, come to my house and stay."

One of the fat cops laughed and got pushed in the arm. Go man.

"*And it came to pass, as we went to prayer, a certain damsel possessed with a spirit of divination met us* . . . and come following behind calling me the man of God. But I turned her away. She was after my powers for her own. And . . . in doing so . . . my friends . . ." He turned his head, shutting the book and looked at all of them. They were listening now. The slur was slipping off his voice. It would get going good when he was preaching. ". . . annoyed me as it did Paul many years ago. I tried to push her away but she would not be turned. She was after the weakness of man. At her own admittance after the weakness of man. And the magistrates were angry for we followed a custom not of their city and they dragged us away. The citizens attacked our bodies with stones, the magistrates tore the garments off our bodies and gave orders to beat us with rods and sticks. And we were thrown into the jail.

"Read it my friends. It is there in the Bible, Acts 16, the Book of our Lord. Paul and Silas in prison because they went against the customs of the land. When in Rome do as the Romans do. But how do you know what the Romans do if the Romans don't tell you? How do you know when they send their beautiful women after a tired and lonesome man? With such lovely women would not a man believe that was what the Romans do? Must a man not believe this is what the Romans do? Or the Petersvillians." He drooled a little on that one. Right down the front of his lapel. Not quite drunk enough to give it his all. Not quite sober enough either. The climate had been better. But onward to victory.

"And they threw Paul and Silas into prison and tossed away the key. They tied and handcuffed them and threw them on the cold, cold ground. And they did not give them water to drink, food for their tired bodies, a pillow for their heads. Ah

my friends, but that was a mistake. For in the night Paul and
Silas began to sing, to sing with the voices of nightingales
the hymns of our Lord. Their voices rose through the ceiling,
over the walls, out to the far corners of the city, to the very
heavens. And our Lord heard them my friends, our Lord up
there in heaven on his throne said, I hear the voice of man.
Man is crying out to me. He is in trouble. He needs my help."

He had them now. Even the old guy at the desk had come
around and was listening.

"And suddenly the floor of the jail began to tremble and a
great crack came in it. The bars rattled, the walls shook, and
rolled like waves on a mighty ocean, and the Lord let loose a great
earthquake that shook the very foundations of the prison. And
the Lord called out 'I'm angry' and the very earth shook with
the force. And the handcuffs snapped away. And the doors
flew open. And the walls fell down. And all were set free.
And the jailer, bloody and dying in the rubble, threw himself
down at their feet. He drew his knife and said 'I will cut my own
throat before the wrath of God comes upon me. I will spill my
blood on the floor because I have sinned in locking up these
brethren because they come to our city and did not know how
we do.'

"And did Paul and Silas allow this? Did they? No, they did
not. They opened their hearts in kindness. Paul cried out, 'Don't
hurt yourself. Do not inflict on yourself a mortal wound. Fall
on your knees and be saved. There is still time to be saved. It
is never too late when there is the very air of life in your body
to fall before your Lord Jesus Christ and be saved.' And the
jailer fell on his knees before them and said, 'Kind sirs, Please
help this poor sinner. What must I do to be saved?' And Paul
said quite simply, 'Believe on the Lord Jesus Christ and thou
shalt be saved.' That is all. And that is everything. I have
spoken. And to you my friends let that be a lesson. No bars made
by man will hold me. No cell can contain the burning fire of
my love of God. Put walls around me and the Lord will tear them

down. Go now. Set me free and the Lord be with you. Bless you."

They went in the back room and had a conference. They called me in away from my fellow prisoners, and shoved me out the door. Said get out of town on the next bus. The next bus was a local but I didn't spend the night behind bars with a bunch of smelly bums. Just spent the night on Trailways with a bunch of smelly bums.

Might have to go back to preaching. Been a while now. But not if I'm spending a spell in Summit. Falissa would have my hide on the wall. Boy, I was wrong about that one. How wrong can you get? Just tells you how a nice ass can lead you astray. One royal bitch that one turned into, tongue zinging at you like a snake, and how long did it take, a year. But won't Jerome one to let the world slide over him. Hanging around that place with Papa Willie thinking he was going to get it for sixteen years. I swear to God I bet I set up in my crib and said Papa Willie is a sonovabitch. Jerome is slow on the draw. Ask him a question and by the time he's answered it you forgot what you asked. Jerome, what you think of the weather? By sundown, you get, 'Barometer's falling. Winds in the west, might rain.' Not very swift that Jerome. Has to start planting a year early to get it in the ground. But give him a pot of dirt. Set his ass in a sandbox and he happy as a Jew on a pile of money. Got me wondering what his younguns are like. Hope the Lord had the decency not to make them look like him anyway. Just see a little girl with a fat lip and a space between the teeth big enough for a cat to walk through. Falissa ain't bad-looking though, just a bit rawboned. Maybe she took after her but she'll have feet like a duck, no getting away from that with them plopping along from both sides of the family. But I tell you about them country gals like Falissa. They put on a big show with their piousness but, baby, they want it too. You can't give them enough of it. Wouldn't tell you in a million

years and think you don't know it. I seen a million like Falissa.
But she can cook some dumplings. And ain't nobody can hold
a candle to her damson preserves. But she is one royal bitch.
Don't know how I called that one wrong. Don't know where
she got those set ideas except what wore off from that prissy
stick of a mother. Broke the mold when they made that one.

But that little Cale is what I'm after to see. Take him out
on a spree that will send his Mama to the altar on Saturday
night. Knowing Jerome he figures it ain't nothing but something to play with in the barn. Jerome never had a live ant in
his pants in his life, just sit there till mold growed on him. I
swear when I used to take him by to Sallie she said my big brother
was going to have her arrested for rape. Just too goddamn lazy
to screw. He does beat all. Summit 8 miles. Man you got to
be one foot in it before they tell you it's near. I thought I heard
my stomach growling.

*   *   *

Roe was in Summit by one-thirty Saturday. The bus
hissed to a stop right in front of the house and Roe got off carrying his duffel bag and a cardboard box. Cale saw him from
the window first.

"He's here. Uncle Roe is here."

He banged out through the front door and Falissa watched
from the window. Jerome was out at the barns. Roe dropped
his duffel bag and shook hands with Cale. They carried his
things to the porch and she slipped back in the shadow watching them as they started toward the barns, Roe with his arm
around Cale. He hadn't aged much. Looked a little heavier,
baggy around the face. That's what all that drinking does to you.
It'll catch up with him sooner or later.

She went into the back room and took out another chair
and put it at the table. And if that chair stays there more than
two weeks there are going to be some words. She went into the
kitchen and took out her flour cloth and started to roll out the

dumplings. With all his faults Roe was a man that noticed what was on the plate in front of him before he choked it down. The bed was made in Sarah Ann's room and he could just see how long he could sleep in there with the frills and the mothballs. Roe hated mothballs. You had to plan ahead when a relative like Roe paid a visit. Yes sirree.

"Mama, there's a strange man out at the barn with Cale and Daddy."

Pearlie looked out of her room, her head covered with one of Falissa's old hats.

"I know, honey. That is your Uncle Roe."

"Can I go out to meet him? Please?"

"Why don't you wait until he comes in? They're probably talking men talk. And I can guarantee you'll get to see more than enough of your Uncle Roe. Don't let all these promises about coming for a visit fool you. When he lights, he sticks like glue."

Falissa had held lunch for Roe and did her usual supper fixings, pie and biscuits. Roe sat down at the head of the table, Jerome's chair, but nobody said anything because he was company. Falissa asked Pearlie to say grace and she started out: " 'Now I lay me down to sleep, I pray the Lord my soul to keep; if I die before I wake . . .' Oh, that's wrong, Mama. Mama, please start it for me. I forget." Roe got tickled and Falissa's face turned red.

"Don't say grace very often these days, Falissa?"

"Just for company."

"Hush, Pearlie."

Roe leaned back in his chair and kept laughing, then Jerome and Cale joined him.

"Now this is not very funny. Bless this food our Father . . ."

"And thank you for our many other blessings. Pass the chicken," Roe said and laughed again. Now he had Cale and Jerome going. Falissa reached for the bowl of dumplings and handed it to Jerome.

"Well, I suppose we should eat it before it gets cold since it takes so much to-do to get out a decent blessing," Falissa said.

"Didn't she smile, Jerome? Didn't I just see a little wink of a smile on that pretty face?"

"Pretty faces we don't have here."

"Why I see two of them, one ripe and one ablooming. I was saying to myself coming down here that I hoped that little girl would be fortunate enough not to look like a Jenkins and sho nuff she was. Just like her mama. Pretty as a picture. How old are you, Pearlie?"

"Eight almost."

"And pretty as a grown woman. Going to be a heart-breaker."

"I'd just as soon she looked like a little girl for a while knowing the likes of you are still around."

Roe began to laugh loudly as he stacked his plate high with dumplings. "Ain't changed a bit, Falissa. I told Jerome when he married you that there was a gal with some kick."

"Pearlie, drink your milk down some. I don't want to see any turnovers tonight or somebody I know is going to leave the table."

"Falissa, you mind I tell Jerome about the war? We got started out back before supper . . ."

"I don't believe I remember if it made any difference if I minded or not, Roe. Say what you please but remember there are two children present who hear every word of it. That's all I ask. I don't want Pearlie having any more nightmares."

"Tell us about the Japs," Cale said.

"The Japs. Now there is a funny race of animals because if you saw them you would see they weren't people in our sense of the word. They aren't big as a minute and they move around like their pants on fire, scuffle along like rollers is on their feet and they squint at you so tight you can't see their eyeballs. They had these guys in the war, you heard about them that fly out on a mission with orders to crash their planes in our ships, suicide flyers. Ain't that something? Go into training just to go out and get yourself killed and crash your plane. Knowing damn good and well you can't come back alive. You know that ain't like us. We got no business getting messed up with people who don't think like us if you know what I mean."

"I seen them in the newsreel, Uncle Roe. They come crashing right into our boats and caught them on fire."

"That's the one and you know them yellow bastards, excuse me, Falissa, them Japs wait there where they take off and if they see one of them come back not crashed, they shoot him down themselves. Now how can you fight people like that, I ask you? I tell you it was different in Europe. You had a gun, he had a gun, you do something stupid and he'd get you or you'd get him the same way, but you let one of them Japs catch you without a gun. He'd put on this big grin and cut you down. Zap."

"You want more iced tea, Roe? There's a pot in the kitchen."

"Yes please. Let me get it, Falissa."

"No, you keep your seat." Falissa went into the kitchen but she left the door open.

Roe started to whisper. "But let me tell you about them little women. Those yellow bastards know how to bring up their women right. They know their places I tell you. They wait on a man like he's a king, bringing you food and warming your feet. Now don't you frown at me, Pearlie. You ain't no slant-eyed gal. It's going to be the other way around for you, men bowing and scraping."

"Hey Roe, what happened to that one you brought back?" Jerome asked.

"Oh. Well, she went back. They sent her back. She didn't have the right papers. That's the last I heard of her. She didn't write no English. Cute little thing."

"Did you really marry her when you had another wife, did you, huh?"

"Believe I did." Jerome started to laugh and Cale watched the tears form around his eyes. "But don't believe I'll pull that one again. No sirree. Like to have put me under the jail. There's hard laws on the books for that one. And I have become an expert on them I can tell you."

"Did you ever get you a French gal? I hear they're humdingers," Jerome asked.

"You certainly have a way of bringing out the best in my husband, Roe. Are you children finished? You have my permission to leave the table and go play."

"How about dessert, Mama? I saw you turning ice cream."

"I'll give it to you at bedtime. You run along now." Cale and Pearlie got up and left the room, Pearlie back to her paper dolls but Falissa could see Cale with his hands in his pockets trying to hear from the porch. No use. She was wasting her time. She couldn't follow them around, for goodness' sake.

"I tell you Jerome. Don't believe what they say about French gals. Cool as cucumbers. It's the English ones that are the best. Give me a gal I can talk to any day. Got little sharp noses like they were whittled and their eyes roll in a bit too close, nice twitchy little behinds, but you got to get used to seeing what pure blood does to people. Ain't got the variety we got. Let's say, they didn't have. They got it now."

Jerome started to laugh again, while Falissa began clearing the table. Roe was still eating so she just cleared it around him and moved the bowls in closer.

"Clean it all up if you like. Save me putting up leftovers."

"Fine meal, Falissa. You're better than ever, if that's possible."

"Thank you, Roe."

"Let me tell you something about that mixed blood, Jerome. You might not believe this but them foreign gals don't know a nigger from a white man."

"Naw."

"I'm telling you. That place is full of half-nigger babies. People over here wondering why we got some uppity niggers now should have seen what I seen. Black buck come in a uni-

form and he could have his pick. I seen one pull a knife on a
white fellow because this red-headed French gal had taken to
him first and this fellow didn't like it, see. They'd have put his
ass in a tree in Yeller County. It was enough to make you sick,
Jerome. We going to have us some trouble. You mark my
words. Should have either sent them over for good or kept them
here, one or the other."

"We know how to take care of that, don't we Roe?"

"Yeah, they see how well we know how. You have any
trouble around here?"

"Naw, Summit don't have no trouble. They know better.
Just sorry as ever. Aunt Bynum makes out like she's smart then
I seen a pile of clothes down in the woods last week, good clothes.
Some Falissa give them the kids had outgrown. They weren't
even hurt. Just got them stinking dirty and throwed them
away. Never thinked to wash them out."

"That's a nigger for you. That was one thing Willie had right.
Should have got them in crates before there was so many and
shipped them back."

"Yeah, just got us stuck with them because them Yankee
bastards couldn't use them. If they could have stood the cold
they would own them to this day up there in them factories,
what you bet? They wouldn't have fought no war to set
them free. Just weren't smart enough to get any work out of
them."

"Shit yeah. But they going to get them. They getting them
now. Man, you just get on a bus going north you'll see where
they all going. And I bet they ain't expecting them."

Jerome started to laugh. "No kidding, Roe. They all moving
up there?"

"By the hundreds. Some of them take the whole crew, fat
mama and her brood with their stuff in shopping bags, going
north. Some of them leave them behind but there is no doubt
to my mind they moving north."

"They be back come winter to eat off us. They can't do nothing in the winter."

"They can work in them factories. That's what they got their minds on. What them Yankees don't know is no nigger ever done nothing longer than two weeks. And what them niggers don't know is when the work stops, there ain't nobody to keep them up. They leaving Summit?"

"I ain't seen no less. We'd make out just fine if they did, just fine. You won't find me complaining."

"You two want to fight the Civil War again or would you rather eat homemade ice cream?"

"She sho has picked up, Jerome. Sho has. She'd of throwed me out on my ass ten years ago."

"She's just putting on for you. She'll still throw you out on your ass and me behind you, you don't watch her."

"Bring it in here, honey," Roe called. "There ain't no nectar of the gods as sweet as your peach ice cream."

"It's apple. The peaches are long gone."

"Apple then. You name your flavor. Don't she move pretty, Jerome? Just as light as a girl."

"I thought it was a slue-footed pigeon the last time you were here."

"Don't she have a memory for the bad? You do look fine, Falissa. People going to ask you if my ugly brother is your papa. Where is the old man? He die?"

"Four years ago June, Roe. I wrote you, remember?"

"Sorry to hear that, Falissa."

"Thank you, Roe. I have gone out of mourning."

"Swish like a snake. That tongue will cut an iron bar in two. What's doing in Summit tonight, Jerome? The usual twenty choices?"

"The same thing that's doing every night for me, Roe. Sleeping. I'm too old for that."

"Where's the boy? There he is. Cale, what's doing in Summit tonight?"

"He has to do his homework."

"Not on Saturday night, Falissa. Caught you there, didn't I. What's doing, boy?"

Cale stood at the door. "Got a ball game in Raleigh and a race over at the oval this afternoon we could get in. And a thing over at the school grounds, a carnival like."

"A carnival. You didn't tell me about it." Falissa said.

"You wouldn't have gone, Mama. I was saving it for Uncle Roe."

"Well, let's you and me go carnivaling."

"Can we, Mama?"

"I just don't want you down at that race track. You're too young for that crowd and one of those cars might get loose and run over you and you'll just eat hot dogs and mess for supper. Ask your father."

"I don't care. You just come in quiet, Roe. You learn him how to leave his clodhoppers on the porch."

"O.K., Cale. Me and you gotta go check out which one is the squeaky step."

*   *   *

Cale and Roe made it into Summit by three-thirty. Soon as they got out of sight of the house, they started thumbing.

Had to fill Uncle Roe in quick on Mama; he stuck out his thumb right there in front of her. If you get a ride you got to ask to get put off before you get there, at least down below Will James' place in case she happens to be out in the yard or she'll give you a fit. You could spend half your life walking and Mama wouldn't care. I told Tommy to look out for us down about the depot and if we won't there before eight to go on without us. But there he was, leaning up against the wall, smoking a cigar. Roe and Tommy hit it off right away. Tommy can talk big like a grown man about women and all and I don't mind it because he don't never make me admit to anything I haven't done in front of anybody. He lets me in on things. He has been wanting me to come in on Saturdays since I've known him and you

know this is the first time Mama has ever let me. I knew it
would be good with Roe coming.

We are at the track now, first place we come to and the feature
hadn't got going yet. Roe paid both of our ways to get in.
We're waiting on them to get started. They're out shoveling dirt
in the biggest holes. There's one right here in front of us that
gets them up on two wheels every time. I been here when
there won't no cars, just an old balled-up wreck with numbers
on it like it was broom painted. But this is something else.
All them cars going around and running the people back from
the fence. It's really something. Roe bought us special seats up
in the bleachers where we could see. Somebody got run over
down here once was what Mama was scared of. I have never
seen such cars. Makes those over at the high school look like
something my mama would drive if she could drive a car. She
tried once Daddy said, thinking it was no harder than the tractor,
and backed his cousin's car into the fence and they laughed at
her so hard she never got in one again. They are out raking the
track now so they won't bust no more tires on the junk that come
off the cars. Dust's not settled yet from the last one.

"You ever been here before, boy?"

"No sir. At least not when a race was going on."

"Uh, don't sir me, boy, O.K.? Makes me look like an old
man."

"You're just the right age, Roe. I won't do it again. Except I
better in front of Mama if you know what I mean."

"I think it's high time you let that Mama of yours know her
place if you want to know what I mean. How old are you?"

"Eleven."

"Eleven years old. You know I left home when I won't but
one year older than you."

"That's what I tried to tell him, Roe. His mama just likes to
hear herself talk. He could light out and she would just flap
her mouth to the breeze. No old lady can't do nothing."

"Well, how 'bout you coming out and taking my whippings

for me. I oughta show you what my old man did yesterday. You slap me on the back today and I'll kill you."

"Jerome beat you?"

"He beat the daylights out of me. With his belt and knocked whelps all over me with the buckle."

"What for?"

"Sassing Mama. Or that's what she said. For not agreeing with everything she says if you want to know the truth."

"I never would have thought it. I never would have thought Jerome would give his kid a mean licking, not after what Willie done to us. That old bastard. I'd give a hundred dollars today to walk up and knock his block off if he was sitting in a wheel-chair."

"Where is Grandpa Willie? I never seen him and he's my grandpa I reckon though nobody wants to act like it."

"He's in a gutter somewhere. He has some property not far from here, might be there. He don't want to be Grandpa or Pa either. Just let him rot and forget about him. I'm sure disappointed in Jerome. He was inclined to be a stick in the mud but I never thought he'd be a mean bastard."

The engines are starting up and the cars are moving toward the track, bobbing up and down in the back. They move like old clumsy turtles before they get going in a circle. The dust is going up again. Gets so you can hardly see the other side. I can't hear nothing people are saying, Uncle Roe's mouth has stopped moving because they are coming by in front of us. Look like a row of monsters in a horror movie. That's all those old monsters are I bet, one of these with a green skin. They move good when they get one side cocked up on the track. There's one won't start and they are pushing it. It blew out fire when it took off and he's coming out on the track. The Blue Turdle. He throwed rocks all over them people down front when he went around, tat, tat, tat, through the parking lot, right through the holes in the fence and into everybody's cars. They done rutted up the track already, and they hadn't even got going.

Roe and Tommy are smoking cigars. Boy, do they stink. Roe offered me one but I ain't taking it here and get sick in front of everybody. I had one over to Tommy's and got sick as a dog. And my whole head is fuzzy inside from the dust. I thought I could stir up some with the tractor but I ain't never seen nothing like this. They got cleats on their tires near about like my tractor. I'd like to get myself in one of them.

They lined up and they aren't as noisy now.

"Keep an eye on the guy with the gun. See him."

He lifted his hand and the engines all got loud till I thought they would bust my head and they took off in the awfulest mess you ever seen. Running into each other, pushing off sideways. "I never seen so many cars in one place."

"Look them bounce back from that fence."

The people all get back from the wire and you can see the sparks as they scrape into the posts. There's color all down every one of them where they left their paint before.

"I got fifty cents on Number Seventeen, the thirty-six." That was Tommy.

"O.K. I take fifty cents on Thirteen. I think Seventeen is going to bust his ass. What you take, Cale?"

"I bet on Zero."

"Way back there?"

"I think he'll catch up."

"O.K., buddy."

Soon the engine noise was a loud whine as the cars dug for traction in the rutted track. A recap came off and slapped around the fence. Zero was sawing at the wheel. Cale could see his big muscles and a tattoo. He had on a gym shirt with "O" painted on the back and he had on Big Mac work gloves.

"I'd like to do that, Roe. I can shift gears good on the tractor without stopping."

"No gear shifting in them. They welded in gear. You let go of that wheel to go shifting and you land on your ass."

"How old you got to be?"

"Oh, I don't know. Old enough to have a license probably.
. . . whoop!" Roe turned Cale's head toward a car up on two
wheels from the hole in front of them. It balanced a moment
then went over on its roof and slid down in the grass. The driver
crawled out the window and ran to the center of the grass circle
and everybody clapped when they saw him.

"He got it that time."

It was a great mass of movement, fenders, body panels,
everything flapping as the drivers fought the steering wheels.

"I seen them back when they didn't use those gloves, come
out with their hands dripping blood. Never lift their foot, just
keep it in the floor. Had me a thirty-two like the red one yonder."

"You did, Roe? I didn't know you ever drove a race car."

"Yeah, when I was down east in Salamander."

"You've done everything, Uncle Roe."

"Not yet. But I ain't finished either."

Cale sneezed and wiped his nose on his sleeve.

"You think it's dusty here, boy, you ought to see it down east.
I seen it in July when the man won who had the biggest air
cleaner. Your nose would be so full up you'd have to take air
in your mouth. And you could feel it shifting in your lungs.
Pick your nose for a week. You think you got it bad up here you
ought to see what it's like in that car. Them fellas take a real
beating."

"My cousin's got one. He ain't out today because he got
busted up by Zipper Jones. I hope he breaks his neck."

"What car?"

"Zero."

"Hey, that's my bet."

"I still hope he breaks his ass. My cousin worked on that car
for two months and Zipper rammed him in the back and made
him turn over. I helped him build it. I got to cut out all the stuff
inside and we welded down his seat. He'd be dead today if we
hadn't welded down that seat for him to hold on to. Rolled over

four times and the gear shift went right up his pants leg and
ripped his britches off. Would have gone through his heart won't
for that welded seat."

"Did it hurt him bad?"

"Naw. Ruint the car. Beat it up underneath. Busted an
axle and rolled off over a post, tore up the rear end."

Roe turned to Cale. "You see, Cale, I told you they weld them
in gear, so they got both hands for the wheel and so it won't go
jumping out when it gets rutted. Well, if they need to change
gears, they change rear ends. Different for different tracks.
What engine he running, Tommy?"

"Flathead Ford. We gon' run it out to High Tom. Got our
other rear end in there."

"High Tom half mile, ain't it?"

"Yeah."

"How big is here, Uncle Roe?"

"Third mile. Uh oh. Watch it. He's smoking bad. There he
goes."

Twenty-one blew his engine and the oil hit the track spreading around the corner. It happened instantly. They were all in
it, sideways, over each other. The cars kept piling up, fourteen
in all, Twelve drove over Seventeen, and Zero took to the grass
and managed to stay in one piece. Twenty-one went to steer off
course and hit a pothole and turned over on his lid, wheels still
spinning off oil.

"Well, he shit in his hat."

"Look over there, Cale," Tommy said. "They are having to
pull one out the window hole. Door's welded shut."

"Is he hurt?"

"Could be real bad."

"You ought to go into betting, boy. All Zero has to do is
finish and he's got it. Nothing left but junkers. Let's cut out for
a while. This will take an hour."

"How come?"

"Because they got to undo that mess and that S.O.B. on the

bottom just wanted to give his mother a scare. He ain't hurt no more than me."

They climbed down out of the bleachers which were thinning now as people moved to their cars for their bottles.

"Don't last long."

"Naw, this was worse than usual. They don't usually all fall in the soup at once. That's the way it goes if they get bunched up. Not going to be much left worth watching. We'll check it out before we go home. Got to see if that bet gets paid off. Now where's this carnival? Over at the school? Hey boy, your old man ever tell you about me over at that grammar school?"

"I didn't know you went to the same one. I thought you went to the country school."

"There won't but one then. I got throwed out in the third grade. Ain't that something? A mere child and they throwed me out into the wickedness of the world."

Cale and Tommy laughed.

"I been throwed out twenty million times but they keep coming over after me. You must know something to get throwed out for good."

"Naw, I didn't know nothing. That was the reason. Except one little poem. One pretty little poem that I recited in my squeaky voice, face round and innocent as a choirboy."

"What was it, Roe? Can you remember it?"

"Tell you how it happened. This old teacher, Miss Cartwright, asked us all to recite our favorite poem for the class . . ."

"They still do that. They do, Roe, they still do that same thing."

"Summit always did have a way of falling back in its own crap."

"Come on, Cale. I want to hear the poem."

"The poem. Yes."

Roe stopped and stepped up on the wall by the walkway and spread out his arms, then clasped his hands together like a preacher:

There was a young man from Vass,
His balls were made out of brass.
He'd knock them together
And make stormy weather
And lightning flew out of his ass.

Cale and Tommy laughed and Roe jumped down, walking
away quickly and pushing them down the walkway. "Move
along, boys. Move along. Your old uncle has plans to sleep
on sheets tonight. That jail floor attracts me like a whore with a
fever blister."

"Mind if I borrow that one, Roe? 'Bout time for another trip
to the training school."

"What's that like? That won't there either."

"Just a big farm. Got the best baseball team around though.
And there ain't nothing much they can make you do in the
winter. You just eat what they growed last summer. Just got a
ball field. Not much doing. Just stand around and shoot the
shit a lot. Know what I mean? Ain't much worse than home
except when you decide you want to stroll on off. We're making
us some plans out there. One fellow out there, he's seventeen,
we got some plans going. I come out to talk to him at the fence
and he got run back in and we didn't get to set no other meeting
time. He'll be out in a month and then we are going to get us
some money."

"You watch your doing there. They put you up at the state
for stealing. They hold you in the training school till you get
old enough then they put you in the state pen. Won't do no ball
playing there. And people forget about you. They get all
excited and weep and wail when you're in court but they forget
about you once you're in. And you stay in. There's other ways
to get money. Just send those cops up a tree they so mad because they can't lay a hand on you. Keep those cops guessing
and you be a hop and a jump ahead of them. But you keep
away from stealing."

Tommy didn't say anything. Cale looked at him but he

couldn't see his expression in the dark. This was the first he had heard of any stealing or whatever Tommy was planning to do for money.

Tommy turned the corner and started down a side street.

"Hey, Tommy. Thought we were going to the school," Cale called.

"Ain't nothing doing at the school."

"You said there was a carnival."

"Sure with lions and tigers and dancing girls right in the boys' john." Tommy came back up to them and said, "Thought I might go off down to the river."

Roe walked over to Tommy where he could see his face. "What's down at the river? Another wild goose chase?"

"Naw, man. There's rooster fighting."

"They'll put you under the jail for that."

"What's the matter, man? You scared of cops or something?"

Cale was surprised at Tommy. Roe was their friend, but Tommy better watch his mouth. Roe would have to take Tommy down a peg if he didn't go easy.

"You got a lot to learn, boy. You remember that. I thought I knew everything when I was twelve but I know differently now. Where's the cockfight?"

"Down on the river bank behind Parson's Store in the hollow. It's off beyond the wrecked cars where you can't see it from the road. They got lantern light going for it and the cops ain't been yet. They don't know nothing. They won't know about it until it is packed up and gone. Besides it's outside the line. Got to be the sheriff and he ain't been to Summit since those two niggers cut each other up over near the dump. Friend of mine found the body."

They walked toward Parson's Store, thumbing a ride in the back of a truck. They thought he was just an old farmer until he turned in at Parson's Store and shut off the engine. He lifted a tarp up off an old hen case and slid the box down the truck bed.

"Boy, stand at the road and let me know when there's no cars."

Cale went to the road. It was clear so he waved O.K.

The old farmer took the box out in his arms and ran sprattle-legged into the woods, the rooster cock-a-dooing at a lantern light in the woods. "Shet up, you loud-mouthed little sonova-bitch. You save your balls for later."

Cale ran back to Roe and Tommy who were laughing.

"Did you hear that, Cale?" Roe asked.

"Naw, what was it? I heard a rooster crow."

"He saw the light and thought it was the sun. That little sonovabitch going to have his claws full of more than sun-shine."

Four more trucks had pulled in and a man came from inside the store and told them to park around back with the wrecks.

"Must be coming off for sure," Tommy said.

"Thought you'd been before."

"I have been but they got chicken shit and took them out of the ring before they got going good."

"Like that chicken shit," Roe said, and Tommy looked at his feet. "If I was running it, I would have a signal buzzer inside, see and if the state men came strolling up, I'd pull the buzzer and all them guys on the bank would run up and set in a row and start sipping a beer and bitching about their old ladies get-ting the tight ass, see."

"Why don't you tell them, Uncle Roe? I bet they never thought of it."

"Naw, they wouldn't appreciate it. These guys act like they know it all and underneath it they're sweating like a whore in church. Naw, let them figure it out. Let's get on down there and you two stay close on me in case we have to get out fast. They ain't going to take to seeing minors down there. If they get caught the law's worse on them."

"You sure know the law, Uncle Roe."

"Yes, son, and it ain't from practicing it. It's from breaking it.

Say you've been at one of these before, Tommy?"

"Nobody seen me. I heard they run you off if you're under thirty."

"They must figure a kid would talk too much."

"Not me, man. I know when to keep my mouth shut better than these old fools."

"We'll watch from the bushes just the same till we see if there are some other kids there. I don't want to miss this. I can get us out down the river and come up over on Eighteen if trouble comes up. I know that trail like the back of my hand. Done it many a time in the dark when Willie sent me into Parson's with his fruit jar."

They went down the path and Roe led them off behind the rocks. He took them over the rocks and they found a place where they could see the whole gathering which was now about eight men with an assortment of covered chicken cages and a circle of light from a lantern. When they got settled they could hear the hiss of the gas lantern that spread white light in the men's faces.

"How come you know this place so good, Roe?"

"I know every backwoods path in twenty miles of Summit. My old man used to make licker on that creek, up to the other end. Half dozen of them up there today I bet. It don't never let you down."

"I didn't know Grandpa Willie made licker."

"He didn't ever make no money off it. He drank up the profits as they say. I remember right before I took off, one of Willie's greatest blunders. He got drunk and let the tobacco barn catch on fire and there he was, drunker than hell, sputtering and screaming at the Summit volunteer fire department to let the goddamn tobacco barn go and save his feed barn. Well, the tobacco barn was near about new and the feed barn looked like it would fall over if you leaned on it and Willie just wasn't getting through to them and then the feed barn caught up and Willie took off running. Didn't burn half a minute till there

was the most god-awful explosion you ever heard and the roof
flew up off that barn and shot a blue blaze halfway up the sky,
showering across that farm like fireworks."

Tommy started to laugh.

"What blew up, Uncle Roe?"

"His licker, you numbskull," Tommy said.

"That's right. How did you know, Tommy?"

"Because I seen my old man pour some in a saucer and light
it and it burned blue to the ceiling."

"That's it all right. Two hundred gallons of pure corn licker
underneath his hay. Never seen anything like it."

"I bet that was something. I love a good fire. We got that
old house nobody lives in on Walnut Street."

"No kidding," Cale said. "I didn't know you had anything to
do with that."

"Yep. The *Summit Weekly* said 'cause unknown.'"

"Hey look. They're getting set up."

The men began to drag old car seats from the woods and
arranged them in a square, four bench seats, their backs in-
ward.

"They put them down in there, Uncle Roe?"

"I guess Cale. That is what they call the pit. They want the
two roosters to know they're stuck in there with each other."

Cale looked in one of the cages where a small rooster was
ramming his chest against the bars. His colors were brilliant
and moved in the light like an oil slick on the road.

"They ain't much bigger than a bantam, Uncle Roe."

"Little bigger. And about ten times as mean. I seen one of
them kill a dog, a hunting dog. He thought he had him a
pheasant cornered up and that little rascal come at him and
got him right up under the neck with his spurs and got him
bleeding. They got some wicked spurs on their legs. Then he
come in for the kill, right on top of his head and tore into his
ears. He was dead before they could get the rooster off. Turned
a hose on him to make him let loose. They'll fight a man."

"I would have thought they would peck each other to death."

"Most people do. I did until I saw my first one down in Mexico but it's a foot fight. Those Mexicans take it big. They even got them fitten with little spurs so they can make it worse. They don't like it unless the people sitting on the front row can go home with blood on them."

"They got spurs here, too. I seen them last time. Man had a set he took out of his pocket."

"I thought you hadn't seen them fight. We ain't got your story straight yet."

"I seen them. I said I hadn't been up close. I seen them many a time."

"They ever ask you to leave?"

"No. But they never knew I was here either. Besides I look old for my age, if they did see me."

"Well, we'll wait and see the crowd just to be sure. This happen every Saturday?"

"Yep, since it got started last July. Fellow come over from Tennessee sold the farmers around here a bunch of the chickens, way I heard it."

"Looks like I might pick up a little pocket change here if I'm getting a straight story out of somebody for a change."

"I ain't lying to you."

"You going to raise a rooster, Uncle Roe?"

"Naw, we'll just let the chicken farmers take care of that. I never was much for shelling corn. I'll just pick my favorites after they're grown-up."

The men opened two of the cages and put socks over the roosters' heads. They clasped one hand tightly around the roosters' legs leaving their claws pointing downward. Roe noticed they wore gloves just the same, thick leather gloves. They went down to the pit, stooping to their knees on opposite sides of the car seats. Then the betting started.

"Man oh man, it's going to kill me to watch this. The frog ain't jumped that I didn't bet on how far he'd go."

The two men held the roosters up over the pits and began to rub their chests together.

"Is that to get them riled, Uncle Roe?"

"Yeah, they'll get them good and aggravated then they'll take off those socks and let them get a good look at each other. They do that to make sure one of them don't decide he's not in a fighting mood and go running off through the woods."

One of the men yelled O.K. and two other men came up and took off the socks. The roosters' feet began to stretch and point and one of them let out a loud squawk that made the men start laughing.

"Shut up you old bastard. You wanna fight with the sock in your beak."

"Looks like your sock took the wind out of him, Carlson."

"Don't kill him on the fumes before the fight starts."

The men continued to rub them together and bump them against each other until one man said, "Can't hold him no more."

"Let 'em go!"

"One, two, three, GO!"

The two men jumped back and set the roosters down in the pit. They didn't go at each other at once, but their pressed feathers began to swell out like a mad cat. The betting was still going on, each flick of the roosters' tails brought a change in betting. Then instantly they were at it, feet first, jumping at each other.

"I never seen anything fight like that, Uncle Roe. Look at that! Boy, ain't that the craziest-looking thing."

"See they figured out a long time ago where the meanest part of them was, that spur on their heels and they figured out where the weakest part of that other rooster was. They'll aim for the neck, right around the craw and the first one to get a good slit in there is on his way. I got my money on the one with the blue ring. He acts like he's done it before."

The roosters squawked at each other now, jumping and sending up a spray of the blue-black feathers. Little drops of blood

were in the air and began to land wet on the backs of the car
seats. Cale could see the old blood there from last time now,
brown red and dried.

"Think your boy has lost his balls, Carlson."

"Shit you say. Not yet he ain't."

"You better start feeding him better corn, Carlson. Looks
like he's ready for the pasture."

"Ain't going to be able to keep the hens in the barnyard with
that one."

"Carlson, you sure that ain't a hen with a comb on? Does
he crow real highlike?" The man crowed in a high squeaky
voice.

The rooster with the red ring was beginning to weaken. He
didn't jump anymore, just fended the blue ring's jumps and
Cale could see his beak, bright red with his own blood. Soon
the other one's feet were so red, you couldn't tell he had on a
blue ring but there was no doubt which one was winning. The
bets were changing fast but nobody would take them, the fight
was as much as over.

"Get out of my goddamn way." It was Carlson. He had on
his leather gloves and he was reaching in for his rooster. The
other cock came at him, snagging the arm of his shirt. He
lifted the rooster up and headed toward the cage with it squirming in his hands. "Do your fighting now, you little sonovabitch.
Why didn't you think of that earlier? Get your ass still or you're
going to be on the table tomorrow."

Cale recognized him now, the same sprattle-legged walk of
the old farmer they saw when they came in. Carlson covered
over the cage and hurried up the path.

"Will he live, Uncle Roe?"

"Probably. And he may fight again. The local boys usually
take them out when it starts looking bad and take them home
and doctor them up."

"See, they're getting out the spurs now. I told you they had
metal spurs," Tommy said.

The next two roosters were held up top on their legs and had leather sheaths over their spurs.

"See Cale," Roe said, "they cover those little metal spurs up till they set them loose or they'll really get messed up. They're sharp as a razor."

"They don't need them do they? Looks like to me they can take care of theirselves without them."

"They can but this makes it different, you wait and see."

"It don't last as long. They gotta bet faster," Tommy said.

The men were visibly more excited. The rooster chests were being rubbed together and suddenly two men on each chicken took off the sheaths and the socks and they were on the ground and at each other. Instantly the blood was flying. It was hard to tell which was getting the worst of it.

"Quick, who's your chicken, Tommy?"

"Yellow band."

"Your choice fellow, fifty cents."

In another minute it was starting to end. No one pulled them apart this time but the yellow one was down, fighting up from the ground.

"You lose, buddy."

Tommy reached in his blue jeans and handed Roe two quarters.

"Keep it buddy. You can buy me a beer sometime."

"Shit no. I pay my debts."

"O.K." Roe took the money and dropped it in his pocket. The winning chicken began to peck around on the ground, calmly like he was in his lot, his green ring colored red with blood. The other chicken had stopped moving, his throat slit. The man who set him out took him up, took off his metal spurs, and put him in a burlap bag. They began to pull the car seats apart and drag them back in the woods. The winning chicken was picked up, docile now, his spurs were sheathed and he was pushed into his cage. One man kicked dirt over the blood on the ground while another covered the swept-off spot with dead leaves. Cale saw the man who had lost his chicken down by the creek, washing the blood from his hands. They waited until all the men had gone, either away in the pickups or up to Parson's for a beer. Cale and Roe and Tommy walked back up to the highway.

"I gotta be going in now," Tommy said and turned and walked back toward town.

"Don't you want to go back and see who won the race? I got your rain check."

"Naw, I ain't interested."

"They got more chickens to fight later."

"Naw, I gotta go." He was soon gone in the darkness.

"Well, do you want to go back or are you pooping out on me too?"

Cale yawned involuntarily and they both laughed.

"I didn't mean to do that, Uncle Roe. That's what comes from going to bed at nine-thirty on Saturday night."

"Come on. We'll head on home. We can see another race another day and I'll find out tomorrow who won it."

They headed on down the highway, Roe holding his thumb out to the first car that passed them by. It went on past and Roe watched to see if the brake lights would glow, they didn't. Then he put his arm over Cale's back.

"I want to tell you something, boy, and I want you to know I don't mean no harm by it, O.K.?"

"Sure. O.K."

"I'd like to see you stay away from that Tommy boy. He's no good for you."

Cale looked up at Roe.

"Now I know you're thinking, why in the world did he say that about my best friend and you're going to have to keep wondering why because I can't put my finger on it yet. I've known Tommy's before and there's a certain kind of poison, I don't know what it is about people like him. But he's just no good. There is something about him that is just no good."

Chapter 23

BY CHRISTMAS, Falissa had been certain that Roe was there to stay this time. He had taken to leaving on weekends with his old cronies, staying gone a week at a time but coming back like that was home. At first she counted the days, hoping that he really had decided to leave, once even going into his room and getting together what few things he left behind so she could send them to him when he wrote for them. But he came back, found his stuff got up and looked at her like she'd committed a crime. Now here it was May and she was sure he was always going to come back. He had draped things over Mama Sarah Ann's doll cabinets, a kimono from Japan with bright-colored stitching on it of a long-tailed peacock, and a towel with a woman painted on it bending over with "D-Day" on the seat of her bathing suit. On the top of the cabinet was a fat white doll with red cheeks that Roe had promised to Pearlie but hadn't given to her yet. On Sarah Ann's white crocheted bedspread was a pillow from the Philippines, bright pink satin. Mama would roll over in her grave if she could see it.

Roe worked at odd jobs in town, loading freight cars, grocery trucks, but never for long. Yet as always, he was not short of money. He played poker every Wednesday night to determine if he would have to work that week and Cale told Falissa he had seen Roe win as much as five dollars betting at the pinball machines. And every week or so he came home with an armful of groceries for her, always the wrong things, until she had to tell him she would rather just have the money and do her own shopping. She regretted saying that because the money came to her much less frequently than the groceries had. And every night there he was at the head of the table because Jerome had never had the nerve to tell him that was his seat.

Roe had one thing in his favor though and though it might be the most artificial of flattery, Roe did notice things. You try a new seasoning, use a special sauce, Roe noticed it. He always complimented her on her cakes and puddings and would come in the kitchen and say, "Falissa, you could serve me that fresh apple pie three meals a day and I would be happy to my dying day." And he noticed things around the house, he bought bunches of flowers from the old colored woman in front of the ten-cent store and though she would never be so extravagant, she loved them. Jerome always fussed and said they brought bugs in the house, but it was her house and he could just keep fussing. It was just that Roe wasn't spoiled by a woman, his kind of woman was of a different type and he was the kind to appreciate what Jerome took for granted. It didn't hurt to be appreciated.

But another person in the house took away your privacy. You didn't feel like you could go around without your shoes and get on your nightshirt early. She never could get it in her mind that he was family. You couldn't forget there was a strange man around. And she just didn't trust him. His mouth had gotten too clean around her. She would like to think it was just growing up but the truth was probably that he waited till he got around the men to let go. And around the boy. Roe would have an effect on Cale. It might be years to come before she could see it, but it would be there. A boy couldn't grow up around a man and not soak up something from him. He could stay around a woman all his life and never hear a word she said but Roe was the kind of man he'd have to notice. Roe did have something and you could see what all those women saw in him even if you wanted no part of him. All the more reason to want no part of him. There is something frightening about him, dangerous. It has been turned over in my mind a thousand times and I can't put my finger on it. When he went downtown to the store with me, I was almost afraid to be around him. Not afraid of him really. Just to be around him. Like he was going to draw a disaster into you. Like he was bad luck. And everywhere we went he charmed people, even if they hated him he charmed them. He could come walking out with horns and a pitchfork and charm people and it wouldn't surprise me.

March, 1953

The days were starting to get longer and Cale didn't need a jacket while he was playing ball until he had to wait his turn to bat. He was hitting left-handed this year and it felt good. When he came up to bat the fielders all started moving back and he got them twice, clean over their heads but his last one went into the center fielder's glove just like he'd planned it. His side won anyway, five to one in three innings. He played first base and the old mitt that belonged to the church was cracking apart inside and felt like catching a batch of nutshells every time he got a hard one from the pitcher. Uncle Roe was going to get him one of his own for his thirteenth birthday.

He played for the junior high team and for the church now and he would get his letter at commencement this year. If they won one more game they got to get out of school three days and go to Cape Fear for the playoffs. Today he had been to softball practice at the church. They had a game in town tomorrow. They would play on the school field with the Methodists and he had ridden down with one of the Sunday school teachers he didn't know to leave off their equipment. He helped unload and the teacher got in his car and left, drove in the other direction with him the whole distance to the church plus home to make. He should have asked. Always having to say they didn't have a car. Mama won't have much to say since a Sunday school teacher did it.

As he walked back through the square he saw someone he hadn't seen all year, Tommy, not since over a year ago when Roe had just come. Hadn't thought about him much since Roe was here to do things with. He was with a bunch of guys coming out of the five-and-ten. Tommy had been sent back to training school he thought but he must have gotten out. Didn't know why he went back but it was probably stealing. Tommy had gotten bad to take things, stuff he didn't need. Took an eggplant off the rack in front of the nigger store once just so he could bust it off the railroad trestle. Didn't come back to regular school anymore so the school probably didn't know he was out again. The guys must have stolen something because they were hurrying to the alley. Cale walked to the alley and looked down.

"Hey Jenkins." Tommy reached under his shirt and pocketed a small blue box.

"Hey Tommy. Where you been?"

"Been up to the training school. Got out last week."

"You coming back to school?"

"Not unless they make me. Not going to the training school no more either. They're getting bad about people coming back. Bastards will beat you and call you a liar if you tell the director. I kill anybody who beats me."

Cale knew the other guys. They lived near Tommy and they were still scattered around in the grammar school grades and they always did what Tommy told them to. One of them was a little kid, Jerky, from the mill houses, who was in the fifth grade and was supposed to be. He was first base on the Little League and Cale had coached him in the clinic last week.

"Tommy's got a gun and he'll kill anybody messes with him," one of the boys said.

"What'd you go up for?" Cale asked.

"Shooting."

"You shoot somebody?"

Tommy started to laugh so all his friends did too. "Naw, man, I just removed all the back windows in Parson's Store. Ping, tinkle, ping, tinkle, ping, tinkle."

"Whatcha get in the five-and-ten?"

"Cards."

He took them out of his pocket and popped the stamp on the pack of Bicycle playing cards. "Wanna go play poker with us?"

The boys all laughed.

"Come on, man. The stakes are low. Real low." The boys all laughed again. Cale didn't know at what unless they were scared not to laugh at Tommy. His face looked different, maybe he had started shaving.

"O.K." Roe had taught him how to play five-card draw and blackjack. He even beat Roe sometimes. "Can't play for money in public can you?"

"We don't play in public, man. Got my own private little clubhouse down by the river. Playing in public can get you in a little bit of trouble." The boys all laughed again. They were beginning to get on his nerves. Tommy always said someday he would have a bunch of goons to do all his dirty work.

Cale followed them down behind the stores. They cut through one of the dirt streets in niggertown and headed down on the river. Tommy held up his hand and they marched single file back through the brambles. The wind was blowing up the smell from the river, smelled like the alleys did after it rained. Soon there was a brown shack, nobody's because the windows weren't closed over with paper even.

"O.K., y'all wait here while I check it out."

Tommy disappeared around the shack and they heard the front door creak open. They heard voices. Then Tommy was back around the shack.

"O.K. Come on round and get inside quick and shut the door."

They all went around and inside, and when Tommy shut the

door no one moved because they couldn't see anything but a few dusty spider webs in the light around the window. Tommy struck a match and they watched him move in the circle of light to a kerosene lamp, lift the globe and light it. The ceiling was covered with gray-white circles where it had leaked and the whole place smelled like rotten wood that had been left in the rain. Tommy set the lamp in the middle of the floor and the good kerosene smell went out. Cale jumped when he saw two other people there, the voices they had heard, two colored girls, one big and one little, sitting on a quilt with their legs tucked up against them like they were cold.

"Blackjack, get in a circle," Tommy ordered.

The other boys followed Tommy and sat down. They weren't surprised to see the girls, Cale could tell that, except Jerky who wrinkled his nose. What in the world did they want to play poker with two stupid little old colored girls for?

Tommy started to deal the cards. He dealt hands for the two girls in an empty space in the circle.

"Come over and pick up your cards."

The girls obeyed and sat down across from them, moaning when their rear ends touched the wet floor. They picked up the cards and looked at them. Cale saw the big girl's hand, two face cards. She didn't know no better than to let everybody see her hand. Guess they saw it too.

"Now the first guy to get twenty-one wins, O.K. Ten cents a hand." The boys put out ten cents each. The big girl reached for the money and Tommy popped her hand and said, "Not yet."

Cale reached in his pocket and said, "I can't play for money long. I don't have but twenty-five cents."

"Me neither, two dimes," Jerky said.

"Gamble, man. You might get rich." Cale and Jerky added their dimes to the stack. Tommy looked at the girls who blinked at their cards. "Now the rules are, when you lose, you got to take off a piece of clothes, and shoes and socks and things in your pocket don't count. You want a card you say, 'Hit me.' You want a card?" He spoke to the tall black girl, the one with the two face cards.

"Uh-huh."

"Well say, hit me."

"Uh-uh."

"Say, gimme a card."

"Gimme a card."

Tommy turned over a card. It was a king.

"What you got?"

"Dun' know."

"Show me your cards."

She held her cards in his face.

"You lose. Thirty points. You should have stayed put. Off with the dress."

The girl unbuttoned her dress, undid the safety pin that held it shut over her bosom, and pulled it quickly over her head. She grinned widely at them. She had on ragged white drawers that her flesh showed through in brown circles. Elastic hung down in loops around her thighs, and her man's undershirt was yellow under the arms.

The boy beside Cale turned to him and whispered, "Man, she's got big teaties." Cale felt chill bumps go all over him. Strip poker. Damn, he was dumb not to know it. Tommy used to talk about it all the time. He looked at the circular lumps her nipples made under the undershirt like two buttons. She was as big as a grown woman.

"I get de dime."

"Naw, you don't get it yet." Tommy looked at the other boys and laughed. Then he picked up the cards and dealt another hand. He asked the little girl if she wanted a card. She said no and her eyes began to shine. Cale thought she was going to cry when the big girl yelled she wanted a card, still grinning. She lost again, twenty-three this time, not even her own fault, and she pulled off the undershirt before she was asked.

"I told you she had big titties," the boy beside Cale said.

"I'm not blind," Cale said angrily. He looked at her dusty

brown breasts, rounder and higher than those in his books with
the pink white skin. And the ones in the magazine posed themselves while this girl just sat, slumped forward, and grinned.

"Cale ain't never seen a naked woman, have you, Cale?"
That was Tommy. Not the old Tommy, teasing at him in front
of everybody.

"No, I ain't, not a real one. But I got pictures. I seen plenty
of pictures." His face reddened. "I bet they ain't either."

"Yes, they have. Every week, all but Jerky. He ain't been before." Cale looked at Jerky who stared at the girl's breasts. Jerky
was real little, not but a year older than Pearlie.

"You want them dimes?" Tommy asked the big girl. He
reached out and rolled one of her nipples between his fingers.
When he let go it was bigger than the other one.

The big girl smiled and nodded her head and her breasts
swung slowly back and forth. The little girl turned her face
away. She was about to cry but the big girl didn't turn to look
at her.

"You know how to get all five dimes?"

"Uh-huh."

"Yes sir, you mean."

"Yessuh."

She picked up her dress and undershirt and slid the dimes in
the pocket of the dress. Then she walked over and sat down
on the quilt, took off her pants, and lay down, facing the
wall, her round hips dimpled with dark shadows. The little girl
ran over in front of her and pressed her face in the wall, crying.
"Shut up, Lucille. Yuh say yuh wan' de dime. Ain't gon' brang
yuh no' mo' yuh don't do fer de dime." Cale looked at Tommy
who was standing up and taking off his belt and he saw Jerky
dart past him and out the door. Cale was right behind him,
slinging the door shut behind him and hitting the outside in
the bright light, running down the riverbank. Jerky ran harder
in front of him, crashing through the weeds as he got off the
trail. He fell down and started crying. Cale saw him roll over
and hold up his fist in front of his face.

"Come on, get up out of here."

Jerky got up and followed Cale as he made his way back to the path. They ran up a dirt street and between the store and didn't stop until they were on Main Street. They walked across the street to the park. There were two old men on a bench, sitting sprattle-legged with their stomachs hanging over their belts, not talking to each other.

"Here, sit down here, Jerky."

They sat on a bench across from the old men who frowned at them while they panted to get their breath. Cale was wet all over and zipped up his windbreaker when the air hit him.

"I thought you was them."

"Naw."

"They was going to do bad," Jerky whispered. "Can that old man hear me?"

"No, I don't think so."

"They was going to do bad with those nigger girls. My big brother beat me . . ." Tears started to pour down Jerky's cheeks. He had skint his elbow and tore the knee of his jeans. "Dammit." He lifted his shirttail and wiped his face. He didn't have on an undershirt and his stomach was shiny with sweat. He was a pretty skinny little kid.

"Yeah," Cale said, "I didn't know that was what they were up to. I oughta known, knowing Tommy Grinnin, that it'd be strip poker instead of plain old poker."

Jerky stopped crying and looked at him. "You didn't know neither?"

"Naw, did you?"

"Uh-uh. Tommy say he teach me to play cards. Took my dime. That was my movie money. Tommy's going to get bugs. I hope he does and they eat him alive."

"Huh?"

"My big brother told me. Nigger girls give you bugs and they eat your peter off and you can't go to the bathroom. You walk over to my house with me? They going to get me."

"They ain't going to bother you."

"Yes they are too. Tommy Grinnin called me chicken shit and gave me a nosebleed. I'll get my big brother to whip his ass. But I gotta get home before they get holt of me."

"Naw, they'll be down there on the river rest of the afternoon."

"Why?"

"With those girls. Tommy's done that before. He snuck up and watched men do it with his sister. His sister showed him how to do it out back of his house in the car. He told me she did. Don't you know what they're doing?"

"They made that girl get naked."

"I mean don't you know why?"

"Uh-uh." Cale looked at Jerky. His face was streaked from tears and the dusty shed. He looked even younger away from them, his feet hardly reached the ground on the bench. Cale leaned back in the seat. His hands had stopped shaking. He believed Tommy would be down there until dark anyway. Jerky sure was a little kid. He had heard guys at school talk about screwing before he got out of the third grade.

"Well Jerky, I'll tell you. You are right that they are going to do bad. But it's worse than you think. You see it's not just bad because you're not supposed to do it. They are going to make babies in those girls."

Jerky frowned and twisted up his lip. "Huh?"

"Make babies. Like mothers and daddies do only they are doing it for meanness. They are doing it because it feels good to them. They don't want the babies but they might get one anyway."

"Nigger babies?"

"Partway I guess. I guess it's the same." Hadn't thought about that. "Yeah, partway. Heard a lady preacher say once that was the way it worked."

"My mama says babies come from Jesus and that he brings them to your house at night."

"What's your daddy say?"

"He ain't there."

Cale looked at Jerky. "You want me to walk with you? You live on Main Street?"

"At the highway end."

"That's on my way."

They went out of the park. Just before they reached the sidewalk Jerky sniffed deeply and ran and stuck his face in the water fountain. He dried his face on his T-shirt and zipped up his windbreaker over it.

"I ain't never going near that Tommy Grinnin again," Jerky said loudly.

"Me neither. My Uncle Roe said he won't no good."

"He ain't no good and he's going to be sorry about those bugs. When I get to be sixteen I'm going to beat up Tommy Grinnin. I'm going to bust him a bloody nose."

"Tommy's pretty strong."

"Yeah, but he'll get old and I'll be able to beat him."

"Hey Jerky, I tell you something. You know where the public library is?"

"Yeah."

"Well, you go in one day past the old lady at the desk and you ask the boy there, he'll be dusting or putting up books, you ask him for the marriage book, can you remember that?"

"Yeah, marriage book."

"Right. And you read it there. It's really something."

"You read it?"

"Yeah, me and Tommy read it one Saturday."

"O.K. See ya."

"See ya."

Jerky turned and went down the flat house row on the end of Main Street where the mill used to be. He ran around a chicken coop and ran his fingers down the wire, scaring up two hens who sent their feathers out through the holes. The sun was behind one of the smokestacks and cut notches in it.

Cale could hear his mama ringing the supper bell by the time he got to Will James' and he saw his Daddy and Roe at the plant bed when he came up. He'd get Uncle Roe to tell him about black and white babies. Never thought of it before but Uncle Roe would know. Wait till old Jerky got his hands on that book.

*   *   *

He saw her there on a bed quilt. He had meant to go home to bed. His mother was going to be mad. It was dark and past supper and bedtime. He had meant to go to bed. He thought sure he'd gone to bed. He even thought he had brushed his teeth and did his arithmetic homework before he got in bed. He did have on his pajamas and he didn't have on shoes but it didn't feel cold. It was feeling close to summer. She was in another room, the shack had another room he didn't see the first time he was there and it was filled up with corn like their crib, just like it, but he never knew about the other room before. The little girl was in there on a clean quilt spread on top of the corn and she had bigger teaties than her sister. She had her legs apart and he saw the place, a big round hole and she pointed at it and grinned and looked just like her sister. He would do it before Tommy got there, it would come out real fast. It was so hot like a fire, like standing in front of a fireplace with his clothes burning him. They set it on fire. Tommy and the others had got him in there and set it on fire. The crib was burning up and his daddy would kill him for letting Tommy do that. He looked at the little girl and she was burned up, gone. He ran in the other room. He had gotten all wet. Both of the girls were in there. And there was the little girl and she didn't have big teaties after all. They had tricked him. She was beside the big girl and she was crying. She looked just like Pearlie. She had blond hair. She wasn't a nigger girl. He was going to beat Tommy Grinnin till he died. He hit Tommy in the face and Tommy swung back . . .

He was awake and in his room. The clock was there, with the light-up face. It was his room. He had clean sheets tonight,

Monday. He was home. The top covers had all gone off on the floor and the bed was wet. Cale saw the door open and a face and hand come around the edge.

"Cale, Cale, are you all right?" It was his mother. He wouldn't answer. She walked in the room and he could hear her picking up the covers. He wouldn't move. The covers settled over him and he didn't open his eyes until she shut the door.

"What is it?" He heard his daddy through the door.

"He had a nightmare. Kicked everything off in the floor like a baby. He seems to be sleeping all right now. But he shouldn't go to so many of those movies. If I had known that he was going to end up downtown and go to that horror movie . . ."

He heard the door to their room shut. It was 11:00 P.M. on the green dial and he was asleep again before he could start thinking.

September, 1953

Cale and Jerome were in the barn, loading the tobacco into a pickup to take into Durham to sell. The smell burned his head as he slid the yellow-orange bundles of leaves off into the pickup bed. It was a good year and the tobacco leaves ripened thick and heavy while the tree leaves skittered across the ground. This was going to be their best load. Jerome had borrowed a truck and two men Cale didn't know were there with it. He got their names as something like Red and Siegy. Roe had been supposed to help but he had gotten a notice in the box that he had a package in town at the post office and had taken off to get it. Jason and Floyd were there too, Floyd had almost grown to Jason's height and he was almost as thin. They were so much alike Cale didn't recognize Floyd anymore unless he looked right straight at him. Floyd never talked anymore.

The door to the barn thumped shut and Roe came running in. "I saved it. Like to have killed me but I brought it all the way from town without opening it so I could share it with you."

Jerome dropped his stick and walked over to Roe. When Jerome quit, all the others did too.

"Whatcha got, Roe? Don't have no return on it?"

"Naw. That give you a hint?"

"That tells me you got something they don't want the post office to trace. Whatcha got. Dirty pictures?"

Roe started laughing and unwrapped the box slowly. He turned his back and took off the lid. "Woo, woo, God Almighty. Would you look at this!"

"Come on Roe, let us see it."

He lifted it from the box, a long limp piece of rubber twisting like an old inner tube. But instead of black rubber this was colored pink with yellow at one end. Roe had laughed until tears formed in his eyes then he held it up full length. They all saw finally what it was, a life-size blond woman made of rubber with her breasts rippling, the nipples bright red as her mouth. Her only clothing was a red garter right above one knee. In her belly button was a valve.

Roe said, "It came from Ohio, see. Them Yankees ain't got no nigger women to warm up their beds first, so they make them one up out of rubber."

"Sh, Roe. Floyd and Jason are over there."

"Shit if I watch my mouth in front of a couple of shines, boy."

When Roe talked Cale smelled the liquor on his breath. It always made him mean and he didn't like Roe as well then.

"It's a hot water bottle," Roe explained. "See the valve there. That's where you put it in."

"That might be where *you* put it in, Roe."

"That ain't where my pappy told me to put it in. No wonder you can't keep no woman happy, Roe."

"Boy, she has got one fine set of titties on her."

"Roe gon' use her to ride the waves at the beach."

"They won't be able to get him outa the water to go to bed."

"She ain't much of a looker in the face, Roe. She's got a bit of a blank look to her. Kinda stupid-looking."

Roe spread out the face in his hands, "She do look a bit blank, don't she? She don't look too bright, now that you mention it. But what do you expect of a gal who comes in a plain brown wrapper, huh? You expect her to bring a diploma? Maybe she ain't too bright but she makes up for it. She's easy enough to keep happy. She wants a simple life. I like her." Roe began to dance around with her in his arms, her deflated legs dangling and her butt jiggling. "Uh-oh," he held her out from him. "'Bout to get me all hot and bothered." He lifted her in his arms and she flopped like a dead body. "I don't care if my family doesn't like her, I'm in love with her. So maybe she's not a good dresser, she's got a nice garter. Won't get old on me; if she does, nothing a few tire patches won't fix."

Jerome beat his hands on his legs, "Roe, you really are something. If you ain't something. You are making me hurt inside."

Roe sat down on the floor and unscrewed the valve.

"Spread her out for me, Cale. Let's see what she's really built like."

Cale walked from over behind Jerome. His face was red and Roe started to say something but shut his mouth. Cale saw Roe wink at Jerome as he took the rubber legs and stretched the woman out. "That's right. Now pull that left ham a little straighter. Right. Um, that's a pretty little limb." He lifted the valve and buckled her in the center. Roe puffed up with air and his breath made a ringing sound as it went inside her, like going way down in a hollow. She still stayed flat.

"Roe, you are going to bust a gut like that. All those alcohol fumes in her. She'll float up like a balloon." Roe reddened and blew for a while more until Jerome appeared with a bicycle pump and held it around the valve. He started pumping in the air and she began to flop like a fish.

"Now she's getting a wiggle on. Look at that hip action."

Roe stood up and watched Jerome and said, "She looks like one of the floppy-boobed Africans. Remember when we would get them *National Geographics* and look them up, Jerome, and that old bitch built like a washboard threw us out of the public library." Cale thought, same old bitch, she's still there. Roe reached down and pinched together the breasts, rubbing them until they squeaked.

"Speaking of Africans, Jerome." Roe looked around the barn. "Where'd them shines get to?"

"They went out back. I saw them out there when I got the pump, taking a smoke out back."

All the men busted out laughing again, loud.

Roe winked at Jerome. "Reckon they want me to give them the address? Why I could get rich. I could sell one of these to every black ass in the county. What you think of that, Cale? You know all about that now. You want to be a partner with your old uncle? Jenkins and Jenkins."

Cale sat beside Jerome on the hay bale now. He nodded his head and smiled. Jerome patted him on the back and he relaxed.

"Ain't your uncle something? I been telling you all these years what we were in for. Don't he beat all you ever seen in your life?"

"He sure does. Ain't nobody like my Uncle Roe."

"That a boy." Jerome patted him again and Roe winked at him.

"But I tell you boy. You got to remember that the law might try to put me and you out of business. They might change it to read 'and facsimile thereof!' You reckon?"

Cale didn't understand and felt a moment of panic until Jerome said, "What do you mean, Roe?"

"I mean we string one up and disball him for getting him a white woman. Don't you know nothing about the law? This my friend is a 'facsimile thereof.' "

They got up to go back to work. Jerome called Jason and Floyd, and Cale noticed they were right by the door. They had heard everything that went on but nobody seemed to care.

That evening after supper Roe had gotten out his bottle again and resumed his drinking. After dinner Cale was helping his mama in the kitchen and when they started to rinse the dishes no hot water would come in the pan.

"Jerome, can you come here a minute?"

Jerome appeared at the door. "What's the matter?"

"Something has gone wrong with the water heater. The water runs cold as ice. I didn't have half a sinkful."

Jerome walked to the back door and started to go out. "I better see if the fuse has blown out." He stopped halfway through the door and said, "Uh-oh. Never mind." Then he started to giggle. He motioned to Falissa and Cale to come with him. They went to the bathroom door and knocked. "Roe, can we come in?"

"Jerome, what is it?" Falissa was completely confused.

They could hear Roe laughing. Jerome cracked the door and then opened it up. Roe was on his knees beside the tub drying off his woman. She was on her side, fully inflated, and her body was wet and shiny. He had filled the tub and held her under to fill her up and his hands were bright red from the hot water. Steam rose off the rubber woman and the paint on her red teaties was running down her stomach.

"Jerome!" Falissa screamed.

"Shhh, Falissa. Don't get Pearlie down here."

Falissa pulled Cale back from the door and pushed him away. "What is that thing? What are you doing with a naked woman thing, whatever it is?"

"It's a hot water bottle, Falissa. See, there's the valve."

"My Lord in heaven above. Mercy on us." Falissa walked by Cale and dropped into the living room chair. "There is no end to it. Just no end in sight."

Roe and Jerome walked through in front of her, Roe with the head end, Jerome with her feet. The water slushed inside her and her breasts went flat as it sagged down in her back.

"Hey Roe, hold up. Look."

Roe turned and looked at her and said, "One, two, three, over."

They turned her and the water ran into the breasts and filled them again. They pointed straight downward at the floor. Jerome was laughing so hard his legs wobbled. Falissa heard them "one, two, three" again and the woman hit Roe's bed with a splash and a gurgle.

"I thank the Lord above that Papa is not here to see this. They have done a lot of things, but this is it. This one is it." Cale looked at Falissa. He had never seen her so mad. He had never seen her sit quiet for so long. He sat with her without speaking while the two men laughed in the other room. Pearlie came in and said, "Mama, what's so funny?"

"Nothing's funny, darling. Come here with me, if you're going to stay down here."

Pearlie sat down with her mother and leaned against her shoulder. Falissa began to smooth the child's hair, undoing her clamp and fastening it again. Pearlie had a loom in her lap and was making a potholder. They heard the door to the bedroom shut and Jerome came out leaving Roe inside. He sat on the other side of the room beside Cale. "We should finish up the top barn tomorrow."

"Yes sir, I think so."

Suddenly Falissa's mouth dropped open and she covered her eyes in horror.

"Uncle Roe's jumping up and down on his bed, Mama," Pearlie said. "You want me to tell him to stop before he breaks his slats like Cale did?"

Falissa dropped her hands and said "No," too loudly, and pulled Pearlie to her when suddenly they heard water splashing and Roe start cussing. Then a loud moan and he was silent but the water continued to splash. Falissa got up and led Pearlie to the stairs. "Upstairs, darling. I'll be up in a minute after I tend to one more thing."

"But, Mama."

"No but's. Upstairs."

She went in the kitchen and came back through the living room with her mop bucket and a mop. When she got to the door of Sarah Ann's room, the water had already started under. She opened the door and threw in the bucket and mop and they clanged across the floor. Roe hollered out, lying in the floor naked, his body red as a scalded pig, but she muffled his voice when she slammed the door. She came back into the living room and Cale and Jerome were both laughing.

"I have one thing to say to both of you, one thing." She spoke slowly, her voice trembling. "He goes. He goes out of here or he starves to death because he is not eating one more bite of food at my table. He goes out the front door and I'm bolting him out of my house."

She left the room and Cale looked at Jerome. "She don't mean that, do she, Daddy? She's not going to run out Uncle Roe."

"Naw, she'll cool off. Bet it will be a while before your Uncle Roe cools off boy . . . Don't you bet it will be a while?"

"He's going to buy out Parson's supply of inner-tube patches."

Jerome let out a howl and laughed again. "Woo, you're going to be just like him. I swear you're going to be just like him."

Falissa appeared at the door of the room. "Over my dead body, Mr. Jenkins." And she turned and was gone up the stairs. Jerome stopped laughing for the first time that evening.

The next morning Falissa sent Cale to the trash pile with the woman. Since Roe wasn't up yet when he left, Falissa had sent him in the room to get it. Roe was asleep atop the wet mattress and sheets and he didn't have a stitch on him. Cale had to pull the woman from under him, finally rolling him over to get her loose. Roe moaned and swung at Cale but his arms fell back down on his hairy body and he didn't wake up. When he was still again, Cale could hear more water dripping to the floor. Cale spread the woman out by the bed and rolled her up before he left the room.

"Did you get it?"

"Yes, ma'am," and he shut the door quietly behind him.

"You don't have to be so careful about waking him up. He is going to get his sorry self up this morning and get that mattress out in the sun while there is some sun."

"What you want me to do with it? It's split about two feet so I don't see how he can fix it."

"Fix it! Heaven forbid that he try to fix it. What are you thinking of? Do you think I'd let that man fix that thing and keep it?"

"Well, I didn't know, Mama. It was his and not ours."

"You take that thing down and put it on the trash pile or bury it, or burn it, I don't care just so it's got rid of. I don't ever want to see it again. And after we get rid of it, we'll just see if we can't get rid of what brought it in."

"You're going to make Uncle Roe leave?"

"He is leaving this house if I have to drag him out with my own two hands."

"I think you're making too much of it. Can't you take a joke?"

"A joke! Who are you talking to, young man? Do you want another beating?"

"I'm talking to my mother. And my father is not giving me any more beatings because you tell him to. And if you touch me you'll be sorry."

"Get out! Get out of my sight!" Falissa came to the door as he went down the steps. "The male members of the household can just fix their own supper tonight because when you get back, Pearlie and I are going to be gone."

Cale walked toward the trash pile, stooping under the fence with the woman rolled up under his arm. He unrolled her head and looked at it. Not a bit like a real person like the body was. He noticed she had rubber lashes attached to her lids that flopped back and forth and her lips were painted red, almost heart-shaped, and they were coming off now like her teaties. She had hardly no nose at all, just a pucker in the rubber. She didn't look like a dead person in the face, more like one of his sister's dolls.

He got to the trash pile and saw it still covered with broken glass that he and Tommy had shot up with a rifle two years ago. Something ran over the pile, a rat, and it made the blood stir in his legs. He took the woman and threw her out on the trash. She unrolled instantly and spread out like a dead person, her chest bloody from the red paint. Her head was to the side and the pink body looked like a real woman, a real naked woman, and he could imagine her breath making her chest heave. He arranged her teaties so they would stick up. He stood there a moment until he felt it, his pants tightened, just like when that damn sister of Tommy's climbed up in top of the garage with him and rubbed on his legs and then ran off and left him. He looked all around himself, quickly. No one was there so he ran over the hill and dropped into the gully to get rid of it with his hand. When he was done he went back to the woman and dragged some burlap bags over her. He didn't want to see her anymore, nobody would ever know she was under there. He started to go back to the house but he felt sleepy. When he ducked in the barn, he saw Roe at the house, his pants on now, pulling the wet mattress across the porch. He heard his mother yell, "Pick it up" from inside the house and he watched Uncle Roe's knees wobble as he pulled the mattress to his shoulders.

Chapter 24

WHEN CALE WOKE UP it was two o'clock. He must have slept right through the lunch bell and would have been asleep still if two old hens hadn't come pecking in the stall. He got up and went to check on Roe. The ground was wet from a shower. Roe must have taken the mattress back in because it wasn't in the yard. Cale walked on to the house, it seemed awful quiet. He found Roe sitting in the front room with all the curtains closed, still dressed in nothing but his pants.

"Uncle Roe? What happened to lunch?"

Roe shook his head. He looked up at Cale as he walked in and sat across from him but there was practically no expression on his face. He looked very tired.

"Hey boy. Guess I really pulled a bad one, huh?"

"I thought it was pretty funny myself, Uncle Roe."

"I mean your mama. I didn't know I would ever make her that mad."

"Aw, don't worry about Mama. She makes a mountain out of a molehill, you know. She gets all excited over things but she gets over them."

"Well, I hope you know more about her than me. She's gone, reason I mention it."

"Mama's gone?"

"Yeah, she left right after lunch, fixed a plate for herself and Pearlie, straightened up the dishes, got hers and Pearlie's stuff together and took off."

"Where'd she go? Shopping?"

"Naw. I mean she got her clothes together. She packed up a box of clothes and left and didn't say where she was going or nothing."

"Golly. I didn't think she meant it, that she really was going to take off."

"She must have. Now you know I didn't mean to come in here and cause nothing like that. I would have left long ago if I thought I was going to cause something like that. I had no intentions of disrupting things, boy, you know what I mean? I didn't come in here to mess up my brother's home. I just got kinda lonesome I guess. I kinda wanted to come home every now and then and see the same people. You know what I mean."

Cale didn't answer for a moment. He didn't know he was supposed to until he saw Roe's eyes on him. "I think I know what you mean, Roe."

"Naw, you don't. I don't mean no harm by it, boy, but none of you can really know what I mean. And here I've come to be a while in the solidest family I know of and I've done broke it up. Just bad medicine from the word go, that's me."

"Mama'll be back. Don't you worry. She was as mad at me and Daddy as she was at you."

"She take off like this before?"

"Well, no sir. I don't remember it."

Roe moaned and put his face in his hands.

"I better go close up the chickens, Roe, I'll be right back. I think I left them undone."

"Cale, wait up. Do me a big favor. Will you take a couple of dollars if I give it to you and go into town and get us some hamburgers and french fries or something all made up so Jerome will have some dinner when he comes in."

"Mama didn't leave nothing fixed up?"

"She said she didn't."

"Well, I guess she didn't. Can you cook?"

"If I have to, but I'm not in the mood, if you know what I

mean. I'll take over until I figure how to get her back but I'm not up to it tonight."

Cale left with the money and walked toward town catching a ride almost before he was at Will's place. He got six hamburgers at the Rebel Bar and got the man to fill an ice cream carton with french fries. He had to wait thirty minutes while he cooked and wrapped them and his stomach was already growling. On the way back he couldn't keep his hands out of the carton and by the time he got there, about half of them were gone and he wasn't hungry anymore. He walked in the living room and Roe was just where he left him but his daddy was on the other side of the room.

"We got problems, buster. I guess you heard."

"Yeah, Roe told me. I got us some supper or lunch or whatever you want to call it. I'll put it out on the table if you're ready."

"Fix us up a pot of ice tea, will you boy. Just boil some water and pour it over the grounds like you do coffee. O.K.?"

"Sure, if I can find it."

"In the pantry. And dash the sugar in while it's hot so it'll melt and cut up a lemon. We'll make out."

Cale went into the kitchen. He could hear them start to talk again so he moved quietly, listening.

"You should have gotten up and out this morning, buddy. You shouldn't have tried her when she was mad."

"I know. I know. But you shoulda gotten me up, Jerome. I didn't have no steam left."

"Just ain't like Falissa to really do it. Not a bit like her. Didn't ever think she'd do it for sure. Looks like she could have said where she went. She didn't have no money to take except what was in the drawer and it ain't been touched. Makes me think she must have gone to a cousin of hers, one of the ones over near Raleigh. Did she say how she was traveling?"

"Nothing, Jerome. Nothing more than I told you. We could ask down at the station."

"No bother. She won't come back until she's good and ready. I know that hardheaded woman. I wish you'd come and got me so I could have gotten holt of her before she left. I wish you had."

"She was out before I could turn around . . ."

"Come eat it before it gets cold or colder, I should say."

They got up and went to the table. At each of their seats was a glass of brackish tea that had already melted the ice, a wrapped-up burger bleeding through the wrapper and in the center of the table was the half carton of fries and a bottle of catsup.

"Why'd you dirty up glasses, boy? That stuff would have stood up without them."

"I could say make your own next time."

"Don't much care for french fries. They give me the burps . . . They cook this beef done?"

"I asked them to."

"Don't look done. Don't want it mooing at me when I bite it."

They all sat down and began to peel the paper away. Jerome and Cale started to eat but Roe just stared at the table.

* * *

Uncle Roe don't want to talk tonight, I can tell that. I sure hate to see him down. He ain't the kind that makes out good down. He didn't say ten words coming in to town. And he has had five beers already, I counted them, and he's starting to slurp them out loud and left the foam on his mouth. He ain't drunk, he is just to that "not give a damn" stage of his, that's what he calls it. He's been good to me, Mama don't give him no credit at all for that because she can't understand it. I ain't never had nobody be good to me like Uncle Roe. I never got to go no place. And it ain't just that. Uncle Roe is good around the house too. He'll throw a ball with you. He can do anything you name and he told me he won't but four years younger than my old man. No sir, you'd never know that looking at him. And I'm not

ashamed to ask him almost anything because he don't make a
to-do over it. He just answers you straight.

"Hey Roe, can you cook pretty good?"
"Huh?"
"Can you cook?"
"Yeah. I told you in a fashion. I'm not much for using a
kitchen but I can fry up a good fish in the woods."
"We don't even need Mama. With a little practice we could
get along without her. Aunt Bynum could do the washing."
Roe looked up at Cale and shook his head.
"That's bad talking, boy."
"How come?"
"I said it's bad. And I don't want to hear it again. You don't
know what you're talking about."
"You don't know her like I do, Uncle Roe. You don't know
how mean she can be. She's the one who makes Daddy mean
about half the time."
"Drop it, boy. And believe me, you don't know. Give it two
weeks and you'll see what that house will be without that
woman."
"I don't like having women around myself. I'd just as soon
it be us men. Can I have another Pepsi?"
Roe waved to the man behind the counter and pointed at
Cale's empty Pepsi bottle.
"You ever drink anything stronger than that?"
"Nope. Well, I had a couple of sips over at Tommy's one
day and didn't much like the way it tasted. Had to chew bubble
gum to get the smell away so Mama wouldn't notice it."
"You got a lot to learn, boy. I got a lesson for you, O.K.? Don't
feel so sorry for yourself. And I know you think I don't practice what I preach but I'm a lot older and I been through a lot
more. And I can tell you that if my old man didn't like what I
did it was tough shit." The man behind the bar set a hot Pepsi
and a glass of ice in front of Cale.

"You don't just go all bad on them at once. You just let them have it easylike, one at a time and let them get used to it. One at a time until you don't ask them, you tell them. First you cuss. Then you light up a cigar. In a month or so you come home drunk. Then you ready for jelly roll. And I'd recommend not knocking up any little fat farm gals like I did. Go visit them that knows how because it ain't worth the money it saves. That, my boy, was your Uncle Roe's biggest mistake. That fellow would have married his daughter to a nigger if he thought he done it. I managed to let my ribs rub my backbone for a couple of months and I won't forget that. Nobody'd give me work because I was too young. You don't know what it's like to get used to looking in the cabinets and at least finding flour and potatoes and one day you ain't got no cabinets and got to spend all your time worrying on food; food and a place to sleep. That ain't no good. Stealing 'cause you got to and knowing people waste more in their garbage than you had to eat all day. You got to have money. And when you can get it, a woman to cook for you. And when you can get it, that too. Food and shelter first, but when all else fails, that too."

Roe started to cackle. Cale thought he was beginning to feel better.

"So you ain't done no drinking. I won't ask you if you've had a cigar or a chew. Shit, boy, I'm disappointed in you. I been here two years this month and you're still as pure as the driven snow. We got a lot of ground to cover. We got to go over to see Sallie. I bet your pants are about to burn up for that, huh?"

"Who's she?"

"A gal I want you to meet. Ought to give her a kick. Second generation of Jenkins. She took Jerome for his first roll. She might be getting tired though and give you to one of the younger gals. And she has some fine ones, I'm telling you. Got a pretty daughter. They're built better when they're young, I'm telling you. Put a white beanpole to shame. And Sal ain't done bad by herself. She ain't put on as much weight as me which she

told me. She said, 'Dere's mo of yo, and dere wuz 'nuff befo.'
That Sal is something. But I think we ought to get you a young
one. Yeah, a slick young thing, um!"

Cale looked down at his Pepsi and poured it into the glass
of ice cubes. The glass curved in at the center and he rubbed
his hands up the cool sides.

"Hey boy. Don't frown so. You like that glass, huh? Caught
you, didn't I? You like them to go in like that? In at the middle,
out at the top. You know what I'm talking about."

Cale looked at the glass and squinted then he smiled. "I got
you. Like a woman. And you talking about taking me to a
whorehouse."

"Yeah boy." Roe started to laugh and then got choked and
turned red in the face. "You foxed your old uncle." People
were turning around on the stools and Cale felt his neck red
around his collar. Uncle Roe could never tell when he was talking loud. And Uncle Roe was going to take him to a whorehouse
tonight, Big Sal's that Tommy used to talk about which was
the only one in town he'd ever heard of, just outside over on
the edge of the nigger section.

"We going over to Big Sal's, Roe? I know where that is."

"You been there?"

"Naw, I been by there."

"Now you ain't making a fool of your old uncle. You been
going rolling out by the smokehouse every Saturday night?"

"Naw, Uncle Roe. You know that ain't true. I never done
it . . . with a girl."

"Now don't go getting down in the dumps on me. Your life
ain't over yet. Life ain't over at thirteen. You got lots of years
left to make up your time in. Don't want to wear it out. What
you so gloomy about?"

They went out into the street and the air was fresh and un-
smoky. Cale saw the night traffic moving around the circle,
around and around and back down through the drive-in for all

the boys at the high school who had cars. There were still a
few old men on the benches in the square, who'd fallen asleep
and wouldn't go home till it got cold, but through one of the
bench slats you could see the sunset orange. They cut down off
Main Street where the sidewalk sloped downhill fast. There was
one big old white house there with the little patch of lawn mowed
and the bushes cut and on the porch there was an old woman
in a rocker. She sat up high off the street behind the leaning
stores, a grocery with the window written on in white shoe
polish and a used-clothes store with nothing on the window,
just a rack on the inside with clothes hanging on it.

"Only one left."

"What?" Roe had spoken in stillness and Cale realized that
no cars moved down here, just up around the square where the
street was paved.

"This was Summit's finest old section, richest people in town
owned them houses. See them loop posts, few of them left.
That's where they tied up their buggies. They had stained glass
windows and the damndest little decorations on them you ever
seen. Looked like church till you saw they were peacocks and
palm trees. A bitch to paint. See them busted off up there,
all them little curlicues. Had a fireplace in every room. That
was before your time."

They stopped and looked where Roe pointed on the house.
The paint had peeled off the gingerbread and most of the
wooden points had broken off or been spattered by pigeons.
The old woman got up and walked to the edge, craning her
neck around.

"See, it's rotted and busted off."

"What's that?" the old lady hollered and turned her head
sideways.

"I say your house needs painting and it's going to rot away."

She grunted and spit a long brown string of snuff behind the
bushes and went back to her chair.

"But you'll probably rot first." She didn't hear him.

"What happened to their children?"

"Depression. And their children didn't want that kind of crap to keep up. Old lady like that can't understand such as that. Like your grandma Sarah Ann. That old bitch thought it was a sin to sweat. Niggers took over this street and they'll get that one too, soon as she dies. They claw you till the last, but any way you cut it, they gonna die. . . . She'll hiss at you and won't turn loose a thing and one morning she won't wake up and people'll be in there throwing out stuff before they get her out. Maybe there's less room for Sarah Ann's in this world than there is for niggers. To tell you the truth, boy, I can find more use for them."

Roe laughed so Cale laughed too when he slapped him on the shoulder. Cale looked at the tall pointed houses, all tight and squeezed up, and tried to see what it was like when that was all there was. All those steps and points and thin windows like the jailhouse; people must have been wanting something different from him. Like a house you wanted to get out of quick as you could.

All the gingerbread houses turned dark at the end of the street, soot-colored or rotten wood, and he saw colored people in the porch chairs. Then there were no more big houses; they passed the last rose lattice broken off from the ground and held upright by a tangle of honeysuckle. They walked by house fronts so close to the street they stepped down in the gutter so they wouldn't pass so close to the people that they would think they were butting in on their conversations.

They walked still further downhill until Cale couldn't tell what level was or whether the houses were leaning. None of them were painted and there were people everywhere staring at them, colored people, sitting on the steps, on the edge of the porch, and in metal chairs on the porches.

"Ever get that 'watched' feeling, boy?"

They crossed the tracks and went into another dark row of houses, more uneven and this time without unkept lawns, smaller and newer shacks with sand in front beaten hard by children playing. Cale had never seen this, had lived in Summit all his life and had never been through this section. He had seen the niggers down by the river because they had to go that way to get to the train station. It must lead nowhere, this street. Soon they were through the houses and on a short stretch of open road and across a wooden bridge. Cale saw cars moving, the back of a store, Parson's.

"Ain't that Eighteen?"

"Sure is. You never come up the back way?"

"Never did."

"You stay here a second."

Cale watched Roe walk in the back door of Parson's Store. Most of the windows were still out and just closed with cardboard. He felt nervous, awful guilty about something.

Me and Roe is going to see Sal. I know why. I hoped and wished for it a thousand times, I told myself that is what I would get Uncle Roe to do for me, take me to a grown woman to learn how like Tommy done. I just gotta do it. I don't want to keep talking big with the rest of them. I gotta do it.

Roe appeared at the door and he had a bag against his chest. "Clear as the morning dew. Best-looking stuff Parson ever had."

They turned and walked back toward the colored section. Soon they came to a dirt alley and Roe said, "This way."

"Are you sure this is it?"

"Sure I'm sure, boy. Your Uncle Roe found this alley in a pouring rain drunk as a skunk many a time. No reason I shouldn't find it sober."

Cale didn't say anything. That goddamn Tommy. That wasn't even Sal's house they rode by. That lying bastard had never even been to Sal's.

It was getting dark and only the occasional flair of a cigarette on the porch steps told him the houses were occupied. There were no lights inside and Cale felt the night coming in hot

like early summer. At the end of the street they turned into a
drive. Cale saw his first light and it hurt his eyes coming up from
a basement, a light on some dark brick steps. The yard was
sweet-smelling, not stinking like the street of garbage and
food cooking, and he saw the flowers, red lilies that rocked and
sent chills on his arms with spider webs when they walked
through them. Roe walked up to the door and he knocked, not
like Cale would have expected but just like he was going visiting. He heard someone coming, a heavy walk that made the
house vibrate and made something tight draw up in his stomach.

"Who dat?"

"It's Roe Jenkins, Sallie."

"I don't know no Bo Clemings. Who sent you?"

"Wash out your ears, Sallie. Roe Jenkins, and I'm going to
swat your ass good you don't open this door."

The door opened suddenly and Cale saw the laughing face
of a big black woman.

"Roe Jenkins, yuh old sonovabitch. Where yuh been? Lawsy
mercy, done got mealy-mouthed 'fore yuh got here. Come in
before the skeeters do . . . Who dat?"

"That's my nephew, Cale Jenkins. Brought him to meet you."

"Well, yuh come on in, boy. Damn yuh, Roe Jenkins. Yuh
bring me that red kimono yuh promised? I heard yuh been
messing around with a white gal lately. She throw yuh out
reason yuh come see Sallie? She got my red kimono I betcha."

"Sallie, I had you the prettiest one you ever seen and somebody stole my suitcase at the bus station."

"Yuh lying dog. Same as ever. Don't know why I put up with
yuh."

Cale watched the woman go to the cabinet and take down
three jelly glasses, her long black fingers running in the top of
each one. He had never seen a black woman talk so forward.
She stopped and snapped her head around to Roe.

"I ain't doing all this for nothing."

"No sirree. Got it right here." Roe held up the bag. "Best-
looking bottle I seen in a while. Doing it right."

"Bleaching it, you mean."

"Naw."

"Got me batch last week wuz. I ain't gon' go selling bad mess. I got too many friends I wanna keep. Lemme smell."

Sallie took the bag and lifted out the jar of clear liquid. She unscrewed the lid and sniffed it. "Naw, I'm wrong. This one good as gold. How come I don't get none like this? Here."

She held it under Roe's nose. "Yes sir. Like a loaf of fresh-cooked bread. Sallie, where you get Cloroxed liquor? If you don't mind me asking."

"I don't mind telling yuh, Mr. Roe, but I don't be knowing his name, red-headed boy from up Hawtown section."

"Red Simson. I know the bastard. You know him, Cale. He worked on the tobacco."

"I know him, the one with the orange hair." He heard his voice, boylike, and he wished he hadn't answered. Why didn't he wait and take his time and keep it down low. He could keep it down low if he tried.

Sallie looked at Roe and smiled softly, shaking her head.

"Yuh sonovagun Roe."

They looked at each other in silence as Sallie poured the alcohol. Damn it, now she knows what a kid I am, Jesus Christ. I gotta do it, I just gotta. I can't wait off no longer. I gotta do it before I go up to the high school.

"You by yourself up here, Sallie?"

"Naw, not with all the meanness lately. I got me two nice girls living in. One real young." Sallie had a soft voice when she wanted it, real pretty and kinda sad.

"She occupied?"

"Naw, don't much do before nine. Ain't but seven-thirty, Roe. Yuh got no watch? Boy, you ain't touched your juice."

Roe looked at Cale. "You want it watered? Sal, you got a Pepsi?"

"I reckon I got a Co-Cola."

She got up and opened the refrigerator. She had an old stove like they had given to Aunt Bynum who kept it on the porch because his daddy hadn't gotten around to the electricity yet. Aunt Bynum, no sirree, not an Aunt Bynum sonovabitching this and that.

Sallie poured the Coke into Cale's glass and he watched it fall through the liquid in a long brown string. He lifted the glass and sipped it and held it in his mouth until he could swallow, worse than apple sauce, and it spread in his stomach like drinking hot water. He kept on at the glass now, drinking more, watching Sallie and Roe laughing at him. They were moving soon, almost by the third swallow and he had to turn to one, then the other, and blink a few times before he could get what they were saying straight. How come it was just like he expected? Big old colored woman and getting drunk. He won't going to do it with that fat thing. He'd fight Roe before he would.

"One's enough, Sal."

"One to go."

"Naw, he's thirteen, Sal. Two and he'll be a dishrag. He might not make it as it is."

He heard Sallie call a name, Becka, Bella, something, and it pressed inside his eyes. Soon there was a tall black girl beside him, thin and long like she was stretched out. Roe popped him on the shoulder and asked Sallie to save this one for him, and Cale got up and walked beside the woman, her tall over him and guiding him like a child. They went into her room and she locked the door. He tried to talk for the first time but no words came. She was busy anyway, over to the window to pull down the shade.

"Sho hot in here, ain't it honey? Get yuh things off."

Her voice, it was dark suddenly. The light, she cut out the light. He was locked in a dark room with her. Nothing's wrong. That's the way it's supposed to. What'd he think? Uncle Roe was going to watch or something? Something hot in his pants, no, nothing.

She undid her robe and hung it over the chair. He could see her form, but she was only a shadow with white behind her, the moon maybe because there were no street lights. No, the porch light.

"Put yuh clothes dere, honey, so they don't wrinkle."

He stood there. He couldn't move. He'd close his eyes so he couldn't see her. The shadow moved across the room to him and he ran to the door, grabbing for the knob. His clothes stuck to him like glue. He was soaked with sweat.

"Boo. I scare yuh, honey?"

He unlocked the door, expecting hands to grab him from behind but none did. He looked into the kitchen. The light was off and he could see the glasses reflecting in the porch light. Roe was gone. He jumped back against the wall as a warm hand lifted his hand from the knob. She pushed the door back together and locked it.

"Now come on." She spoke gently, she wasn't impatient. Her arm closed around his and she led him to the bed where they sat down. "Ain't gon' be a soul here till eight-thirty, boy. Yuh take yuh sweet time." She began to undo his shirt. "Yuh Unca Roe gon' be gone a spell. Me and yuh just stretch out here by the window. Yuh clean? How 'bout yuh wash yuh thing. Pan's dere."

Cale unzipped his pants and began to wash himself. Water was cold as ice. Made his head clear a second, then it went again soon as he dried off on her towel.

"Smoke?" She lit two cigarettes that were in her mouth, he didn't even see her pick them up and the match flared over her face, hard-boned and shiny. He saw her breasts as she shook out the match, smooth, earth-colored, not near as big as the girl in the shack, and in his mind he could see Roe's woman, the rubber woman with the big red circles on her. He started to giggle.

"What's tickling yuh, boy?"

"My Uncle Roe. He got him this hot water bottle woman . . ."

She didn't answer and he felt her slide his shirt over his

shoulders. She still had both cigarettes in her mouth. "Yuh get off yuh pants and get o'er by de window."

He undid his belt and pulled down his pants leaving his shorts inside them and fell back on the bed. There won't no sheet to cover up and keep her from seeing him. He was getting dizzy. He sure was sleepy. He couldn't get up if the bed was on fire. The room turned in darkness, the foot of the bed, he wished the room was empty so he wouldn't have to close his eyes to be able to see nothing. The bed pressed down as she crawled over to the other side of him and when he reached up he touched her body, warm but not wet and sticky like him.

"I'm all dirty and sticky."

"Naw, yuh fine."

"Did I finish telling you about Uncle Roe's rubber woman?"

"Yeah, told me all 'bout her."

"Where's my cigarette?"

"Burnt out."

"The ceiling is flying in a circle. It's making me sick. I'm gonna upchuck."

"Rub one foot on the floor."

Cale dropped one foot over the bed and scraped it. "Like that?"

"Yeah, put on yuh brakes fer yuh. Stop that spinning business."

He felt fire hit his stomach and reached to knock it away and it was her hand.

"What's that blue light for?" He pointed at the Christmas tree light in the baseboard.

"Keep from stubbing my toe . . . Yuh first time?"

"I'm drunk."

"Naw, yuh ain't."

"I'm drunker than shit. Quit it. I'm getting sick again."

She kept rubbing him and everywhere he reached for her hand she was gone somewhere else.

"I am. I'm going to pass out."

"Naw, yuh jest fine."

"I don't wanna do it."

He heard her laugh and turned his head. Her laugh was muffled but there was no pillow. His head was gone from his body.

"My head just come off. I don't wanna do it."

"Yuh better tell the rest of yuh."

"Huh?"

"Yuh better tell the rest of yuh yuh dun' wanna cause it dun' know."

The darkness moved over him and he felt her body getting sticky on top of him, they were together and he felt her knees in his side as she sat down on him. She began to move up and down pressing her hands in his stomach. He was starting to feel it. Couldn't hold it back. His mind was gone, as he tried to hold back and it was over. There were sounds of them sticking together as she lay down and then it was quiet. They fell sideways and he could feel her breath hot on the top of his head. She had done it. He hadn't done nothing. Tired. Over. He didn't do it, damnit. She did every bit of it. That won't fair. He'd tell Uncle Roe.

He opened his eyes as a hand pushed on his shoulder, thin sharp fingers. He looked up and saw her with the robe back on.

"Get yuh clothes on. Near 'bout eight."

She sounded mean. He looked and saw himself naked and jumped up quickly for his clothes. Something hit his head like an iron bar. But she wasn't there, she was on the other side of the room. There won't no iron bar there neither. He pulled on his pants, undershorts still inside them. He put his shirt around his shoulders and started for the door.

"Shoes."

He walked back to the bed and picked them up, laces still tied. When he stepped into the hall, he could see Roe and Sallie, back at the table drinking. There was music coming from somewhere, and a whole row of blue lights on down the hall. Roe saw him. He looked excited.

"Hey boy, you O.K. Yes sirree, you made out fine. O.K., Bella?"

"O.K."

Cale turned and saw the dark woman leaning against the door. There was a faint smile but her face was smooth as stone. Boy, she was a big woman, six feet tall at least.

"Goddamn, boy. First time. Took your old Uncle Roe three times and him falling all over hisself, didn't it Sal?"

"If I 'member correctly yuh eleven year old."

"First time. How you feel?"

Cale squinted in the light. Then he sat down on the floor to put on his shoes.

"Too much licker, Bella?"

"Jest rite. Yuh pay Mama for me?"

"I pay double you take me."

"Roe, yuh sonovabitch. Ain't Sal good no more, getting old for yuh?"

"Now Sal, when did Roe Jenkins slight anybody?"

He took his money out of his wallet and held it up and Bella nodded and Roe was gone to her room.

"Wait on me, Cale," he called from the door.

"Yuh partial to the floor, boy?"

Cale had his shoes on and was trying to tie the laces. His head fell sideways against the wall and he felt his face slide on the wood, cool. He saw the light bulb over the table and it left a spot before he closed his eyes.

Sunday morning when Cale opened his eyes his first thought was water, getting in it up to his chin and drinking a gallon of it. He was in his underwear instead of his pajamas. Roe put him in bed, that was it. He drank that glass of lightning, with a Coke mixed in it. And he got drunk and passed out and Roe had to tote him home. It happened so fast, just like something put him to sleep. How did Roe get him this far? Were Mama and Daddy awake when he brought me in? He stood up and started toward the bathroom and felt a weight shift in his head. In the bathroom he filled a glass with water and drank it while he peed, in one end and out the other. He wobbled and his hands shook, must be what it's like to be an old man. As soon as the water hit his stomach he felt drunk again, it lighted his head and relaxed the pain behind his eyes. He ran a tub and when he sat down in it, Jerome opened the door.

"So you decided to come home?"

"Huh?"

"What time did you and Roe get in?"

"I don't know. I don't have a watch."

"Don't get sassy with me. I'm not your mother. I'll jerk a knot in you."

Cale scooped his hands full of water and splashed his face, rubbing the crusts out of his eyes. Roe appeared at the door in his shorts and a gym shirt. "What's going on? Family reunion?"

"I just come in to take a bath if ya'll don't mind." When Cale began to soap himself, the water dulled and a skim formed around the edge of the tub.

"I think you're carrying it too far, Roe. You stayed out too late. What is there to do that late? I know it was four so don't lie."

"You dressed for church?"

"Quit changing the goddamn subject. My temper gets short when I don't eat well."

"Me and Cale went in and messed around town."

"And you got him drunk because I heard him puking in his bed in the middle of the night. Never had that sort of thing under this roof before."

"So we had a few drinks. It seems you've had a few drinks in your day, Jerome. I got to explain my doings to my own brother?"

"While you live under my roof you do. You stretching your welcome a little thin in my book."

"Look Jerome. I'll go get Falissa back if that's what's riling you. I'll get a room in town at the boardinghouse and deliver your chief cook and bottle washer to your doorstep. That make you happy?"

"Keep me up half the night."

"Since when you worried over anyone? Since when has Jerome Jenkins lost a night's sleep?"

"Roe, tell me the truth now. I want the straight honest truth out of you. You been taking him to women?"

"What do you mean?"

"I mean did you take him in to one of your whores? He's not but thirteen years old and I want to know if that's what you did last night because there ain't a goddamn thing going on in Summit after one o'clock with decent people but sleeping."

"What if I did?"

"He didn't. We just went in and had a few drinks with some girls Roe knows. I done had my first smoking and cussing. Now I had my first drink."

"You don't have to lie to him, Cale."

Cale looked puzzled. What happened after the drink?

"What you getting so high and mighty about, Jerome? Somebody tell you that's how to be a family man? You pissing me off, Jerome. Hell yeah, I took him in to a whore, a good one, and a pretty one, and he has got one goddamn itch out from under his hat that you would have left there driving him crazy till he was twenty-one if you could. What you think having a youngun is for? Getting you a free work mule? Where you think you'd be now if I hadn't seen to you? I'm telling you, you wouldn't have figured out how to have any younguns. You and Falissa the two most selfish people I ever seen. Treat your younguns like they just around to make you look good. But you remember one thing, that is you need to start subtracting years off a kid's life because it don't take them half as long to grow up anymore. They know more than you do about some things."

"You took him to some dirty whore."

"She won't dirty. She made me wash off."

"I thought you said you didn't go!"

"Well, I don't remember good. I guess I did. I did, huh, Uncle Roe? I did it."

"You damn right you did it and Bella said you won't half scared and she ain't never seen such a little character as you. She had fine things to say about you."

"She did?"

Jerome grabbed Roe's shoulder and shoved him in the bathroom. "Now you listen to me, you bastard . . ."

"Watch it, Jerome. That's a reflection on our parents."

Cale laughed and Jerome tossed a bottle of aspirin off the sink and hit him in the forehead.

"Ouch, that hurt." He touched it with his fingertips and there was blood.

Then Jerome turned to Roe and hit him across the face with his hand, a loud slap, and Cale was sure it hurt Jerome worse than Roe.

"Now you listen. I'm going to church. I'm going to get Falissa and bring her and Pearlie back home. And I want your ass and everything that belongs to you out of here when I get back. And you boy. You go out and get you some kerosene and take you another bath. It might be too late . . ."

"Lay off him, Jerome. They were clean."

"You do as I say, boy. Your Uncle Roe has wallowed around in filth so long it don't bother him."

Cale didn't answer but held the rag to his head.

"Answer me, goddammit."

"Yes sir."

Jerome turned and left and they were silent until they heard the front door slam.

"I messed us up good, Roe. I'm sorry."

"You didn't mess up nothing. I guess I don't know my fucking brother."

Before church let out Roe had his things packed up. He had collected more belongings than he thought, five large cardboard boxes full, things he had brought from overseas or won at the fair or gotten from mail order houses. He threw out a toy dog he had bought from a man on the street. It had barked and turned flips, then when he got it home, he found out the man was throwing his voice and it didn't make a sound. But the rest he couldn't stand to give up and Cale took the toy dog and put it on the bed pillow in Pearlie's room. He and Cale carried them out to the packhouse to store them until he could come for them. Roe left down the highway, dressed in a sport shirt and slacks with his duffel bag over his shoulder, thumbing toward town to the Shady Lawn Tourist Home where he had called and gotten room and board for five dollars a week. Cale was to meet him down at the river after dinner at six-thirty and they were going down to check on Red Simmons' still. If Cale wasn't there by six forty-five, Roe was to know he couldn't get away and go without him.

Cale dressed in his Sunday shirt and pants even though there wasn't time for him to get to church. Might rile Mama if he sat at the Sunday dinner table in his overalls. He went into the kitchen and cleaned up the pile of dishes that was already collected and scraped his daddy's stuck egg out of the pan and carried out the bag of garbage that was already drawing flies. He threw it across the trash pile, right on top where the rubber woman was hidden. Roe never did ask what happened to her. He took his and Roe's sheets and rolled them in a ball on the back porch after he turned the hose on them. He got gagged all over again when he smelled them, but nothing came up this time but water that stung the top of his head and in his nose. By the time he heard a car door slam out front, he had the table set for the whole family. He looked through the window and he saw all three of them getting out of somebody's car they'd gotten a ride with, just like always only he wasn't with them. Mama wasn't smiling and she looked very tired but Pearlie was the same as always. She ran and jumped on her swing and started pumping.

"Pearlie, change your clothes first. I'll switch you good if you snag that dress too."

Pearlie jumped out of the swing and ran up on the porch. She was the first in the house. Her crinoline was already hanging down on one side and she hitched it up when she came across the living room.

"He gone?" she whispered.

"Yeah, he left this morning."

"That's good because Mama said she was leaving again if he was still here."

"Did you want him out?"

"Uh-uh."

"Well, that's good to hear. Mama is acting like a fool if you want to know what I think and if you tell her I said that I'll beat your ass."

Pearlie stuck her tongue out at him and giggled. Then she ran upstairs to her room pulling her dress over her head on the way up. As she ducked around the corner he saw Sunday written in red on the back of her underpants. The front door shut again and his mother and father walked across the living room. His mother walked directly to Roe's room. The bed was stripped, the spread folded, and the room was empty. Cale watched his mama walk across the room and run her finger through the dust on the dresser. They had forgotten that when they packed up and there were circles of clean wood on top of the dresser where his Kewpie dolls had been sitting.

"Cale, you'll dust in here while I get dinner ready?"

"Yes, ma'am."

"And run the carpet sweeper a few times. That should hold it until I have time to give it a thorough going through next week. Does that mattress smell musty to you?"

"No, ma'am."

"Does to me. Might be the rug. Take till next spring to get the dampness out."

"I put the sheets in the dirty clothes basket on the porch, and his towel and washcloth."

She stopped at the door and shut it behind her. "Cale, I want to speak to you a minute."

"O.K."

"I know right now you're thinking I'm the meanest and most unfair person in the world."

He didn't answer and when she started talking more he looked at his feet so he wouldn't have to see her eyes on him.

After a while, she stopped talking. This must have been her day to teach Sunday school, had to be, because she brought that voice home with her, that was her primary school voice. Roe just didn't know. He would hate her as much as I do if he could be the fly on the wall in this room right this minute. I don't want Daddy to spend more time with me, or her either. I want them both to leave me alone.

"Mama, since I didn't get to Sunday school today do you think it would be a good idea if I went to the Training Union tonight after supper. I hadn't missed since I had the measles."

"I think that is a wonderful idea, Cale. In fact, I would like to see you start going regular."

"Yes, ma'am."

Chapter 25

CALE WAS DOWN BY THE RIVER at six-fifteen. He took an afternoon nap and felt better. His daddy hadn't said word one to him all day but he won't mean, just quiet. Truth was, bet he kinda missed Roe and was sorry for what he said. He had felt itchy all day. His damn old man. Now he would have to worry about bugs. He won't going to wash in kerosene. He did last time he got into chiggers and it like to have set him on fire. Rather have the chiggers and the bugs. He kept looking at himself every time he went to the bathroom but it didn't seem any different. In fact nothing seemed any different. All this time waiting and planning on how the woman won't going to know it was the first time and she would have known anyway and then get so damn drunk you don't remember what really happened anyway. Won't five minutes. Couldn't have been five minutes he was with her. But he passed out. It did get to be eight o'clock somehow. Couldn't even see her in that dark room.

Wouldn't I like to tell Tommy? I should have asked if he'd been there. Then wouldn't I have it on him? You don't even know where Sallie's is, Tommy. I'll take you there sometime. She's got a Budweiser light in her kitchen with Custer's Last Stand on it and she drinks out of jelly glasses. She's got blue Christmas tree lights that light up all along the hallway down on the baseboard so you can find your way in the dark. And

Bella's got one in her room. Pretty as a picture, tall and got straight hair and a kimono with white balls hanging on it. What you know, Tommy? Shit, you don't even know where she lives. I'm going back to see old Bella again. Bet she'll remember me. I hear Roe cracking through. He'll be surprised to see me I betcha.

"Hey boy!"

"Hey, Uncle Roe."

"I'll be damn. I didn't expect you to make it."

"You would have been proud of me, Uncle Roe. I am attending the Training Union at Wet Springs Baptist Church."

"No lie. Wondered why you had on a clean shirt."

"You know where it is?"

"What?"

"The still."

"Oh sure. It's half mine. I set it up and got it going but it smells like to me somebody's been using it in the off hours. Can't you smell it in the water? Bad time to run with no rain. Getting too sparse in the trees."

"No, at least I never noticed it. To tell the truth, Uncle Roe, I don't know nothing about it."

There it went again. It was so easy to tell Uncle Roe you didn't know something. One of the days I'll tell him I don't remember how I done it with Bella. That oughta tickle him.

"Well, why didn't you say so? Let me go from the beginning. Start on off down the bank path."

Cale walked in front of him feeling the silk of spider webs tickle across his face, just like last night in the canna lilies. The leaves were starting to thin and he could see all the way around the bend of the river. Water was kinda low.

"You start with drums, see, big fifty-five-gallon oil drums, and you put the stuff in there to work it off. That's about fifty pounds of sugar and fifty pounds of cornmeal and some baker's yeast to get it moving. That's how my old man got caught once, 'fore he even started the making. The old fool went into the general store, downtown mind you, not Parson's because he was pissed at Parson for what he paid him on his last haul, he went into the general store and asked for five hundred pounds of sugar and all the yeast in the store, standing right beside the sheriff's wife who happened to have the recipe in her collection. You see why I'm surprised you got good sense with relatives like that? So they hauled him in for questioning and me and Jerome slipped out like we didn't belong to him and run home on foot and covered the whole business up with a load of horse manure and put the barrels of meal in the barn like we was going to feed it to the cows. And Papa Willie come home with half the sheriff's department following his wagon in a twenty-seven Ford, our old mule just plopping along and stalling, and me and Jerome was just like deaf and dumb. Didn't know no nothing they asked us. Willie had done told them he feared a war was coming and he was stocking up on his sugar. And you know that sonovabitch got off. Willie could haul the Confederate Monument out and put it in his front yard and they'd let him off. Hey, slow down a little buddy. You got more spring in your legs than me. So he went back and hauled off the sugar, five hundred pounds, and a big pack of yeast. And he put it in the barrels, he had near 'bout ten of them and started throwing in the horse manure to get it to working faster, that's to get the yeast going, and that stuff foamed up and Willie drank it right off the top of the barrels, right out of that horse manure. The truth is, that's beer foaming on top is what it is anyway and Willie got so goddamn drunk that he passed out and the whole batch turned to enough vinegar to open a pickle factory. Let me stop and get my breath."

Cale stopped and turned around. Roe's face was red and he was panting and choking on his laughs.

"Old man can't take a night like last night too often."

"I felt better myself."

"Damn old Willie. I can talk about him to beat the band but

I don't want to be in the same county with him. What time does your Training Union let out?"

"I think it's safe to go till nine."

"Anyway I was telling about the still. I told you how to make vinegar, now I got to tell you how to make liquor. Now after you got the stuff ready in the barrels, that's one of the times you got to watch it by the way, one of the times because it can stink to high heaven and it don't take a bloodhound to find it. In fact a sheriff with a head cold can find it. Then you got to run it through the still, that's when you make the stuff, keep walking. I get a smell in the air that ain't pleasing me. That's where the river comes in if you want to do it right and this is a bad time down here to do it right. What you do is cook it on one end, send it through a coil and catch it at the other. Had to be damn simple or Willie would have messed it up. He'd heard of people getting old radiators out of cars to use for a still so he got him about ten and started running it through and it ran off full of lead and antifreeze and crap with enough poison to kill a mule. But Willie wouldn't throw it away, just sold it and kept the next batch for hisself. I'd like to know how many people pushing up lilies over Willie's liquor. Anyway after a while he got to doing it right, after he like to have burnt his own guts out. Pissed in his pants a few times until he figured he'd rusted out his plumbing. Then he figured he'd better plumb his still right. Best thing is water pipe, copper it better be or it'll be poison as a black toadstool. What you do is find a tree the right size and wrap it around it and cut down the tree and pull it off. That's what you do after your stubborn old man breaks up about ten feet of that expensive stuff trying to coil it by hand because he's too goddamn lazy to cut down a tree. Then you hook up to the boiler and pump it full of stuff you done worked off and you throw the wood to it and get it going good and if you're making it right you get a stream off big as my little finger. That's all there is to it. I'll show you how some day. Me and you could get it going and the money's the finest around, I'm telling you."

"Won't we get arrested?"

"Aw come on. You oughta know that if we get caught, we'll get put under the jail. There's ways not to get caught. It ain't the law you worry about. Law gets you then you got to donate a few quarts to the cause, that's all. It's the people you got working with you. 'Bout to get a lesson in that."

"Why they on the river?"

"Oh, forgot that. Got to keep that coil cold so the alcohol will come through, drip off like sweat on a tin roof, can't let it get hot or it quits, floats out and makes lightning in the sky Papa Willie used to say. That's what I was telling you about, last night at Sallie's. Those bastards tried to do it too fast and burnt it. And poor old Sallie. She don't know no better than to drink it. That's what burns me is some bastard passing off the bad on her 'cause she don't know no better. She knows now and will throw his ass in the street next time. You just can't run it too fast. It will scorch like a shirt, get brown as muddy water. Many times as I told Sallie, look for a smell like a fresh-cooked bread loaf and she'll mouth it back and drink the first bad bottle she gets. I don't know if she knows no better or not. I'm getting it in the air, boy. You getting it in the air?"

"I don't smell nothing."

"Try again. Get still a minute. Get your cheek in the breeze, got it."

Cale stopped and breathed deeply. Roe was panting hard from the walking.

"I guess I smell something."

"They just took off the low middling and are sending the rest downstream. I bet you money. Those bastards thought they could get off a quick one. Stretching out on me on my day of rest. They'll be a nervous bunch till the air clears. They getting the lids on the high run now and that bastard Red is loading in the wagon to take up to the barn. Hear them. Listen."

"Uncle Roe. There's a man. And I think he's got a gun."

"I think I'd stop right there, boy, and turn myself back around the other direction," the man said.

"Hop Simmons. Shut your goddamn mouth."

"Roe Jenkins?"

"Yeah, you sonovabitch. You sure is acting suspicious. What you up to? You squirrel hunting?"

"Yeah, I'm squirrel hunting."

"Well, I'm the game warden and it's out of season."

Roe shook hands with Hop. Almost like they shook hands so they wouldn't have to fight.

"How you been, Roe?"

"O.K. My nephew Cale, here. Red with you?"

"Yeah, up there a ways."

Cale shook Hop's hand.

"Shouldn't have brung a kid up here. Talk too much."

"He don't talk too much. He goes everywhere I go."

"Kid caused Parson's fights to shut down."

"How come?"

"Shot off his mouth at the school. Kid told his old man. Old man was a do-gooder and that's all brother. Don't like no kid around."

"This kid don't talk. Except to me. Looks like something's going you're trying to hide from more than kids. You and Red are running, aren't you?"

"Yeah, I guess we are. What's it to you?"

"A goddamn lot if Red ain't bothered to tell you. Walk on through." They walked through the bushes and the odor became definite.

"Hop, your nose must be worn out. This is going to carry to Main Street. Ya'll out of your heads?"

"We closing up here today."

"Oh? How come?"

"Got a betta place. Packing up and moving."

Roe walked over to Red who nodded but didn't shake hands. He was over a row of wide-mouthed Mason jars and he had a bottle in his hand, like Mama soaking the collars of their shirts, Clorox.

"You bastard, Red."

"What's it to you?"

"You are a goddamn fucking bastard. Looks like I shoulda taken a walk every Sunday afternoon. Somebody I know don't celebrate the Sabbath."

Red continued to pour the Clorox. "Hop, show Mr. Jenkins the way out."

"Just wanted to see for myself. Thought supplies thinned out fast."

"When you get so hot? You get you a nigger jar? I ain't got to explain my time to you. These is mine and Hop's nigger jars. We don't use any of the good stuff here. We do all the work. What's it to you?"

"It's an agreement we made, that's what it is to me. I don't like nobody trying to slip around on me. And it don't take that much longer to make it good."

"Not when I get two for the price of one."

"Got one more thing to say to you, Red, then I'll be going."

"You might be going before that. Get the gun, Hop, and put on the rest of the lids. You are standing on my property in case you forgot."

"You get this straight, Red, and don't let it slip your mind. Not much there for it to slip over so hang on to it. You give Sallie good stuff. You give Sallie another bottle of bad stuff and I'll kill you."

"How you planning on killing me, Roe? Looks like I got the cards."

"You know goddamn good and well who's got the cards. You got a wife. You got a record. And you got a witness." Roe turned to look at Cale who had moved in close to his elbow. "And I ain't got nothing to worry about taking care of but me. Let's go, boy."

Cale turned and started to walk quickly back to the woods. When he got in the cover of the trees, he got away from Roe.

"Slow down, boy. Don't let old shit mouth scare you. Take it easy. He ain't going to do nothing."

"What'd you go there for, Roe? Now they'll be after you."

"They were already after me. See I figured they were running extra on my stuff but I hadn't figured they were running bad stuff. Sloppy bastard."

"What are they after you for?"

"I'll have to keep that my business for a while. You just don't forget what you saw in case I need it. You keep it inside your head word for word and don't you mention it until I ask for it. Nobody else, just me, you understand."

"I understand."

Cale nodded his head. The woods were getting dark and he started stumbling but Roe walked ahead like he had been through before. *He has been bootlegging all along and I didn't know it.*

When they got back to the bank behind the farm, Roe looked at his watch, close to his face in the dark. "Eight-thirty. You back early. See you later boy. I ain't used to all this exercise. I'm going to go to bed. Remember where I am if you want to come in visiting."

Roe slapped him on the shoulder and was gone. He felt funny, real empty. The leaves were coming down fast on the path, maybe a storm stirring up. Chill in the air, needed a jacket. Winter would come in fast now.

Just something was wrong. Something felt all wrong. When he saw the back side of the barn and the porch light he felt really alone again, just his own walking he could hear.

August, 1954

Cale didn't go back to Bella's. He was sure he wouldn't the night after he and Roe went to the still. He was scared, scareder now than he was before he went. When he was in town twice on Training Union night, he skipped out and went by the Shady Lawn Tourist Home but there was no one there both times but an old man in a rocker on the porch who said Roe wasn't there and that he had never seen anyone there who matched Roe's description. The man didn't act bright so he never was sure if it was the truth. Roe didn't show up at the farm all winter and by the next spring the place was back to normal. The outside work picked up and by summer he usually sat on the porch at night, sometimes falling asleep in his chair, listening to the outside noises that could drown out people talking. But then he would get in bed and toss about from the heat, never as restful there as in his chair on the porch, on and off with the sheet, waiting for the breeze that never seemed to blow and the rain that never came. Lightning filled the room silently and out-lined everything like day then fell into dark. He couldn't keep his eyes shut until it quit. He watched through the window to see if the light would ever catch anything sneaking around but it never did, once a possum maybe, but he wasn't sure those were glass eyes looking at him. Then it broke all at once and the rains came and lay in red ditches between the rows, sagging the tobacco leaves like rags and washing all the roots above ground.

And it wouldn't stop coming. All they could do was wait and hope it would quit and hear his daddy say over and over, "Only two things sure to come in this world, taxes and bad weather." So you sat on your ass and took it, just watched it come and do as it pleased. His daddy moved with a slow, dull resistance to everything. He hadn't even raised his voice since that day Roe left. The whole barn would collapse and he'd shake his head and say "Damn." Everything in the garden was swollen and breaking out of its skin and his hands broke through the vegetable flesh, the cucumbers, tomatoes that he picked for his mother and his hands stunk with a rot that wouldn't wash off. His feet broke like the vegetables, swollen, split and yellow and his body was cut in half at the waist when he sat in the tub, brown top and white bottom, rusty feet, and the grit cut him under his tail. He even smelled like a goddamn farmer. Not like hay and corn but like green weeds, ragweed. His feet grew out the bottom of his jeans and his ankles stretched longer, white, and he didn't get no new pants till next year, or till school anyway. He was going into the high school this fall a clod, and he had already seen the guys wearing black pants with buckles on the back, pink shirts, tassel shoes and he was going to be a goddamn starched-shirt clod with creases in his blue jeans with his collars ironed out flat with the points clean to the shoulders because that was the only way his mama knew how to iron. He'd wear T-shirts till it got cold. His hair was long though, she didn't mess with that, just bitched at him and he ignored her, and his old man didn't care and he ducktailed it with water.

Then one day in late August everything that had settled into place changed again. He wouldn't have let it happen but things had gotten so slow, so dull. He was in town taking in a deposit for the money from the first tobacco load. It was cash — two hundred and fifty dollars — and he was always nervous about money. He started straight to the bank, he wasn't even stopping off for a cold drink until he got it in when he saw Roe, standing in front of the drugstore. He looked funny, old like the color had washed off the sides of his hair, almost like his old man. Roe called to him but he ducked in the bank and got in the line for deposits. Roe came in behind him.

"Hey boy, you not recognizing me these days?"

"Hey Roe. Yeah, I saw you but I got this money and I wanted to get inside with it. You know what I mean?"

Roe looked angry. "Well, I hadn't remembered stealing from my kin."

"I didn't mean that, Roe. I just didn't want to stand out on the street with it. I promised the old man I'd take it straight here and I don't want him to ever say I didn't if something happened."

"I got you."

He looked at Roe close now. He hadn't shaved, his shirt was dirty. Roe wasn't doing well. Looked like when he got off the bus the first day, only older.

"Where you been, Roe? I come in to see you at the Tourist Home and they didn't know you."

"Yeah, well, they don't see much of me." He looked around the bank. "Getting fancy in here, plastic plants and the rest."

"Been like that awhile."

"Yeah. Well, I'm not at the Tourist Home. I won't there a week. Old bastard wouldn't give me a key and locked me out so much I might as well of not had a bed. I been down at Sallie's."

"You been living in niggertown?"

"Your turn."

"Oh." Cale turned and handed the money over. It was rolled with a rubber band around the bankbook. She stuck the book in a typewriter and started to count the money.

"It's two hundred fifty dollars." She kept counting and didn't look up.

"Hey, how 'bout you meeting me for a beer tonight, boy?"

"Can't. No way I can go off on week nights."

"Next Sunday then."

"No beer on Sunday."

"I can get beer on Sunday, boy. You meet me at Parson's Store and we'll talk over the latest. I want you to catch me up on your doings."

"I will if I can, Roe. I don't know I can get away."

"Please boy. I'd like to talk to you."

"O.K. Roe. I'll see you about six-thirty out front of Parson's unless something comes up I can't get away."

Roe slapped Cale on the shoulder and was gone. Almost like he was begging him, lonesome or something.

Sunday night he left with a longer excuse, a party over at one of the girl's houses after the Training Union to hear some missionary talk. No, he didn't know where, he'd find out when he got there. Yes, he would wear a white shirt since he would be walking by the road late.

It was good to get outside because he had been working on a

drawing since he left Roe and his eyes had gotten fuzzy. Last week he had shown his shop teacher, Mr. Smith, one of his houses he was drawing; the one with the open rafters but he didn't say much. Acted like his feelings were hurt because he couldn't read the plan and said go show it to the drafting teacher, said it like he was mad. So that was the end of that because the drafting teacher didn't think there was anything in the world but rulers and tracing paper and somebody else's plans. There were some books in the Public Library but none you could take home except for the one on Frank Lloyd Wright. That was the one. He was really something. Trouble was the book didn't tell enough and the librarian said there wasn't enough interest to order more, that he was the only person who checked out the book they had. Still you could tell a lot from the pictures; you could tell the houses would make you feel good if you were inside them. To make you feel as good inside as outside even in good weather, that was the best thing. Papa Lonza's old house wasn't like that, like it was meant to make you run out first chance you got, squeezed you in so many little rooms you didn't even think it was big until you looked at it from the outside. But anything else would be a long time coming to Summit. They all drove by and stared at the new ranch type house near town and whispered about how terrible it must be to have the bedrooms right downstairs next to the living room, and imagine everything on one floor. That was Summit for you; Raleigh was already full of them. They'd be out of style before Summit built another one. He'd have to remember to ask Roe if he'd seen it.

He got to Parson's early, six-fifteen, and sat on the concrete wall that was on the river bridge. All part of the same river that snaked through Yellow County, full of everybody's waste, somewhere in that foam was the washout of their tobacco field, the rain downtown, probably still was getting Red's "low middlings," the foul last run that wasn't fit for anyone, even niggers. Would probably kill the fish, might not be any fish now up this far. He hadn't been back there either, to the clearing with the brown-rusted barrels, spewing foam, woodsmoke. Didn't want no part of that, somebody else could make his money that way. The river was clear once, dull in the twenties from Soloman's dumpings, cleared up in the thirties, clean clear when he was a little boy and he and Papa found the fish; smelly now with sewer strings hanging on the crayfish, growing on the bottom like green hair. The deep woods was still good, there was still some fishing in the deep woods where smoke came off the water after a rain and all the runoff came through the pinestraw. But you didn't swim no more, even in the deep woods. If you swam it was in the fish pond where you knew where the water came from and you didn't go in until you got your typhoid booster. You didn't go into Raleigh to swim in the park pool because of polio, it was shut down they heard. Summit had had three cases, one died, one came to school with a short leg on a shoe like a stump, a girl who kept her hand in her dress pocket. His mama checked them every Saturday, made them bend their necks and touch their chins to their chests while she rammed her cold fingers into the backs of their necks, hurt here? here?

The cars swished across behind him but he didn't turn around, tried to guess them by their sound and caught their shape in the curve below the river to see if he was right. They sucked his sweat-wet shirt away from his back and settled it back again, cool. Clod Mama, look at the clod sitting on the river bridge, spitting, chewing 'backy. Rotten teeth, hayseeds in his hair, and we are going to Florida on Highway 18 and stay at a motel. We are going where we can pick oranges and coconuts, where the palm trees grow like the clods wear on their shirts. Pen leaks ink in the bottom of his shirt pocket, no, he won't have a pen till he gets older and sells shoes. You won't ever marry a clod honey, you won't listen to his name if he's from the country. Where you from? I'm from Charlotte. Well, I'm from Summit, City of Tomorrow.

"Penny for your thoughts, buddy."

Cale jumped and felt his body rock on the bridge until

his fingers held him. He almost fell, god, that would have been stupid.

"Hey, Roe."

"Didn't mean to be late on you. What you thinking on?"

"Nothing much. Mostly how I want to get out of Summit before I'm from Summit."

"You already from Summit. I'm from Summit."

"Yeah, but you been places, Roe."

"I been places but I'm from Summit. And I'm back."

"Why you back, Roe? Why don't you get out of this place and tell people like Mama to go to hell? You can get out. You done it before. I wanna go somewhere where you don't just farm and barely make it through the winter just so you can start all over again."

Roe jumped up beside him and dangled his feet on the road-side. He was cleaned up but he still looked older. Looked a lot better though.

"I been out, you right about that. And I don't say everybody hadn't ought to do it once in his life. But I got scared and figured it was time to get back. I ever tell you about when I got scared? You want to get some beer?"

"Not really. Not unless you do."

"O.K. I'll tell you about it. It was in Atlantic City, right before I come home when I got scared. I was out walking and I got cracked on the head. Simple as that. Got hit on the head and felt it stinging and wet and I lay in the gutter all night and got to shaking right before sunup and couldn't find my mouth and couldn't find my legs and didn't nobody know I was there until the garbage man shoved me with his foot. I looked up and this nigger was pushing me with his foot, 'If you alive, buddy you better get going, cop through here at seven, and I got scared. I was up and out fore he got the can turned up. I got the shakes for two days everywhere I went. In the amusement park, in the cafe and in my room, I just kept looking for people to talk to, acting like one of them lonely old bastards who runs a rooming house that I was always trying to shake, you know the kind I mean? That's when I sent Jerome that telegram. I couldn't stand myself anymore."

Roe was silent. "I'd get scared too, Uncle Roe, if somebody hit me in the head. I'm scared to death of that when I got the tobacco money and it hardly ever happens around here."

"Naw, naw, that ain't it. You awful young, yes sir, you are. I just got scared I was gonna be lying there dying in some strange place, boy, it won't the dying. I just won't sure I had any friends. It was going out all puny and weak, draining out on the ground like somebody pulled out the plug and not having no voice. That got me about the voice. Not having no voice to say I'm Roe Jenkins, buster, and don't you forget, waiting for them to roll me over and go through my pockets and scratch their head and put a tag in my ear and send me off for the state to put in the ground, not North Carolina's, either. New Jersey it was, or Japan or Germany or wherever they didn't want me stinking up the place and drawing flies on top the ground and they put me under. That ain't no way to go out. No, to stand there and say I want Cale Jenkins to have this guitar and Pearlie Jenkins to have this music box and damn right my name is Jenkins and I got kin to be notified. You want to see why I did, boy. Now don't you laugh at this because I done it serious."

He reached in his pocket and pulled out a card. "My name is Roe Jenkins," Cale read, "upon acident or dying call Jerome Jenkins, Summit North Carolina, 5-7298."

"You ought to do that, boy. Everybody ought to do that. You got any identification, boy?"

"No, but people know me around here. You spelled accident wrong. It's got two c's."

"Might not end up dying around here. Might die here and get thrown on a boxcar and end up in New Orleans where nobody knows you. You can't ever tell about that."

"They could look through your black book, Roe. Get one of your gals to come identify you."

"Gals forget. Quick as you forget them. I got to go taking off again, Cale."

"Aw, how come, Roe? I didn't know you were getting at that. When you got to leave?"

"Real soon. I got in some trouble."

"With the police?"

"Naw, I'd rather it be with the police. With somebody the police don't protect you from and I got to get going because there ain't but one of me and a bunch of them. You know what I mean."

"They going to gang up on you? Why don't you tell Daddy? He could get a bunch of men together for your side. You ought not let them run you off."

"It's real bad what I'm in, Cale. Well, not to me but to him. He don't want his name associated with it. I'm not ashamed to leave, you see. I just hate to go off and leave my friends."

"Can you tell me what it is?"

"Naw. And not 'cause I don't trust you. 'Cause I'm ashamed. Anyhow, that's why I wanted special to see you tonight. I'm heading out on the morning bus."

"Where to, Roe?"

"Thought I'd try the Everglades. Always wanted to see the swamps and they say alligator hunting is where the money is. I'll keep you posted. I'll send you a card soon as I get there."

Cale watched the last edge of the sun through the trees. He looked down and found it in the water, spread out like a broken egg. The heat wasn't leaving with the sun, just the light and some of the stinking dusty smells of the dirt-coated road flowers, bitterweed. The lightning bugs were out, popping on and off. He closed one in his hand, the red-black split-wing insect lighting up between his fingers before it lifted off again. Mosquito on Roe's arm, pop, broken body and a red squirt on his skin. Roe had on a spread-collar shirt and pleated pants. Roe smelled like a farmer too.

They started down the road. A headlight slid under their

feet as a car went by. "A thirty-six. Nice one. Was it blue or black?"

"Black, I think. Been down to the track lately, Roe?"

"Not recently. Hear Jones is getting whipped regular."

"I'm glad of that."

"He busted a tire first of the summer and rolled over and broke his arm out the window. Ain't had the cast off but two weeks so he might pick up."

A truck pulled out of Parson's, loose tail gate with the chain jingling. They could hear the gravel go against the rain barrel and across the Coke sign, tat, tat, tat, just like at the track as the truck came down the road behind them, engine sounded like one from the drags. Roe stopped still, his hand clawed into Cale's shoulder.

"Jesus God, boy!"

As Cale swung around he saw the lights of the truck, bright beams coming right at the shoulder. He jumped and Roe pushed but something sharp cut his leg before he fell over the side of the ditch. Roe's hand snapped away from his shoulder and he went across the hood of the truck, bouncing into the glass with a dull crack and over the other side onto the highway. When Roe hit the highway, the truck was gone, roaring and popping like a dragster, one red light down the highway. Cale was in the shallow ditch. Nothing hurt but his eyes were shutting. The ground was all around him. Truck was blue-black and there was a red devil driving it, glowing in the dark like the one he saw walking in the chicken lot.

* * *

Got no way to put it back like it was. Got no way at all to make it day before yesterday and make it not happen. And I can't find no way to sleep anymore. I slept clean through last night and part of this morning and now my foot is hurting and my head just won't quit turning. I'm all hot and sore around the eyes like I been crying when I don't even remember it. The last I remember was Uncle Roe, going in the air, and a light, red, somewhere. The front door has opened and shut a thousand times and people keep driving up, slamming doors. And nobody has asked me to explain nothing. Mama and Daddy just stare at me and ask am I all right. Don't want me to explain nothing, tell them where I was, why I was with Roe. They're saving it. They are going to come in at me with it hard and fast and I don't know. It was on purpose. That truck run off deliberate and hit us. And he just kept going. Sheriff's car has been, I seen it but he didn't talk to me. He talked to Mama and she wouldn't let him I bet. They put me off up here by myself and won't none of them there. It was me there with him. And Uncle Roe is already at the funeral home in town. They aren't going to keep him here like they did Papa. I'm not going to get to see him. Mama said I wasn't going to either.

Pearlie sat in there all night while the people were here and wound up that little dog and let it run down and now I can hear it clacking like it is right inside my head. She is such a little kid. She doesn't even know it's supposed to bother her that Uncle Roe got run over and she just cried tonight because she saw everybody was upset. She wasn't crying over Uncle Roe and Mama patted her on the back and took her into her room and talked to her like she had the sense to know what happened but she don't know. She just believes everything everybody tells her and Mama says someone dying is supposed to make you sad so she starts crying. Why they make like it matters to her? It was me it happened with. It was me that seen that truck bust Uncle Roe all up. And it was done on purpose. Ran off the road to get him. I'm sure of it.

The door to Cale's room popped open and the light spread in slowly. "Go back in your room." Pearlie stood in the square of light. She shut it and came inside. "You're not supposed to be in here. You're supposed to be asleep."

"Cale, can I sit in here a minute?" She climbed up on the edge of his bed. She had on her white nightgown but she hadn't put on her slippers. She must have just got out of bed.

"What you want?"

"They're all downstairs talking and I can't sleep. I got scared and I don't want Mama to come in again."

"What are you scared of?" She whimpered so he talked easier.

"Uncle Roe."

"Well, you got no reason to be because he's dead and isn't going to be able to do anything anymore to scare anybody. When did you ever have any reason to be scared of him anyway?"

"Did you see him? Mama said I couldn't."

"No, I didn't see him since it happened and I'm not going to. Pearlie, I don't want to talk about it anymore. I told you this afternoon. It was a very bad thing. He got run over. You've seen things get run over before. Somebody run over a loose pig right in front of the house once, remember? That's what happens to people too. Uncle Roe walked out in front of a car."

"Mama says he went to heaven."

"Uncle Roe? He wouldn't have nothing to do with heaven. He went to hell. And I know it because I saw the devil get him."

Pearlie balled up in a little knot on the foot of his bed and started crying, not loud.

"Pearlie, cut that out now. I'm sorry. I was kidding. Don't go crying again, please. What did I say wrong and I'll take it back?"

"I don't want him to go to the bad place."

"Well, he wouldn't want to go to the good place. He didn't like those people. I didn't think you cared anything about him anyway."

She started crying again.

"Pearlie, please stop. Don't cry. I don't know why you're crying. I wish you would tell me."

"Uncle Roe is hurting."

"No, he isn't. That's not right. It's living people that hurt. My foot hurts where the truck hit me but Uncle Roe doesn't hurt. He doesn't feel anything anymore and he's happy and resting. Dead people don't hurt. Whoever told you that?"

"I heard Daddy say he was bust in a million pieces."

"He was not. I seen it better than Daddy. I oughta know. He died real quick, Pearlie. Like that pig. You couldn't see a mark on him. It hurt for an instant then it was gone and nothing felt anymore. Now Uncle Roe is like when you're asleep and the only difference is that he isn't going to wake up."

She sat up and looked at Cale, wiping her face on her sleeve. She wasn't putting on, she really was crying. Mama got her all upset about it. She messed up on telling her what happened. Got to go and make something religious out of everything. Why didn't she just say he was dead and say what dead was.

"Pearlie, he's gone where Papa Lonza is. And Grandma Sarah Ann. And where we will all go someday when we get old and die or if something happens to us. And it isn't bad. The getting sick and hurt and dying is bad but after that is good. You believe that, don't you? That things are going to be even better than they are here after you die? You don't have to hurt anymore then."

She sniffed and nodded her head.

"O.K. then. That's all there is to it. Uncle Roe is up there telling jokes and buying things for the little girls in heaven . . ."

"You said he didn't go there."

"Well, I don't know for sure. We can't know for sure. He don't know what we know and we don't know what he knows. And he isn't going to be able to talk to us about it anymore so we have to guess about each other. But it's not bad, Pearlie. To hurt is bad but to die isn't. O.K.?"

"O.K."

"Can you go back and go to sleep now?"

"I think maybe."

"O.K., and if you have any more questions, you ask me, O.K. Don't ask Mama, just ask me. I know the answers usually and if I don't I'll find out for you, O.K."

"O.K."

Pearlie jumped to the floor. She opened the door slowly and

waved to Cale and was gone to her room, leaving a crack of
light showing in his door. He got out of bed and pushed it to.
When he walked he felt dizzy, like getting up to go to the bathroom when he'd been asleep. Pains shot through his foot each
time he put his weight down on it. He got back in bed and tried
to think but his mind was getting slow and jumbled. He
had to remember tomorrow, to think about it tomorrow. Did
Roe go to hell? That wasn't right. It couldn't be. Roe didn't
believe in any of that stuff. He never went to church and they
couldn't make him go where he didn't want to. There couldn't
be any such place as heaven and hell. Where were they? They
were just made up like all the rest of it. They just make something up to keep you from really knowing about things. When
they run out of answers they start making things up.

*   *   *

Willie didn't come. In all the papers, first hit-and-run in
Summit since a child was run down with a buggy in '02, and
Roe was his own kid and he didn't even come. Only a half
dozen people that knew him did, and all those bitches from
Falissa's circle that never miss a burying. The only white people
there. There was a bunch of niggers outside in the bushes, all
women. Roe's black women. Even a bunch of whores had the
decency to come see him in. More than his own father had.

Jerome couldn't keep his hands still. They twisted at his hat
until the brim was ruint, wet and collapsed. Falissa pushed
them away once but they went back. She held his wrist and
he pulled away. He was going to have to go breaking. When
it was all over and he was back home, he would go breaking up
bottles and timbers out in the barn where it didn't matter and
nobody could make anything to do over it. Where there won't
nobody around. Nothing was coming out here. Not in front of
these people, nobody. Goddamn Willie. Willie can rot in hell.
I hope he rots in hell, right here in the church I hope he rots
in hell. And it was done a'purpose. Whoever kilt Roe done

it a'purpose. The boy seen it, they come clean off the road
and cut in on them and done it a'purpose. And kept going. No
need to keep going if it was an accident. Unless you were
drunk.

Jerome looked at the floor at the boy's foot swollen in a sock,
no shoe, black and blue from something, bumper probably.
Cale's mouth was open, face blank, sense be knocked out of him
for a while. Said he seen a devil driving the car. Cale face down
in the ditch didn't see no devil, face down when we found him.
One of Roe's cronies come after him for doing him. And Willie
didn't even come to the services. Threw him out of his house
when he was twelve years old like he won't his kin. Threw him
out. Lord God, I threw him out. I threw him out and sent him
downhill.

"Falissa."

"Shhh, Jerome. He is about to start the reading."

"Falissa, I got to get out of here."

"Jerome, you sit right there. You'll be all right. It won't last
long."

"No, I got to get out. I'll wait for you by the grave."

Jerome was out of the row and to the door before the preacher
spoke. He went through the black women who waited outside.
He walked the road home, past Parson's, past where they found
Roe with the card in his pocket, Cale face down, lying like dead,
out cold and away from it all until Roe was gone, carried away
in the doctor's car, broken in every direction, arms on backwards. Nobody oughta die that way. Never thought Roe would
get hisself in dying trouble. 'Cause I threw him out. 'Cause I
let that bitching woman make me throw him out. That's the
cause of it. Got no more brothers. Got no more family. Willie
drunk somewhere. Wouldn't bat an eye if you told him. So,
I didn't know he was alive, Willie would say. That's all you'd
get out of Willie.

Jerome went to the hill where the grave was, not close to the
others because the old graves weren't all marked and they didn't

want to hit one. He didn't dig it. Come from in town and then they make measurements. Got to measure everything. Way it used to be not good enough.

He sat down to wait by the grave until they got there, up under the locust tree. Had to bust through two big roots digging that hole, won't kill it though. No more coming to visit. Nope. Everytime I go thinking he's coming in, I got to look up here and say there he is, going nowhere. Wish you'd never come in, Roe. You was doing fine till you come in home. Took home to kill you. Go around the world in one piece and come home and it kills you. They all teamed up against you and got you, Falissa and your friends, all of them got together and said let's get Jerome Jenkins.

Book Four

Chapter 26

"YONDER it is, Cale. Down at the bend."

"I ain't blind you know." Pearlie stood beside him in her red raincoat, one sleeve empty so she could hold her book sack underneath, and white boots. She had to have white boots, nothing else would do, in other words all the other girls had white boots, so they became the only kind that would keep your feet dry. They were already orange around the soles from Yellow County. Yellow County was yellow slick today, the ditch running high and foaming.

"Mama says you ruin the King's English. You're not supposed to say ain't. It's isn't."

"Thank you, teacher. How come I don't learn as much at school as you? Now you can shut up, Miss Priss. I'll step on your white boots."

Cale dragged his loafer across the top of her boot, making a mud streak.

"Quit it. I'll tell Mama. You've ruined them."

She squatted by the road and rubbed the mud away from her boot top, her book sack bulging underneath her raincoat.

The rain was coming harder and Cale had just his Windbreaker on with the collar up, mainly because his mother had followed him halfway out the door trying to make him wear his raincoat and put something on his head. He used to wear his baseball cap but the lining shrank up and it wouldn't go on his

head. Water was trickling down his back and it was getting
damn cold. He could see the yellow-orange form coming,
smoking and steaming through the rain, with a funny kind of
glow for something as ordinary as the school bus. Wouldn't
go over thirty flat out, leaning way over where Highway 18 was
getting worn down along the edges.

He was going to get that old A-Model truck of Papa Lonza's
running if it killed him. Sat in the barn until the tires rotted
and the chickens shit all over it. Soon as he could buy the rest
of the parts it would run he thought. Keep on crapping
around, bus, so I can get good and soaked. Like to take my own
sweet time coming across 18 when we get off, see them cars
squeak to a stop, don't hesitate on the first one, walk cool and
slow or you're chicken shit. Tried it in town one day and almost
got my ass run down. What is the number one worse crime you
can commit in North Carolina? Pass a stopped school bus.
I've seen people who'd smother their mama while she was sleeping but they'd stop for a stopped school bus. Uncle Roe said
that. He used to talk about that. He loved to talk about laws.
Read something cool on colors in the science book, about red
and green and how they change when it gets dark or right
before a storm, how green gets bright and red gets dull when the
light changes. Already forgot why. Got to look that back up.

That's right, Pearlie, run up the steps and bust your knee.
Aw, she made it, set a new record, hadn't knocked that same
scab off but three times. And sit with the row of girls with
the white boots, don't you have nothing to do with the ones
with red ones and there is one with yellow ones, heaven forbid.
Snotty little shit.

"Hey, Cale."

"Hey, Jigger."

Cale sat halfway back beside Jigger.

"You seen this?"

"What?" Jigger handed Cale a news article, death vehicle.
Truck with a dented hood.

"Read it. They think that's the truck got you and your Uncle Roe. They think they're really on the right trail now."

"Aw, that ain't it. That's an old stock A-Model pickup. I told them it was set up. That thing has been rotting there five years. I seen it before."

"Might of had gutted mufflers on it."

"Naw, that was a big engine I heard. I know cutouts when I hear them. I'd know it if I heard it again."

Cale glanced through the article. They had found an old truck dumped off in the woods, dented up so they figured that was it. The Yellow County Sheriff's department had a record of never solving a crime. Summit had a murder once that they spent five years looking for the guy and never found out till he told an old nurse when he was dying. Those guys were probably out of the state a week after it happened and they think over a year later they got it figured. I been back over to Red Simmons' place and looked through the woods and there won't a trace, nothing, not even a jar. It must have been Red. Other than his mother, Red was the only person who had anything against Roe. And Roe didn't like Red either. Roe was real mad about that Cloroxed liquor. But let them figure it out. Roe wouldn't have wanted him squealing. But Roe was awful scared, scared enough to be planning to leave Summit. But he didn't know they were after him that night, couldn't have known or he wouldn't have come out on the road. I thought through it a lot, about who it might be. Told them all I know, truck, blue or black with one light and a hot engine, and I swear it looked like the devil driving. It didn't look like red hair; it was a red face and everything. But I ain't going to say that no more. They put me in the looney bin. Just let them figure it out. I'll believe them when they tell me who it was if they can let me hear that engine, that was a smooth-running V-8. I'd like to know sometime. I really would. I'd like to go in and talk to Sallie and see if she don't know something. But not now. I been having too many bad dreams of what is going to happen when I go looking. I don't want nobody coming after me. I'm flat scared. I'm not ashamed to admit it, though not out loud, but it took me a while to want to walk by the road again. I don't like it now. Don't think I'll never like it again.

"Naw, I'm sure that ain't it. Got an old junker, and trying to call it the one because they can't do no better."

Jigger took back the article and folded it into his pocket. Jigger's got this game that you play, clue, when you try to find a murderer and he loses every damn time. He is really not too smart. Don't but two people know who done it anyway. Roe and the guy who done it. And Roe is dead. Got to keep saying it. It is like he is just gone off like he was before when I couldn't find him. Seems like it's going to always be like that. But that ain't true. He is dead. Roe is the first person I can remember good dying. It is hard to remember Papa and besides I didn't see him die. I just saw him at the viewing and I don't remember that good. But I saw Roe go up in the air like he won't real, like somebody was slinging off a doll. That is the part I won't forget. To my dying day I won't forget hearing him holler at me and go flying over like somebody snatched him up on a rope. Really makes you feel people ain't big at all, their house could decide to fall and squash them alive. Seems right easy to kill a person.

The bus stopped at the elementary school. The boys got off, then all the white-booted girls got off, followed by the red boots and yellow boots. Cale watched the colored feet move through the rain, he blurred his eyes and they bounced along like balloons.

"My little sister is so pissed at my mother she won't even speak to her," Jigger said. "The old lady got her yellow boots instead of white boots. See her, the only one getting her feet wet because she put them in her book sack soon as she got out of Mama's sight. And there's another one with yellow. Watcha bet she hates her mama too?"

"Jesus, her too? What is it?"

"They think they look like majorettes, man, didn't you know. All those little pimple-chests think that makes them look like the majorettes over at the high school. My little sister will be wearing undershirts when she's eighteen. Shoulda heard her the other day," Jigger mocked, " 'at least I don't stuff them full of Kleenex like some people I know.' "

"Oughta be like mine. She got her first bra with her own money and had a screaming raving temper throw-up because Mama made her keep wearing her undershirt."

"No kidding." Jigger began to laugh. "Hey, did you get your algebra?"

"Yeah, all but one wouldn't check out in the back."

"Jesus, how you do it? Mine didn't come nowhere near checking out. Can I copy yours in homeroom?"

"Sure, I don't care."

"I should have took the business math. That stuff is so simple it's funny. I could have done it in the fourth grade. But my old man makes me take algebra because of college."

Jigger always talks about that, about college. He wants to go to State he said and be an engineer, build roads and bridges maybe. Jigger don't have to farm. His old man don't even have to work. They have tenants enough to do all the work and he goes to camp most summers down at the beach. He even knows how to sail. They have money, Mama said, said they'd always had it and his daddy didn't have to make it. But Jigger don't ever have any. He borrows off me all the time but that ain't because he's poor. That's because he's stupid and he either forgets it or loses it.

The bus unloaded at the high school, consolidated now with the county and city in one and going ten through twelve, but the city kids didn't have much to do with the county kids because they were there first and they pretty much thought they were better. The only ones they had anything to say to were the athletes since they were number one in football now the county boys had come in. They didn't care about anything but football and basketball, they wouldn't even come out and watch baseball and track. You could have a home game and ten people wouldn't be there. The cheerleaders were so snobbish they made their alternates do the baseball games.

Cale and Jigger went to their lockers and hung up their wet jackets. The hall was full of open umbrellas drying till old lady Tindell, the typing teacher, came through saying, "Pick it up, pick it up, pick it up." Cale heard one of the boys holler, "Who's looking for a pickup? Old lady Tindell's trying to get picked up. Here's your chance. Any man over sixty stand up and be counted." Then he heard them laughing, he didn't hear the rest of it. She acted like she didn't hear the first of it as she whipped back in her room. Teachers were deaf when you were wising off and they knew they couldn't do anything about it.

"Hey Cale, got word from the up-tops that there is going to be a locker check today."

"For what?"

"Library books."

Cale and Jigger took down the pinups on the insides of their locker doors and folded them up. Jigger's crackled because it had a plastic lift-up with clothes drawn on it.

"Put it in the lab manual. We don't use it today."

The first bell rang and they went into the homeroom. The teacher was already passing out something mimeographed. Jigger took the stack and slid in his seat smelling it. "Um, cheap drunk."

"What is it?"

"Pep rally Friday. Got the cheers written on it so the Freshmen will get them right, it says. Hot dog, we get out of part of first period. That old bastard will have to change the algebra test. Sonovabitch. You got it again."

"What?"

"Honor roll."

Cale looked up on the blackboard. His name was there with

three others. That was a surprise because English didn't average out that good.

The teacher called the roll and asked for the devotion. Jigger
said "present" when she called him, that always riles her. She
looked up at him, like he'd said shit. It was Jigger's turn to do
the devotion and he had gotten one of the girls to do it for him.
She was a bad one, little weak face, pimples with plaster on
them, floppy skirts and her socks rolled over on top, one of them
with a red rubber band showing, a real believer.

"Hey, Jigger, how much did you pay her?"

"You know the type. This is part of her crusade she tells me.
I would be most happy to read the Word of the Lord Jesus
Christ, she says, if you will take this booklet. Give it to me,
I say. The four ways to find Jesus Christ. You know them?"

"Listen for the flap of his sandals. Look for the guy in the
white robe. Look for the guy with long hair and a beard. What's
the fourth one?"

"The nail holes in his hands, you nit."

"James! Excuse me, Brenda Sue. James, if you won't give
the devotion, you can at least respect those who do give it and
those who want to hear it. Go ahead, Brenda Sue. Excuse
me for interrupting."

Jigger's ears turned red. He tries to act cool but it really gets
him to get called down. Brenda Sue finished her devotion with
a prayer. Jigger and Cale looked around. Most of the other
guys were looking too, checking out the God Squad, to see which
ones really had their eyes shut. During the devotion Jigger
kept tapping the girl in front of him in the back. She kept
trying to sit up so he couldn't reach her and wouldn't turn around
until finally he said, "Hey, I didn't know you had a broken back.
When did you break your back?"

She turned around and snapped, "I don't have a broken
back."

"Then why you got that brace around it?" He popped the
back of her bra.

*

Jigger has got more nerve than I have.

Algebra I. Five days a week, forty-five minutes of doing problems around the blackboard, about half of them wrong on the average, then we get a new example for the next day. Then comes the test and we forgot the one we done the first day but we just memorize every third problem because that's what's on the test, does it every time, always the third problem. I seen guys trying to knock their books out of the desk or even write it on the floor before class and keep their foot over it. Anybody ought to know old Armadillo never picked anything but the third problem. This is Mr. Armor, veteran, shell-shocked Mr. Armadillo, the American burrowing nocturnal mammal. We get in our seats and he looks over the roll book at us like he's watching from a foxhole, zip, zip, his eyes have surveyed the enemy, they are all here, but he has to rip off the roll anyway like we're lining up for attention. Last week he come in carrying his fishbowl and put it on the desk, the one that sits in the back next to the door. Only one thing wrong, you couldn't see the fish. The water was dark blue. Somebody had dumped a whole bottle of ink in it and did old Armadillo go running to the head to wash it out and save his precious goldfish, naw, he gave us a twenty-minute lecture on respect for other people's property while they both floated to the top.

The best one was in September. He had this fan. He was always getting sweaty, great big circles right through his coat, they used to make bets they'd meet in the center, so he would set up this fan to blow on him during class. Only trouble was none of the plugs in our room would work so he had to run an extension cord across the hall and go run and unplug it right quick before the bell rang so the guys coming down the hall wouldn't pick up the cord and drag the fan through the door. Anyway one day old Armadillo's watch was slow and the bell went off and his fan went bouncing up the steps and he went running up after it and got his tie in it. Damn near strangled him before the plug came out at the other end. Funny as hell and not a soul tried to help him. That really got him.

Jigger has gone up with my paper to do a problem. He won't get to me anyway. He just goes right down the rows in military order, only changed once with a big "A-ha" and went in the other direction. Now we get the demonstration where Armadillo comes out with the answer that isn't like the one in the book and it's always the book that has a misprint. He really gets excited when he slips and gets one right. Get to watch him splinter up chalk. Squeek, squark, couple of the girls really going crazy on that, there he goes, busted it in a million pieces, dust all over him, dust left over from yesterday. He even starts out with dust all over him, got two suits, dusty brown and dusty blue. Last year a guy dropped a book, a friend of Jigger's in the tenth told me about this, and old Armadillo hit the floor behind the desk and started pelting them with chalk, erasers, anything he could get his hands on and he come up once swinging the chalk on a string he uses to make circles in geometry class and yelled "Charge" and went back again and didn't come out even when the bell rang. That's when they got a substitute for a week but old Armadillo came back. He'll be teaching here till somebody blows him apart with a hand grenade. That's what they say done it to him, one went off right under his butt and he's been like that ever since. Damn if he isn't doing the same problem we had on Monday again. He must have gotten back a page by accident. Not a soul will tell him, that's for sure unless one of those dumb girls does. The bell.

"Thanks, Cale."

"Sure. Did you see what he did?"

"Naw, what?"

"The stupid S.O.B. did Monday's example again and gave us the same homework."

Jigger squinted at the blackboard. "No lie? Then we ain't got none tonight. Hot damn. I'm going to get to watch 'Inner Sanctum.' "

Cale went into English. This was Miss Sammons. She was O.K. His favorite. Crummy course though. The poetry and stuff was better than the grammar and the diagramming but it was all pretty bad. She was young, just out of college, and had a nice way of dressing and pretty hair to her shoulders. She really liked the sad stuff. Especially that Evangeline searching for her lost love Gabriel and she searched through a hell of a lot of pages. Miss Sammons acted like she was going to cry the day she told them about Longfellow's sad life, all his wives dying and leaving him alone with his poetry. One of them burned to death but he kept on writing. That old bitch he had last year could have done that stuff and he would have laughed his ass off. But Miss Sammons really liked it. She made him feel kind of sad when she said she liked his book report on *Tale of Two Cities* because he got it out of the *Classic Comic*.

Here we go again:

> Blessings on thee, little man,
> Barefoot boy, with cheek of tan!
> With thy turned-up pantaloons,
> And thy merry whistled tunes;
> With thy red lip, redder still
> Kissed by strawberries on the hill;

Cale was thinking. There was another barefoot boy poem:

> It was midnight on the ocean,
> Not a streetcar was in sight,
> The sun was shining brightly
> Though it rained all day that night.
>
> A barefoot boy with shoes on
> Stood sitting in the grass.
> Along came a snake and
> Ran right up his ass.

That must have been one of Uncle Roe's. Here come the dumb questions.

"What does Mr. Whittier mean when he says 'knowledge never learned of schools'?"

"Of the things of nature that just come naturally."

"Why does Nature have hands and a face?"

"Because she is a person."

"Not exactly."

"Because she is Mother Nature."

"No, more than that. What is the word we learned?"

Silence.

Personification. Nature is a woman like a ship and a country are sometimes a woman. Damn what a stupid class. She skipped over the verse in "Trees" about the sweet flowing breasts of Mother Nature and it was printed right there in the book.

"The word is personification." Miss Sammons writes it on the board for the third time this year. "Now put it in your notebooks." I got it already, twice. "Nature here is personified as a woman just as we often find a ship and . . ."

"Now what is he saying in the last stanza?"

Silence.

"What does he mean when he says, 'Like a colt's for work be shod'?"

Silence.

"Now that isn't so hard. Let us put the sentence in the order we use today. We have shod a colt for work. Not a full-grown horse now, a colt. Anyone want to guess?"

Silence.

"Cale?"

That's it. She always does that when she's giving up. "I don't know. I guess it's like he has to grow up, I mean the boy has to put on shoes and go to work someday like the colt has to put on shoes and go to work when he's a horse, and it's not going to be fun anymore because he isn't a little kid and can't go barefoot and act like one."

"That's right . . ." Look at that old face light up. That really wowed them. She won't ask any more questions now.

She'll act like I said it all and she'll resay it. Let her try to pick the whole works out of us and we crap it up good.

The bell.

"Cale, wait just a second, please. I'll give you a late permission if you need it."

Uh-oh. She wants something.

"Cale, I don't know if you are aware of it or not but the tenth grade drama club is going to give a play. I want to do *Our Town*. Do you know of it?"

"No, I guess I don't. I don't know much about plays."

"Oh, it's a wonderful play. I know you will just love it. But we have a problem. There is just no one in the group that can play George properly and I just hate to do it if it can't be done right. Would you come and read the part for me?"

"Be in a play?"

"Surely. Why not? You've been in plays before, haven't you? Besides that doesn't matter. It will be a new and exciting experience."

"Naw, I couldn't."

"Oh, why not? I just know you would be perfect. It doesn't matter if you've never been in a play before. You have such a nice voice and I know it will carry well."

"I got to go to Biology, Miss Sammons."

"I'll write you a late. Do think about it, Cale, please. We are having tryouts this afternoon. I really do think you would do well at it and I would love to have you come read."

She took a blue slip and checked in the square that said "held by teacher" and handed it to Cale.

"Cale, you don't think acting is sissy do you?"

"Huh? Well, I don't know really. I never thought about it."

"Do you think the other boys think it's sissy?"

"I don't know, I guess they might. Yeah, they probably do if you want the truth."

In biology class, they all had out their clam from the formaldehyde jar. Nothing left but the starfish and the earthworm.

They cut the crawfish in a million pieces. Boy, do the girls hate this class. They went crazy when the teacher had a grasshopper on a pin. Cale handed the slip to the teacher, Mr. Caldwell, and he grunted, "Get your clam," and stuck it in the drawer.

"Hey man, where you been?"

"Miss Sammons held me after class."

"Oh, so you got something going with the queen of Summit High."

"Yeah, she wanted my expert opinion on the nature of barefoot boys with strawberry red lips."

"Huh?"

"The poem. John Greenleaf Whittier, my boy."

"Oh, we ain't there yet."

"James."

It was Mr. Caldwell. Damn Jigger would carry on a conversation during a funeral at full volume. His whisper was like a steam engine.

"Yes sir."

"Do you have your clam ready to dissect?"

"Yes sir, but I'm afraid mine's still alive. I went to spring his lid and he spit in my face."

The class started to laugh.

"Well, if he's alive, James, you have just witnessed the greatest scientific wonder of all times."

Mr. Caldwell passed around a diagram of part of the innards of a clam with fill-in-the-blank spaces. Jigger sniffed the paper again, "With this and the stiff juice, I'm going to be drunk as a skunk when I get to lunch. Or sick one or the other." Jigger burped out loud but Caldwell didn't hear him. "What did you tell old Sammons on the barefoot boy, huh?"

"I told her I wasn't real familiar with many barefoot boys with strawberry lips but I thought they were awful sweet." That got old Jigger. He really thinks I said it.

"Strawberry lips! Must be a messy eater. Tell her I seen one with a milk ring on his mouth and he was the sweetest thing but he couldn't stand strawberries. Wonder who the sonovabitch was who decided to put this class so near lunch?"

"Didn't you hear? We got clam soup today."

Cale pulled open the shell with his lab tools and looked at the ugly gray insides that oozed around. One of the girls went running out, then her best friend asked to go too. Why do girls like to go watch each other puke? This was the class with the good-looking girl, Janet Grover, and she just took her tools and busted that old clam open like it was nothing and started picking out the parts, didn't crack a smile, like she was bored as hell.

They cleaned up, dropped thirty-five smashed clams in the garbage and handed in their fill-in sheets, Jigger's with half the spaces empty. Mr. Caldwell had separated their seats so Jigger had to get by on his own in here. Mr. Caldwell would correct the diagrams, give them back for them to memorize and give them a copy to fill in on Friday as a test. Almost anybody could pass biology, even Jigger, because you didn't have to remember things long.

The bell rang and they headed down to study hall, big old fat Mrs. Peters who was O.K. She taught shorthand and spent most of her time keeping study halls. She would give them an excuse to get out about half the time and let them read magazines as long as they weren't movie magazines or something and you could read them inside another one. She got a copy of *Nugget* away from Jigger and was keeping it in her desk until the end of the year. Old lady Crimpton, the other study hall they got transferred out of used to come around snatching away anything that wasn't a school book and you had to come back after school to get them back. Old Crimpton would have torn that *Nugget* in a million pieces. She kept it so quiet in there it would drive you crazy when you didn't have anything to do.

Hubbard was in this study hall. When Hubbard got out of the ninth grade he was eighteen years old and his whole family came to see him get his certificate because he was the first one in the family to ever get one and they all got together and stood up and clapped when he came across the stage. That really got old Hubbard, he was so proud, and the principal was madder than hell. He figures he'll get out of high school when he's twenty-three because they got social promotion. They won't keep you but two years then they send you up or try to talk you into quitting and they'll never make Hubbard quit. He loves school. He don't ever miss a day. The bell rings and no Hubbard, there he is. Knew he wouldn't miss.

"Hubbard, you're late."

"I'm sorry, Mrs. Peters. I had to finish doing something down at the head."

The class starts to laugh and Mrs. Peters holds her short fat finger to her mouth, Shhh.

"That's all right this time, Hubbard, but get an excuse next time."

"Want to see what I was doing, Mrs. Peters?" Hubbard whispers loud enough for everybody to hear.

"Let me call roll, first." Old Hubbard's got her worried. He'll say anything. On Hallowe'en Hubbard shit in a paper sack and lit it on old Armadillo's porch and Armor come running out and stomped it all over his foot. She calls roll and Hubbard stands right there by her desk. She gets to his name and has to call it three times.

"Hubbard, answer the roll."

"Didn't you know I was here, Mrs. Peters?"

Duh. Jigger really digs Hubbard. He's always mocking him after school and he's so tickled now he's about to fall out of his chair.

"Can I tell you now, Mrs. Peters?"

"O.K., Hubbard, you can tell me."

Hubbard really loves Mrs. Peters. He picked her a bunch of goldenrod and she sneezed all day long but she kept it right there in a jar on the desk. He already come in with a fifty-pound pumpkin for her and set it on her desk. He turns his back on the class so they can't see him. He's rolling up his sleeves. Hubbard's B.O. will knock you back ten feet.

"Hubbard! You go right down to the rest room and wash that mess off this minute." She starts to write out a slip. We can see it now. Old Hubbard has drawn all over his arms with a ballpoint pen. He can draw real good, he's even colored some of them red, hearts and ships and naked women. Hubbard loves ships but the Navy wouldn't take him because he flunked the test. He said he might even quit school if the Navy would take him. He even wrote "Mrs. Peters is my favrite" on the back of his hand. That really broke old Hubbard up. He thought she'd love that. He hates awful to make Mrs. Peters really mad.

After about twenty minutes old Hubbard is back. His arms are blood red where he has been scrubbing. Mrs. Peters makes him roll his arms around so she can check all sides.

"All right, Hubbard. You can go to your seat now."

Old Hubbard is grinning like crazy. He's up to something.

"Hubbard, I said to your seat."

"Mrs. Peters?"

"Yes."

"You didn't say nothing about this one." Hubbard yanked up his shirt and stuck out his stomach. Drawn around a patch of red hair, a full-rigged schooner sitting on the waves, a naked woman on the front, red and blue sails with a pirate's flag on the top.

After lunch Cale had American History. They had sat outside on the wall during lunch break and shot the bull until time for the bell. The weather was still pretty nice but in a few weeks they'd get stuck inside until lunch was over. They couldn't even go out in the halls because they had to have two shifts and people were still in classes. It was really funny to watch the girls who had come over from the junior high with him. They were used to bunching together at a special table and not letting anyone sit with them unless they were in the right group and wore the right clothes and they almost went crazy before they got their own table at the high school. But they were settled now and going after the junior-senior boys so they could have a steady in time for the prom in the spring. They wouldn't have anything to do with the sophomore boys and were trying to get a senior so they could wear his ring with a big pile of wax under it. If you were rich and pretty you were in the group automatically, pretty and poor you might get in because they wanted to keep an eye on you, that's where Pearlie would probably come in, but if you were both ugly and poor, you sat over in the corner with the rest of the uglies. And you had to dress right. That was the most important part. They already had out their cashmere sweaters and were burning up in them and went around feeling each other's sleeves to see if it was real cashmere or some kind of scratchy wool. All the poor uglies wore these thin baggy sweaters that stretched all around the buttons and didn't have white collars with silver pins through them. They didn't have three colors of suede loafers and some of them wore their bobby socks rolled over which was an automatic out. They were all getting their hair cut off one by one, as they got the nerve except for the ones with long pigtails who were chicken and whose mamas wouldn't let them. And they were putting away those crunchy petticoats they wore under their summer dresses that rattled and popped when they sat down in class and were wearing pleated wool skirts. The boys weren't that bad but most of them wouldn't wear jeans anymore but wore those pants with the hiney-binders across the back that cut grooves in the backs of the desks when they sat down and they didn't wear anything but button-down collar shirts and white socks. They weren't like the girls though. You could wear jeans especially if you played ball. It's no different with the guys. They're always talking about those snotty little girls, how they won't give you a date unless you can pass their test.

*

This American History class is really bad but I get to just listen today because I already said my Presidents. You got to get up and recite them and their Vice President and party and how long they were in office. Jigger isn't in this class but he told me he has already had two tries and messed up. But he'll pass. He always does, gets bad grades all year and in the end he always passes. His daddy is talking about sending him to military school so he can get his grades up for college. He got to do his notebook on Theodore Roosevelt who there must be a million books on, and me, I get Chester Alan Arthur who wouldn't have been President if Garfield hadn't gotten shot and there is absolutely nothing on him anywhere but the encyclopedia and I've got to find five references at least. There might not even *be* five references on Chester Alan Arthur in the entire world. I bet I have to thumb to Raleigh just to make that damn thing. This guy is a real fairy, a student teacher from Raleigh. I told him there weren't any books in our library and asked him to give me another name and he wouldn't do it, said we all can't be privileged characters or some such shit. Jigger said somebody dropped a rubber on the floor by his desk and he picked it up and said, "Whose little plaything is this?" Damn he's a stupid queer. We got it planned the last day he's here we are going to turn all our desks around facing the back and refuse to turn around and see what he'll do. We got everybody promised now but three girls and one guy up front who's as big a queer as he is. His waist is up to his armpits and he wears shaving lotion that smells like girls' perfume.

I got Shop last period. We had to take Home Ec the second month and they made all the girls come over and take shop for a month. That was funny as hell. We had to fix a meal for a teacher so we asked Coach Beale, our coach, and it was really bad. I spent all morning rolling up these carrot strips and putting toothpicks through them and putting them in water so they would curl and he looked at them like I'd put turds on his plate. Cracked him up. Nothing got through at the same time and I burned the hamburger rolls into little black rocks. We had to pay for it so we had hamburger and they shrunk up about the size of a half dollar but the teacher had to grade us so we all got an A because Coach Beale wants us to keep our grades up and come out next spring. He's a cool guy, got this big fat belly that his pants slip down under and he's skinny everywhere else and his belt is always hanging down and his pants about half unzipped. He's always turning around in his World History class, that's what he teaches, and pulling his zipper up. He doesn't really teach World History, he just makes you read a chapter a week and gives a multiple choice test that we all fail but nobody ever fails the course. I get to take that next year. I hear we spend most of the time watching him outline the football plays on the board. A girl hardly ever takes that course unless it's by mistake. It's good too because he always slips and cusses in class. That Home Ec teacher ought to hope she never gets guys again. She got her ass sunburned at the beach and she hiked up her dress to show us, I couldn't believe it, like she forgot we were guys. She's supposed to get married to some guy next summer at the funeral home and quit teaching. Coach Beale asked us if she had a nice ass when we told him. He's got a wife that weighs about two fifty.

The bell rang and the teacher made them sit until one of the girls was through her Presidents. She got nervous and started fumbling and asked to go the next day. Cale walked down the stairs to the shop room. The wood and stain smell was good, almost like outdoors. He went and took his lamp down, it was almost done. Sanded and stained so all it needed was fine sanding and oil. He sanded and piddled and finished it up and got a ticket to get out of shop and go to the head. There was sawdust on him everywhere, in his cuffs, under his fingernails, behind his collar, his own and everybody else's; he could feel it around his eyes when he blinked them. It could really make you itch if you stayed in there long. Made you want to take your clothes off and jump in the water somewhere. Mr. Smith was a pretty cool guy but most of the other teachers didn't have much to do with him so he usually ate his lunch in the shop or came and ate with the guys.

Cale bent over the sink and splashed water in his face and stood and let it run down and drip on his shirt front. Didn't matter, it was his second day on it and he was out after shop. Felt better, almost like waking up in the morning. Wiping back and forth on those little pieces of wood until he wore through the sandpaper, bet he could do it in his sleep. You got a bunch of blocks and dowels that fit together into a lamp that was pictured in the manual, about hard enough for a first-grader to do, with an iron pipe to go up the middle and run the wire through, everything all cut and fitted and you just had to put it together like a bunch of Tinkertoys. So he had sanded and stained and rubbed it with steel wool until the wood was as smooth as flesh when he decided he would take the corners off so it would be like flesh, nothing better to do. He did take the corners off and waxed it in the first forty-five minutes of shop and got up to leave for the head when he saw something that really surprised him, what the others were doing. They were all still working, struggling with fitting the pieces in the holes and one guy had accidentally gotten an extra dowel and was trying to put it on the lamp when there wasn't even a hole for it, cramping it in the center even though the thing stood on four corners in the picture.

Cale went back to the shop and went ahead and wired his, he'd done that at home enough, and there just wasn't anything left he could find to work on on the damn thing. He took it to Mr. Smith and got permission to carry it home to Pearlie. Man, it was like working in a room at the nut house. It was. Made you want to jump out the window and run. Jigger was smart compared to these guys. They hadn't done anything in shop he hadn't been knowing how to do since he was ten and poor Mr. Smith had to tell them the same thing fifty times. He raised an eyebrow when Cale showed him the lamp, turned it around in his hand, and put a check plus in his grade book. Maybe Mr. Smith would let him work on something else. He said he built engines for two of the guys down at the oval. Cale had really looked forward to shop when he heard about that. Maybe he should ask Mr. Smith when they were going to get to the engines. He might laugh at him, with a class like this he might have to laugh at him if he asked about an engine. These morons couldn't do an engine. Are you crazy? An engine? They couldn't shoot a rubber band.

Jesus, you get that feeling just to quit, to get out of this damn place as soon as they'll let you, you know? When you know you could really do something better and would like to but as long as there is no need of it, why bother. Just do better than anyone else and keep it so you don't have to work too hard. I want to get out of here and do something, like Roe did. But I don't want to get messed up. I don't want to go out and get messed up and end up in some gutter. I'm going to do things nobody else can. I got to stay here till I know for sure what is right. I got to wait till I know where I'm going. But it would be good to do something different here. It wouldn't be bad to have to work harder if it was halfway interesting. I really wouldn't mind. This is something there was no one to talk to about. I might be able to tell Mr. Smith but I don't know for sure. Sometimes it seems like Mr. Smith doesn't want to work harder than he has to either, like he doesn't really care about doing anything but what he has to. And you just couldn't be sure if Mr. Smith was smart or not or just like everybody else except Uncle Roe.

You never went anywhere here. You just had to stand around and wait for the rest of them to catch up so you could get on. Made you start feeling like you were sliding backwards too because you couldn't remember when there was anything new. It was better than the other stuff though; at least there was the wood and tools and something to do with your hands so you could stay awake. But you never got to make your own plans for things, just took what Mr. Smith said or the stuff he gave you and put it together. He spent more time worrying that somebody was going to get cut up on the machines than he did on what they made.

Jigger couldn't take shop. He really wanted to because he did so bad in the other stuff but his old man wouldn't let him. His old man was worse than a woman about letting you go around with dirty hands and clothes, like if you went to college you never had to change a tire or take out the garbage or anything. Every time he and Jigger were working on something they had to dodge him until it was time to clean up for supper. He paid to have things fixed that even Cale's old man could fix.

Cale knew what he wanted to say, that he was smarter than anyone else around his house and most of the ones in his classes, he thought, but you don't say that, you just think it. Because these people are so dumb they don't know it. He really ought to go home and say that. That would go over real big. Go home tonight and say: "Dad, I've come to tell you I'm the smartest person around this house. You see, I know everything you're going to say before you say it. I can think things out the way you're going to do them before you can. I know all your answers and they're not bright answers, old man. They just fit for you and you just stumble along like you're walking down a row behind a mule and the only thing that happens is that the dirt parts and the mule farts in your face . . . boop, pucker, boop, pucker, boop, pucker, and you bring the news to us at the supper table that John Mule had never farted more than three times in succession and Mama will say, 'Hush, Jerome.'"

And Mama, you're more than just dumb. You whine. You keep saying the same things. And you watch me out the window. But I can work you now. You feel sorry for me because of what happened with Uncle Roe because I was on my way to church on account of you. And I can make you defend me in front of the old man. You think I'm going to knock up some girl and you'll know her mother. What you don't know is, you don't touch these queens around here, not if you have to wear blue jeans. You don't know nothing about what it's like over here. I'll say to you, old lady, "I'm the smartest person around this house," and you'll say, "Shhhh! Your father will hear. Don't start a row. Save it to say some other time when things are smoother. Do it for my sake."

And Pearlie. Dumb little bitch. No, that's not fair. She hasn't got a chance either. Just a little girl who wants to be a little girl where it's safe and pretend she's a woman now and then when nobody's paying any attention. And you don't know nothing. Mama's not going to let you know nothing. Comic books and movie magazines and true confessions you read on the school bus and at your girl friends' houses. The ones you wore out reading over and keep under your mattress. Rolling off a sled in the snow, Kid Colt reaching for your hand and pulling you into his arms out of a pit, the world stops with one kiss, just like Doris Day and Rock Hudson at the end of a movie. If you knew what happened next it would scare you to death, if you knew what men did to women next. And the way to be right and safe is to have white rain boots. You are so mixed up, Pearlie.

"Cale, what do you do with girls?" she asks.

"I beat them and tie them to trees in the woods and the buzzards pick their eyes out."

"Cale, quit. You promised to tell me so I could tell the girls at school. It's important for me to tell them because they don't have a brother and I promise I won't tell them you told me on purpose. If you want me to. That I just knew all along and didn't have to ask you."

Pearlie, you're not my problem. I don't have to worry about you. "Why don't you ask Mama? That's what she's supposed to do." Then little Pearlie laughed in that way of hers, that way that said even though you don't tell me, we still have a secret. We know about Mama and that she doesn't know enough to tell me.

Now will I go up there and ask Mr. Smith if he'll let me build

an engine or do something different anyway? He let me build
a birdhouse first month that won the Civitan contest for five
dollars. Or is he going to get mad as hell with me because I'm
sitting here trying to keep busy until the bell rings, with my
lamp already put together and steel-wooled down and waxed
until it shines like an apple? I can always steel-wool it again
and wax it some more and maybe by then half of these morons
will have the pieces together anyway. The bell.

Cale ran up the steps to his locker. Forgot about the locker
check. Here they come, down the line, sticking their noses in,
making you want to slam the doors on them. And there's Miss
Sammons, checking her homeroom. She is going to be watching
for me to come to that play tryout, I know her. She can watch
all day. Nobody is going to make me stay longer at this school
than I have to, except Coach Beal and that's all. I'm going down
and watch the nigger bands practice for the Christmas parade
and watch those black girls strut, me and Jigger. They make
our majorettes look like they're sick but if that band director
caught them strutting like that he would throw every one of
them out. That's where I'm going after school. Damn, she
saw me. And smiled at me. Damn I wish I could do it for her.
I know she's hoping I will. I can't, Miss Sammons. You won't
ever understand. I just can't.

*   *   *

July, 1956
Pearlie had had a twelve-year-old birthday party, the first one
at their house where more than her best friend got invited.
Since she was going to the junior high next year she thought it
was all of a sudden important to ask an equal number of boys and
girls but that got all messed up and there were too many girls.
Falissa said no more, never again because Pearlie had been so
particular about the favors and cake that it wore her out before
they even got there, then they really made a mess. They had

played spin the bottle and one of the boys got scared and ran home. Falissa saw him running off down toward the highway but he was out of sight, and his mother called Falissa wanting to know what was going on over at her house. That was what really did it. She was ashamed because somebody had called her down and didn't want any strangers in her house again. She hadn't paid any attention to what kind of silly little games they were playing. Then the kids had gotten in a popcorn fight and Falissa was still finding it, under the cushions, over the cornices.

Acted like little animals. Just went wild with no respect for anybody's property. And the party had certainly caused a change in Pearlie. It wasn't clear at first, but now it was. She was more grown-up or acting that way anyhow. She didn't seem so much a child. She wouldn't go outdoors, she couldn't stand to have her hands dirty. She wanted to iron her own clothes. Not so much that she was growing up, that wasn't it. She was growing away from them, into herself, into herself so much you couldn't tell when her mind was going like a child or like an adult. She never brought home friends or talked about them or school. She wasn't going to let a soul know anything about her. A girl shouldn't be like that with her mother. She didn't carry on so when she was a little girl. Maybe it's just a notion. Just a stage she will grow right out of. She was a pretty little thing in her own way and all that frowning and long face wasn't going to make people like her. She'd come out of it though. She'll come to me and talk about it. I'll just wait until she's good and ready. I won't push her. She can take her time. I'm not one to go waiting over her like Mama did over me, like a buzzard. I'll just pretend I don't notice a thing. Little girls can feel all kinds of funny ways when they're about to go through the change. Cale just doesn't know how much harder it is to be a girl. He learns swear words and his voice goes down a note and he thinks he knows something. Listens to a bunch of big talk from the men and believes he knows everything.

The Lord might strike me dead but that Roe going was a blessing. Let him do his growing without that to model by. The
Lord won't strike me, Roe was the devil's business.

*   *   *

Pearlie closed herself in her room and didn't play the radio
anymore when she did her homework. Cale found her too
quiet these days and it bothered him. She didn't even try to
tag along with him anymore. And something else about her
was bothering him. He knew she was going in to talk with the
preacher and his mother didn't. She was up to something.

"Hey, what do you do at that class at the church? How come I
didn't have to do that?" he asked, walking up from the bus.

"It's a new idea. The young preacher, Mr. Royster, you don't
know him I suppose . . ."

"You suppose. Don't talk so fancy to me. Of course, I know
him as much as you do."

"Anyway, he plans a special study for us. We are going on a
spiritual trip to find Christ."

"Oh, bull shit."

"Cale! Cale, you are going to be in real trouble someday. You
can't say such things about Christ's word. You will be punished."

"What do you go to that preacher's office all the time for? I
know you aren't just going to the classes because Jigger's sister
told him and he told me."

"Oh, you just can't trust Betty Ann."

"So you are trying to hide it."

"I have nothing to hide. He and I are doing a special study
that is more difficult than the one he does in class. Besides the
Lord Jesus Christ knows and sees everything and . . ."

"Pearlie, would you cut it out? I didn't know you'd joined
the God Squad. Forget I asked, O.K.?"

And that's the way it kept going. Every time she wanted to
make her mind up about something, she would get out the
Bible and look it up and if she couldn't find it, she would go to

the preacher and ask him. Cale was really getting angry with her but he couldn't let her know it because it would please her too much. She was just too damn good. She was trying to act like some damn saint or something. He wanted to grab her and shake her until she said shit. But she never made any noise. She just sat in her room and read her Bible and she had gone out one day with all of her movie magazines and true confessions and put them in the trash basket and she got him to set them on fire because she was scared to.

"What are you going to do if something bad happens to you?" he asked her. "What if you get asked a question that isn't in your answer book? What if some man comes up and grabs you? What are you going to do? Tell him some Bible verse? Tell him thou shalt not do that?"

Then she pouted and shook her head like he was some kind of moron. "Trust in the Lord, Cale. You can't believe that, can you? I pity you but hope someday you will find Christ as your Savior."

"Now you listen to me, Miss Twelve-Years-Old. You think you have all the answers but you don't have half of them. You think everything that happens in this world can be answered if you just go down and talk to that preacher . . ."

"Are you a disbeliever, Cale?"

"Shut up. No, I'm not a disbeliever. I just want to tell you that you have a mind inside your head, O.K.? That thing between your ears that buzzes now and then. That you don't just go around and listen to everything Mama and that preacher say and think that's all you got to know. They don't know everything. They don't know half of most things. You let them get to you. You are really sure aren't you? You are right and the rest of the world is wrong. You better not let them get to you. You want to be like Mama? You want to spend your life shut up on an old farm keeping house and never go anywhere or do anything?"

She didn't answer for a moment, then she said, "I'm going to be a Christian Education Director. I'm almost sure of it. At first I thought I would be a missionary but now I think I want to stay right here and help the people around me."

After that he let it go. He wasn't going to go running along in front of her to protect the people from her either. People had to look after themselves. And so did Pearlie. That's what he thought, that is until she went into the next stage. The other stage hadn't even lasted long enough for him to get used to it until she was in another one.

He would hear her calling his name, loud and squealing like something bad was wrong. The first time he had almost broken his neck getting to her. He got there, already wet around the neck from hearing that squeal that sounded like something was tearing her apart limb by limb, and there she sat, nothing wrong with her and with this expression on her face, it wasn't hers at all, maybe out of the movies, maybe the face he had seen on her little friends when they would ask him to do something for them.

"Oh Cale, can you put the chain back on my bicycle," or "Cale, I would so appreciate it if you would get the lid off this jar. I just can't budge it." It really bothered him, seeing her looking like that. She was teaching herself another lesson. The Bible was in deep, now she was teaching herself to be a girl, to fool boys was the way he had it figured now. Boys who didn't have sisters, that's all the fooling she would do.

He heard her one afternoon. He was up in the loft and decided not to go running down like a fool. Then she wouldn't answer him, just kept squealing until he got real worried and ran and found her, sitting beside the smokehouse. There she sat on the ground with a skirt on no less, spread out over her knees, her hand held to her mouth.

"Oh Cale, look how awful!"

He had looked, unwinding inside, still unable to get mad because he had been so frightened. Knew her that well and still she scared him to death. There it was, the cause of her terrible fright, a perfectly normal, fat, freckled toad frog sitting caught in a peanut butter jar.

"You mean all that screaming was about a goddamn frog. Shit!"

"But Cale, look how pitiful . . ."

"Shit!"

"Cale, he can't get out. I saw him jump up and jump up and get hung halfway over the top and squirm and squirm and just dump out this slimy blood till I thought he would die and he couldn't get his other leg over the top and he just stretched all out of shape and his mouth was hanging open."

"So why don't you dump him out?"

"Oh, I'm so afraid of him. What if I turned the jar over with him half out and squashed him? I wish I'd never seen him. I couldn't stand to see him squashed and spitting up his insides. I don't know why I even saw him if I hadn't thought he was a bird and was drowning. I wish I had never known about him."

The frog sat in an inch of slimy water, half peanut butter, half algae, with his sides moving in and out. He was a tired old frog. And this was Pearlie who not more than a year ago had even let him put a mouse in her shirt.

Cale reached for Pearlie and pulled her to her feet. She started to cry now.

"Dump him out!"

"Oh no, oh no, Cale. I can't. No, Cale, don't make me do it."

She was getting hysterical.

"Just reach down there and pick up the jar and dump him out and stop trying to act like those priss ass girls . . ."

"No!" She was screaming now and when he took her arm and tried to make her dump the frog out she pulled away from him and ran to her mother in the kitchen.

He reached down and dumped out the frog who just sat there like he was still in the jar. Cale watched him till he jumped once, dumping off globs of peanut butter, and then went to the house while the frog went down the path toward the woods.

He was planning on going up to catch hell from his mother but he would tell her what caused this one, a damn old harmless frog. Yet when he saw his mother on the steps, all she said was, "Cale, please be easier on her. She's going through a hard time."

Chapter 27

CALE AND JIGGER spent July and August working on Papa's A-Model truck. Cale had been thinking about it all along, looking at it, lifting up the hood, wondering why they had left it there all those years and trying to figure what it would take to get it going. Then Jigger got this book on restoring an A-Model that his daddy bought for him, fifteen dollars just for the book but as soon as Jigger said "book" his daddy bought it. They set to work, using mostly Jigger's money since Cale was working on the truck on weekends when he used to pick up extra money. Jigger got an allowance anyway for doing nothing, just had to bother his father and he would pay him to leave.

They rolled it out one Saturday for its first inspection in the sun and had to kill a chicken snake that was curled up in the seat. Then they had to scrub out of the truck bed what his prey had deposited while roosting in there. The truck had been dark green with black fenders, not all black like Cale had guessed and the spoke wheels had been yellow once and there was a black stripe down the side. Jigger started calling it the old June Bug because of its colors and that was its final name.

The upholstery had rotted out so Falissa repacked the springs and made them some slip covers when they promised to get all the snakes and spiders out before she started to work. Then she lay on her back and stitched gray felt to the ceiling. The little clock in the rear view mirror had a string, she pulled it and discovered the one thing in the truck that still worked. No one could remember why Papa had decided to park it and what broke it in the first place so they took the whole engine apart. Cale sorted out the parts on his workbench, covered with black sludge and slime. He put Jigger to work cleaning and he started to examine each part. The inside of the engine was perfect, the cylinder walls smooth and unpitted. Cale was glad he tore it down, he had never gotten a chance to go from the bottom to the top, just a few tune-ups and adjustments that Roe had showed him down at the track, but he was almost sure that Papa had retired his car for about ten dollars' worth of parts right on top, a burnt-out coil and distributor cap. And to think they had walked all those years. This truck could have taken all of them to the ocean.

The engine was back in place, he had topped it up with oil, put fresh gas in the tank, they had a new battery from Sears, re-built the starter, done everything the book said. It was time to crank it up. Everyone was there, Jerome, Falissa, Pearlie, Cale and Jigger. Jigger got to press the starter button while Cale watched the engine. The starter ground and it caught, just like it had been running all along. Jigger got out and Cale sat in it, pressed the gas, listened to the engine, his hand hit the gear lever and he stopped, turned the switch off. Four flat tires was all they had, forty dollars it would cost to ever move from that spot.

That afternoon he and Jigger made the move. They sold their bicycles and went to Sears and ordered four tires and tubes. By the end of the week they were going down the road, three lug nuts on the two back wheels, two stripped studs each, Cale with a license from Driver's Education at school, Jigger with his third learner's permit because he had flunked the written test. They had had two small setbacks but all seemed to be under control now. It had caught on fire once and they didn't notice it until the paint started bubbling on the hood. Falissa had come running out and smothered it with baking soda. The copper gas line had vibrated and broken, dumping gas that ignited as soon as the starter turned over. The loss was a twelve-cent distributor wire and about four hours to clean off the baking soda. And it was back to the book that said put a loop in the gas line to prevent breakage from vibration. They had an oil leak at the back of the pan and Cale discovered a horseshoe-shaped gasket that he had forgotten. He had left Jigger to change the pan gaskets and put it in when he had to go in with the to-bacco. It was Jigger's first major job. When he got back he found him coated with oil, Falissa with his head in the sink trying to scrub it away because Jigger had let down the pan with-out draining the engine. Cale went into the yard, rolled the car off of its black puddle and sat down to scrape away the cork gaskets from the rim of the pan. He put the horseshoe gasket in place at the end of the pan when Jigger walked out, his skin blazing red from scouring powder.

"Hey man, I hear they're looking for a chief mechanic for the Parson's Store racing team."

"Kiss my royal American ass."

They put the pan in place, bolted it up and filled the engine with oil again. It was ready. And Jigger had done the one thing he claimed to do really well. He had gotten them a couple of hot dates for that night.

They went to the drive-in movie, all four in the front seat, Jigger's date in his lap so Cale could get to the gearshift. Cale was trying to figure if both girls had on the same perfume or if the mixture of the two was what was making him sick. He had both windows down and rolled out the windshield. His date really loved that rolling windshield and kept opening and shutting it. The fumes from the gas tank rose up inside until Cale suggested they go outside and made a mental note to get a new gas tank gasket. When he stepped down on the bumper, his side felt cool where they had sweated together. They sat on opposite fenders with the speaker on the outside but they could hear the people in the cars talking and slapping mosquitoes better than the movie. Mosquitoes didn't like Cale much but they really loved his date, until she asked him if they could leave. The movie wasn't worth watching anyway except when the monsters came on. The rest of the time it was people running around in police cars. Jigger took the best-looking one, could count on him for that. Cale's had really frizzly hair that he couldn't tell if it was dyed or just naturally that ugly. Her face wasn't so bad but she had a million curls on her head, but you didn't go many places in Summit with a date that anybody would see you anyway. Jigger had told him this was one to take to a drive-in. They had been planning to go to one all summer but Jigger's old man wouldn't let him have the car until he got his license. And they hadn't figured on what it was going to be like to double in a one-seater, at least Cale hadn't but when he picked up Jigger, he made him drive by his barn and he got a quilt and threw it in the back.

"We'll take them down by the river after the movie. I know just where to go," Jigger had said. He had had a steady for four months last year who had her own car. They broke up when she told Jigger she thought she was pregnant and she really wasn't and had scared him to death. Jigger made Cale drive through the filling station while he went in the rest room and bought some rubbers.

"All set," he said and slid them under the seat. "Wait till you see these two. They won't even make it through the movie."

"Where did you find them?"

"They wait on tables out at the 18 Cafe. One of them went to Summit High but she quit. I don't think you knew her."

"You're sure you picked the right kind?"

"Sure, I'm sure. Man, I told you. I know how to pick them. I'm just planning on being a little smarter, that's all. Nobody is going to make me get married."

Cale didn't recognize the girl but she knew him and she never stopped talking about things that happened in their English class. She must have been there because she remembered all right but he never even saw her to know he was looking at her. In fact he didn't remember any of the girls in Miss Sammons' class, just Miss Sammons. He had heard she wasn't coming back this year but there she was, same as always, but he'd never get to be in her class again.

So here was Lavonda Rigsbee and Jigger's was Jolene Pedigrew. Things went fine after that first night of fumbling around down at the river. But the first night was bad.

He remembered trying to get the latch undone on Bella's door but this time there wasn't any door, just Jigger down there on the riverbank waiting for him to say he was through. They had done some pretty heavy necking last year with Jigger's cousin and Jigger's girlfriend but Cale wasn't around when Jigger laid her. And this Lavonda girl expected it, she wasn't out to get you all hot and bothered and say no. She wasn't even insulted because he had a quilt and had made plans. He was about to panic when he got an idea. "Lavonda, I've never been out with a nice girl before."

"What do you mean?"

"I mean I've just been with prostitutes. I don't know how to treat a nice girl."

Then she laughed and the panic was over. Lavonda showed him how and August was a good month. After school started up in September, the girls wanted to go to ball games and places where they would be seen together and Cale found Jigger more concerned about that than he was. He had gotten to like old Lavonda. He told her he thought she was prettier with no makeup and her hair straight and she did it for him. He was trying to figure out a nice way to get rid of that perfume. They would sit down on the river bank and after the first night when she had told him her whole life story in about ten minutes, how her cousin had been the first to take advantage of her and how she liked waiting on tables because the truckers were nicer than the old bitches who came in the dime store where she worked before, he decided he liked old Lavonda. She just told you straight, no lying and hiding things and she always wanted him to talk, asked him questions soon as he quit. She laughed a lot. She wasn't too smart but old Lavonda was good company. Then Jigger would holler it was their turn and they would get the back of the truck. Jigger's girl never said a word after that first night at the drive-in when they both giggled and talked about people Cale and Jigger didn't know. Cale was sure now that Jigger had taken the wrong one. Lavonda kept telling him she just might like him better than she did her regular boyfriend who was nineteen and in the service that she never got to see anymore because he was in basic. Then right before school started, she said something that really scared him. Right out of the blue while he was telling her about trying to find Uncle Roe's killer she asked him, "If I broke off with my regular boy-friend, would you like that?"

"Huh?"

"Do you want me to give him his ring back? He gave it to me before he left. He wants to marry me when he gets out in November. But I could give him back his ring and he wouldn't bother me anymore."

He couldn't say anything. He really got scared. What did she say that for?

Then she said, "Jolene was right. She said you didn't have no intentions of marrying me. You don't have no respect for me. I want to go back. You take me back right now."

They started up the path and met Jigger on the way. They took them back and Lavonda slammed the truck door so hard Cale heard the window glass shatter down inside. Then Cale found out it had all been a plan. Jolene wouldn't let Jigger touch her either and asked him the same thing and he told her, Hell no, he wasn't going to marry her. They started to drive home when Jigger said, "Ten-thirty. Shit, I can't go home at ten thirty. You know what it was. Those bitches' boyfriends are back. We been filling in during basic training." Then he got tickled and they decided to go get drunk. They went over to

Parson's Store and Mr. Parson made them go around back to get a bottle. He handed it out the back and took their money and told them not to open it until they were off the premises. So they went back to the riverbank and between them they emptied it. Jigger drank more than his share and when Cale stopped at his house, he watched him all the way up the drive to make sure he made it through the door. Jigger was walking on the tops of his feet and Cale heard him fall over the garbage can by the garage and cuss out loud. Jigger had a room of his own out over the garage and didn't even have to go through the regular house. Cale drove home slowly, concentrating on the road and counting the gears. He counted the stones in the walk, the porch steps, steps to his room and he made it before he fell asleep in his clothes.

October, 1956

He didn't date again or touch another drop of liquor until October, after the football game. He had asked Brenda Sue Gutton who he had walked to the movies downtown once. She was sort of pretty he thought and Jigger agreed. Only trouble was she was a different kind of girl from Lavonda or the girl Jigger had and Jigger tried to pull the same procedure and the date was over soon as they pulled up at the river. He took Brenda Sue home with her mad as hell and not speaking to him and waited on Jigger by himself on the riverbank. Then Jigger took his date home and he and Jigger got drunk again. He remembered driving back by Brenda Sue's house and blowing the oogha horn several times he thought. But that was all until he got home and ran into his old man.

That morning when he got up, he went to the window to see about the truck. It was sideways in the drive and he saw tracks through his mother's chrysanthemums where one wheel had smashed down about half of them. He went down to breakfast and found the dishes done and his food cold in his plate. There was a note, "Wash your plate and split the kindling." He ate the food and sat there nauseated for about a moment before he rinsed his plate and went to the shed for the ax. When he split the first piece and the wood chips went tinkling down across the yard, he began to wake up.

He heard a chicken flutter, rushing ahead of an imaginary flock to grab a wood chip. The flake rolled around her beak while she made a whistling sound like a question and let it drop back to the ground.

"It wasn't corn, was it?" he said. The hen saw him and the ax and chop block, her neck stretched up into a thin white stalk before she left with a squawk, leaving two curls of down drifting in the air.

He was watching the down stay suspended like a windseed when he started to hear the other sounds again; no longer the clunk and snap of his ax and the wood but the clucking chickens and a chain saw rasping and chewing into the trees deep in the woods.

As he chopped into the logs, for the first time in his life he realized why he didn't hate to do that job, why he never really hated any job he could do alone. He stood a log on the chop block, balanced it on its end and swung the ax around with one arm, splitting the log before it toppled over. If it fell over before he got the ax around he would hit himself in the leg but he swung even harder when he thought of that so he could hear the sound of the wet wood pulling apart, the sound that somehow made his heart beat faster and made him feel he had done something he shouldn't. The wood was yellow with bubbles of sap on it and it stuck on the palms of his hands as he picked up the smaller pieces, before splitting them as thin as he could. And all the while, he thought of the wood, of nothing but the wood on the block because if he didn't he would hurt himself bad. Then when it was all done, he split each piece as small as he could. He stood there dumbly, looking through the thin strips for a larger piece, knowing there was no more and waiting for the ground around him to come back into focus.

His name came through the air, so thin it was no more than the other sounds. Falissa was soon behind him, talking to him but he never really heard her, never really noticed she was there until he saw the yellow flowers of her dress when she walked around in front of him. The skirt hung smooth and straight but the top sagged as shapeless as the body beneath it.

"You acting like you can't hear me. I been calling you for the last ten minutes," she said.

"You ought not come walking up behind me when I'm chopping, Mama. I could have hit you and not meant to."

He had dropped the head of his ax by his foot and looked up at her. She was so easy to defeat, one quick, hard word and her eyes clouded up.

"I didn't mean to run down your flowers last night. The steering wheel bracket came loose and . . ."

"Let's not worry about them. They were about bloomed out."

"I left it down there so the noise wouldn't wake you up."

She frowned at him and shook her head. "I just wish you wouldn't chop so reckless, Cale. You scare me to death you're going to bust your leg wide open."

"You don't have to go watching me when you send me to do something. I do what you tell me to."

She kept looking at his leg and wouldn't look up when he spoke. "I was by the window, Cale. I was putting in the wash and just happened to be looking out. And the way you swing your arm up with that ax, I know that wood could slip off and you'd cut yourself in two."

"I done it a thousand times, Mama, the same way. Do you want it done or not is what I'm asking."

"Don't you forget I got you stitched up from that sickle last summer." She pointed to his leg and he felt a pain in his groin when she spoke, not the pain of doing something but the feeling of waiting for it to happen and knowing you can't stop it. And it was always the sickle she mentioned, not any of the other times he messed up and cut himself and he had to think of

that blade again that made him ache to see it on the wall of the
shed. He never did know how to use it right, blade didn't seem
to fit on right. She really knew how to get to him again and
again the same way, something he would die with if it didn't
die with her first. The scar would be there too, not like the
small lines in his skin with a score of pen knives and glass, so
small he couldn't remember all of them but the ditch in his leg
with the skin pulled across it like tissue paper, its smoothness
seeming so fragile he was afraid to touch it direct except when
he sat in the tub and could touch its smoothness like a foreign
thing that wasn't him and it glowed red in the hot water. His
blue jeans felt too tight for a while and the pressure was only
gone when he put his pajamas on at night.

He had almost bled to death after it happened, sitting in
the doctor's office with a rag pressed up against his thigh with
that stupid feeling that he had changed the direction of his life,
worse than it was after Roe was killed, and he could never turn
it back so it had not happened. His mother had stuffed the gash
with spider webs and he had watched her short body move behind the bushes, reaching into every corner of the underpin-
ning, trailing the gray silk down her arm. She had come through
the bushes toward him, popping at the spiders on her arms, and
he wanted to run from her but he couldn't move. She buzzed
around him like a yellow jacket and he drew up tight, waiting
and knowing she was going to light on him. He watched her
rip the leg off his pants, hearing its wet rip in his own blood
and he saw her long hands stuff the gray into the bubbling
blood, but there was no sting when she pressed inside his flesh,
just a moment when he felt the touch of something very cold
inside him. That was the last he saw of his blood running because she waved down a car and in ten minutes he was in the
office of the doctor in town and his leg was black with soot.
He first felt it when he tried to step up on the doctor's bench,
like somebody slapped him. It hurt bad when the doctor tried
to clean it out and shook his head at the mess, muttering about

home remedies. Cale knew his mother was in the waiting room with her hands clasped in her lap.

He had looked back at the ceiling because it seemed to hurt worse each time he saw the doctor's hands move toward him. There was an ice cube tray light that hurt his eyes so he shut them and listened to the muffled sound of the doctor working. When he raised his arm to cover his eyes, someone pulled it back down. He remembered the sound when it happened, the dull rip as the sickle cut through his pants, the sucking sound when he pulled it out, and the silence of everything but the stinging noise in his head as he watched his pants turn dark red. He had wanted time to turn back, take it away and not do it again, but when he walked back to the house sweat ran into his eyes while the sides of the cut rubbed together.

He was sure of the silence of everything when her pan of beans hit the porch and rolled down the steps like a ball. When she came running to him, he knew he didn't have to move anymore, that all that he could do was over.

That morning hadn't been the first time that he had thought back about the sickle. She wouldn't let it leave his mind but it wasn't all her, it was him too when he found himself running across the peak of the barn and sliding down across the edge, knowing he might have done something stupid again and waiting for the hurt to come as he went off toward the ground, further away than he thought and felt the pain shoot through his ankles, then waited to see if it had happened again, if he had moved again unaware of what was before him and would have to stand the consequences of it. But that time the pain had drained away, that was yesterday.

He watched her walk to the clothesline with a basket on her hip, her feet rolled over in her bedroom shoes like they had once held up more weight than they held now. Year by year she seemed to grow smaller at first as he grew taller. But now she was even small away from him, flat-footed beside her friends and always having to pull together the neckline of her dress with a pin. She started snapping out the clothes in the basket, popping them again and again, not because they needed it he thought but because she liked the sound, and taking a long time at the line because she liked being out of the house.

He picked up a big wood chip and threw it at her, striking her on the rear. She screamed and leaped forward, dropping the towel she was hanging up in the dirt beside her. Cale walked toward her laughing when she started to pick it up and dust it off.

"Now I got to wash it again," she said and laid it over the handle of her basket. "You're not very funny, young man."

"Oh, I don't know. I enjoy me a great deal."

"Well, you're one of the multitude, I can assure you." She lifted up one of his plaid shirts and snapped it out full length, pinning it up by the shoulders.

"You starved me and crushed me and pinned me on the line."

She looked at him blankly, then shook her head, slinging out what little of what he had said that had made sense. She wasn't paying any attention to him and she was surely more cross than usual.

"You should have heard what your father said this morning about what Mrs. Gutton said about you. She called before you got up, you know. That certainly didn't fill me with pride. I don't know where you get the money to get lickered up but if it's coming from me and I find out where, I'm putting a stop to it."

"What are you talking about?"

"You know fine well what I'm talking about."

"I wasn't lickered up, Mama. Mrs. Gutton can't tell her ass from a hole in the ground."

"Well, you broke up half my house last night in that condition if I remember correctly."

Cale started to laugh but it didn't sound real not even to him so he got quiet. He went over to the porch steps. He did get into something last night. It was starting to come back. He did, it was . . . that china clock that never had the right time but was excused for its faults because it was antique. He had told her just because some nigger bought it off a junk peddler a hundred years ago didn't make it valuable. Half her house he hadn't broken up, just one of her treasures—now he remembered. It was get home soon or sleep where he was. Jigger was already gone when it hit him bad. He cut off the motor and coasted the last fifty feet and into the drive. Just as he had got in the door he heard that damn clock of hers start bonging and he could hear her and his father start mumbling and groaning in their sleep from the noise, and somehow from his father the words "What's that?"

He had planned to tell her he had tripped on the table and that was why the clock was busted but he knew he had picked it up and smashed it then listened to it finish striking twelve times though it was strewn all over the floor.

It was still ticking and he was on his knees looking for the part that made the noise when the light came on in the room. He squinted and put his fist in his eyes then looked up at the vague figure of his father with his little black pistol in his hand.

"That's the last time that clock will wake you up, Pop." The words floated out, then he belched and he could even smell the liquor. He saw the anger come to his father's face and he wanted to rise, to prove he was taller even though he was not bigger but his father had kicked him in the side. He hadn't expected it and he doubled up with pain and nausea as soon as the bare foot hooked under his ribs. He felt the broken bits of the clock against his side and didn't know how many times he was kicked with the hard foot that didn't really hurt so bad but wouldn't stop coming back and that made him do nothing but shrivel up on the floor and watch the black pistol wave in his father's hand, making him cold each time it pointed at him.

He had no right to do that and he told her before he went upstairs while his father was in the bathroom.

Cale went inside into the living room while she put in another load of wash and found the broken clock swept up in the corner. He started gluing the clock back together, remembering how it felt in his hand the night before, all that was really crystal clear to him about that night, how he reached through the air for it as though in a dream and how he thought it would feel like a jellyfish, soft with all of its curled leaves and roses coming off of it like tentacles but it seemed to turn to rock in his hand. When he felt its hardness, he wanted to see if he could break it. He looked at the fragile bits of china that morning and wondered why he could have ever doubted he could break it. He looked up and Falissa was in the door watching, smiling faintly at him. She took the clock from him, turned it in her hand to see the pattern of the seamed nicked surface, then she had laughed but only because she had to react and if she hadn't laughed she would have cried. Then when the tears came to her eyes, she wasn't ashamed and he knew she didn't have to explain them.

She put the clock in the china cabinet and its seams were lost in the darkness. The stubborn ticking had stopped, leaving its bent hands to stare out like some cross-eyed moron.

"You remember your carving, Cale, the one you were so proud of?"

"Yeah, right on the tabletop." He had made a scene, trees, little cars, and felt so excited to see the curled shavings roll up from the tabletop.

Then Falissa turned and went back to the clothesline. He watched her at the line now, squinting as she picked the dirt off the towel she had dropped. He went back out and walked up behind her.

"What did old lady Gutton tell you I did, huh?"

"Oh, you scared me. She said you just put Brenda Sue out right down at the gate and didn't have the courtesy to see if she got to the house safely."

"I watched her. She got in O.K."

"You know how to act better than that. If that's the way

you're going to act when you drive the truck you can just walk your girls on your dating."

"You act like it's your truck or something. That thing would have rotted in the ground if it wasn't for me."

"Nobody ever said that truck was yours. I have told you time and time again just how far a little manners will go. That's the last time you will get to take her out if it's any lesson to you."

"That saint can sit on her butt and count her beads the rest of her life for all I care."

"She's not Catholic, Cale."

"Oh, that's a shame. Do you suppose it will keep her out of the convent?"

His mother shook her head again and he saw her eyes rock dumbly. "You are getting to be such a smart aleck in the last year, I don't even like you much anymore sometimes."

"Well, if you'd just stop picking me. When I take a girl out I'll dump her in a ditch if I want to. There is nothing you can tell me what to do about that goes one inch beyond this crumby farm."

"There are plenty of things I can tell you what to do as long as you sleep under my roof and eat my food and I wash and iron your clothes and pick up after you. And there is no girl you can dump in a ditch if you want to, even if she was to be sorry. The law don't allow that."

She looked at the line and his row of shirts moved together like a chorus line, laughing at him. Five shirts in one week.

"Besides I said I watched her get to the house and didn't leave till the porch light came on. The last time I walked a girl to her door her old lady threw the door open and pulled her in and glared at me as soon as we got there like I was planning on raping her on the porch."

"Cale Jenkins, the day you get some girl in trouble is the last day you live here if I come to know about it."

She looked down at the dirty towel in her hand then walked to the clothesline, hanging it up with the rest before she wheezed and started up the steps with the basket on her hip.

"Someday you are going to see you've cut off your nose to spite your face when there isn't a decent girl left you would have as a wife and you have messed up every girl for miles around."

"Is that what you think I do?" He was surprised.

"Yes, it is. You don't fool me as much as you think. You changed the very day that truck started running. And you remember once you mess them up they just don't care anymore and they're as good as anybody's." She was almost ready to cry.

Cale took two steps back from her, as if he wanted an arm's length from her before he spoke. "Is that the way it is, that once Pa messed you up, you didn't care who done it then?"

The blood shot into her cheeks and stayed where the bones pressed out. She looked like she had just come in from the cold. Cale had never seen her change like that and she almost scared him, like an animal you reach out to play with and it jerks back and snarls at you. Not big enough to be scared of but you just aren't sure.

"You are dirty-mouthed as you can be. You are not fit to live and be called a son. What makes you so hateful? I won't ever talk such trash with you again. You can just go talk with your licker-mouthed friends if that's all the kind of things you can think about."

"You would be a liar to stand up there and say you love having him around you, wouldn't you?"

She walked closer to the door and her hand fumbled for the handle. She was crying now but she wouldn't turn her face and let him see her. Cale could see the creases deepen in her hand. Too far. He had pushed her too far. This was his fault.

"Your father has times when there is nobody on God's green earth who could be as good as him. He is black as tar when his meanness comes out but maybe that was meant for his goodness to show better. And there are times now when I think he's making up for the disappointment you've been to me. If you want to say he's all bad you'll just have to find somebody else to talk to because I won't agree to it."

She looked at Cale but he couldn't say anymore. Then she turned and went in the house and the screen slammed shut. Cale walked back to the woodshed. All the kindling was split. He started to pick up the ax but when he saw the same pieces, he couldn't do it. His leg hurt and he was scared.

Falissa went upstairs tossing the wash basket into the back room for another week and walked straight to the window above the chop block. She stopped there, jumping back a bit when she saw her shadow spread in the glass, but noticing below her that Cale had not seen her come there because his back was to her while he picked up the pieces of kindling, cupping them against his body and carried it to the box under the porch, the top of his head disappearing from her sight each time he went up the steps.

She didn't know for sure why she kept doing this, waiting and running for her chance to watch her boy from a perch where he could not see her. She couldn't stop herself anymore, even if she had wanted to.

His face turned and her body tightened up when she saw his eyes, clear, unseeing. But she remembered Cale's words the night he and Jerome went in to sell tobacco and left her home with too much cash in the house. "You can't see in a dark house if it's light outside but you can see in a light house if it's dark so you get yourself back away from the windows if you're worried by yourself. There's nobody to know you're by yourself."

But that was two years ago before Roe died which seemed like a long time now because Cale had changed so. And not so much for the better as she had hoped with Roe gone. Too much of Roe had taken hold before anybody could stop it and it would be a long time washing out if it ever did. She told him that, she told everyone that but nobody paid her any mind and they all suffer for it. She didn't think he was unconcerned for her; she just couldn't know how he felt—that was what truly hurt, the kind of hurt that comes when the preacher talks to you after a death, numb and spreading through you because you know you're not really special. He didn't tell her more than he'd tell his schoolteachers. Shut out. She guessed she watched him now hoping she would see something. That had to be it, hoping she would see something that would let her in on something . . . what he was thinking, where he was going, why he wouldn't talk to her anymore and why if he did he made it in a language she couldn't understand. It wasn't plain old nosiness, not fair to call it that. She wanted to know about the good thoughts he was having. His patience with her was gone but she had to keep scolding him. He was making her. You can't ignore a teen-age son coming in drunk at 2:00 A.M. and breaking up your house and Mrs. Gutton carrying on about her daughter. Why's she so sure that girl didn't bring misbehaving on herself?

The kindling started sliding from his arms and Falissa jumped again when he threw it all at the ground. His anger had become so quick; now his anger got in his way and he said and did things before he thought. That's the Jenkins in him. Cale started picking the wood up again, snatching at each piece like he wanted it to know he was mad. He could clap them together one at a time but they could swarm in to overpower him and make him a fool if he didn't watch out. He was fighting mad now. Try to act grown-up one minute and every bit of the child comes out all at once. He's got a long way to go yet.

She heard him come in downstairs and heard an armful of kindling crash to the floor beside the wood stove, then he was back outside before she could move from her spot. Just as well, nothing you could say to him would amount to a hill of beans. He was throwing corncobs at the oil barrel now, making silver dents through the rust as he threw and a singing sound in the air. It made her uneasy to watch him but when she closed her eyes the sound was as bad as the sight, not because he would rupture the old tank but what she always feared, Jerome, still she feared him, seeing him appear, seeing his dark thick body there watching Cale, Cale with all of his childishness exploding from his man's body. And his words, she never had to think hard for any of his words, she could say them for him had there ever been any need to, but there wasn't with him living nor would there be with him dead because they were such waste. "Got too much energy have you? Got yourself a body like a man and nothing between the ears to go with it. Guess I'm not giving you enough to do if you've got nothing better to spend your time on than destruction." Spit it out like a snake.

And Cale would want to hurl everything in his hands at him, to jump on him and beat the stuffings out of him just to see if he could win if he had to. And I'm so tired. So tired of standing between every row. Making him stay out of Jerome's way. Those two ever went at it one of them would go. Then she would be alone, her and Pearlie because people let nothingness bust up a family. She would crawl on her belly like a snake before that would happen. No shame to admit, she wanted to keep them both.

There were still times it was good, she kept reminding herself of that but it was true. A mother would lie to say it wasn't sometimes good. When she could tell Cale of things he didn't remember, when he listened and laughed at the stories of him as a little boy, treasure she didn't mind giving away because they would never go dry, she had seventeen years' worth of them all the way back to his coming into the world, getting bad as Papa, like the world don't go no way but backwards. Ought to tell him the day he was born it felt like he wanted to walk out and do it by himself even then, and hurt her because she wanted to help him. Little snake in the grass. And she had near about forgotten she had a life before that day.

She could tell him stories now that like to have killed her when they happened. Maybe that was the peace she should have now for this boy who tormented her, the time he painted Mrs. Gutton's cow green, he was only eight and only painted half up her side because that was all the far he could reach but he painted her teats and they were afraid the paint remover might poison the milk so they milked her while she was moaning in pain and dumped it away for weeks before they felt it was safe. She had to give up her own cow's milk to Mrs. Gutton at a time when she needed the milk for the baby girl, and knowing they were so fancy they were throwing out what was probably perfectly good. There were many bad things about it. She whipped Cale good, and watched Mrs. Gutton spill out the milk on the ground, watched it soaking away like it was no more than water, and leaving its precious white foam for the ants and Pearlie just starving for milk.

Cale told her all he remembered was the whipping and that it hurt, and sure enough he had gotten a whipping when she thought Jerome was going to let him get by on her switching. But the boy remembered that they both whipped him, that was proof enough for her that he felt alone, that there was no one to turn to if she whipped him too. Who was it that was telling her, somebody at the church that they loved you better if you whipped them? Not a word of truth in it. Maybe when they're grown but what does that matter to me now? And that Jerome used to say she was making him a sissy. There was nothing in her boy that any sane man could call sissy. He could make you mad as a snake with his trifling but he wasn't going to back down on a thing. He could cry, she had seen him do that, it had been a long time but she had see him. Like the day when the rabbits were screaming under the mower blade and they could all see them, cut up or trying to run with their legs gone and he kept mowing because Jerome said to. The hay stood up it was so thick. It wouldn't fall enough for him to feel it was being mowed and she saw him crying and he told her it was like all he was doing was killing, that the hay wouldn't fall enough for him to think he was mowing, and that what he was doing was killing the rabbits for his father, and he didn't want to kill them. He was ten then, the year they first got the hay mower for the tractor.

But there were good times too, when she could hear him singing above the tractor engine and she had told him and he was embarrassed because he could hear himself and thought no one could hear him. But they laughed about that. She would have to make herself think about the things they laughed about until she could see clear what to do. There was no good in staying down and thinking over and over what put you down. No good in it. There were things that she ought to have been able to laugh over. The others laughed.

Like when that hating radio broke. Should have known that ugly thing wouldn't give up the ghost in a quiet way. When the war was going, Jerome played it until her head split. It got like they were making up things just to have something to pop and scratch at you and Jerome was one to make like he cared about something he knew good and well won't going to affect him and let something come up that did, like the tobacco allotment, and he would close up his ears. Something wrong about a person who has to pretend he's caring when he has more than enough to care about. Couldn't help but think of all that killing and ugliness that used to come out of it even if there won't nothing but those silly morning soap operas and that was all there was. She heard them all talking about them at the church sewing circle, making just like they were real people and her asking, "Joy who?" and them laughing at her like she was a child. Some people are so idle they want to listen to such. Can't iron a shirt without racket going. She liked to know the birds were singing herself or to surely know when one of the children was calling her.

Falissa listened through one until the advertisement came. The voices won't a bit like those that Cale found in the afternoon and at night on his Christmas radio where the sounds with all that bumping and shooting and horses running just make you sure somebody is putting on. They were just like they were sitting right there in the living room, talking out loud about things they got no business telling anybody outside the family and getting mixed up in things. She had never heard such people and such meddling in others' affairs like day in and day out they had nothing better to fret about. But she wouldn't tell them that at the circle. Just let them go on about it and she would get on with her mending. Troubles enough of your own not to go getting into others', goodness. She had turned it off and looked out the window at the quiet. Could hear the wind rattling twigs off the roof. And it wasn't two days later that Miss Stevens from the church came visiting about pledging and just couldn't miss what happened today and turned it on and that ugly brown thing picked right then to blow up like a skunk cabbage, sending out enough black and filth to make you think she had used it for a coal bin. With Miss Stevens screaming, you would have thought she had dumped a scalding pan in her lap, and her trying to get behind the old box with a towel to pull out the plug before it burned the house down. It was just awful. Not a piece of it touched that big fat thing and she scared her half to death with her hollering. And it couldn't have happened to a bigger mouth and it was all over by the next circle.

She carried that hating thing out on her own steam before Jerome ever knew it was broke and had to set it down twice before she got to the packhouse and in there was every last thing she had ever sent Jerome out of the house with, as far as he got. And he wouldn't give one single thing away if it was broken in a thousand pieces, her old hot water heater with the bottom rusted clean through, the living room lamp that popped out three good bulbs in a row, the biggest pile of junk you've ever seen, and she told him to give it to Aunt Bynum or somebody who could find some use for it and there it lay. And he was one to accuse her of saving and the day had not come when she saved a single solitary thing that didn't have some use to it.

Why it was just selfishness and if she had a notion that he might not go snooping in there, not one speck would be left tomorrow. But he'd find out sure as she was standing there and tell her to go back to worrying inside her house. So he could keep his old junk shop there until the day he died and have folks come looking and find what a mess he kept things in and laugh at him with him in the grave.

Cale was still throwing below her when she saw Jerome coming up the hill to the house. Before she thought she tapped the window, and Cale looked up at her, seeing her finger point to the dark man coming closer. He nodded his head and she moved back from the window, frowning and pressing her hands because she had done it again. Stood right there thinking about it and turned right around and did it again.

The ringing of the last ear of corn faded from the drum, the sides swelling in and out, humming now as the red cob rolled down the hill behind the smokehouse. The drum had stopped vibrating by the time Jerome walked into the yard. He looked at Cale and at the drum so Falissa knew he must have heard the sound from the bottom of the path.

Cale hadn't been afraid or decided not to appear so since he stood with a handful of cobs in the yard, tossing one in the air and catching it. She watched the two of them, saw Jerome speak and knew the words so well she felt her head would burst from the silence like she was a crazy person, a bug sealed up tight in a mason jar, running up the sides and falling on her back to the bottom. Falissa went quickly back down the stairs and waited in the kitchen for Jerome to come in.

He came through the screen door and set his hat atop the refrigerator.

"You going to lie down or do you want to eat right away?" she said, without thinking, so easy because those were always her words.

Jerome walked across the room, silent. That's the way he was. Could scare you to death from a distance but let him get up close, and the fear of him faded like night breaking and sending out the morning. He's looking gray and old today, up close you can see all the creases. His hair had sweated up in little tufts around the top of his head from his hat and he looked like a messy-haired child with soap in his hair. He washed his hands and sat down at the table which was his answer, and she started to dish out his food.

"Just as soon eat now. Don't matter one way or the other. I got no craving for nothing but to rest my bones and it'll have to be night before they'll allow me that. Got to be night before I can sleep and keep face. Head's stuffed up, got some cold."

"Talking like an old man. Didn't you sleep good last night? I didn't see you squirm a muscle."

He looked old again, drawn up, as he waited for his slow words to come, even weak now she thought, like he would shrivel to a dry skin if she were to hold the food away and refuse it to him.

"Lie awake half the night waiting to hear him come in knowing there is no sense falling off till he's put for the night. He never had a thought for no one that don't get to sleep his mornings away. Come in stinking sorry drunk and busted up the house."

"You mean Cale?"

"Well, I hope there is no other man sneaking into my house when I'm sleeping."

"You don't have to act so smart. I thought you got plenty of sleep since you went down at nine o'clock."

"You know I mean him, so quit acting like you don't know nothing of it. Or are you going to lie for him?"

"No, I'm not. You didn't leave him anything to do so I had him split up the kindling."

"There's plenty for him to do. Getting him to do it is another story. He hadn't been worth what we have to feed him since school started. Where's Pearlie?"

"Helping at the church."

He waved his hand then clamped it on the edge of the table. She put his plate in front of him, the food already dished out and poured his coffee, splashing his arm.

"Ouch, you watch out scalding me."

"Well, wake up and eat your food before it gets cold."

"Sure stunk up the house."

"If you want me to stink up the yard I'll cook your greens out there."

Jerome looked up at her and smiled. "Boy, if you ain't been eating razor soup today."

"Jerome, there are times when your picking just gets to be more than I can bear."

"I just come in here to eat and you light into me about picking at you. Nobody's picking at you, honey. Has the boy done something else to upset you?"

"Five minutes you been here and you have been through Cale and my cooking and the way I pour your coffee and you don't even think to taste the food that's in your plate. Just stuff it in your mouth like I could put anything in front of you . . ."

"It always tastes all right to me."

Falissa looked at his plate and asked, "You want more?"

"No ma'am, I'm done."

He stood up and his chair scraped back with him, leaning against the cabinet. She took the plate and put it in the sink, looking out the window as she set the chair straight again. She felt tired; Jerome always made her feel tired. Cale wasn't to be seen and he had left the ax against the chop block instead of setting it inside the shed. She'd have to see to that before Jerome went back out. But that would be a while; he might sleep all afternoon.

Cale came around the corner swinging a stick at something gray that fell to the ground. He flipped it up with the stick and swung at it again, hitting it this time and sending it sliding across the yard. It was the cone of a wasp colony, broken apart from his stick and with the little cells broken by the hatching wasps, only the dead ones still sealed over with a thin gray skin. Cale walked to it and poked it with the stick, breaking the sealed cells one by one and waiting for the insects to rise up out of the hole. He stood back from it, almost like he was afraid, she thought, and the wasps would not be living, not this late. But maybe he wasn't thinking at all, it could be an ash of a paper or a cow pile that he poked at and his mind was somewhere else. No, you could see it in him. He was still afraid, as afraid as he was when he was a little boy. She had seen his skin twitch before when the stinging insects were around, his memory was as good as hers for that, for the time when every inch of his body was burned by them. He would remember someday how she looked after him. These were bad years now. He would come back someday after these bad years were past and remember what she had done for him.

Chapter 28

THE BIG BIRD flew breakneck into the trees, diving through the mass as though the woods were made of feathers instead of limbs and trunks that could snap his skinny neck. Stretched out in the grass above the pond, Cale waited for a noise, a howl or a long cry as the bird drove his head in a tree like a nail but he heard nothing more than a quiet wind moving through the branches, a few clattering leaves that hadn't let go yet. No sooner had he figured the bird had been swallowed up or had slipped out the back side than the woods spit it toward the old locust tree that grew by the spring. Hard to believe it could have woven through the holes in the woods no better than it looked like it could fly, sideways and up and down, dodging imaginary bullets. It lit on a limb in the locust tree overshooting it and almost pitching off, a jumbled pile of bones and feathers that relieved itself with a splash in the spring before it got its balance. Cale laughed when the bomb hit the water, picturing his old man running down the hill cussing and waving his arms at the bird knowing damn well the turd was already in the water. That's what his old man would do, then he would cuss the turd and try to fish it out on a leaf like he had never touched a turd before. Cale imagined the bird creaking over to the edge of the water like an old man, raising one foot ever so gracefully to hold it for Mr. Audubon, Great Blue Heron. Goddamn crane to his old man who had no use for any animal larger than a sparrow. "Don't see how they call that a bird. It's too big to be a bird." Then he would dissect the turd with a stick and say, "See! Trout eyes. Look at that fur, gobbling up the little rabbits whole. Bet it ate every salamander in the spring, stop off the water. Won't be a little animal left on the place." All because the crane shit in his spring.

He had seen the bird before this fall, always by himself waiting for fish, so still it looked like a statue you buy for the yard. It waited with its neck folded down in a flattened S, holding its breath probably, not moving a feather until something swimming and beaksize was caught in the yellow eye. The neck straightened out and down like the stroke of an ax, up with a stretch, then still again, something, a crawfish or a tadpole caught too fast for you to see until a bump went swimming down inside the bird's neck.

But there the bird wobbled, still on the limb opening its wings to grab the air for balance, then settling back to a slow, rocking perch, sucking its ruffled feathers back into place before a draft got under them. Cale wondered if it could think, trying to decide if there was going to be good picking in the lake today, just taking its time because nothing mattered but eating and building tree houses and dropping eggs and white bombs whichever one happened to be on the way. Making sure it didn't mistake the feeling and shit in its nest.

Maybe it sees me. That's why it's sitting there. Maybe it thinks I'm here for the same reason it is, to slurp up those nice, soft slimy tadpoles and slide them down my throat. Really hard to figure how things can eat what they do, birds eating worms, horses eating hay, really strange things when you stop and think about it.

Can't tell if it sees me. Better not let anybody else know I'm here. Nice sitting here and knowing no one cares you're here and no one hollers at you to do something. Goddamn bird. I was here first. I don't know whether you care or not but I can't just sit here and not think about it, since you decided to

flap in and look at me. Stare at me, that's what you're doing.
Like a blue buzzard on the bedpost, waiting for the death rattle
so you can get first shot at the eyeballs.

"Hey bird, I don't even *like* tadpoles."

The bird fluttered again, losing its balance at Cale's words
and each time the wind hit Cale's face, spreading his hair across
his forehead, its wings would open, reach in the air, and relax
when its toes squeezed shut around the limb.

So if he is that chicken-shit, he can sit up on that limb and
starve to death and crumble away because I'm not leaving first.

The bird took off across the sky like a woman on a trapeze
swing and stopped at the edge of the water, driving its legs down
into the mud and freezing still without so much as a splash.
Just like somebody shot an arrow.

Time to play statue for a while, so still you can check me
out up close and make sure I don't have a rifle. A little braver
than sitting up in the trees anyway, bird, though I could have
picked you off up there too.

Around its legs were the white bellies of tadpoles, poisoned
when the cattails were sprayed. The bird's head twisted at
the dead bloated things while before, right side up, they had
wiggled away to hide from the crane in the shadow of the
rushes. One foot lifted from the water, funny somehow, it
bent the wrong way like an arm not a leg, then stepped back
down, sliding into the water, not a sound in its step. Its beak
reached down, slowly, picked a dead thing up and slung it on
the bank. Not right, they're supposed to wiggle through the
water and smell washed not dead.

Damn it, bird, I'm sorry. It was the cattails I was after.

Suddenly the water flew up and fell in droplets. The bird
was gone with a scream, more scared than hurt, probably not
hit, up over Cale's head, the beat of wings like a sheet flapping
on the clothesline, his neck stretching out, spearlike. The water
was still being torn up, rising up in shoots. Not from underneath, on top. Cale looked across the lake and saw him; it was

Floyd, throwing something, clods. The bird was gone now, hidden somewhere in the trees.

Floyd had taken to walking around when he didn't have work to do and Cale would see him, never up close, always hanging around the edges of the field or the yard. Cale hadn't even felt him come up and even now when Floyd scooped up dirt and threw it across the water, his brown skin and brown clothes were only there if you made yourself notice them. Most people wouldn't even be able to see him. He wasn't quite old enough yet to scare his mama with his wandering around but his father had started to wonder whether his restlessness would grow out of him or up with him. He was going to keep an eye on this one. Floyd never talked to anyone and his eyes had gone behind thin slits. He never smiled, just stared.

Cale's mama had once said to him, "You might find them by the white of their eyes on a dark night but I don't want them messing around my house in broad daylight. There's too much bad business going on now in the schools to suit me. I don't like the sullenness of that boy, doesn't have a laugh or a smile in him. Was the cutest little button around when he was little but he's grown off and left it. He's took up a mean streak." Cale remembered that because it was about all his mother had said about Aunt Bynum and her family since he used to play with Floyd.

She counted heads every now and then like chickens in the chicken house. Aunt Bynum had quit having her own but her children were showing up with children. And Jason was gone.

If his old man found out Floyd didn't stay put at night, he would have to work him down until he did. If he started looking like trouble and that didn't do the trick he was going to have to be put off, but the old man would wait until the last minute because you can't throw away something worth something to you just because it makes you mad. "You grow to ignore his fiddling around, boy, as long as he stays put at night, and get what you want from them without it bothering you. Aunt

Bynum had too many girls. We need some male hands around here. That's my complaint. One man in a house of girls." That is what his father said about Floyd and when Cale told him about catching him throwing a knife at a fence post his father laughed at him and said, "If he throws it at my cows you tell me about it, boy, but you just let him get it out of his system on my fence post. He is strong as a little mule, that young nigger," and Cale had felt a moment of jealousy before he was able to laugh at himself.

Floyd had stopped throwing now, maybe disappointed because the bird had flown off so fast or maybe because he thought Cale might start throwing at him. Then he turned and walked off slowly and Cale felt something inside that ached and made him madder each step Floyd took and the slower and more deliberately he moved the more it pulled inside him. If he hadn't been covered by the trees in the woods he felt he would have had to yell or throw at his brown back and make it move faster.

Cale could hear a crackling sound in the little woods. That might be Floyd still there, just deep enough to hide himself, breaking twigs with his feet, still watching him. Or maybe it was just the wind. Cale felt like he had lifted something heavy and all his muscles wanted to rest but they were stretched out inside him. He would like to close his eyes and sleep but would have to keep opening them to make sure his father didn't catch him here stretched out in the grass. He couldn't let that nigger get by with that. That was different. He was sorry Floyd had done it because he didn't want to have to think of something. But Floyd had an edge and when that bird took to the air, it was like sharpening an edge across a stone. Floyd couldn't get by with that.

*   *   *

October, 1957

At the State Fair in Raleigh, Cale sat in a little restaurant with shavings on the floor and hinges in all the corners. Next week it wouldn't even be there. It'd just fold up and they'd jack up the prices on the wall and take it up north. Cale was drinking again tonight but he knew he wouldn't be drunk by the time he got home because he hadn't had enough money for but a pint.

It had gotten so he could drink a little and not have much trouble at home as long as they didn't see him. The tobacco sold bad and his father had started getting drunk a couple of nights a week but he got mean drunk, right at home and never went out and had any fun, just stayed there where his mother could put him to bed. He was starting to slip, his mother said. Couldn't take it like he used to.

Cale kept the bottle in the pocket of his Windbreaker, sliding his 7-Up over the edge while the waitress fixed four hot dogs for this fat guy. The bourbon slid in with a fizz like it was going to dissolve the ice then eat the bottom out of the cup. He set the discolored liquid back on the counter, breathing in the alcohol, it wasn't a very good bottle, while he spun the lid back on the bottle in his pocket. He took a sip and his eyes watered while the bourbon spread into the corners of his stomach like a heat blast. Should have filled the space with food first. That fat S.O.B. has eaten three hot dogs already, smell the onions down here.

This year he had wandered through all kinds of exhibits he'd never seen before because when he came with the guys it was to the front of the girlie shows, never with enough money to go in; then on the way home they'd make up a bunch of stuff about the livestock to tell their fathers when they asked them about the fair . . . the Herefords were not as good this year as last year and they had a cow with a hump on its back like a camel and the number one prize bull just turned his ass toward the judge and dookeyed like the rest of them, which was just about as much as they would have noticed if they'd really been there.

He laughed out loud then smiled and the waitress turned to him.

"You got a funny you're holding in?" she said, half to him and half to the paper plates she was cracking in two and ramming in the trash can.

"Not fit for telling, huh?"

"Not fit for telling," he said. She smiled, he thought because he used her phrase, used it like that was the way he would have said it. She was kind of old but she didn't care, no makeup and her ass jiggled like somebody's mother's. If somebody would ask her to do her number in the strip show, she would put her hands on her hips and say, "Are you shitting me?" and then laugh and jiggle some more, laugh at dirty jokes, that's what she would do. She was O.K.

He'd gone over to one of the art shows and was looking at all these paintings of fruit and stuff. There were these two old ladies having an argument with some man about hanging this picture and he walked around them until he could see what it was and it was a picture of a naked woman stretched out on a couch. Those two old women were screaming something about all the little children who would be looking at the show since a children's exhibit was included and this just wasn't the place for that sort of thing. The man kept calling it art but Cale could tell he was losing. He always used to wonder about the guy who got to take the picture. He thought of a bunch of things to say to the little old ladies, like all the little kids are down on the front row in the strip show so don't worry about them coming to see your dirty art show.

Cale heard a humming noise and looked down at the end of the counter where a girl sat. He couldn't tell how old she was but she was slurping at a Coke like a little kid. Her hair was frizzled and blond, he hated that frizzly hair, was it baby blond or dyed blond . . . he never could tell that unless the roots were real black. It made him mad, sort of mad like it did when his little sister told him about this girl he thought was stacked, how her little sister borrowed her bathing suit and had the same figure except the falsies kept floating out in the water.

Old Pearlie got a point for that one. That humming was beginning to get on his nerves; she must know everyone could
hear her. And she left the crusts of her sandwich in her plate.
That always made him mad too, the best part. Guess she thought
it made her look dainty, she had a little bow stuck over her ear
by this little curl that was spit-stuck to her face, yeah, she must
be trying to look dainty. Too many little frills all around, curls
she played with with one hand, kept wetting her fingers and
working on that little curl.

He heard her drink slurp from the bottom of her straw and
decided to put her on the chop block. He had to hit her before
she fell over, a dead hit and she opened up so easily, all in how
it is hit, the whole stroke smooth and straight, zap. Now he
would split the halves, ax in one hand but she was so skinny he
missed and hit his shin with the ax, not a bit of blood, just a
bunch of little gold wheels that kept ticking and turning inside
her even though she was split in half. He looked at the girl
again and was almost sure she was still humming. For a minute he thought he was humming.

Too black at the roots for baby blond. It's dyed. But he knew
she had long since decided he wasn't interested, he had looked
at her hand once, not quite his best sneer, and she could tell
he had decided she was too ugly to bother with, so it was over.
Now he would have to see her without looking at her, looking
over and around reading the menu above the counter, watching
the people go by with cotton candy, pink and glowing in the
early dark. How could anybody eat that stuff? He didn't have
enough money to pick up a girl, not this early in the evening.
He couldn't entertain one all night and she wouldn't be out by
herself if she wasn't looking for it. He kept looking up at this
noise then he saw it was the door, each time it opened this funny
little bell would ring, not the right place for that kind of little
bell, ought to be for some rich bitch to call her maid by. Something like Grandma Sarah Ann would have in her cabinet.

He had had half the bottle and that was enough for now. He

hadn't had enough to eat, hot dogs just wouldn't hold him, and
he was really starting to feel it. The music that came through
the door each time it was opened had taken on that roar inside
his head, that roar that all loud noises started to make when he
was drunk that turned inside his head so fast he couldn't close
his eyes, not for long anyway because he would get sick and
there'd be no stopping it. More noise on the outside than the
inside. All the sideshows going now, the whores standing out
front with enough off and on to get the kids inside, giving them
a few sample bumps and grinds. Girls go to those things, why
the hell do a bunch of girls go to those things? Think they're
going to find out things they don't know. Makes them feel
good when they go back and sit their fat butts down in the
office on Monday morning and hope someday somebody will
make a pass at them. Asked Pearlie once . . . why do girls go to
those things and she had told him, "Every girl secretly wants
to be a nun and a prostitute." How about that from old Pearlie?
He didn't even know she knew what a nun was, much less a
prostitute.

Even old Pearlie wouldn't come with him to the fair. Pretty
bad off when you have to stoop to that. She said she didn't
want to spend the evening smelling pigs and she knew Cale
wouldn't take her on any of the rides. He told her she was
damn right and now he was sitting there wishing he hadn't
said that, that even going on a bunch of damn rides with your
sister was better than this, having to look a certain way so no
one would know you didn't want to be by yourself. This
wasn't one of the things that was any good by yourself.

Cale paid the woman behind the counter; she smiled at him
funny and he knew she knew he had loaded his drink. But
he had a card; borrowed it off a guy. He could buy beer if he
wanted to. He had just been a buck-fifty short of a fifth. And
he wanted to go to a show, so he held it. If the pint wouldn't
hold him then all he would be able to go see would be the
hogs. That's what his old man would ask him about, if he saw

the livestock because he was too damn lazy to go himself and too crummy a farmer to have any of his stuff there.

He was drunker than he thought when he got outside because he knew it had turned off cold and he didn't feel it. He wasn't staggering yet but he didn't worry about bumping people and he knew he was. All he needed was a fight. He'd go watch the waterfall for a while; it had colored lights on it so it changed a lot and he didn't get tired of looking at it. They had a bunch of fancy ducks swimming around in the pool at the bottom; that was what got him . . . how they could sit there and swim under that waterfall with it making an awful roar. Those stupid ducks weren't even scared but he was waiting until one of them swam under the water and came out nothing but busted feathers. It could happen. Don't know why nobody thought of it. Just didn't go together, that waterfall coming down and those ducks in that calm water right under it swimming between a bunch of floating paper cups and crud.

"That big duck has got one eye gone."

I'll be damned. Cale hadn't noticed her, not since he left the café but there she was beside him and he didn't know how long she'd been there.

"Probably got it poked out with one of those damn peanuts. Damn peanuts floating all over the place like they are a bunch of monkeys or something." Goddamn stupid people, he thought, what does it mean if a duck happened to eat a peanut you throw in or it just sinks? What in the hell was this girl doing following him around?

"I wouldn't like to be a duck at the fair," she said.

He didn't know why he had bothered to talk to her and he could tell by her voice that she didn't mean that to be funny. What the hell would a nice girl come to the fair by herself for; she wouldn't, and why was she here talking like they'd been friends all their life? He looked at her again and her bottom lip was out, pouting because she was sorry for the ducks he figured and looking pretty silly but there was something nice about the

shine of the lights from the waterfall that went across her eyes.
But she couldn't pass for good-looking, little pointed chin and
nose that looked like it had gotten whittled down too much.
Bones in every direction, nothing, she did nothing for him
unless he wanted to work on looking at the lights in her eyes
but that wasn't her, that was the waterfall and he was still
drunk and it was too much trouble to find some interesting
things about her. She could beat it. The long silence, he knew
she was thinking that it was his turn now to speak. It was hard
to sustain the silence; he could insult her but he didn't feel
mean either. Wouldn't like to be a duck at the fair, what
would you like to be, but a question would mean he would be
stuck with her. He had gotten drunk too soon; he should have
seen everything first and then gotten drunk. But he was cornered now. He had to talk back to her.

"What would you like to be?"

She turned her little pointed chin up and the lights slid
through her eyes and disappeared.

"Nothing at the fair, I can tell you. No matter how poor I
was to ever get, I wouldn't get up and do what they do." She
nodded toward the sideshow but the girls had gone inside for
their act. "That one who was on the end, you know she isn't
but seventeen years old and has ruint her life. I was meaning to
talk with her and ask her how she can stand to ride all over the
country with that show. They let their costumes get filthy dirty
and live out of a bunch of trailers. Why they're no better than
gypsies. I just work local. I don't go all over . . ."

Cale quit listening to her talk but he knew she was still at it,
her thin little voice somewhere down below him and all the
noise of the water and the music on the rides above him. He
had thought before in the bar that if she had opened her mouth,
he would know all there was to know about her and here he
was couldn't tell if she was a second rate whore or the daughter
of a Baptist preacher and if she got up in one of those shows
they'd laugh her off the stage, seventeen maybe younger and

twelve years old except for the wrinkles pinched between her eyes. Jigger would be ashamed of him.

The air was getting hot around him and he saw that they had been trapped up against the fence by a cluster of people, he couldn't stand that, to stay in one place because he had to not because he wanted to. He started pushing his way to the outside, not knowing or caring if she was with him or not. He went through all the crowds around the rides and had to turn his face away from the Ferris wheel; he was at that bad stage of drinking when he didn't know whether to get sick or try to drink more. But he had shaken her, she didn't come after him through that.

He looked up at the rides on the Midway and they twirled and spun until it all seemed to be one big ride, the rocket and the Ferris wheel and the Tilt-a-whirl, all rolling in a figure eight with hands dangling from them and people screaming like they were loving it. Cale looked back at his feet again and shut his eyes slowly; he had almost done it that time, he felt the liquor rise up in his throat. He waited while his stomach stopped churning, pressing his hand against his eyes so no light could get through. If he could make it to the livestock barns then he would be sober, the rabbits or the chickens, if he went in the hog barn he would be sick. He better do something or one of the cops would get him.

He stopped by a cage full of spotted rabbits and looked all around him. She wasn't there. Was he running from the crowd of people or was he running from her? Both of them. They must not like rabbits. The only female he had seen who didn't have a bunch of friends with her, they were impossible that way if you were alone. Would have been a bad night for him and Jigger, too many in a bunch. Couldn't get them to break up for anything but if you could take them by the pair. He looked into the cage beside him and saw the split pink nose of a rabbit pushing through a circle of chicken wire. It moved up and down and its whiskers twitched.

He touched the rabbit on the nose, expecting it to pull away but it pressed up closer against his fingers. Its eyes were closed and it settled down in the haunches, like a cat by a fireplace, feeling completely safe and secure here with a stranger touching, and it was stupid enough to trust him. He could kill it, he could pinch its nose together and kill it and the rabbit didn't even know it. He scratched the rabbit under its chin and it folded its ears down against its head.

She wouldn't like to be a duck at the fair but she would like to be a rabbit he guessed. He crossed through into the cow barn and when he heard a kid crying he knew he wasn't drunk anymore. That was good. He'd just as soon not have to worry for a while. He watched where he was putting his feet down and he felt the ground hard and then softer where the sawdust was thicker. O.K. He saw the kid who was crying, too old to be crying in public, must be at least twelve so something bad had happened.

He walked to look in the stall behind the kid and he saw what had happened. His calf was lying on its side, one leg bent. The mother had stepped on it because she wasn't used to a tight stall. Cale stooped beside the calf, pulled its lip away from its teeth and felt the bristle around its mouth. The calf pulled back from him and he looked at the saliva on his hand.

"Mother stepped on it?" Cale said.

The boy didn't look up but answered, "Yeah. And it's busted up bad inside."

"Got no blood at its mouth."

"That ain't no sign it's O.K. It can't stand up. They won't give me a ribbon now even if it would have won one."

"Look at how easy it's breathing. It couldn't be hurt too bad. It's just half scared to death."

"It won't stand up and it ain't been judged yet," the boy yelled and started to whimper.

Cale felt a hand on his arm and stepped aside as the doctor for the cow barn went in. The mother cow kept eating like she didn't notice the doctor or her crushed calf, but Cale saw white in the edge of the calf's eye when it saw the doctor.

Cale started to walk away when he heard someone call, "Hey." He turned to see the boy, tears still shining on his face. The boy stared at him a moment, trembling too much to speak, then he shouted, "Get out of here, you sonovabitch." The boy started crying again and went in the stall and stood beside a man Cale took to be his father. The man turned slowly to the boy, took him by the collar, and hit him in the mouth with the back of his hand.

"You watch your mouth," the man said. "You're in a public place."

Cale turned away quickly when he saw the boy's face; he knew the boy wanted to kill him. He walked to the end of the cow barn and looked for a door out so he wouldn't have to walk past the boy again. Just as he stepped through the door he realized how the animals had been crying. The sounds of the Midway rattled and tinkled with music and the barn behind him burst with too many sounds for so little a space.

He had brought a calf to the fair once. He wanted to win more than anything and had spent days brushing his calf. He thought it had to be the most beautiful one there but that was before he knew that everyone else had spent just as long as he had brushing their calves. And it only got a red ribbon, it wasn't a good enough color. And that was just the beginning of its problems. It got hookworms later that balled up in knots under its skin and one day when Pearlie was tossing down hay, a stick hit it in the eye and it went blind. It wasn't her fault. Could have happened to him. Then he knew they would just kill it for beef. You couldn't tell his father anything, that it was good stock inside even though it did look beat up. So his father slaughtered it. That was when he had the pony and he left and rode off and had come back later; he hadn't cried. He saw the slaughtered cows from the distance, there had been two of them, and they were pink and hanging from a pole so their blood could drip out. There were two of Aunt Bynum's little children under the cows and as he rode closer he saw they were playing in the blood. It was on their hands and they were drawing on the ground with it.

There was a little girl with blood on her arms. She came running up to him to tell him how warm the blood was she smeared on her arms. Her eyes were bright until she saw his face; at first he thought it was his fault that she was frightened. She said, "Cold, I'm cold," though it was summer and the dew hadn't fallen yet. As she had run it had gotten cold he figured and when she got beside him, she started to shiver. Then she looked down at the blood and began to cry. It had started to dry and tightened on her skin. She cried more and more as he got down from the pony and took her to the spring to wash her. There were tears spread over her face when she pointed to each splotch and made him get every spot off. He picked her up to carry her back to the road but she squirmed and clawed like a kitten who wants to be loose. She pressed her little palms against his shoulders and pressed herself away from him until he saw what it was. She saw the blood she had gotten on his shirt. When he set her on the ground it was like he'd dumped a rabbit out of a gum and she fell and scrambled away and would never let him near her again. Aunt Bynum straightened up and watched him hard when he came near her. It was bad when a little kid did something like that to you. He didn't like to get along bad with a little girl.

He went by the cloth signs, their colors aged away but never replaced because they didn't need to be; people were just as big suckers now as they ever were and a woman with 1920 eyebrows and frizzy hair was fine as long as she was stacked like something out of *L'il Abner*. "See Woman Turned Into Gorilla," and in the picture her legs were bent and hair-covered and she had this look like she had just seen herself in the mirror as she looked down at her big boobs and held them with her hands.

Then the next one looked like a painting of the same damn
woman only this one had red hair and her bit was "The World's
Biggest Feet," same gorgeous body only she had these big stupid-
looking feet with huge red toenails. There was one, "See the
Torture of Joan of Arc," a woman tied to a flaming post with her
jugs popping out from under the ropes. And you had to hand it
to them; they were smart putting those big boobs on them. Nobody would pay a quarter just to see a fat ugly woman burn up
or turn into a gorilla or look at her big feet.

He came to where a crowd was gathered, one of the three bur-
lesque shows. Here they didn't count on a bunch of old beat-
up posters to get you in, here they brought out the real thing,
wrapped up in a bunch of furs or feathers. He looked for the
one, the seventeen-year-old but he didn't see a one who was that
young, in fact there was one old dame whose hands were shriveled and knotted with veins like somebody's grandma. He
watched the barker, it was a woman too, middle-aged in about
as conservative a gray suit as you would see on a preacher's
wife and she bulged under it, shapeless and sticking out in all
the wrong directions. She had on these black boots and he could
see between her long skirt and the top of her boot a pretty
good-looking leg. Then she turned around and what looked like
graying hair was really bleached blond. She had painted eyebrows and a smile on her face that made her look like a clown
wearing a surprise mask. Nothing moved but her mouth.

"Now we ain't got no unicycles inside, nary a one." 'Nary a
one' with a Yankee accent. Now that's real good, lady. "And
we ain't brought a single juggler to toss up bowling pens."
She stopped for a minute to smile at her audience and wait for
them to make some noise.

"Well, what have you got, lady? Not much that's showing,"
one of them called and they all laughed together, her with
them.

"Oh, I might have something to keep your feet warm in the
winter . . . or anywhere else that gets cold."

They liked that and started laughing and yelling but Cale noticed the row of girls sitting in folding chairs and wearing knee-length pink satin coats didn't crack a smile. They'd heard it a thousand times before he guessed and nobody paid them to smile.

"Or I might say it's a good thing you have such warm fall nights down south or we'd have us some frost-bitten girls."

He walked on down to the next one; it had a man barker and he was telling dirty jokes. This looked like a more expensive operation, they even had a neon sign which said "Paradise Inside" and a five-piece band. Just as he got there a spotlight flashed on the tent entrance, a snare drum and a flat trumpet tried to work up an exciting fanfare. Then she appeared. "And here she is, the gal with the two forty-fives, Paradise Sloan." There she was, and he won't lying.

"Goddamn if she ain't wearing the world's strongest brassiere," one of the boys called out. Cale couldn't help but laugh and he saw old Paradise got a kick out of it too, winked at them. She wasn't like the rest of those deadpans, old Paradise had some life. She was gorgeous. And she cost fifty cents more. She stood at least six feet tall and had the longest legs he'd ever seen on a woman and her hair was piled up in one of those foot-high styles that made her look like even more of a giant. He never saw a woman like that in his life. He watched her walk up and down.

"Hey man, what's your Paradise got my girl hasn't got?"

Cale looked over at the drunk who had hollered that and saw his arm was around a flat-chested girl in a Beethovan sweat shirt. She swung and hit him on the cheek and went off crying, holding on to her hand.

Paradise winked at him and said, "I'm a natural blond." He laughed and said "Be back in a minute," and ran off after his girl.

"Yeah, go get her back." The barker was going again. "Old Paradise here has got a few things to tell you girls, ain't that right, Paradise? Or maybe I should say Paradise doesn't do much talking, she's got a lot to show you."

The boys all laughed and whistled on that as he went on. "Now girls, you shouldn't be jealous of Paradise here. She's your friend. That's right, she's the best friend a girl ever had. Now you come on in with your boyfriend and Paradise will show you what a good friend she is. She'll show you more tricks than you ever dreamed of. She's one of you. You know why? I'll tell you why, gals. I guar-ran-tee when you take your man home from here tonight, he'll be ready!

"So come on fellows, let's go inside." And Cale watched her go inside and found himself in the line giving the man his dollar.

He walked on in, the third in line and to his surprise the tent was already packed with people and he had to take a seat in the third from the back row. There was a lot of noise inside and a man up front selling Cokes. The front of the place was almost all boys but back here he saw a bunch of old women, four of them old colored women and the one in front of him had on a white blouse with little holes all over the collar stitched up, even a little strip of lace sewed up and a friz of gray hair tightened into a bun no bigger than a plum. What in the world are a bunch of old ladies doing in here? They sat without talking, their hands moving fans back and forth like they were waiting for a sermon to begin. Cale sensed the boredom in them and realized what he had gotten himself into. That guy kept taking Paradise back out making like it was time for the show and it wasn't going to start until he got this place filled up. He leaned back in the seat and let his chin drop and almost went to sleep. Finally a man walked out on the stage and everybody started clapping and cheering, like they did at school just because something was over or just because they wanted an excuse to make some noise.

"Ladies and gentlemen. I am sorry to report there has been a change in our program."

He held his hands up when they started hissing but Cale saw he was smiling. It was part of the act.

"Ladies and gentlemen, our whole troupe of jugglers and uni-cycle riders got stopped at the Mason-Dixon line and they wouldn't let them cross. That's right. So we haven't got a thing left to entertain you with but girls. That's right. Nothing but beautiful girls."

Everyone started cheering and he looked over his shoulder backstage and decided to stall a little longer.

"Yeah, it used to be that we did fancy tricks on this show, balancing acts, acrobats. In fact I used to saw a woman in half right here on this stage. That's right. The audience loved it. But I had to give it up. I was the only man in the business who sawed a woman in half and got left with the half that eats."

Everybody hissed on that but it didn't seem to bother him. Cale could tell he didn't give a damn about the bunch of clods out in front of him and he could hear him after his bit was over, "Did you see that bunch of grits?"

"Well, ladies, and gentlemen, our first girl is ready. This little gal comes to us from Sweden, doesn't speak a word of English. But she knows how to say everything she needs to say, yes sir, this little gal can twist her body more than I can twist a rubber band."

The music started, canned and scratched and Cale wondered what happened to the live band except maybe they were still outside getting people in, not Paradise too. Man, if she isn't in the show, I'll tear down the tent.

"Here she is from Sweden, Astrid Copenhagen . . ." The spotlight hit the stage. He saw a white-skinned girl with blond hair in a short skirt and top with fringe. Cale watched her start moving, slowly at first, frontwards, backwards, until the yelling on the front row reached a peak when he saw her reach for the snap on her dress and go down to a bikini that glowed in the dark. She moved a little more until the yelling built up again and she reached for the snaps and there was another shiny bikini, smaller than the other one. By now Cale could see that she was really pretty flat-chested but she was moving harder and faster to make up for it. She got on her knees on the floor and started bending over backwards, once with her crotch facing out then she turned around and let them all see her breasts move up and down. Pretty vacant up there. The boy next to him laughed and said, "Look at that! She shook them so much it's all slid down to the end."

"Like two baseballs in a pair of socks," he heard himself say and he and the boy laughed.

Then she was to her feet and reaching for the center of her bra. "Damnation, if they got her one smaller than that one I'd like to see it."

And for an instant they did see it, three tiny patches of sequins on the vital spots and a tassel stuck under her belly button, and then she was away, the spotlight running after her and catching on her naked fanny. The front row stood up and clapped for the light man who took a bow from his platform.

"Damnation, if he ain't got a fine job. I bet he's been chasing that butt with that light all season."

For a moment Cale sat there not moving and he felt like everyone around him was doing the same thing. It was a funny kind of shock. They really did it, they stripped down to absolutely nothing just like they said they did and they didn't get arrested. Boy, that would never happen at the movie downtown and they did it here in real life. He didn't want the boy beside him to know this was the first time he had come inside.

"Ain't it something, they can strip down like that to nothing," Cale said. "Every time I see it I'm amazed all over again."

"Ain't that something really. They get bare naked. This is the first time I ever been in one of these."

"No lie?"

Cale felt his voice just sliding out, easy because he could still feel what he had to drink and this guy wasn't ashamed of anything. He was easy to talk to.

"Woo-ee, look at that one." The man had announced something about a gal from California. "Woo-ee, we sure do make them better than they do in Sweden," the boy said. Cale tried to imagine California which was as foreign as Sweden and he knew he and this guy had about as much chance of ever seeing one as the other.

The girl from California had a better body he thought but she could dance about as much as he could. She got louder music, like the hell drivers, the announcer always got real excited and loud when they were doing something crummy. She was such a crummy dancer she kept stopping like she was trying to remember what step came next and every time she stopped they yelled at her to take something else off. Finally she just started undoing snaps and shaking till the clothes fell off. She was good at that. She never smiled a bit.

"Damn if she ain't a haughty bitch," Cale said.

"Yeah, I bet she wouldn't laugh at Emmett Kelly. She's probably his little girl turned bad. Man, but wouldn't I like to work at gitting a smile out of her, I sure would. I'd work all night long for one little smile."

"Hey, what you reckon holds on them little shiny things?"

"God, I don't know, glue I reckon."

"Oooee, I bet that smarts to take them off."

At that the whole row of old colored women in front of him started bouncing up and down, like laughing had started up a bunch of little motors inside of them that made their elbows poke each other when they got warmed up.

"Hey, those old darkies liked that one," the boy whispered, then he got a puzzled look on his face and Cale knew they were both thinking that same thing.

"What in the world do they come to this thing for?" the boy asked.

"You know I was wondering the same thing. Now if they were black men . . ."

"Yeah, if they was they'd throw their asses out of here."

"Yeah, they might but you don't know what them damn Yankees will do to make a buck. I bet they would take a buck off a nigger man as quick as they would off me or you."

"Shit, you better believe it. They don't even own a front yard to burn a cross on, they'll pack this place up and get out stealing half the town, you wait. They don't have to answer to nobody. They don't live here. My pa says the niggers get uppity for a week after the fair." The gal from New Orleans was out there now but she was a little slow in taking off and she looked like she was about to get tickled.

"Damnation, look at that. She's got her button stuck."

One of the boys in the front row jumped up and said, "I'll help you." He looked back at the others with a surprised look, Cale figured they'd made a plan, when I say "three" we all jump up and unhook it for her. Then two big men walked out of nowhere and he slid back in his seat and they disappeared and it was almost like it had never happened. By now the lady from New Orleans had it undone and they were all cheering again.

"They sure build them O.K. down there in New Orleans. I'm going to go down there myself one day."

"You have to really watch the women down there. They are all part nigger and they'll get you in bad trouble. My Uncle Roe said they say they're part French and part Indian and he said not unless Columbus was more screwed up than he thought and landed on Africa."

The guy liked that. "What's your name?"

"Cale Jenkins."

"I'm Harold Seeley, nice to meetcha."

He shifted the bottle and they shook hands and about that time New Orleans undid the last hook and she danced around awhile.

"Woo, look at her. Naked as a jaybird. Give me my ticket to New Orleans."

She had her tail to them and the guy on the spotlight was

playing like she was shaking it too fast for him to keep up. Cale saw a man walk out and shoo her off like she was a little kid and she gave her tail a big shake toward him. She had some spunk, he'd say that. The guys on the front row jumped up to boo him and the two big guys stepped out again.

"Hey, you reckon they planned that?"

"Naw, he probably saw the cops come in."

With that they both turned around to the back door and Harold turned back but Cale saw something he couldn't believe. That goddamn Floyd. That goddamn Floyd was back there.

"Hey, hey," he poked Harold.

"Hey, you see a cop really?"

"Naw, worse, I see a nigger. One of the niggers from our place."

"No lie. Goddamn, there are a bunch of niggers back there. You sure were right about those Yankee bastards."

Floyd looked at Cale like he always did, like he had never seen him before and wasn't seeing him now. Not even a trace of recognition went over his face.

"Hey man, don't miss a second of this. He's telling about Paradise Sloan."

Cale turned around and saw the man back out. ". . . the gal with the two forty-fives . . . she'll make you shift in your seat, fellers, but don't be embarrassed . . . look at the guy next to you . . . he's ready and she ain't even come out yet."

"Man, we didn't pay to see your ass. Bring on Paradise."

Cale could see that made the guy really mad. "Son, you're just about ready to miss the last half of the show . . . and without no raincheck."

"Shut up, man," one of them said to the guy, "let him do his bit."

Harold said to Cale, "Damn, if he didn't sound like the principal getting ready to introduce an old maid music teacher, didn't he? And here he is bringing out strippers. Man, a principal like him is one we gotta get. I'd stay in my seat and keep my

hands in my pocket if this is what he'd have for us at chapel
. . . hey, did you hear about the stingy Scotsman who cut holes
in his kids' pockets? . . . God Almighty!"

And there she was. About twice as big-looking now as before
after those other girls. "Boy, I bet she just names her price."

And old Paradise didn't have no canned music, just a guy
beating on a drum. He couldn't look away from this, not for one
damn second and there was that nigger Floyd back there watching everything he could see. Man, that won't right to do that to
Paradise and there she was just smiling up a storm and that
nigger thought she was smiling at him too.

"I wish she would put on a bathrobe and say I'm not going to
do another thing until every nigger man is out of here."

"Ain't it the truth," Harold said, "but I bet that Paradise would
go down for a nigger as quick as a white man if he had the
money."

Cale felt the heat come to his face. "Goddamn, you ain't
got no right to say such a thing." He was mad now, but he knew
he was about half drunk and had better watch himself. "She
isn't that common."

"Damn, if you don't act like she's your little sister. Big
sister." Harold's voice had an edge on it too. He didn't like Cale
jumping on him. Little sister. He thought of Pearlie for a
minute but he was too drunk to even see her in his mind so he
knew he had better not press this.

"Well, she better get her a bigger nigger than those back there
or he'll fall in." Harold laughed at that, but Cale didn't think
he was funny.

Paradise was really going now and the place was as still and
quiet as a funeral except for that drum beat.

"I wonder if that hurts her, slinging around like that." Paradise stopped spinning her boobs and made the little tassels on
the ends spin by themselves. "I bet I won't ever in my life see
anything like that again. She's got more muscles in her jugs
than I got in my whole body."

Harold could say the craziest things. Then the front row started squirming again. "Paradise, you are going to give yourself a black eye!" That cracked her up, man, that Paradise had a sense of humor. They still stared at her in amazement and Cale started trying to put things through his fuzzy mind. There is a naked woman up there with the biggest boobs I'll ever see in my life. She has taken off all her clothes and is slinging them around. That is real skin, and that is real fat around her waist where she took off her waist cincher, and that is real sweat shining on her and she would be hot as fire if I touched her. His own head felt hot but he was too drunk for it to do any further. She suddenly disappeared and he realized the curtain had dropped. Jesus Christ.

"Dirty trick," Harold jumped up and yelled. Then he got scared and quieter and said to Cale, "They just turned it off like that so you wouldn't be ready and would buy another ticket."

The commotion started on the front row and Cale saw a bunch of guys pull up another guy on the stage, sweat dripping off his face and all of them pointing to the bulge in his pants. Then the bouncers came back and ran them off. Cale looked to the door and saw the old colored women going through the flap almost like they had just come in to get out of the sun. What he was really looking for was that damn Floyd but he was gone.

He looked down at Harold who was pouting and holding his bottle in broad view.

"Hey man, put that bottle out of sight." Harold obeyed but continued to pout. "It's all over, let's go."

"Not me. I'm staying until the next bunch comes in."

"They aren't going to let you. They'll clear the place out and I bet it takes him two hours to fill it up before another show. Come on."

"Not me. You can go on. Nice sitting with you."

"See you then."

"See you," and Cale started toward the door thinking what a strange guy Harold turned out to be.

The lights outside hurt his eyes but everything was going on the Midway now. He looked at the Ferris wheel as it stopped. He could see every light separate so he wasn't bad drunk anymore but he felt his skin draw up tight on him when he heard people laugh. They were laughing dirty and he didn't know what they were laughing at which made him want to fight. He was trying to remember what he'd done tonight but he was pretty blank. He wasn't mad at anyone really. And he was too tired to fight, he didn't want to do something like that. At home on the farm he would just get whipped with his old man's belt, but if he got into something here he'd end up in jail. He'd never done that. He was pretty careful about never doing things that would get him put in jail.

He walked toward the gate, trying to decide whether to go on out because once he left they wouldn't let him back in without another ticket. They had fireworks going now but he could see them from home even and wait for their noise like thunder, later than the flash. The people were getting sparser and he saw a head over in the light near the game stands that made him stop. It was that frilly little girl again, the one he'd left over at the waterfall. He started walking over toward her when he saw she was in the center of one of those games, in the middle of a little box with a broom sweeping the nickels that missed the saucers into the center and standing under a ring of pinky teddy bears.

He walked into the light beside her stand and waited for her to turn around. She didn't look at his face but when she saw he wasn't going to throw a nickel she looked up.

"What do you want?" she said. "You can't just hang around here without playing."

Her voice cracked when she said that, and he knew she had been trying to sound mad.

"Can't I just stand here and talk to you if there ain't much business?" He realized that didn't sound like he wanted it to. "I mean, what are you going to do, call a cop and tell him I'm not allowed on this spot of ground unless I'm throwing around a bunch of nickels?"

"You can stand where you please I suppose."

"Does anybody ever win one of those?" Cale pointed up to the bears.

"One tonight, but he'd put something sticky on the nickel. I ain't telling the boss that or he'll put me back on them duck things with the numbers on their bottom sides where I got to keep my hands in the water till they chap off."

"Do you have one?"

"Do I have one what?"

"Do you have a teddy bear?"

"No, I got a stuffed dog I got at Myrtle Beach, a poodle. I had to buy it though, with my own money after my boyfriend throwed away enough money to buy me ten of them. He was trying to knock off those wooden milk bottles and I could have told him he couldn't."

A nickel rolled under her feet and she jumped and knocked off one of the saucers. Cale heard someone laugh when she bent over to set it back up and say, "Oh, bend over again, honey."

"Where's your boyfriend tonight?"

"Oh, he's in the service. But I sort of broke off with him anyway before he left. We write to each other though."

"You got a way home tonight?"

"I was walking since it ain't a mile even. Can you drive me?"

"I can't drive you. I wrecked my car last week, but I can walk with you."

"I ain't off until twelve when it shuts down."

"You wait here and I'll be back then."

Cale turned away and started walking behind the booths out of her sight. He walked along the edge of the fence and felt the vines stick and pull on his sleeves. When he stopped he heard the sound of the horses coming by in the sulky race and he looked through a crack to see the tight veins moving under their skin, their ears pressed back as the whips singed their

rumps. The clock over the grandstand said eleven-thirty. He
guessed he would wait for her. Yeah, he would wait. He
could have left her alone but he didn't intend to be mean twice.

He hadn't really expected her to be that easy. He just sort of
felt sorry for her all the way around. She had said a lot of
things at first that made him think she was testing him, letting
him know that she was different from the rest of the girls who
worked there. But when he went to get her at twelve, the
first thing he noticed was how she had respit all those little curls
around her face and dumped on enough perfume for him to
smell her before he could even see her good. It kind of made
him feel sad when he first saw her, putting on lipstick by looking into the bottom side of one of the ashtrays you threw nickels
in.

He found out she didn't work local after all and that she lived
in one of the trailers there but when they got to the trailer, her
roommate had locked her out. She dragged him between the
trailers until they got to this car that belonged to a friend of hers
she said and they got in and locked all the doors. Cale was
about to get mad at her because she was pulling him around so
fast that he asked her if she was trying to get rid of him and she
got mad and accused him of calling her a whore and said something to the effect that she didn't ask him for any money which
made him realize that she damn well expected it.

The girl asked him to "rape" her and refused to take all
her clothes off; she wanted to leave half of them hanging on
"because it's more exciting that way." She was crazy in the head
and he started thinking about bugs but she smelled like soap
powder after working in that place all day.

That wasn't the only thing that happened that night. He
was walking with her back to the trailer when they came up
on about six black boys, and she grabbed hold of his arm and
said, "There are them niggers again. We got the law after them
last night for messing around here, and the sheriff was so nasty

to us, said if we didn't have no better sense than to sell tickets
to them for the shows, then they were going to come after our
women. One of them said let that big woman Paradise hold on
to one of them if she caught him looking in her window and if
she could hold him till they got there, they would lock him
up."

But before the colored boys had rustled away like black rats
around the trailers, one had looked at him and he had seen
him back. He knew it was Floyd and it was almost as if Floyd
wanted him to know it was him, but that couldn't be true.
They would lock him up, all he had to do was say the word. No,
Floyd didn't want him to know it was him running behind the
trailer. He couldn't have. He did when they were in the tent
but this time Floyd would have liked to have gotten away without him noticing him.

When he caught up with Floyd going to the store the next
morning, Cale found out that he was right.

"Up mighty bright and early to have been out so late last
night, ain't you, Floyd?"

Floyd didn't answer.

"It's not good enough for you to see them take off every stitch
in a show, is it, boy. You want to see them when they don't
know you're looking."

Floyd still didn't answer but his face wasn't blank anymore;
this was the first time Cale had ever seen that smooth blank face
tighten up and his eyes turn away like something had struck
him on the side of the face. He wasn't nothing like he was when
they were little. Nothing at all.

"You know I could turn you over to the law, don't you?"

"I ain't never been there before. I was to home night 'fore
last."

Cale felt a shock go through his body, to hear Floyd say so
much and to know he had caught him. He had caught him now.

"Never before, huh? But that was you last night, won't it?

Thought if those white women were sorry enough to go around naked in front of everybody then they'd go the rest of the way. But that wasn't true, was it boy? They'd go straight to the law if you were black. Even your money wasn't any good, that right?"

Floyd was twisting his face now. He was mad, really mad. Cale felt nervous, but it was daylight, bright daylight. It didn't matter.

Floyd turned to cut through a field.

"Hold up. Don't you turn off till I'm through talking to you. I'll tell the law, boy, don't you mess with me."

Floyd stopped still.

"Turn around."

He turned around and looked once at Cale, not Floyd anymore, but one of the shy little children who couldn't stand to look a white man in the face when he talked to them, his eyes suddenly weak, lost. But he had to be filled with hate. He had enough sense to hate his guts.

"I got me one last night. Didn't cost a cent and she would have gone all night long."

Floyd's expression changed. It was slight but it was different. He squinted then his face relaxed and he was still. Cale heard his words, so damn stupid. Sounding like a damn kid in front of him. He wanted to take them back. What was the matter with him? Floyd still didn't move, he still stared. Cale turned away and started toward the house, confused. He could hear Floyd walking through the dry cornstalks, rustling away from him. He stopped and turned around but Floyd was gone, the stalks didn't move. He had made Floyd hate him. He had never made anyone hate him before.

Book Five

Chapter 29

EVERYTHING was in now. Cale had nothing to do. A few red peppers and tomatoes hung on their dead vines, bright to look at and rotten to the touch. The bushes were heavy with berries; a hard winter Papa Lonza would say, nature's way of readying the birds and squirrels for a hard winter. This would be one of the last days to walk like this; the radio said tonight would be heavy frost and tomorrow the ground cold would come through the bottoms of his shoes and he wouldn't be able to sit outside away from everyone. The only green left was winter green, the last sprouts on the fallen tobacco stems, turnip tops, unreal green like crepe paper. He wouldn't have to bring in the last of the turnip salad because he had picked it gritty last time. After a rain he had gone after them, he was late and a shower had come across hard, taking down the last of the colored leaves and spattering the dirt in the turnip patch. He snapped off the dirty greens, then the sand in his basket ended up in his supper plate, even after his mother washed and washed the leaves, running out the water and washing again, so afraid of Jerome. And sure enough, Jerome hit the first grit and they heard it crack all the way across the table at suppertime. They watched him reach in his mouth and pull out the green blob. His mama was so damn scared of his daddy, apologizing like it was a crime or something.

Cale walked to the end of the turnip patch, dragging his

feet through the leaves looking for a purple-ringed top. He saw one, pulled it out with a pop and busted the dirt off on his leg. He went toward the woods behind the lake, sat down under a tree and started to peel the turnip with his pocket knife. The hot white chips were dry when they hit his mouth then the fire started up through the back of his nose. Hot. He ate slowly until the inside of his mouth was soft, slick like a burn. Then he rolled the turnip toward the water, watched it collect dirt until plop, it bobbed through the reeds and disappeared.

Saturdays were a pain now that school had started. The ball games were all on Friday night and they always lost now anyway since Summit High had been promoted to the bigger league. There was nothing to do Saturday except go to town and shoot pool and go to a movie and try to pick up a girl, that is if you had enough money to do anything at all. He used to ride some or go shooting but it was all too damn much trouble. The last time he had decided to ride, he went out to Jigger's stable, and the only two horses they had were mud-caked from wallowing in the lot. Jigger didn't have much time anymore. He was studying and getting scared that he wasn't going to pass the College Boards. He was going to Carolina because his daddy had been there. They were afraid he wouldn't get in because he failed a course last year and had to take it in summer school. So all you could do now over at Jigger's was call out the questions to him from this College Board answer book and listen to him miss them. Jigger wasn't going to make it. He wasn't even good at cheating. It was too late because what Jigger really needed was to go back and learn the multiplication tables and stuff like that. At first Cale had thought that Jigger really didn't want to go, the way he talked about it. But then his daddy gave him a car, a '57 Chevrolet and he put a blue Carolina sticker in the window and started saying that was where he was going and asking people where they were going. That was when he asked Cale.

"I don't know. Nowhere I guess."

"What do you mean? You got grades good enough to go up north to a big school where they got a good football team. Or Georgia Tech. They beat Duke every time."

"My parents don't have enough money to send me I don't think. I'm not going to ask for it."

He was sorry he said that and wished he hadn't. He didn't like to let anybody know that much, especially someone like Jigger who talked all the time. And Jigger looked surprised. He was so dumb he probably didn't know Cale wouldn't have enough money.

Then Cale thought that Jigger had started getting kind of snobbish. He started hanging around with the guys at lunch that were going to Carolina next year and they talked about the ball games. Jigger went to one of them with his Daddy and he wouldn't stop talking about it. It didn't really matter that much to Cale. There were other people to have a good time with and that's about all Jigger was good for. Besides he didn't figure Jigger would last very long at Carolina unless the same sort of teachers were there as here, the ones who knew his daddy and wouldn't fail him except for that student teacher last year who didn't know any better. Most of the teachers knew to flunk him along the way to get him to work hard and to pass him in the course.

Later he thought about what he had said to Jigger. His parents didn't have enough money. He wasn't going to ask for it. He wouldn't have asked for it if they had had it. He wouldn't let his daddy go around saying he had given it to him. His mama asked him a lot what his plans were but he didn't answer her, he said he didn't know and walked away because she would bother him more if he told her anything. His father didn't ask him, he just figured that he would work on the farm and get a job in town in winter, get a job instead of going to school.

What was wrong was there was nothing in between, between working with that bunch of morons who loaded trucks in town and going to college. And he didn't want anyone watching him, like his mother did everybody; so-and-so made out well or so-and-so didn't amount to much. You couldn't do anything with them watching, not just anything bad but anything good either. Nobody who didn't have money had ever been to college from Summit, nobody but one girl. He remembered her. She came from the poor side of town and she was real smart and got a scholarship. But he wouldn't be able to get one of them. You had to pay to take all these tests to find out about them and he didn't know anybody who ever got one. It was sort of like someone had to ask you to take them and if they didn't, you forgot about it, or that was the feeling the teachers gave anyway. Anyway they didn't like people who took shop instead of Latin. Coach Beal said he might be able to play baseball somewhere but there was nowhere in the state would give him enough to go on, just for basketball and football. He could play pro ball in Durham if he could pass the tryouts. But that wasn't what he wanted to do anyway. Of all the things he had thought of, doctor, dentist, lawyer, he wanted to be something Summit didn't have and wouldn't want if they had. He wanted to draw buildings, be an architect, build a house like the one he saw in a book over the river. Like Great-grandpa had wanted to do, down over a river. You would find it behind the trees and it would look like it grew there. But he couldn't talk about that around any of them, never his Daddy. He'd say, "You wanna build something, do you? Then get you a hammer and nails and go fix the chicken house I asked you to fix last summer." Then he'd look around and try to find someone to laugh with him. Maybe he could talk to his mother but she would talk about it too much and call attention to him and ruin things. He would have to keep it quiet until he had done it. And he would have to go off by himself somewhere before he got started, where nobody who knew him would be watching. So then if he messed up a few times no one would be there watching to make fun of him. He would make the money to

get going doing anything, it didn't matter and put it in his savings account. He already had a hundred and sixty-eight dollars.
He could get lots of kinds of jobs. He could work on a construction crew, he could even do some carpentry work if he
wanted to or work for an electrician and he learned how to lay
bricks his junior year. He could work on cars, do anything before he would work on a damn farm again. Work all the damn
time and get nothing for it. "You get your damn food on the
table and a roof over your head, that's what you get," his old
man had said when he asked him to pay him an allowance.
That was after he laughed at him in front of everybody.

He had thought about the house a lot and he had some
drawings of it hidden in his room. To make one with the sunshine coming through all around without having to cut down
the trees, glass everywhere there was light so you wouldn't have
to use electricity in the daytime and it would be set so people
couldn't see inside. Colors like out of doors only you would
be inside, orange, yellow, brown, and where there was glass in
the ceiling it would have blue wood around it the same color
as the sky. He had done a paper on one sort of like it for his
junior English project, on Frank Lloyd Wright. The teacher
found a lot of stupid things wrong with it, didn't like his sentences, wrote all over it "topic sentence," "fragment," "subordinate," just all the crap she had talked about in the grammar
book and didn't say anything about what it said. Like she
made him write a paper just to grade his grammar and what
it was about didn't make any difference. Jigger saw it and got
all excited, "Hey man, you got back a bloody paper. God, she
wounded it on every page," he said as he flipped through it.
"Now you know how I feel." She started giving him B's all
the time and wouldn't call on him when he raised his hand,
only when he didn't have anything to say. That was when he
decided to take it by to Miss Sammons. He had been glad to find
her out when he got there so he could leave a note with the
paper under it. Then school was out for the summer before he

saw her again. He had seen her before assembly last week and she came right up to him and said, "Cale, I would like to talk to you about your paper. Come by any afternoon after school." He was sure she had forgotten about it. Every day that week he had thought about going by, then he would find himself walking out and getting on the bus. Every time he would almost go, he made himself say it wasn't important, just a paper and one he wrote last year at that. She may want to tell me the teacher was right, that I did a bad job of writing it. And then the bus would start moving and he would feel sorry again that he left, and get mad at himself. She would know he wanted to be an architect, that he was practicing drawing because he put three in the paper. She already did know. Old lady Cummings that scribbled on it could read it fifty times and not do anything but find another topic sentence in the wrong place. He had imagined asking Miss Sammons sometime if she ever wanted to be anything else, a nurse maybe, or a singing star, or even an actress. She loved those plays and she would do parts, like that Emily part and it was like she was another person up there in that long skirt with her hair done up. She was really good only everybody laughed when George talked because it was that queer Freddie Crawford but Miss Sammons just kept on like they weren't even there.

Cale got up from the pinestraw and felt his pants hit his butt, wet from the ground. He walked through the trees holding his jeans out from his crotch so they just rubbed damp against the back of his thighs. Beggar lice began to dot the bottom of his pants legs. Briars, twisted and bending in loops like barbed wire set up on a battle field, sent him weaving through the field. He saw a horse once that got it in the barbed wire. Her shoe got hooked over a strand and she went wild, kicking her foot so nobody could help her and the wire caught deeper until she shredded her leg. Might be true what that book said about animals, that a hog had more sense than a horse. A horse looks cocky as hell, pretty and slick muscles and you yell beep and it goes wild. Floyd. Just like that goddamn Floyd. Cocky as hell and you catch him at something and he crawls up on his belly. He had a knife probably but he was scared to use it on a white person. Wonder if Floyd's ever cut anybody.

He smelled something mildewy, the trash pile where he used to shoot. There was glass busted all around it which pissed his old man off because he backed up to dump a load of trash and punctured a tire. There was glass busted that he didn't do. Somebody else was using it for shooting. Somebody had dumped a pile of clothes, still smelling like sweat and piss though they had been rained on. He took a stick and poked at the pile. He saw his old Windbreaker that his Mama had given to Aunt Bynum's family and Floyd had worn until the cuffs were up to his elbow. He saw the edge of something, still brightly colored though it had rained on it, Pearlie's dress with the velvet top and the taffeta skirt. He took the stick and poked it down until you couldn't see it. Pearlie didn't ever come down there anyway. Her mother had made her scared of the woods and the trash pile because of the rats and snakes and people that might be hanging around.

Somebody must have brought all the crap from Floyd's house, probably Floyd. His old man always went over there once a year and told them he was going to put them out if they didn't clean it out and once a year they brought all their dirty and broken stuff down to the trash pile. He had been to the house once. There wasn't anything to see, it was just two rooms and built just like everything else his old man built, except for this one he used scraps and made it two layers, one for the outside dobbed like the tobacco barns and the inside just boards. His old man didn't know how to make dobbing like his grandpa had and most of it fell out anyway. He had seen them one winter all out stuffing the cracks with rags and newspapers. That made his old man happy though because the house looked worse. He worried the whole time it looked new about somebody throwing off on him. Never washed his tractor just so nobody would know he bought it new.

Floyd must not sleep at home much yet you always saw him

around somewhere, usually so far away you couldn't see his expression. When I was a little kid, Floyd was spindlier than I was. Once we were putting our jelly glasses on the edge of the porch and Floyd's little arm looked like a black snake. We had had ice water. If the water was cold enough the sulphur taste from the well would be gone and you could see the yellow-brown sulphur settled in the bottom of the ice water jar. The glasses were different sizes. The niggers took the ones with the squares on the bottom and me and Pearlie had the ones with the lines up the side. We were still to put them in different places on the porch. Mama had come out and called him away from the ballgame and whispered though the others were away off down the hill, "Cale, do you recall which glass you drank out of?" I did, I do now even, the one with the lines on the side and she carried the glasses in and scalded the ones the niggers had drank out of. She asked me to scald my plate if I let the dog eat scraps off it. But she never asked me which plate. It didn't matter that much about the dog, but Mama was never going to let us eat after the niggers. And me and Floyd used to drink out of the same Tru-Ade many a time.

All he knew of Floyd now he could think in a minute. He really was surprised to see him over at the fair because he hadn't thought before that Floyd was just as old as he was and had probably had him a girl. Wonder if Floyd still liked to throw? Could say what you wanted to about him but he had never seen anybody who could throw like Floyd. He only knew one other thing of the way Floyd was. When he was little he went inside Floyd's house, well almost inside. Floyd didn't want him to go in and his little skinny body had got stiff. He started running off in all directions trying to get Cale to go play and keep him away from the house. That was when he found out that Floyd didn't have a plug in his house. That's why he outgrew playing with Floyd because Floyd didn't have enough around his house to do anything but play in the yard like a little kid.

Then he probably just stopped playing and went off looking for something to do. He didn't think about Floyd or any of this until it was almost winter and he wasn't working so hard and getting so tired his mind wanted to sleep. Those days in the summer when he had wanted to make plans when he was working, driving the tractor, throwing hay, his mind wouldn't do it. It wouldn't stay on the subject and he would have to start over and over just like when he was trying to read his history textbook and his mind wanted to daydream. It was only now he could make it go on and on, put things together, start in one place in his thinking about things and sit down by the woods and put things together.

But now he was starting to remember as good as he could make up things, remember how his mama and daddy and Pearlie had been and what they had come to now, how his mama and daddy didn't ever really change, that things around them caught up and shoved them back and forth but they were always the same except they were getting slower and they weighed more. But Pearlie changed so fast he couldn't keep up with her.

And Floyd. Him more than the other niggers because he was the same age. And Floyd didn't seem anything like he was when he was little. He figured Floyd was getting ready to take out away from there and never come back again. There was something told him Floyd was going to and that it was going to be easy for him, nobody would come out looking and he could forget any of this damn farm was there because he didn't have to own any of it anyway. He figured he didn't worry about his mama or any of his little sisters. But he wasn't going to find it easy. It would never be easy for a nigger boy to find work and though Floyd got off with no parents or farm to go after him, he wouldn't get any job. Everybody would try to catch him at something. Like he did, catch Floyd messing around those trailers. Getting all those laws changed wouldn't make any difference to Floyd. The law can't be everywhere; besides nobody down here cared. Just those that kept stirring them up.

Aunt Bynum didn't care. She probably wouldn't care if Floyd took off and never came back either. She'd tell him to get a job and send her money just like she did Jason. And Cale could get the job right out from under either of them if he wanted it, almost anywhere down here anyway and maybe even up North. Floyd would see. It was easier for him to take off but then it would be harder going.

Chapter 30

CALE AND PEARLIE got off the school bus. She walked up to the high school to ride with him but she always sat in a different part of the bus and didn't talk to him while they rode. She was in her last year at the junior high and Cale was a senior so they hadn't been in the same school since the elementary. Pearlie was strange now, hardly ever said anything. He could remember when she was noisy, even on the bus, talked too loud. Now she just sat and stared at the window and it wasn't that all her friends were quiet, they weren't. They chattered constantly about who was going steady and who wasn't and how they thought it was terrible to tie themselves down with one boy, and how so-and-so had five cashmere sweaters and three pairs of suede loafers. They wouldn't go steady until they got to the high school. He figured that was mainly because they couldn't catch one and because their mothers wouldn't let them. Pearlie never had a date or talked about a boyfriend; she didn't ask him about the girls he took out anymore. Pearlie wasn't ugly or anything, she was just sort of strange looking, but that was mostly her own doing. Her face was a little bumpy in the hollows of her cheeks and her hair was straight and dark and she wouldn't curl it, just put it up in a ponytail with a rubber band and half the time got it up sideways. And she wouldn't wear lipstick. He thought she would have been the first to put it on. Pearlie had changed fast and not just the way she looked; she had even gotten scared of him, would start to tell him something then just shut up and say "Never mind." She was getting tall and her waist was longer than most of her dresses. She wore the same thing a lot and didn't care about clothes like she had, always an old green plaid dress or one of her corduroy jumpers. She walked in front of him, quickly on her thin legs, carrying all of her school books home and two library books, eight books propped on one hipbone. Falissa had let the hem down on the jumper she wore and it had a white ring around the bottom of the skirt. Something about her looked older than her friends and in some ways she was younger. Pearlie hadn't gone through the first date with Falissa bothering her and watching her. The other girls had done more things on the outside, but they had never been quiet long enough to get all balled up inside like Pearlie. And she was all balled up inside over something. She never talked to him anymore or asked him questions but she didn't fuss much either. She did more than her half around the house and she had quit telling on him. She wouldn't take up for him exactly, she just wouldn't say anything. And Mama seemed to like her like this, working all the time and gloomy. She didn't have enough sense to know that something might be wrong. For some reason Pearlie didn't want to let anyone know anything about her.

That night after supper Pearlie was washing the dishes and he was stacking and drying. Pearlie had a clean pan of hot water that she slid each dish into after she washed it and he fished it out and dried it, his fingers glowing red. Falissa and Jerome were in the front room and the door to the kitchen was shut.

"You know what I heard today?" Pearlie said. "You know all that business about the niggers going to the white schools?"

"Yeah, they are in some places."

"Well, I heard today that it is going to happen here. It has over in Durham."

"Not enough to matter. They'll come once then they'll go back. Not their idea."

"What do you mean?"

"I mean somebody put them up to it. Somebody up high in the government. They got their own school. They didn't want to come to ours until somebody told them that other niggers were doing it and the law said they could get by with it. They don't want to go. They just want to spite us."

"Where do Aunt Bynum's children go?"

"Some of them don't go. I don't know. Floyd used to tell me they had to ride the bus about ten miles out in the country and he had the same teacher three years straight but you can't believe him."

"Do you think Floyd would come to your school?"

"Floyd? Hell no. Floyd wouldn't go to any school unless they made him. He don't want to come to our school."

"How do you know he doesn't? Have you ever talked to him?"

"About what? He hasn't got anything to say. Do you think he does or something? What gave you that crazy idea?"

"Well, why not?" She walked to the end of the counter for the rest of the dishes. "You don't have to yell at me. I was just asking. I was wondering how you know if you don't ask somebody, if you don't ever talk to them. We don't ever talk to niggers. We don't know what is going on inside their heads."

"Next to nothing."

"You don't have to be smart to have something going on inside your head."

"He can have meanness going on, stealing and eating and screwing."

Pearlie's neck began to turn red. She was quiet again. Cale hadn't meant to say that. Every time you said something like that Pearlie got embarrassed and wouldn't talk.

"I don't know Pearlie. I really don't. I just never thought about it much. But with most dumb people you do know what they're thinking, like Mama for instance. You usually know what she's thinking, don't you?"

"Yes, I guess I do." Her voice cracked a little.

"That's why I don't like to hear you going around repeating her, because you've got more on the ball than her."

"You go around repeating Daddy," she snapped.

Cale took the pans to the pantry and began putting them on the nails. What did she mean by that? He didn't begin to repeat his daddy.

"I don't see how you can say that."

"Well, you do. You talk just like him sometimes. Like about Floyd. You admitted yourself you never thought about it. That's just what he would say, that he doesn't want to go to our school. You don't know that."

"There are some things that you just know and that is one of them."

"I don't believe you."

Pearlie hung up the dishrag and went through the door. He heard her go up the steps and walk over his head into her room before he had the silver in the drawer.

Pearlie was getting to be a nigger lover. Maybe that's why she was so quiet. And it wasn't the fault of that preacher down at the church. He's long gone and she had already moped around about that. It wasn't at school either, she had the same teachers he did except for Math. It was all those books she was getting out of the library. When they'd go downtown, she'd spend all her free time in the library reading magazines. She had already gone around pretending she was English and answering everything with an English accent, trying to talk fancy and making you want to punch her in the mouth. All her ràthers and potàtoes and tomàtoes. Always talking about somebody she read about in a book, like they were a real person. No reason for her to be a nigger lover except she didn't know any, that's why. Aunt Bynum didn't have any girls her age and she didn't ever get around them much anyway except for some hopscotching with the older girls before they all started having babies. He could remember her hopscotching and seeing them all get tickled and listening to them jumping, the-monkey-and-the-baboon-were-sitting-in-the-grass-the-monkey-stuck-his-finger-up-the-baboon's-ass-the-baboon-said-doggone-your-soul-keep-your-finger-out-of-my-ass-hole, that's what he heard them saying and when he walked up and caught them hopscotching to it, all the nigger girls went running off laughing and Pearlie stood there scared to death he was going to tell Mama he heard her talking dirty. But Pearlie didn't play with the niggers much. She just watched them. She didn't play much with anybody, just stayed in her room and sometimes was pale all summer long because she worked with Falissa in the kitchen. Mama wouldn't let her go off and play with the tenant children, not when there were any boys in the bunch.

Pearlie had always talked about Floyd. She asked about him more than a normal amount, Cale thought. Cale and Floyd were the same age, but Floyd got muscled up sooner. He was about as old as Pearlie is now, about fourteen, when he started outgrowing himself. His daddy always laughed when he walked by and whispered to them on the porch that Floyd's pants had gone "high water." When Floyd worked, his insides looked like they were balled up tight inside of his skin. He got shiny with sweat quicker than Cale and long-waisted sooner, and his veins got swollen hard when he lifted. Pearlie was always talking about the veins, said she couldn't stand to look at them or the ones in her own wrist because of the knots when you strained. But she must have kept looking at the nigger's because she had talked about it more than once. Cale wouldn't forget that. His mama would have gotten a lot madder about that than about the dirty poem. When she was little, Pearlie had even asked Floyd to let her touch one of them and he was going to since that was something to him, her asking to touch. He stuck out his arm and she reached and jerked back and Cale turned her around and whopped her hiney harder than he meant to because she had bit her tongue and made it bleed. They were all down at the barn, handing tobacco and the grown-ups were in the field except Aunt

Bynum who was tying. Pearlie ran off but he caught her by her shirttail by the smokehouse and she fell down to make him feel bad and she accidentally skint her knee and cried even more. Together they had made it out a whole lot bigger than it was, he figured, but he couldn't help himself.

"You don't touch niggers, you hear. Unless it's a nigger woman that is old and you have got good reason but you are too old to even have good reason for that. But don't you ever touch no nigger boy, you hear me. What's the matter with you, thinking about doing something like that?"

He was so mad he could hardly keep from hurting her more, mad that she was as old as she was and still did something like that. And he had to watch her cry and cry until she could control it except for gasps. By then she was able to look at him and it was a look like she hated his guts and would have jumped on him if she had been a boy. It was not many times that Pearlie looked mean like that. She would cry quick for anything that hurt because she was so chicken-hearted, she felt sorry for everything, but when she really got mad it was an ugly kind of crying that she usually went to her room with and wouldn't come out to eat and would even strangle on what her mother took up to her.

She didn't cry mad like that anymore; she hadn't done it since the dress thing happened. It was because of the niggers again, and she was in the white sand of the road beating her fists so hard she scraped herself and sealed her wet face up with sand. This does make Pearlie out to be a hothead though she's not, just at those certain times. She just used to not be able to stop her temper. It was all over that little nigger girl in the field in her Sunday dress, the one he'd found last week and poked down in the trash pile. That's all it was when it finally came out of her in words so he let her go again and roll in the dirt, made like she didn't have good sense because he knew it was nothing big then, and he hoped nothing big would ever happen to Pearlie because of the way she took it. But she didn't do that much, he didn't worry about it all that much then, just mainly that time when she wanted to touch Floyd's veins and when the little nigger, he didn't ever know her name, came out in that candy-striped dress.

By the time Pearlie had quit crying over the dress and had a new jumper she liked better that little nigger had a swollen belly and it was told all around that it was Floyd's and he was her brother. Cale didn't know about that. They could always turn up pregnant and he never saw them ever touch each other. That's the way they were different from the whites down at the barn, handing tobacco. The white kids would get in a row so they could rub against each other and try to touch the girls but the niggers never paid enough attention to each other for you to even know who was whose and then one after the other they would turn up with a belly swelling up under the baggy clothes.

Floyd was like them but he was different too. Floyd was smarter. Maybe that's why Pearlie always paid too much attention to him. But you couldn't figure out his face any more than the rest of them; there was just something there and he didn't mind looking at you. Cale remembered last summer how Floyd stared him down and he had to look away at a noise that didn't happen because his eyes were starting to sting. It wouldn't have started with any of the others, just with Floyd because he was always looking at you, half the time making you say things you didn't mean to. His daddy always said things like restless or trifling about Floyd and didn't give him credit for anything but being a wiggle worm, like a little kid. That wasn't right. There was more to Floyd than that. He was thinking about something if you could get him to tell you.

Floyd had a way of winning too. He would stay far enough away so he could beat you out and never say a word like going through the orchard and taking one bite out of every apple and throwing it down. Cale had even seen him do that once, bite each one and screw up his face and throw it down, sometimes even spitting out the green pulp. You could know something

was going on inside his head. You could know there was
nothing in their minds when the others ducked down their
faces but not Floyd. There was more than being smarter in his
face. You knew that Floyd was never going to pick an apple
down to the core.

Winter came hard in Summit. The fall had come without
rain, only wind, and the roadsides had rattled with drying things,
the corn fodder and the tobacco stalks that didn't get cut in.
The fire danger was high and Cale had been up twice to clear
the roof so his mother wouldn't worry about a spark from the
fireplace setting it off. She would run out the door each time
a glowing piece of paper sucked up the chimney, just to make
sure it scattered out gray and cold when it landed. She had been
like that ever since they replaced the tin with shingles. A cigarette thrown by the roadside had caught up only two miles below the city limits of Summit and Jerome had to go with the volunteer firemen and work six hours to get it under control. He
said snakes were running out of the burning grass and the pave-
ment on 18 crawled with them. He said you could smell animals
frying in the woods like somebody was fixing them to eat and
the little birds were flying away and might never come back.
Traffic was stopped and backed up through Summit all the way
out to their house because the road was smoked over. Florida
tourists, one of them probably set it because he didn't want to
get the ashtray dirty in his Cadillac. He's probably stretched out
on the sand down in Miami now, slurping on a drink. That's
what Jerome heard down at the fire.

Then the rains came and the ground got soft before the high
winds hit and they lost three trees, two chinaberry and one pear.
The pear had fallen like a plank dropping but the chinaberry
limbs circled and twisted and fell in giant knots. It was a bad
fall and the winter it brought was worse. They had spread the
basement with potatoes, Irish and sweet, and Falissa checked

them each week to make sure they weren't starting to rot from the dampness because the storm rains had come under the door. She had wrapped all the green tomatoes with newspaper when the early frost took the plants and Pearlie went down each night and unrolled until she found a red one for supper. The rains had spoiled part of the hay and Falissa saved her grocery money in a jar for the hay she knew they would have to buy before spring to keep the cows fed; such a humiliation to have to buy hay. Other people were suffering but though they worked harder than most, they always seemed to suffer the most.

The white farmers were all going in town to work so most of the tenants couldn't find work. Jason was long gone, up north somewhere Aunt Bynum said, and she would get a check from him directly, soon as he got a little bit ahead. Jerome couldn't make her curse Jason as hard as he tried. Floyd cut wood every day, and the trees were getting so thin around the tenant house that they could see it from theirs. Jerome was watching and getting angry. "Twenty years it takes for a tree to grow that high and they cut it down and burn it up like it was planted yesterday and there'll be a new one tomorrow. Too damn lazy to walk down and get the wood where it's thick. Afraid they might have to carry it a little ways." And Aunt Bynum's little girls took a bucket and went down to the railroad track and picked up what coal fell off the trains.

"That's what they say," Jerome said, "but to my mind that much never fell off a train, short of it turning over. Think they can keep it up so long as they send the little ones, think the law won't mess with them."

One week it hadn't been over twenty degrees for three days. Cale and Jerome were in town with the truck and Falissa had gone to the church. Pearlie was up in her room when she heard someone screaming, at first almost like someone was just calling the animals but then like they were afraid. She went to the window and saw Aunt Bynum coming up the path, her arms stretched out in front of her like the old colored women who walked down the main street in Summit, preaching the Lord was coming.

"Lawd God, Almighty. Lawd, Lawd, hep me, Lawd."

Pearlie opened the window, the cold air hit her face as she spoke.

"Aunt Bynum, is something the matter?"

"Lawd God, Miss Falissa. I done hurt myself bad."

"It's Pearlie, Aunt Bynum. Mama isn't here."

Aunt Bynum walked to the middle of the yard below Pearlie's window. "Hep me, Miss Pearlie." Her arms began to drop and her hands dangled.

Pearlie ran down the stairs to the porch. Aunt Bynum stood in front of the door, her arms still outstretched.

"Hep me, chile."

Pearlie reached for Aunt Bynum's hands but she pulled them back.

"No Lawd, Lawd, honey, no. Don' tech me. I done got burnt bad."

Tears were pouring from her eyes. Pearlie looked at Aunt Bynum's hands as she walked in the door and the skin was loose. She hadn't seen it until she got close, the skin was burned loose.

"Honey, yuh git me some lard. I couldn't pull the lid. Git me some lard."

Pearlie ran into the kitchen with Aunt Bynum following her. She took down the lard and scooped up two handfuls and put it in Aunt Bynum's open palms.

"Oh Lawd. That is the onliest good I ever felt."

Pearlie saw the side of her face shiny with sweat and her breath came deep like she had been running. She put her cheek on the cool refrigerator and smiled.

"Lay your hands in the barrel, Aunt Bynum, so you can get the back sides."

"Naw, honey. Don't want to mess up yuh mama's lard barrel. I make out now."

"Here."

Pearlie took her by the elbows and lifted her hands into the barrel.

"Now you stand there and I'll call up the doctor. You need looking at."

"Naw honey, don't bring him up. I got no money for the doctor."

"My daddy'll pay for it."

"Naw honey, naw he won't. I be all right. By tomorrow I be all right."

"I burned myself once on Mama's iron and it took a long time to get well. I don't think you'll be well tomorrow, though I don't know how to tell on colored people's skin."

"I heals fast. I lucky that way."

"What did you do, Aunt Bynum, to get burned so bad?"

"Acted like I didn't have good sense. Told my younguns a thousand times then I turnt right around and done it. Throwed kerosene on the stove. Got the bothers cause the babies was hollering and the fire goed out. Tried to knock the chill off that house and get that coal going, and it come out at me like the gates of hell with the devil hisself a pushing it."

"You shouldn't have done that, Aunt Bynum. People get burnt up that way. A woman in town caught her coattail doing that once. I read it in the newspaper, and her little boy went running after her and he breathed it in and died too."

"I know, honey. She was a colored lady. I know that story. Now I am in a fix. I declare I can't wiggle my fingers enough to scratch my head and I got three hungry babies to fix for."

"You want me to cook your supper for you? I can cook. Mama showed me how. Let me come fix your supper."

"Now I don't want to put yuh out none."

"You won't put me out."

"I'd be obliged if yuh'd get the pots going. Floyd can take it off when he comes in but I am needing yuh to get the pots going if it won't be a bother."

Pearlie went with Aunt Bynum down to her house. She had

never been inside, only to the door to deliver things, a box of
clothes once and extra stuff from the garden. She went up on
the porch and the house shook, the boards brown and rotten
and giving under her feet. Inside was dark, there was one
light on a string but it wasn't pulled on.

"Pull the light, honey." She pulled the string and when she
did all the little faces turned toward her, three little children,
two girls and a boy.

"See what everybody left me with?"

"They're real cute."

"Why thank yuh, ma'am. Can't yuh say thank yuh ma'am?"
The little children mumbled thank you and turned away from
her, toward the stove.

"Now didn't I tell yuh not to get in so close? Yuh going to
get scorched. Yuh see what it cost me setting that fire. Lawsy,
I can take the cold but them are cold-natured younguns."

The children slid back from the stove a few inches and Pearlie
realized how cold it was. She decided to keep her coat on inside.

"Floyd, he's my third oldest, he got hisself caught up sleeping balled up there, had the hole wide open and near about
crawled in with it. Burned a place big as a saucer on his backside. He always was the coldest natured one but yuh couldn't
keep a hat to his head if'n yuh nailed it on."

Pearlie looked around the room. All the furniture was on
the porch to make room for the pallets on the floor and she
could see one big bed in the other room with more pallets around
it. The walls were covered with pictures, most of them old cal-
endars with colored people on them or pictures of scenery with
a lot of yellow sky and pink flowers in light green grass. They
must have all been by the same person. In the kitchen was a
worktable and the wood stove but no refrigerator.

"Haven't you got a refrigerator? You have the electricity
now."

"Got the 'lectricity, honey, but that don't put in a frigadaire.
My husband Jason promised me one soon as he gets on his feet,

he said he was going to buy his old wife a frigadaire. Lawd, I tell you the truth, the front porch is cold as any frigadaire I know. Honey, I don't want to keep yuh. I would be much obliged if yuh would just cut up them cabbages and start me a hunk of fatback frying. I get it in the pan but I declare I don't reckon my hand gon' shut about that knife." Pearlie took that cabbage and started to peal off the outside leaf. She rolled it up and looked for the trash can.

"Don't throw that out, honey. Wash it off in the pan."

"Daddy says you ought to take off the outside because it's got bug spray on it."

"It'll wash off. Them are good ones got down the market. Come in on a truck from Florida. No bug spray on them."

Pearlie began to cut the cabbage up on the tabletop. Aunt Bynum nodded her head and smiled then went back over to the stove. She began to hum to the little children and Pearlie heard them start to giggle when she sang them a song and nodded at the stocking feet of the little boy.

> Dis little piggy gon' to market,
> Dis little piggy stayed to home.
> Dis little piggy had roast beef,
> Dis little piggy had none . . .

Pearlie looked through the window and she saw Floyd coming up the path from school, two hours later than her. He didn't have any books, just a notebook with paper sticking out. He picked up a rock and threw it on the roof.

"Dis little piggy went wee, wee, wee all the way home . . . Is that Floyd I hear busting up housekeeping?"

"Yes, ma'am, he's coming up the path."

The door swung open, "Hey Mama," and he stopped and stared at Pearlie.

"Where yuh been?"

"Around."

"Yuh mama don had a bad accident and you not here to help her."

"What's that?" He still stared at Pearlie who had started cutting cabbage again.

"I burnt myself bad. Miss Pearlie is getting supper on for me or yuh sorry mouth won't have got fed."

"Now ain't that nice." He threw his notebook across the room and it landed open on one of the pallets. He was around and out the door.

"Where yuh going?"

He was down the steps and up the path.

"Might as well talk to the dirt on the ground. Don't know where he is 'cept when I see him sleeping yonder. 'Spect to come awake one morning and find him gone from there."

Floyd was out of sight when Pearlie placed a hunk of fatback in the pan and set it on the stove. It slicked up and slid to the side of the pan and she smelled the good smell that often floated up from Aunt Bynum's house.

*   *   *

Cale met Floyd on the path. Floyd didn't speak and turned off through the woods.

"Hey, Floyd."

He stopped, "Yeah, man."

"You seen Pearlie?"

"Don't know no Pearlie."

"You know. My sister Pearlie. She's supposed to be at the house."

"What she look like?"

"Kind of tall, long hair in a ponytail. She had on a green dress I think."

"Believe I saw a girl look like that get in a car with a man."

"Where?" Cale was afraid now. "Where and when? Jesus!"

Floyd shrugged. "Down the highway. 'Bout an hour ago."

"Do you remember anything else? What kind of car? What did he look like?"

"Didn't pay no 'tention. You lucky I even saw her."

"You don't even remember what kind of car?"

"Naw, man. Green maybe, blue, don't remember."

"Floyd, you got to help me. I can't tell Mama. We got to find her. Could you tell if she knew the man? He didn't grab her or anything? Maybe it was somebody she knew."

"Man, I got things to do."

"Cale."

It was Pearlie, coming up the path.

"Cale, we got to get the doctor to come to see Aunt Bynum. She has burnt her hands bad. I'm afraid she won't take care of herself and will let them get infected."

"Where have you been?"

"Down at Aunt Bynum's getting her dinner on. Why? Something wrong? Mama and Daddy aren't home yet are they?"

"You been down there all the time?"

"I hadn't been there long, not more than thirty minutes."

"That lying bastard . . ." Cale turned to the woods where Floyd had stood, not a sound and he was gone. "He told me you got in a car with a man."

"Who did?"

"That sonovabitch Floyd."

"He saw me ten minutes ago in his own house. I wouldn't get in a car with a man. Do you think I'm crazy?"

"I ought to kill him for that. You see where nigger loving will get you?"

"Nothing happened to me. I don't know why you're so mad."

"You don't know why I'm mad! Because I got lied to, that's why. I thought we were going to find you in a ditch somewhere."

"I can take care of myself." She turned and headed toward the house.

"You think it's perfectly all right he lied to me?"

"I think I'd lie to you too if you hated me that much."

"Ah shit. You don't know what you're saying. You better watch yourself. You're going to get in real trouble. You just

don't know what you're playing around with. Where'd you get
that business? At church? What you going to do? Go to
Africa and be a missionary and get cooked in a pot? Be a do-
gooder and get Floyd to drag you off in the woods. Why don't
you answer me?"

"Because I don't have anything to say to you. You don't
know what it's like to be poor and cold and near about freeze
to death and get hurt and not have the money to pay for a doctor. You ought to see how they have to live. They don't have
enough light to read by and do their homework. They are going
to eat cabbage for supper with nothing to go along with it but
old salty fatback and nothing to drink but water."

"Jesus, when did you decide to be a preacher?"

"I'm just saying I feel sorry for people who have to live like
that no matter what color they are and I think we ought to do
what we can . . ."

"What do you know about what it's like to live like that?
Maybe they like to live like that. That was a new house and
they messed it up. Mama and Daddy got lots more money
now than they did when I came along. You get new stuff all
the time if you want it. I never got nothing that wasn't second-
handed."

"I don't see what that has to do with it."

Pearlie walked away and went up the steps to the porch. He
saw her ponytail swing and she was in the door before he could
say anything. He didn't want to say anything anyway. He just
wanted to throw a rock at her or something. Now she thought
she was too good for everybody.

Chapter 31

I CAN SEE through the soapy water, just popping up in spots all over my hands. Would that I could sit and look on the stitches at the back of my white church gloves, the smoothness of them when I touch my arm. Mama said age would do it to me, she told me if I didn't take the proper care, it would come out, spots as white as a skint onion and then brown, dark as a mole. I declare I can pick up a nylon with my fingertips. It's good there's not to be another baby for me to touch, scare him like the boogie man. Mama knew I wouldn't take care. I could have told Mama straight then — how long has it been, twenty years? — that Falissa Jenkins was never a woman to be careful about the looks of herself. Now I would never go dirty, no one could accuse me of not scrubbing myself to the bone. And I never let a child of mine go dirty if it meant I had to wash out their little things twice a day, my children were clean. Falissa Jenkins' children were clean. Oh, but I let time take its toll. Worrying and fretting with them and Jerome, I let myself go. I saw those creases coming, I balled up my face in front of the mirror, fifteen years ago I saw those lines that didn't pop back out, like little threads then but the light catches deep in them now. And the skin coming loose at my throat when I turn my head. I don't fool myself. I don't go around saying I'm a young woman still, forty-six years old, I'm done. I'm done doing anything but drying out and bending. Women at the church that have never done a hard

day's work in their lives, hands and legs like a girl's. I worked
myself too hard. There were people who said it to me, Falissa Jenkins, you work yourself too hard but I didn't listen. I
didn't see no other way to be if we were to ever have anything
and this is what it's come to. Dried-out woman looking every
day of sixty to my mind. If you got nothing pretty worth aging
on you, you end up with nothing pretty. But I'm not going on
feeling sorry for myself. I'm not going out caking my face up
with rouge and powder like an old fool. I never expected no
better of myself. I expected it of others, you mind, but not of
me. You make do with what you have and the Lord as good as
told me the day I was born, I wouldn't bring men to bickering
and bargaining. You start with something and you end up
with it and you don't change it and that's a fact before God.
There is not one living thing under the sun I ever had the
power to change but a turnip and a tomato into a stew. I am
believing now that things are set out in the beginning, the Lord
keeps a book and he sets out in the beginning where you're
going and your children and your husband and that is that. I
set out to make my children into the finest on the earth and I
get just what the Lord set out for me. Pearlie. Lord help that
child, she is going to have it hard no matter what I tell her. I
told her from the very start, as soon as she was old enough to
do her share, not to expect nothing from a man but trouble
and bother but to learn to put up with them because you got
to have them. That's what this world will tell you. That you
got to go out and get you one just as quick as you can or you
should be ashamed to call yourself a woman and then you go
your life putting up with his trifling ways. And you are to
satisfy yourself with child raising and housekeeping. What's
there to man and woman loving? Maybe a year or two for some,
not enough to notice for most of us, and you get used to having
them around to remind you nothing's going to change. It makes
you wish another world at times, one where you could go and
get along by yourself and nobody would make nothing of it. I'm

not ashamed to admit my mind has thought on it, but I keep it to myself, no sense working to make it worse. The Lord didn't set it down that way, for woman to make do for herself. The Lord set woman down to get her a man and make do for both of them.

I remember that sermon given by that fine old preacher from Fayetteville who come visiting. He took a wedding to be his sermon; he took a young man and woman joined in the sight of God. He took the young man to be liken to our Lord Jesus Christ and all of us earth souls to be his brides, a wedding of the spirit with salvation in the eyes of the Lord. We say to him, yes, I do, I take him to be my savior. And at death we will not part but will come together. And is that not woman? Is not woman the one who gives up herself to man, yes I do give up what was mine till this day and no matter how hard life comes in upon her, no matter what her man may ask of her, she does her best. The Lord just asks that we do our best. Pearlie will be all right. My little girl will grow into a woman easier than it come to me, before she has a baby in her arms, and it will all be inside her head and in her heart where she will carry such thoughts of being by herself. And she will make a good wife. She will play her part for the Lord's salvation and maybe the Lord will give to her a boy child.

Boy child. Lord, the very sound of those words has come to a change inside me. I said that in my mind until I made it all too high for me to get holt of, until I made the boy child in my mind more than mine could be, more than me and Jerome had to give him of us. And more than the little feller had been given of his own cooped up inside hisself. Me wanting him to step above his raising like it was as easy as falling off a log. Give a child a peck and don't expect ten pecks back for it. I could tell them mamas with their bragging, hold on. He'll do with what he gets and you are as much to blame as he is. Who was to know? Who was to snatch off my dreaming? I looked at that mite, again and again I looked and watched him grow and kept him on my mind until it had little else there, until it just had hands that worked and he lived on my mind like he curled up inside it. And look at him. Oh Lord God, tell me I don't see right. Keep telling me to look at his good features, he brings home good grades and gets most of his chores done. Tell me I don't see a boy that is to come to no good. He walks like on the edge of a cliff, one slip, he is so near to one slip, and he will topple away from all that I ever dreamed for him. Lord, he may have already. He said to me once, Mama, Daddy told me never to stand in an open door and today, Mama, I went and stood in the cow stall door and looked at her as hard as I could and I could hear my heart beating in my ears. So there, see how I disobeyed my Daddy and no harm came to me. Jerome told him that, scared him into thinking he was going to be run in the ground, and that little boy, I declare I think I can see him in my mind, just one dark shadow standing in every door he can get his hands on. And do you think he would have done it if Jerome hadn't told him not to? No sirree. I worry to my dying day of being a proper mother but is that the work of a proper father? To say not to do so much that it gets through the skin of a child until he is spending his days looking to find all the not-do's he can.

I try to be a good wife to Jerome, sick as a dog and I have a hot meal on the table, wash his clothes, put up with his rough-handedness that I would never tell to another man or woman as long as I live. Jerome did not know how to treat a woman and I was not to be able to teach him. I was a woman to cry out to myself and put up with it and not draw attention to myself. It was in the book. He has not changed a hair since I married him. No, that's a fib. A wife and two children weren't made to change him. But Roe, that sorry brother. That did some changing, maybe in the two of us if the truth were known. That was a time he didn't find him a meal and a woman to come to. I showed him that I could do it if I had a mind to. I was not a woman to be particular, the Lord above knows I had to put up with more than my share, but I knew when the living in this house went out of kilter. I put it all in kilter myself with my own two hands and when it went out, I knew it. And this here is my house. That foul-minded, foul-mouthed Roe Jenkins, and forgive me if I speak of the dead and gone, but he left his mark. He is rotting to bones on that hill but he put his mark as deep as if he was sitting on the mantelpiece laughing, saying you are a fool Falissa Jenkins because you didn't lock that door when you saw the bus stop out front. You tore up my husband's mind, put him in guilt for turning you out. You told this whole town what kind of family name we had, didn't you, shamed us. Made Jenkins the name of that man run down by some of his common cronies, not a decent enough man for anybody to bother to find out who done it. I always heard the criminals would kill their own kind. Shamed us with your whoring black women lining up outside our church, took my boy with you into your ugly world and he won't never come out again. You make me fight hate, Roe Jenkins. The Lord says not to hate and he put you there to tempt me because there is nothing else on this earth I could despise like the devil itself that come into my house. Was doing well on our own, thank you very much, and you come and put a streak in my boy that is as evil as your hide. Them streaks don't scrub out and Lord, if time hadn't told me they don't grow out either. But the devil got his due. They hushed my boy when he said the devil drove that truck, shaking their heads and calling it the fever, but don't you think he was just seeing things. The devil has ways and he come after Roe. Roe was showing him up. Can't have nothing on this earth that is worse than him and he come to cart him off to hell where he could make use of him or burn his hide to an ash. Set my boy off that way and now this world around him has become devil enough itself to finish your work. It has with its killing and stealing and meanness and turning over things that have never bothered a soul.

A child is not yours to raise. My mam told me a lot but my

mama didn't tell me that. And she couldn't because it won't
that way then. Mama had more than enough hand in my raising.
I was off and running in my woods and fields, imagining myself
a princess in flowing dresses and I never went past the mail-
box that my Mama and Papa didn't latch on to me and keep
me away from evil. And then my own poor Papa, as innocent
as the newborn baby, took my boy to those picture shows that
filled his head with wild ideas and didn't see it coming that the
world was going to raise him as it saw fit. Papa could tell him
flower names and jumping frogs until it thundered but he
was after other things. He was after guns and killing and talking
ugly and naked women with their clothes open to their waists
showing themselves. I can't stand to look at it. And it's gone,
Papa. Every last thing you knew is gone. It has gone to waste.
Me and my flowers and pictures and Dutch boys, gone to waste.
The world hasn't time for such anymore, just big cars and fancy
clothes. Clean thinking and doing the Lord's will is just for
old people to sit in the parlors and talk of, some as old as you
Papa, smelling like snuff. And I'm to sit down with them now,
not out on the porch with their loud talking, just sit back and
have to push myself to get up before you know it. You'll look
down from heaven and see your little girl, sitting and listening
to their words, their fancy ideas, like a mosquito in the dark,
craning my neck to hear them but knowing good and well there's
nothing new to come to rest in this woman's lap. I declare
I can't be out and about, I can't go prissing out and pick me out
a new frock and curl up my hair and put on big round earbobs.
I can't. I got to sit. I done what I can do. I put down in front
of my children all that I intended to say and be it bad or good,
it's over and done with, the best I knew how. And I see him
throwing things and breaking them and calling me names and
he cuts me up like a knife. But pretty soon there won't be any
more to go cutting on. And he'll go off from here and I will
wait and watch and listen until something comes, I know not
what, but I pray You'll take care of him where I fell short.

Chapter 32

CALE put up the tools in the shed and walked toward the pond. He found that as soon as the weather started getting nice he headed toward it without thinking. He supposed it was becoming a kind of refuge from his family though it hadn't seemed so before. It was always alike. Things just turned different with the seasons but it didn't get worn out and beat up and never replaced like their furniture in the house. Nothing was there but what grew there naturally, just the cattails that went further out and shrunk the pond. No buildings except for his birdhouse that his daddy put on the drain post. So stupid. Cale made the house in shop and his daddy said he wanted to put it up for the pond birds so he put it there, standing sprattle-legged in the row boat. His daddy told Roe that was to protect them from the cats and foxes and Roe got tickled and told him only trouble was they'd have to learn to swim before they learned to fly. His old man with all his bird books just looked at Roe like he was the crazy one then come spring and the mama pushed them out and every last one of them drowned. Plop, plop, plop, and they sank. No more of them would build there though because it was full up with the last nest. He might get it down someday and find another place for it before it rotted. It was a pretty good house and he had put a trapdoor in the back side so it'd be easy to clean.

Nothing to remind him of the farm but one end of a stretch

of fence, it was rusting and streaking from the nails but it wouldn't fall down, at least five more years. Then it would be, "Cale, go fix it." Maybe Cale just might not be there to say that to. They wouldn't be able to believe that, that Cale just might not be there. Just go down the list of what Roe had done—riding logs, working in the oil fields, driving a taxicab. There was more than enough out there to keep him busy thinking about it. It was nice to walk the land here by himself but new places didn't bother him. Sometimes he liked to walk new land or even just a new street in Raleigh when he had time to kill after selling tobacco. You can like old places but you can do without them. And the people too. That might be a pleasure to get to do without the people.

Neither of his parents knew where he was when he was down by the pond. He was sure they didn't know he was there, not like his place behind the barn when he was a kid or the best one, that hole in the ground. He remembered the hole big enough for his body, with a wooden barrel lid and he had sat down in the cool dirt for hours with all his clothes off in the summer, reading comic books with a flashlight. His batteries went dead one day and he was using a candle; that was how Jerome discovered the hole and made him fill it up before somebody fell in it. That was what was nice about the hillside over the pond, he wasn't really hiding because he was right in the middle of everything that he liked and couldn't see much of what he didn't. It was just that no one would ever have any reason to look that way.

And he could think there or just do nothing at all like the night he had watched the day lilies twist up and felt like he was in on something no one had really seen before. Thought about telling Pearlie; she would like it. But talk too much and then she might want to come to his place and sit and talk to him. She had a way of getting just like his mother. You'd like to let her in on things now and then but she'd always want too much. She was just real lonesome. He had seen the flowers open and seen them twisted up but never had seen them petals moving before. He could see him telling his old man about something like that; that would give him grist for his goddamn mill if anybody was so idle he could see such as that. But Papa Lonza had often spoken of sitting on the porch and watching the tobacco grow. Papa had seen some things people like his old man would never see, even when they were old. There was a lot wrong with that old man, he'd be in a fix if he had to get by today, but he had something special. His father didn't have it. He was just a bump on the earth, a nothing. That's why he never enjoyed anything. He just bullied everybody around, especially his mama.

It was funny how when he was a child his mama seemed so large, now she was a skinny thing in baggy clothes. Maybe it was because she used to be big enough to get between him and his father and make some difference. He could laugh at that now, actually she was a short woman around other women but he wasn't so dumb he didn't know why she used to look big. Because she always got up when she thought his father was going to hit him. More than once she made things worse, his father's face drew up at the sound of her voice. He could remember many a time hearing, "You'll have him so he can't fight his own battles." But that was about all his father ever did, gripe about it. It was almost like he didn't really care enough about him to win him over from his mother. When his father didn't whip him, he walked off and left him with her and sometimes her whining was as bad as a beating. Sometimes he took his father's side in their arguments, nothing special his father did really, just there was always something weak about her way of thinking. Most guys bitched about their mothers and said they didn't do anything they told them to and bragged about their fathers. It wasn't really his own idea to go to his father's side. He wasn't much. He would just make his mama go weak and crawling and give up, begging and giving up a fight. Wasn't much to that. That was easy to do. But it meant he couldn't take her side.

That afternoon there had been a whole load of little tenant

children out in front of the house, their mama come to help Aunt Bynum set out tobacco. They were shut up in an old Buick with the windows rolled up because there wasn't anyone to leave with them while their mama was at the plant bed. His mama had fretted all day, "They are going to smother in there. I've read about it, little children smothering in shut-up cars," and every half hour or so she would go out and look in the car, tap the glass, to assure herself that they were all still alive, and a row of sad black faces would come up to the window when she came, smearing the glass like little dogs. He was working on the steps and had to lean back for her long skirts to pass by then listen to her mumble in the kitchen, half out loud.

Jerome had come in for lunch and by then she was really worked up about them. He didn't look up from his food when she told him about it.

"Why don't you mind your own business?"

"It is my business when somebody's little children might be dying out there in my own front yard."

"Nobody's dying in your yard. You've gone around all morning and gotten yourself all worked up over nothing. Why don't you get something to do to occupy your mind or do you want to come down and give us a hand where it's needed."

"You know I never refused to help you when I'm needed but I'm not going out bending over and setting tobacco. I'm just not able anymore. And my house has got to be cleaned."

"Well, that's exactly why you've got that little load of niggers in the yard because you're not able and your house has got to be cleaned. I need the help and they've left them kids in every yard in the county and and not one of them has died yet. You can't kill a nigger that easy." He rolled his eyes round to Cale and grinned, but Cale looked down. He didn't want anything to do with this one.

"What about something to eat? Did anybody think to leave them something to eat?"

"Look goddammit. I don't want to hear another word about

it," Jerome sat up straight, pushing back his empty plate. "They all got a nigger mama somewhere and it is her duty to feed them. She's getting paid for her time. Every last one could die and we'd never miss them. So shut up about it. They're not your concern."

Falissa turned her back to him and went to the sink.

"You hear me," he shouted and left the table, slamming his chair and turning over his glass. His mother set the glass back up and picked up the ice cubes. He watched her thin hands work, pale and speckled as a guinea egg, her face sideways and sad. It was almost as if he had struck her a blow. But she had a way of taking the old man's outbursts, he couldn't have taken that. She had never understood why he couldn't take that.

As soon as his father was to the barn, she had sent Cale out with five jelly biscuits for them. He opened the door quickly and put them on the seat. He looked; no one had seen him but his mother at the window. Their mother came back no sooner than he had gotten back to work on the steps. She caught them eating the biscuits and whipped every one of them. Then the rest of the afternoon he had to listen to crying and whimpering in the car.

"I'd carry them some of yours and Pearlie's old funny books to look at but if she caught them she'd take out her meanness again as sure as I'm sitting here. And I could let them out here in the yard and keep an eye on them. They could find plenty to play with. She has broken their little hearts."

"Daddy said for you to mind your own business, Mama. You've already been the cause of a whipping."

She had turned to look at him and her mouth dropped open slightly, then she turned back and started to cry very softly. She didn't cry much, at least he didn't see her. Wasn't really fair for her to cry at him and not his father. Like she was trying to make him feel bad for something he didn't want anything to do with. The children in the car were still whimpering and he could hear her sniffing as she washed the woodwork in the living room. He finished painting the steps and built a barricade of chairs around them. Then he jumped off the porch and ran out to the barn.

"Did she turn them niggers out?" His daddy was at his workbench, oiling the hand planter, opening and closing the rusty lid.

"No sir, not that I know of."

"Wonder what makes her do such stupid things?" He wasn't really asking Cale a question. Cale knew that he didn't want an explanation, he was just trying to get him to agree that she was stupid.

"She doesn't know any better, I guess." That was the wrong answer; he knew it soon as he said it.

"Doesn't know any better! She damn well better learn before she dies. I'll learn her to tend what's inside those doors and windows and mind her own business if it's the last thing I do."

Cale had taken a wrench and gone into the tractor stall and started to change from the big disks to the plow blade. He had waited a moment, hoping his father wouldn't follow him and start talking when he heard the barn door slam.

Mind your own business. He told her the same damn thing. Cale's hand had begun to shake and he had to use both of them to move the frozen bolt. You sound just like Daddy. Pearlie had told him that a million times and made him mad. All afternoon that had bothered him, everybody pushing to make him take sides when he didn't want either one of them. At least he thought he didn't. It was like he took both of them. And he really didn't know if he would have ignored the little children in the car or not. Like everything around here, one word and it bounces off everything and everybody gets in on the act but nothing ever leaves and goes outside their acres to find out what somebody else might think. What had sent him to his placed by the pond today was his mama, the final blow.

"I don't think you have an ounce of respect for me anymore, Cale."

He didn't answer her. He couldn't really because he couldn't think of anything but something mean, like shooting fish in a barrel, like using a call to get a mourning dove. She didn't have a chance. It just seemed like some kind of kid's game to talk back to her, like cheating to win.

He walked on down beside the pond and heard the frogs start hitting the water, one by one as he got closer. They had filled the edges with slimy eggs as soon as the frost stopped. The water was black now but he could see streaks from the sky light still in it. He stood a moment until the frogs were all gone and quiet and there were just the bats moving way up overhead, bouncing up and down in the air. The water was still. Something white shone back at him from the rushes so he walked over, his feet squeaking in the wet. He parted them; some of the green blades were bent and broken. He saw an open eye in the side of a white face, the big blue bird, dead, its neck limp and twisted. He stooped and touched the gray and dusty-looking feathers, and they felt strangely warm but the bird was dead. Just dead today, but dead. Its feet were underwater like it was still attached to the ground, pushed over like a tree. Where the thin neck went into the body, Cale saw the blood, a black-red spot, a small bullet hole, a twenty-two right in the craw.

He stood and looked across the water at the woods. They were quickly turning dark as the sun fell below the trees. No one. But somewhere in the dark was Floyd and Floyd was laughing over what he had done.

*   *   *

Cale sat in church, on the end with Pearlie between him and his parents. He had been watching her run her fingers over the gold letters on the hymnal with her name on it that she had won for perfect attendance at Sunday school. Her skirt hung over her knees and he could see the light brown hairs on her legs pressed flat under her stockings. He had been thinking all morning about yesterday and the dead bird, about what made Floyd want to kill it. But what was most strange was that he hadn't been able to get mad about it since right when he found it. He was sorry, and sort of sad like losing an old pet that you weren't really proud of but kind of enjoyed, one that made you laugh. Last night before he went to sleep he started thinking that maybe it was his fault the bird was dead, not that he was letting Pearlie and all her preaching about making Floyd mean get to him, just that if it hadn't been for him, maybe Floyd never would have killed the bird. But the bird didn't matter, there were lots of birds. Maybe Floyd shot him because he could get away with it and he would go to jail if he shot a person. Maybe Floyd had gone off in the woods and looked at him right down the gunsight, aimed to shoot him through the head. He's a good shot getting that bird in his thin neck but Floyd could knock the head off a sparrow with a rock. Floyd might have been aiming at him for a long time.

Early this morning when his mama had sent him with a pot of soup for Aunt Bynum, he had thought to ask if Floyd had a gun. But he never did because maybe she didn't know and Floyd didn't want her to. His mama had sent him off down the back path and told him to try to keep his daddy from seeing him to keep down a row. When he got there, Aunt Bynum was on the porch, much too chilly a morning for her to be sitting out. She had on her Sunday hat and shoes, ready for church. Her hands were in her apron, palms up and white like they had turned to stone on her. She smiled when she saw him and nodded as he came up the steps. Even her face was whitening, turning gray like ashes. She told him she had come out to look on the sunshine, though it was cold the sunshine warmed her inside with its yellowness. He set the soup pot beside her and sat down on the steps. She smiled at it like it was a child, moving her legs close to its warmth. He didn't know why he had sat down really, the cold came through the seat of his pants. Maybe he didn't want to go back to the house. She talked a lot, mostly about Floyd who she said was her brightest and so would be the one to bring the most grief upon her. He was restless and not to be satisfied with what was there and she said she hoped Mr. Jerome won't counting on him as a worker because he was likely as not to take off. Cale had put it together then, he and Floyd taking off and the only thing either one of them knew was right there. And his daddy would have to do some of the hard work for a change. He told Aunt Bynum he was going to take off too but not to tell anyone and she smiled and said, "Chile, I glad you ain't black." And he thought that he was glad too. But that wasn't the most important thing she said, it was when she was talking about his family, the goodness of his mama, the hardness of his father, and the gentleness of Papa Lonza. She said he would find them hard folks to leave; she had considered it and come to that thought. But she wanted Floyd to leave for both of them and she would stay home and pray for him until her dying day, even if she never saw him again. But she wanted him to leave.

Cale took her soup pot in and set it on the worktable, bringing all the little children running out of the darkness as he scooped each one up a cupful. He went back out and she had been getting her words ready because they came at him fast, "Don't mean no harm by it, Mr. Cale. You understand." He said he did and she rocked her chair and her white lips moved slowly. "The Preacher told us there is a new day a'coming to this earth. And I seen in a dream my boy saying to the Lord, 'I ain't going spend my day just keeping alive. I'm going make things.'" Then she wrinkled her nose and looked up at him with her bottom lip out and nodded her head just like she had when he came up.

The congregation sat down from the last song and Pearlie closed her hymnal and put it back in her lap, still running her finger on the letters. The clock in the back said he had twenty-five minutes left for his sermon and Cale shut out the preacher's voice before he even told what he was going to talk about. He heard his daddy clear his throat like he did before he went to sleep in his chair at night but here his mama would punch him each time his eyes closed. He just came because he had to and so he could go out of the service and talk with the men about the crops and the government and complain about the allotment size for tobacco. None of the young boys were allowed to say anything because their fathers thought they knew it all, just like his. He even heard his father say once that Floyd would be old enough to take over most of the tobacco work soon and here Aunt Bynum had said he was leaving. And there she was, hands hardly good enough to button her clothes and set out plants and not worried. His father would put them off. Soon as Floyd left he would put her off because she didn't have anything but girls and she was too old to get anything but an old man to live with her. Her talking about a new day. Some shiny black preacher put up his arms and told all those old colored people about a new day just because they can sit where they please on the buses and every last one of them still goes to the back. And Pearlie there thinks it's a new day, that she and a bunch of missionaries can go around with baskets of food and make everything change. Just like a dollar for gas, you burn it up and you're right back where you started and you tell Pearlie that and she starts talking about lighting candles in the dark. And suppose you make Aunt Bynum's house good as ours, that would just make my daddy hate them worse. Pearlie doesn't know what she's doing and she hasn't got enough to go giving away. She's too tenderhearted. She ought to have known Papa Lonza, not me. She's just like him. I'm not waiting for any new day. Nobody's going to give you anything. And you can't stay out of trouble with people because you can get in just as much trouble not doing things as you can doing them.

Cale was outside the church. It had warmed up so he had his coat off and his sleeves up. He didn't wear a tie today and he knew his mama wanted to tell him to but she didn't have the nerve anymore. Pearlie was on the wall out near the parking lot waiting for them to leave, turning through the pages of her hymnal. She was pouting and Cale could tell she was almost mad because of this woman, one his mother knew from town who had come to their service today because of the visiting preacher. She was fat, over two hundred pounds he was sure, and she drove around alone in a black Cadillac, just like the ones at the funeral home. He looked at the car in the lot and saw Pearlie staring at it too. The car was new but it already sagged down on one side from her weight. She lived alone and they said she had more money than anyone in town. She said she had ten guns in the house and that anyone who broke in would be electrocuted. Her house didn't look like a rich person's, paint peeling off and the yard grown up in more weeds than grass, down near niggertown. She bragged about not being afraid and she said she carried her protection with her in the car, too, under the seat, a hose poured full of lead because the law wouldn't let her carry a gun.

Cale walked up behind his mother and said, "Me and Pearlie are going to start toward home."

Before she could answer he was walking quickly toward the parking lot and motioning to Pearlie.

"Hey," he said when she caught up with him, "what did the tank say to make you mad?"

"Who?"

"The tank. Miss Stevens. I saw you walk off from them."

"She said that when she got depressed she got in her Cadillac and drove through niggertown."

Cale shook his head and whispered, "Damn."

"I'd be ashamed to say such as that on the Sabbath. Mama ought not to have such friends. She just stands right there like she agrees. Scared to death of Miss Stevens just because she's got money. Poor people are to be pitied. She doesn't think it's a sin because they are colored people but it is just the same."

"You don't know the half of it. Poor people are to be pitied all right for being so stupid. You know where she got the money for that car? She got it from that row of houses down below the mill that don't have any paint and all look just alike. She owns half the nigger houses in this town and she told Daddy one day she'd own all of them."

"No."

"Yes she does too. You didn't think they owned them, did you? She owns them and goes down in her Cadillac to go rent collecting."

Pearlie wrinkled up her nose, confused, then said, "We're poor people. We don't have a Cadillac or a car either. Why doesn't she want to come out and drive through our place? If she wanted to be hateful, she could make us feel bad just as easy."

"That's why it's not poor people. That's what I'm telling you. It's colored people. Besides they got too many places to hide out at our place. Every colored kid on the place would throw a rock from the bushes till he got her fat ass out and could rock it. I seen Floyd hit a sparrow so don't think he'd miss that fat ass."

Pearlie started to laugh. Cale liked her better then, when she didn't take all this too serious. They heard a horn blow behind them and his body chilled as he took Pearlie by the shoulders and pushed her away from the road.

"Look, it's them in the car."

Their mother beat on the back window looking frantically for the handle. They heard it hiss when the fat lady rolled it down from up front. The brakes squealed as it slowed to a stop.

"Cale, Pearlie. Come ride home in this fine car." She opened the door and Cale shook his head.

"I'd rather walk."

"Me, too," Pearlie called and started back down the road. Cale watched his mother's face through the open window as they started away, her hair blowing around her face until the window moved slowly up in front of it. He looked at Pearlie and she was still smiling, then she pranced along with her nose in the air. "Mama and Daddy didn't listen to the sermon."

"Me either. What was it?"

"Cale! Shame on you." Then she laughed again. "It was about materialism. That's what I'm going to ask them, ask them if they listened if they start fussing with me because I wouldn't ride with them."

Before they got to the driveway, the black car had turned and come back out again, passing them, stinging Pearlie's legs with dirt as it went by. She slapped at her legs and frowned again at Cale. "She's a hateful woman. If I was a different kind of person, I'd hit her with a rock."

As they turned up the drive, both of them looked up. There were three black birds soaring, buzzards making a circle over the little woods.

"Something's dead," Pearlie said.

"Yeah, over near the woods. Must be a fish left out." Then Cale stopped. "No, that's not right. It's the bird. It's the bird I saw yesterday, dead by the water."

"Not the one that comes back every year? He didn't die, did he?" Pearlie was talking loud, like she did when she was afraid.

"No. Just an old crow somebody shot." He lied to her; he didn't know why, he just did. And she wouldn't go look, he didn't think she would. She didn't leave the house much.

After lunch Cale went down by the pond. His mama and daddy hadn't even mentioned the ride in the black car. He stopped in the shed for a shovel. The bird had started to smell, maybe it was dead longer than he had thought, and the odor grew stronger as he walked to the spot by the water. He saw the legs first, the color already faded. He quickly began to throw dirt in its direction before he looked at the body because the smell was already making his lunch rise in his throat. He covered until there was nothing, even covered the feet in the water. He beat the top with the shovel so the dogs wouldn't tear into it. Then he heard something he hadn't expected, a gun cracking in the woods, a small gun, twenty-two probably. He stuck the shovel in the ground and walked toward the sound. It was down at the trash pile where he shot; he could hear the glass breaking. He walked up behind Floyd who didn't hear him until he ran out of bullets and stopped to reload. He looked up at Cale as the first three shells slid down the chute.

"Hey," Cale said.

Floyd nodded and continued to drop in bullets.

"Didn't know you had a gun?"

"Yeah. Had it." The gun was an old one and hadn't been cleaned up; there was rust on the barrel.

"You ought to oil it. Rust will stop up the barrel and hang up a bullet on you."

The chute was full and Floyd slid it back into the gun. Cale felt his arms tense when he saw the gun was loaded again.

"You ever hunt with it?"

"Naw. Naw, I ain't done no hunting yit."

Cale tried to remember the bird, to see him as he had by the water but the picture wouldn't come to his mind. He just saw the mound that he had made. He couldn't make himself see it but he could still smell it even from under the dirt. Wonder if Floyd smelled it. He started to ask him, to say somebody shot a bird down by our pond but he didn't. He turned to walk back toward the house when Floyd took aim at another bottle and broke it. Drops of water sparkled in the air then settled to the ground.

Cale stopped and said, "Can you hit things good? I mean moving things. Like you used to be able to get a bird with a rock off the wires?"

"Man, I can get them on the wing. Won seven dollars on the betting thing out to Raleigh."

"No kidding. You going to the army?"

"Ain't nothing to shoot at. Luster says ain't no war. They got no use for me yit."

Floyd was suddenly silent. He had done that before, started talking and then shut up when he heard himself.

"What would you think if I told you I was going to the army? Just go off and leave this farm that's supposed to be mine some-day?"

Floyd squinted and shrugged his shoulders.

"I mean if I just packed up and left here."

Floyd stared at him in that old way, the way he did that made you talk if you didn't look away because you knew he wasn't going to say anything. And if you started opening up he would stand there and listen making you jabber like a fool and never say anything back to you. Floyd didn't give a damn what he did.

"I just might do it. I just might pack up and leave."

He turned away from Floyd's stare and before he was thirty feet down the road, chills went up his back when the bottles started to break again. He could go talk to the pond or the dead bird mound, that's what it was like talking to Floyd. Like when they were building the roof on the new tobacco barn, two years ago and he wrote down the name of the girl in his Biology class, he had forgotten her name now, he wrote it on a leaf with his fingernail and nailed it under the tin. That was what it was like talking to Floyd, like telling something you had to tell but you knew nobody was ever going to find it. But Floyd wasn't like the leaf in one way; he might be taking it inside his head and turning it around. He just might do that. You would be crazy to believe Floyd didn't think about things. He didn't have anything else to do.

Cale wanted to clear his mind, to do something to get it off leaving for a while, before he told the wrong person and gave himself away. He ran through the woods, dodging around the trees with the briars snatching at his pants. He ran out into the lower field and the scrub trees went by the side of his eyes too fast for him to catch their shapes. He got to the main road and he could see spider webs floating around him, stuck to him. The rifle crack in the woods grew fainter, either Floyd had stopped or he was too far away to hear.

Cale decided to spend the afternoon playing softball at the church field. He had heard the noise through the trees as he walked down the highway. It had warmed up so his mama and daddy would spend the afternoon talking on the porch and Pearlie would go to her room. Before he left to cover the

bird, he had looked up and seen her sitting in the window with
a book. She noticed him and waved as he went off, leaving the
whole house and everything around it in the kind of droning
buzz that the bees had started up in the flowering trees.

On the highway the cars moved with a quick swish of Sunday
afternoon riders and the noise of the ball game got higher. He
felt his heart pick up, the way it used to when he was a little kid
and saw them playing and wasn't sure they were going to let
him play with them, knowing he was going to have to play
twice as well as they expected for a little kid. He had to hit
the ball way out and turn all their heads before he got chosen
on a team and some days nothing would go right for him. But
now he was the best, he got the Player of the Year award at
Summit High the last two years. They would see him walk
up and know the team that got him would be the one to win,
he would change the whole game for the afternoon, the other
team might get an extra person in his place to make up for it.
Some of the guys would be happy when they saw him and some
of them wouldn't like it a bit.

He pitched awhile but he had rather play first base. When
he was sure he had the best team and they'd win anyway, he
switched. After he started hitting deep it felt good. This bunch
made a lot more mistakes than the one at school and he started
hitting to the weak fielders, watched them drop it as he ran,
watched their throws fall short of the bases. Some of them were
fat, as old as his father and their shirts pulled out at the waist
when they ran, their stomachs bobbing, not moving after the
ball until it was already too late. Some of them were the younger
guys at the church who had played on the team when they were
in high school but Cale had the edge on them too. They were
really trying, harder than the old men because they knew everyone had forgotten they were once good and they were being replaced. It was a good afternoon, Cale had nine of the twelve
runs when he started home and they had won twelve to three.
He spoke to Coach Beal's brother who was out playing just before

he started home. He had a message from the coach, it looked good on the scholarship for next year at State.

Cale shrugged his shoulders and walked off, it wasn't that he was sorry Coach Beal was trying, it just wasn't enough. And he'd like to see Coach Beal get credit for getting an athletic scholarship for Summit. Nobody from Summit had ever gotten the baseball scholarship and the colleges didn't really want baseball players anyway. He walked slowly back to the house, looking at the fields starting to green. This was always the time that he got that feeling, that school was almost over for the year, just over a month left. Only this time it was it. No more school and people who had been just alike all along were going different ways. That's what all the girls got silly and cried over and the guys didn't talk about much but it was the truth. Jigger was going to summer school at Carolina to see if he could get up enough to be a freshman. He didn't tell everybody about that, just that he was going in the fall. Cale didn't think he would make it. He figured Jigger had gone as far as he could and that his brain couldn't do more no matter what everybody tried to do with him. So his old man would get him a job, coat and tie, at the bank probably or selling houses. All that damn money just looking for somebody to spend it on and Jigger wasn't even smart enough to be able to use it.

Cale slid his hands in his back pockets. This didn't make him mad, knowing Jigger could go to college and he couldn't, not really. He had never let himself think he was really going. There had been a time when he thought of the ball games. This fall he had been by the campus when they were getting the feed ground in Raleigh and everybody was walking around outside with books, stopping and going when they pleased and not shut in one building. All the stores had "Welcome Wolf-pack" in the windows. And that afternoon when they were getting loaded up at the feed store he saw the traffic, bumper to bumper and the girls with the big white flowers with red and white ribbons pinned on their suit coats. When they started to leave, he watched the girls go up the gravel drives on the campus, wobbling and bending their ankles on high heel shoes. He heard the sounds from the stadium, the bands and the people yelling and halfway back to Summit, sitting in the open back of the truck, he could hear the drums beating from the football field, the sounds coming through the barren trees. It had never seemed so far away as when he was there in Raleigh, like he couldn't even go walking on the inside of the campus when he knew anybody could; Jigger went up to Chapel Hill all the time to walk around in his Carolina Windbreaker and pretend he was already there. It was strange to see that many people not much older than him and not know any of them. He hadn't really planned on going to school there yet. Maybe sometime but he wasn't going to go walking right into it, not until he knew what it was all about. He was going to go out and get a job, not hundreds of miles off like some of the guys talked who weren't going to college, just Durham or Raleigh or maybe up to Greensboro. You didn't have to go hundreds of miles off to get away from his parents, just get out of Summit, because they never did. Then when he figured he was ready to go to the university, he might go. Might not. Might just learn how to build houses and bridges just by getting a job and working on them, start out with something not too hard and go up to something harder when he was good and ready. School would have to be a whole lot different than it was in Summit for him to learn more in classes than he could by just doing something. Jigger wasn't going about it right. He was going flying into that university and he would come flying back out twice as fast and end up stuck in Summit the rest of his life with people whispering about how he couldn't make it, that money wasn't everything.

Cale turned up the back way so he could come in around the barn and not have to go up the drive in front of everybody. He walked around the shed and wrung his hand around the corner post, flaking off the cedar bark with his palm. He stood on the stoop and leaned against the open door, picking the flakes

from under the calluses in his hand. One of the cows was in
there, slopping at the food in her trough. He watched the
birds in the lot, invisible in the gray-brown mud until they
fluttered, scooping up hair from where the mules' winter
coats were chunking away when they rolled. He caught a movement in the corner of his eye, then he heard a laugh.

"If I'd been a snake, I'd a bit you. I was there all the time.
You didn't even know it but I was there all the time."

The cow jumped in the stall behind him and bumped her
head. He leaned against the frame in case she tried to run out
but she went back to her eating. It was his father, Sunday tie
pulled loose at his throat, his Sunday suit coat unbuttoned and
sagging. He could smell liquor, probably the bottle he kept hid
in the barn away from his mama. He looked at Cale, waiting for
an answer. He wanted to talk, Cale could tell that by looking at
him. The truth was he probably just wanted somebody to listen
to him and he stood open-mouthed waiting for Cale to say something. Cale felt his face heat up, almost like getting caught doing something, like all those dreams he had and woke up with
his skin burning because he had been caught at something.
Then he got the relief of finding himself in bed, and knowing
it wasn't real, but here was this grinning little man. He was real
all right. He would have worked harder at staying hid if he had
known Jerome was going to be here. Or worked harder at not
coming home until he had to.

"Yeah, you're real sneaky. Too bad there ain't no demand
for somebody to go sneaking up on people." Cale smiled after he
spoke, it had to be just right because when he got smart with the
old man, he would stare at him hard, looking for something in
Cale's face that would say, you've gone too far, boy. Cale didn't
want to make him mad but he didn't want him to think he was
pleased with his company either. Jerome laughed, a little forced,
but he had a full stomach, maybe he wasn't looking for trouble
today.

"Where you been? Out wasting time?"

"Playing ball at the church."

"Yeah, out wasting time. Just like I asked you, out wasting time. Stinking up your Sunday clothes. Why didn't you change if you can't rest on the Sabbath like you're supposed to." Then Jerome squinted at Cale's shirt, "Oh, I forgot. You didn't bother with your Sunday clothes today. You figured you could get more attention if you went out looking like a bum."

Cale didn't say anything. The old man was picking for a fight. Let him get out of Falissa's hearing distance and he would pick a fight every time, over almost anything. He kept staring so Cale shrugged. Probably the wrong thing to do because Jerome's face reddened. Yeah, that was being disrespectful.

"You don't shrug your shoulders at me, boy. You answer me yes sir or no sir. But none of that smart ass shrugging, hear?"

Cale closed his eyes and recited the words inside his head, how many times the same words, slamming doors, scuffing feet, don't take your temper out on the door of my house, pick your feet up if I have to buy your shoes.

"Look Daddy, don't pick a fight with me, O.K.? I was just standing here, minding my own business and I'd just like to be left alone. If you want here, I'll just go somewhere else."

"Don't you go telling me who can mind whose business. Not standing on my farm and wearing the clothes I bought you."

Cale didn't answer. Jerome looked up at him, squinting, unsquinting like a flash of light was hitting his face. But it wasn't; he was just chewing around inside, waiting for Cale to say something, anything so he could leap out again. Say a word to him and it was like poking a stick at a snapping turtle. Jerome snorted and walked a few feet away, looking out at the field.

"I wish you'd get serious, boy. You're distressing your mama and me. I wish you'd start putting some thought into how much of the work here you going to take over for me and how much you going to do in town. We got to know these things and we ain't young as we used to be. This is too much farm for one man and I'd hate to give up any of it. You ain't going to get your keep for nothing. Not when you start taking home a paycheck. You going to find out how much you cost and give us a hand."

Cale still didn't answer. Next he figured he would get it about the land, what land was worth to a man, something his old man must have seen in a bad Western twenty years ago. No, he never saw movies. Something his own daddy told him that he was dumb enough to believe. His mama would have said when we die this will be yours but not his daddy. He just had children so he wouldn't have to hire help. His daddy didn't think he would ever die and he wasn't going to give anybody anything. He wouldn't even get rid of something old and broken if it belonged to him; the burnt-out water heater and furnace were still in the barn; he'd let them rot before he'd pass them on to somebody like Aunt Bynum who could use them.

"You thought it out, boy?"

He had never asked him directly before. "Yeah, I guess I have."

Jerome looked up quickly, squinted again. "What is it?"

"I'm leaving as soon as school is out."

"You're leaving what?"

"I'm leaving here, home, Summit."

Jerome walked over close again. His breath instantly began to come in snorts. "Where you think you're going?"

"Not sure yet. I'll let you know."

"Don't you talk cock assy to me."

Cale shrugged again. He couldn't help it. There was nothing else to do and it did just what he thought it would. Jerome got madder.

"What happens to you now when you don't have your prissy-skirted mama to take up for you?"

"I don't need her to take up for me."

"You'll be just like your grandpa, let some prissy ass woman get holt of you and make you walk the straight and narrow. I seen you slick down your hair for them, smelling high like you perfumed. I seen you wearing that bracelet with your name on it to school. What's a man doing wearing a bracelet? Let a woman make out you just like them. You wouldn't be gone two weeks before some woman had her claws in you. You know what I could do? I could go down to the courthouse and fix it so you never touch a handful of dirt on this place."

"So go! I give a shit."

"Boy, you talk big now when you've got a full belly. You'd change your tune if you missed meals for a couple of days. What you think is out there? You going out and get rich? Don't nobody get rich honest. They cheat and steal from people. Don't you think you get rich by living right. No man ever did. You spend dawn to dark making enough to stay alive."

"What do you know about it? What you know about further than the driveway?"

"I been out long before you was in this world. I seen more in ten years than you seen all your life. I know what's out there and what don't change. People don't change."

Cale thought a second then said, "Thought I saw you propped up in Miss Stevens' Cadillac. Didn't see you figured it'd get the seat of your pants dirty."

"What you talking about?"

"I'm saying that's dirty money. You don't have to leave Summit to find dirty people. My parents got dirty rich friends right here in Summit. Staying here don't make you clean."

Jerome shook his head. "Boy, you're mixed up. You're mixed up inside. That's what they do at school? Where'd you get that? Miss Stevens keeps up those sorry niggers who don't work and don't pay their rent half the time with a roof over their head that they got no right to. If she threw them out, they'd sleep in the street. Don't shoot your mouth off about what you don't know."

"She doesn't ever fix the houses up. They all leak and got rats."

"Rats go to filth, boy. You live a little longer you learn something. You see how fast a nigger'll make a house a pig lot."

"I'll talk about what I know then. Come the first of June and graduation and I'm gone. I'll take what I paid for and you can keep the rest. That's all I got to tell you."

Jerome grabbed his arm and when Cale snatched it away he grabbed at him again. Cale caught the shorter man under his elbows and pushed him, hard. Jerome lost his balance, scratched for the side of the barn and fell to the ground. He hit hard and his breath cracked out. He lay still and groaned. Cale thought of kicking him, if he tried to get up, he would kick him. He felt the air hit him on the backside through the open stall like something was rushing up behind him. He jumped from the door before the cow came out and went around the barn, through the short stretch of woods toward the road.

He didn't hit him. He didn't go after to hit him. He couldn't have done anything else. Maybe let him sling on his arm and yap in his face. No, he couldn't have done anything else. That old bastard couldn't touch him, maybe when he was a little kid, but not anymore.

Cale got to the road but he didn't walk on the shoulder. He moved at the edge of the woods so the cars going by wouldn't notice him. The old man didn't get right up and come after him. Must have knocked his breath out good. He went to the creek by Parson's Store and sat on the bridge, facing the road so if anyone came up, he would see them. He put his hands on his thighs and looked at them. They were shaking pretty bad. He hadn't hit him, he just shook off from him. He had no intentions of starting a fight with him. Wonder if he got up and started after him. It couldn't have hurt him bad. Cale looked back toward the woods, watching to see someone come out. No, he wouldn't come after him. He would go running to the house like a little kid. Tell Mama. He wouldn't come. He'll just wait there for him to come back. They could sit up waiting and he wouldn't come back at all and they'd call him to get up for school and nobody would be there.

Maybe the old man didn't get up at all. Didn't hit his head.

Don't think so. Not hard anyway. Why didn't he get up? Faking to make him come over so he could jump him. He's back in the house now, beating on things and telling Mama. Cale shook his head. He didn't want to go through that, trying to think out what they were doing, it didn't matter. Why did he let them matter so much when he didn't want them to? It didn't matter what they said or did. He could do what he wanted to. He could leave on the next bus. But they could come after him. Until May 10, 1958, they could come after him and make him go home. He had thought of that before. That's what he told Floyd, that he just might pack up and leave. Shit. That goddamn Floyd can pack up and leave any time he pleases and nobody comes after him or nothing. Aunt Bynum would just sit in her chair and rock and say, "That boy gone. Just like the others. Up and gone." And his old man would say, one less nigger to feed. And if he didn't come home in one hour from now he would be out looking for him and asking people if they seen him until he would have to go hiding like a rat and knowing the longer he stayed hid the worse it would be. He would go find somebody to stay with, somebody who didn't give a damn about him. Willie. He just might go find Grandpa Willie and stay with him, and tell him the reason he came is that his sonovabitch son Jerome is his father and that he hit him. He had seen Willie. He was still alive and he knew where he was. He saw him walking down the road with three mules and he was stepping on the bottoms of his overalls. He buried his mules. Cale knew where that was. Way out in the country and if he could get his truck he might go and tell Willie what happened.

But I don't even know Willie. He wouldn't know me if he saw me. Who? Jerome's son? He'd shake his head and walk off. I don't know anybody. I don't know anybody I could go to and tell them I was getting out. I could tell Pearlie. And I think she just might know what I mean. She didn't used to but she would now I bet. But she'd want to go with me. I know her. She would get all excited and want to go with me, and we'd get halfway out of town and she'd want to go back and mess up everything.

Getting cold and I got no jacket. See it getting gray and it's going to get colder. I got to get home in my room and get my stuff. If I just get a jacket I can make it to winter, fall anyway. Roe sat here. Right here with me on that spot. Right before he was dead. And I saw that sun right there in the same place. I remember good that. But the trees were thick and I didn't see the smokestacks there. I got to keep my mind going so I don't start thinking it's colder than it is. I wish they'd fall and sqush the whole town of Summit. I'm sorry, Papa Lonza, but I do. I wouldn't go to no trouble for them.

Nobody around my house goes to any trouble for anybody. My old man hasn't sent me to Will James' since I went and told him the President was dead. I remember and he looked scared and so did my mama and daddy and the next thing you know the President has his picture on a dime. I didn't know who the President was. I do now and my Daddy is just the same. He wouldn't throw water on Will James' house if it was burning to the ground.

I'm going to have to do something. I got to go to school to-morrow. I don't have but one more month and I could fail every subject and still graduate and if I don't go back I don't get to. I'd have to do the whole year over. And I got no house and if I took the truck, he'd have the cops come after me because of the license plate and put me in jail. I'd have to buy my own food in a restaurant or fix it myself. I wouldn't have any time left to work or do what I wanted to. He would make it hard. He would get up in front of me and try to knock me down if I go after anything I want to do. I know him. He's not going to die and he's not going to leave me alone so I'm going to have to get away from him. He's going to tell me all wrong about things. You can't believe him because he's got things mixed up

and won't think about them and change. He doesn't know about
Pearlie. He thinks he knows but he doesn't know what she's
thinking or me either. He don't even know what Floyd is thinking. Or Aunt Bynum or Mama. He thinks he can just tell them
what they're thinking. He don't know good from bad. I show
him my paper on houses that Miss Sammons thinks is great and
he doesn't even read it all the way through and he looks at
me and says, "Learned a lot of big words, ain't you? What she
make you write a paper on that crazy guy for? She couldn't have
made me do it."

And Mama is so dumb. She doesn't think anything is good
except that I got an A on it. She'll read it but she can't understand it. And if it's a B she says I ought to do what the teacher
says to make it an A. I asked Pearlie and she said she liked it
but she would do it different if she built a house. She would
build it back off in the woods too but she would have wild
animals that would eat out of her hand and banks full of flowers out front and have a whole wall that was a fishbowl full of
long-tailed goldfish and she would keep things like she wanted
them and not let anyone live with her but her animals. I told
her I liked that and that made her happy because she thought I
was going to laugh at her. I don't think she really means it
about being off by herself, not all the time anyway, but I don't
laugh at her because that's just the way I thought I wanted it
one time.

There are some good people in my mind. There's just nobody
I want there all the time. Miss Sammons would have been like
that. She would have listened but I just got to imagine her
listening in my mind because if I really went to her she would
get scared and I would get scared and we really wouldn't say
anything. She goes thinking I don't like her because I don't
come read for her play and join her drama club, things like that
I mean just because she didn't know why I couldn't. I would
like to make Miss Sammons real small and put her in my pocket
and take her home with me long enough to listen to my mama

and daddy because if she was there full size, they would be different and she wouldn't learn anything. Then Miss Sammons and I could talk if she knew what it was really like and saw it for herself. And I think she really cares. I really do. She wouldn't if she didn't think I was smart but she cares because I'm smart and she gets so tired of teaching dumb people and having to make it all so easy. I'm going to tell her some day, more than just in my mind. I thought it through. I did it in my mind enough, going by her office and saying, Miss Sammons, I want to tell you what it's like at home. And I can't go away yet because I haven't got enough money of my own in my savings account and they don't know I got that much because if they did, they'd make me spend it on clothes and things that they been buying and use it all up. And I haven't got anywhere to go yet though I can think of places I'd like to go. But I really don't think I know enough yet about what I want to do because I haven't been away from here and I don't want to go away and just lay bricks and drive nails and things I already know how to do. That's what I would tell her and she would think of something. I know she would and if she would just tell me, I would work harder than she's ever seen. I don't think she would think I was just a little kid whining, I've thought about that. I just gotta have somebody to tell me because none of them tell me anything right.

If I go off and learn something maybe I'll come back and take those smokestacks down in right fashion for Papa. Maybe I'll just do that, come back to Summit and have a meeting with the mayor and draw plans and tell them just how to get them down. Summit wouldn't ever stop talking about that if they looked up and saw someone taking them down and then one day they watched the sun come down and they were gone and not making those long pointed shadows.

And she would tell me Mama and Daddy don't know any better which is right but they never tried to know any better. But she would make me not be so mean to them I bet, she would say be nice outside and think what you like, that her parents were wrong about a lot of things, just put up with them because they're trying to do right. She's too nice to people. And I would tell her I have to do that anyway. If I went to her house right now and told her that I didn't hit Daddy, I just pushed him off me and he fell down but he's going to say I hit him, what would she say to do? I don't know. I really don't know. I don't even know if she would believe me. I don't know anybody that well.

I'd like to tell her about Papa Lonza's daddy, how he come here on that boat and almost died getting here and had enough in him to start all over again when nobody he had ever had around him was alive. But he found him a pretty place and he wanted to build him a house down by the water but the first thing he did was go marry a woman who started talking about snakes and mosquitoes and mildew and there it sets, up on the hill away from the water so far you can't even hear it except in the morning after a rain and only then if everything has been fed and is not making racket. And now my daddy is telling me I'm going to end up married before I get what I want either. And all those things that happen and come that make everything different and you have to go kick yourself when you start thinking what would have happened if that woman and those two little children hadn't died on the boat and if Uncle Roe hadn't got hit by the truck because there is no way you can know. Most important it won't make any difference anyway because that's not the way things are. I know what things are. I can see in my head if I want to just what things are at my house right this minute and if I try I can see what is in people's heads too. And I can't make it different. I can talk all day explaining things and I can't make it different. Nothing is going to be different because Mama and Daddy are the way they are always going to be. And I needn't bother telling the truth because they hear what they want to.

Maybe Uncle Roe would have been just as bad as Daddy only in a different way. Maybe he would have tried to make me like him and like the same things he does just like Daddy tried. And there were a lot of things about Uncle Roe that I didn't want to be like. There were things he didn't want to be like either. He didn't want to die alone. He was scared he was going to die alone off in a ditch and nobody would know him. He even had a name card. But he didn't. He died in a ditch and everybody knew him. Not many came to his funeral but some did and were real sad. I was. And Daddy was. He liked Roe better than any of us. I don't know why. I don't even know why he doesn't like us. Mama would say he does but she would say that because she knows he's supposed to like us. That's not the same. But there's no need to try much. And I used to try but now I think maybe if he starts liking me then I'm no good anymore. I'm going to think everything he thinks up in my mind so I can think just the opposite. I'm going to do that for a while and see what happens. Then I'm going to do it to Mama. Then I can really find out what I want to think. I might just talk to Miss Sammons. I'll think on that tonight. Daddy would say don't talk to no female teacher. That's sissy he would say and he'd make fun if he knew. And Mama would say don't go spreading our family affairs around, keep it inside the family and let people who care about you work things out. I just might talk to Miss Sammons.

And I got to go back home. I'm sleepy already. I played hard this afternoon. And I'm hungry. Seventy-three cents in my pocket. They can't do anything to hurt me. They can fuss and yell and Daddy can try to beat me and Mama can try to stop him and they can tell me I can't go anywhere next weekend and make me do some more work or do something Daddy has put off for three years. He might even hit me with his belt. But they can't do anything to me. I can stay and work and get what I need until I got it planned out where I'm going. Then I can get together what I want to take and tell them I'll be back for visits and go down to the bus station and go. I don't know where but it won't matter as long as nobody knows me.